Shade of Night

Shade of Night

Stephen R. Deppermann

Prominent Books

Editing: Writer Services, LLC (WriterServices.net)
Cover Design & Book Layout: Writer Services, LLC

ISBN 10: 1-942389-19-1
ISBN 13: 978-1-942389-19-4

Prominent Books and the Prominent Books logo are Trademarks of Prominent Books, LLC

TABLE OF CONTENTS

Chapter 1.. 1

Chapter 2... 9

Chapter 3.. 19

Chapter 4.. 31

Chapter 5.. 51

Chapter 6.. 67

Chapter 7.. 77

Chapter 8.. 91

Chapter 9.. 103

Chapter 10.. 117

Chapter 11.. 127

Chapter 12.. 135

Chapter 13.. 145

Chapter 14... 159

Chapter 15... 173

Chapter 16... 183

Chapter 17... 199

Chapter 18... 209

Chapter 19... 219

Chapter 20... 229

Chapter 21... 241

Chapter 22... 257

Chapter 23... 265

Chapter 24... 279

Chapter 25... 285

Chapter 26... 295

Chapter 27... 307

Chapter 28... 323

Chapter 29... 335

Chapter 30... 355

Chapter 31... 363

Chapter 32... 375

Chapter 33... 387

Chapter 34... 403

Chapter 35... 417

Chapter 36... 427

Chapter 37... 441

Chapter 38... 451

Chapter 39... 459

Chapter 40... 475

Chapter 41... 489

Chapter 42... 501

Chapter 43... 509

Chapter 44 515

Chapter 45... 537

Chapter 46... 555

Chapter 47... 561

Epilogue 573

About the Author... 591

Disclaimer

This is a work of fiction. Names, characters, businesses, places, events, locales, and incidents are either the products of the author's imagination or used in a fictitious manner. Any resemblance to actual persons, living or dead, or actual events is purely coincidental.

For Lidia, Brad, and Spencer.

CHAPTER 1

He was late, elbowing through a thinning crowd. He had miscalculated time and distance down East Lake Road. He hoped the reporter would understand. He had to. Tonight's concert was extra. A preliminary celebration before Friday's conference. Then, afterwards, Newsome's feature article on Sunday, the ensuing media exposure, the guaranteed acclaim ... Ross was ecstatic.

He froze, jolted from the reverie.

Arriva's new security guard appeared behind the glass door. No more than a brief apparition, a shadow, but it was Signet, gone as he dissolved amongst the auditorium crowd. The man had been studying Ross as he hurried up the outside stairs.

What was *he* doing *here*?

A totally unexpected encounter, the man a dark presence, unfriendly from their introduction a week earlier. Ross detected impatience now, cold fury in the darting, judging gaze. Startled, he paused before opening the door.

Beads of sweat soaked his brow, a stab of fear overpowering. But he had done nothing wrong, had followed the guidelines almost to the letter. His project was supposed to be successful. Why send this intimidating person? Why now?

Ross refused to be distracted. With rekindled purpose, he pushed against the emotion and stepped into the foyer. A grey and withered usher led him through the throng and up the side stairs to Tier 9, where he held the door. Occupying a middle seat halfway up the noisy crowd, Mr. Newsome waved him on. Ross tingled. A journalist from The New York Times. No question. It was his time for the spotlight. Time to join his future.

"Hey, Daniel. What kept you?"

"A late patient," he said. "And, traffic."

He inched past yielding knees to reach his seat and settled in, noting the expectant buzz. It wasn't everyday a Juilliard pianist came to Clearwater. A Beethoven program. It promised to be quite a feast.

They shook hands, both men immersed in the pleasurable event. Twenty rows down, an elegant concert grand occupied the bare stage. He breathed a sigh of relief and apologized again for his tardy arrival.

"Not a problem," Newsome said, laying aside the gazette. Hard to miss, the headline screamed out in bold print:

DEFENSE TAKING TIME ON ERITREA. DIPLOMAT HOSTAGE. WHITE HOUSE DITHERS.

"Our military is so damn indecisive. It's obvious what to do. Send in the Seals. They'll handle those damn insurgents." He shook his head. "Sorry. I get carried away. This is a no-brainer. We already send Special Forces into Yemen. Eritrea lies only twenty miles away across the straits of Bab-el-Mandeb. But, hey. We can't allow problems in the horn of Africa to distract us. Let's talk about Glaucon, your project. I have a midnight deadline and have to get this right."

"Why don't we talk at dinner? We'll be more relaxed then."

In addition to the concert, Newsome had reserved a table at Bonefish Grill. Ross could already taste the chardonnay, the pricey Dumol his favorite. The New York Times would pick up the tab. A perfect omen.

Newsome began to scribble notes.

"Tell me more about the surgical device and the secret biological agents, you know, the ones that do the trick. Both the readers and my finicky editor will also want to know how your micro-motor actually works. I have to get this right. It's my first piece for the Sunday Magazine. Got to impress if I want more assignments."

The urgent tone surprised Ross. During prior interviews, he'd described everything in great detail: the unique implant tubes and motor, the three agents to stabilize and actually cure glaucoma, the various patents plus a detailed video of the actual surgery. The guy had taken copious notes, recorded their interviews. What more did he need?

He directed their attention to the vacant stage. Getting the clue, Newsome put down the pen.

"You're right. This can wait. What I really need are background tidbits. I read your bio. You once gave recitals in college and later in Boston. I'm impressed."

A sheepish grin, a knuckle bump, the connection reestablished. The fact was, they needed each other to advance: the journalist, hungry for plum assignments, the doctor desperate for recognition.

"There's not much to say," Ross explained. "I came to a fork in the road. Music school beckoned. I went in another direction. I liked to read and study. I wanted to be a doctor."

"But to leave a lucrative practice in Massachusetts to pursue, what some might call, a flyer in Florida..." Newsome feigned a sigh. "I have to say, you're brave to tackle a terrible disease. Didn't you tell me the best minds were hard at work trying to unravel glaucoma? Yet, here you are curing the darn thing. You're a true entrepreneur. I'll headline you as one of the young titans transforming medicine. "

Ross squirmed under the journalist's intensity. Yet, he was spot on, reading Ross like a book. Except for one glaring detail: the source of his motivation.

A painting.

Because, more than money, any prizes, even a trip to Stockholm, Daniel Ross's most cherished goal was to have his portrait hanging alongside the many greats on the wall of the Boston Eye Infirmary library. A life-size gilded oil, gaze focused on a distant horizon.

"Well, that might be going a bit—"

"And a bachelor, to boot. Tell me about the divorce. This private peek at the man behind his tubes. Readers will love it."

He hoped not. He had intentionally abandoned that messy business in Massachusetts. The unfinished Vermont getaway. The lonely skiing trips. And the reason for this unhappy agenda? His new wife had run off to France with his so-called best friend. No. Impossible. If readers wanted that sort of fluff they should consult the tabloids, not the New York Times.

The pianist appeared on stage, bowed, and took his seat. Soon the lights dimmed, the incessant buzz died off, and the magnificent music blazed into Ross's soul, quieting the turmoil, realigning him again.

A discordant note intruded. The damn security man again, this time down at the far left-hand side of the stage. Emerging from behind a giant plant, Signet directed his black eyes at Ross. A frightening individual, angular, hard. He'd come for Ross. Why else make his presence so obvious?

Rattled, Ross wiped his brow. A special ops warrior at a piano concert? More disturbing, Signet had known exactly where to find him. Newsome had dropped off the tickets only that morning. A last-minute invite. Not mentioned to anyone.

The soulful descent of familiar chords recaptured him. Yielding to the music, he stepped past the veil of threat to reenter the near endless domain of creative achievement. It was here, during the many moments of doubt, including the present special ops invasion, he sought refuge.

First up, *Les Adieux,* a late middle period sonata. Ross took tonight's opening Goodbye movement, *Das Lebewohl,* as a symbol of his leaving a difficult research period behind him. Goodbye indeed, to the storm of mishaps and delay that plagued his efforts from the very start.

Most troubling to accept, the early corporate dismissals, the complete lack of interest in his proposal. It shocked him. A cure for devastating blindness? *Sorry, buddy. No money in it.* An "orphan market," he was told. Too small to support investment. Dozens of refusals. Finally, Arriva Incorporated of Tarpon Springs pierced the gloom. Rather, its generous founder and CEO, Samantha Campesi, did. She had offered to help patent, finance, and develop his new device.

Almost blind from glaucoma herself, she jumped at the chance, however remote, to save the small amount of remaining vision. Because her company manufactured a full panoply of growth factors and other biological agents, it was perfectly positioned to supply the agents he'd chosen for Glaucon, the name of his three-tube gizmo. If caught early, glaucoma was a preventable form of blindness. Mrs. Campesi's disease, however, lay on the opposite side of the spectrum. Naturally, she had a strong interest in his curative technique.

With her assistance, Arriva established equity arrangements, hired contract researchers, submitted new drug and device proposals and, later, conducted the premarketing approval process, a set of endless meetings with the FDA, interspersed with an exchange of tricky letters....

There was a muffled commotion in the side aisle. One of the ushers handed in a piece of paper, disturbing sniffy patrons who reluctantly passed the folded note along until it reached Newsome. He gave it a quick glance then abruptly scuttled to the aisle and exited the auditorium.

Seconds passed as distraught patrons resettled, then, just as the mournful *Lebewohl* ended, Ross heard another, muffled thudding sound to his right. He inspected the empty aisle. There it was again, a heavy thud from beyond the aisle door.

Alarmed, he crabbed sideways until he reached the aisle. The door didn't budge when he tried the handle. Conscious of disturbed whispers, he hurried up to the 10th-tier door and stepped out. Head at an odd angle, Newsome lay silent on the carpet below.

Ross descended and felt for a pulse. Nothing from the carotids. The chest was immobile. Either a heart attack or stroke, he decided, commencing, after a chest thump, a rapid CPR. Three frantic minutes later there was still no pulse or breathing. The man was gone, as unresponsive as the herd of ushers on the surrounding steps, paralyzed by the spectacle at their feet.

He retrieved his Samsung and dialed 911. He described the situation, gave the address, and returned to the lifeless body. It had been so sudden. But, reasoning clinically, the man was overdue. He brought fast food for interviews. A heavy smoker, BMI thirty-plus. The perfect prelude to an abrupt departure. Probably an episode of ventricular fibrillation followed by cardiac standstill. A terrible loss.

The situation suddenly hit home. Newsome, ticket to fame and immortality, was *dead*. Why now, on the brink of success, in the middle of a Beethoven concert? So unacceptable. The timing awful. Ross needed that public forum.

What now?

He stared at Newsome's twisted neck, too aware not only of the tragedy of this unexpected death, but of what he, despite all his dreams, feared most:

The specter of defeat.

CHAPTER 2

The police were quick and thorough. After the first arrivals, a Detective Leeks took charge. Tiers 7 through 12 were cordoned off, the distant foyer roped as well. Following a hushed conversation with the Eckerd manager, ushers were dispatched to corral a gathering crowd of onlookers.

Finally, with intermission approaching, they blocked theatre doors on this side of the auditorium, directing traffic to the wine and pretzel concession to the north end. In relative seclusion, the police photographed the crumpled form while forensic uniforms attended details, measuring the body, its position on the steps, the contents of mouth and pockets, erecting, as an afterthought, a low screen to conceal the gruesome task from the foyer.

Ross became increasingly detached. Swept by a vague guilt, he turned away from the action. Meanwhile, the detective took notes, dismissing Ross's proffered diagnosis: dysrhythmia and fatal myocardial infarction.

"Sorry, Doc. We reached another conclusion." He hiked

up undersized trousers, and studied his notes. "The victim did not suffer a fatal heart attack then fall and break his neck. Someone did that for him. Sad, really. This guy was murdered."

"You can't be serious. Morbidly obese, Marlboros in his pocket. My bet is either a heart attack or stroke. Maybe both." Ross shook his head. "For all his charm, he was a catastrophe about to happen."

"Yeah. Maybe. But, the blow was primary." Leeks raised a hand to his own throat, indicating the hyoid, a horseshoe-shaped bone just above the Adam's apple. "Death was fast and brutal."

"I can't believe it. *Murdered*?"

The detective sat beside him on the steps of Tier 2.

"It's a shock. I can see that. Were you close?"

"Not really. He was a reporter. We were listening to the concert. It's so hard to accept."

"We found the note you mentioned." Leek's eye darted around the scene. "Look, my men need me for a moment. Should I send someone over? We've got trauma shrinks on call. Just don't leave. I have a few more questions."

Ross declined the offer. He didn't need a psychologist. He needed something else. In a fit of desperation, he shot to his feet.

"Could you do me a favor?"

"Can it wait?"

"It's more of a request. Mr. Newsome was a reporter for the New York Times. When he was in town, he stayed at the Marriott on Gulf to Bay in Clearwater. What I need—"

"Don't worry." Detective Leeks patted his shoulder. "We'll go through his things with a fine-tooth comb."

He then hurried up the steps toward the other cops.

What Ross wanted was simple enough: Newsome's laptop. It was only Monday. Plenty of time for inclusion of his article on Ross in the Sunday Magazine section. All the detectives had to do was locate the file and send it off.

At the last moment, good sense prevailed. He sat back down, his attention drawn again to the lifeless body the cops were then placing in a black bag. They zipped it up, the mournful maneuver another reminder of the magnitude of the tragedy. This polite and helpful reporter, a stranger really, had been prepared to make him a public figure, to label him Medical Innovator of the Year. Instead, Newsome lay there in a crumpled heap on the floor, and guilt, a new companion, continued to assail Ross, demonstrating, as if it weren't clear enough, how he dwelled primarily on his own predicament instead of thinking about the man's wife and family. What about them?

Someone was calling out his name. Waving an arm, a woman summoned him from behind a sprawling plastic planter near the front of the auditorium. Curious, he walked over.

"How is the concert, Doctor?"

It took a moment. With a sinking sensation, he now recognized Zina Palaeologus, the granddaughter of a patient. Except, it didn't quite look like her.

He scrambled for focus, struck not by the absence of cutoff jeans and baggy tee shirt, her customary attire, but by a transformed image: skyscraper heels, a sleek, low-cut outfit, and peculiar eyeliner. She resembled some classy, eccentric model straight off the runway. A big change from the scrappy, half-washed urchin with spiked hair who always accompanied her granddad on tumultuous office visits.

"Is that you, Ms. Palaeologus?' He noted a strange, new tremor in his voice. "What are you doing here?"

Moist palms, heart racing, his agitation traceable not to a dead body back on the steps but to a very live and disturbingly dressed young woman in front of him.

"What I meant to say, I didn't expect to see you."

She ignored the stupid remark. Cool and well poised, Ms. Palaeologus had morphed beyond his imagination. Radiating confidence and throbbing appeal, she placed a lacquered nail against painted lips. Deep red. Purple. He couldn't decide which.

"Do you like my new look, Dr. Daniel?"

Danneee-el. A mocking tone, seductive.

Batting extravagant eyelashes, her warmth flowed like hot lava. Swept back into a braided pineapple and colored red, her hair contrasted sharply with purple eyebrows and lips, the overall design aeronautical. She cut an exotic image.

She was also flirting, and with a nerd in striped tie and trousers? The idea was outrageous.

"You think me theatrical?"

"What? No. Well, a little."

His emotions ricocheted inside his skull. First, the terrible murder, the trauma of loss, not only of Newsome but of his future plans. Next, Ms. Palaeologus slyly taking his measure, tossing him off track, deviating from their accustomed script.

He shifted weight, pulse uneven.

"What is wrong?" she purred. "You seem … uneasy."

"It's nothing," he murmured. "Your outfit. It's so, I don't know, peculiar."

"Hah. I take no offense. In the court of Justinian and Theodora, every female dressed this way. Next to Krav Maga, I have found ancient Byzantium helpful."

"Isn't Krav Maga a form of martial arts?" he asked. He had no idea what else to say.

Ignoring the question she leaned forward to offer a tantalizing pectoral inspection. He strained to look away. In any direction, not down. Her skintight, lavender blouse left little to the imagination; it magnetized his gaze, his entire brain. Not once, for even an instant during her many trips with grandpa, had she presented herself as available. Or, had he been misinterpreting? Was he misinterpreting now?

"Do you like my new perfume? It's called *Shade of Night*."

Using a fly-by to sample her scent, he took a whiff, then hovered closer, bedazzled. The spell she wove, her velvet epidermis ... With a lurch, he pulled back. What the heck was he thinking?

Wasn't he crossing some boundary? The age disparity. The nature of their relationship. Whatever. Renewing his concentration, he focused on her perfume. Jasmine and pine. Curious coupling. *Coupling*? What was happening? Forcing the provocative image from mind, he turned to Newsome's crumpled body. There. Finally. A reality check. Or, maybe not. Zina tapped him on the nose, her outstretched arm dismantling his composure.

"After Opus 81 he will play Opus 57, the Appassionata. Can you just hear energetic triplets and cascading fifths?" She waved the program notes in his face. "It is here, Dr. Danny-boy. I know all about your precious composer."

Bait-oh-ven. Ay-pass-see-oh-naw-ta. Strange but hopelessly engaging. And then the explanation of her taunting behavior became obvious. It concerned Father Palaeolgus, her grandfather. Following his sight-saving surgery, he'd undergone an unexplained but remarkable change of personality and behavior, one which greatly disturbed the granddaughter, who placed the blame squarely on Ross. She'd disrupted the office many times.

"Thanks to Doctor Dannyee-ell, Father Palaeologus is not

the same. Before surgery, he cherished icons shedding tears. Now, he cherishes girls shedding clothes."

At the moment, however, she was more interested in activity across the lobby than delivering complaints.

"What's the commotion over there?"

He saw no reason not to tell her. A journalist from the New York Times had met with foul play on the auditorium stairs, a conclusion reached by the police after inspecting the poor man's body.

"A mystery," she said with relish, "I'll add it to my collection."

She produced an iPhone from a small handbag, snapped a few shots, then replaced the phone in her handbag and prepared to depart.

The gesture made Ross wonder what else the strange young woman had observed. "Hold on," he said, "How long have you been here?"

She shrugged.

"I arrived just as you stumbled down those stairs. I watched from behind this dusty plant. Why do you ask?"

"Did you see anyone besides me?"

"Only the Fathers Time over there." She nodded towards a group of ushers, stooped and muttering like zombies in a movie.

"Think, Ms. Palaeologus. It's important. The reporter was

murdered a very short time ago. Perhaps when you were walking across the foyer you saw a man or woman dart up the stairs, or run for the front door...?"

Suddenly, Detective Leeks hustled across the foyer and stopped, slightly winded, before Zina. He homed in on her small handbag.

"Who's this, Doc, your date?"

With a look of horror, Zina stepped back, aeronautical eyebrows arching up a notch, ready to launch. She paused, glancing first at the detective, then at Ross, her green eyes penetrating like a laser.

"A *date*?" She spat it out, as if finding a nasty Aviva beet in her salad, "You make me laugh." Her voice then dropped to a husky, Lauren Bacall register. "This man does not have dates. He is married to his eyeball gadget." Her eyes flicked coldly over the detective. "Who are you to barge into our conversation?"

When Leeks did not immediately reply, she spun on her heals and, with an inscrutable pout, aimed in the opposite direction.

"Not so fast, little lady. Why are you taking pictures?"

"'Little lady'?" she snorted derisively "Well, *little man*, it's none of your business."

"I can sure make it that. You want me to arrest you?"

"On what charge? Because you, a man wearing awful plaid, can harass a citizen?" Her eyes flicked over the detective. "Where do you shop, on the moon?"

The situation was going downhill fast. Collecting his wits, Ross intervened.

"Let's back up here. Detective Leeks, meet Zina Palaeologus. Her grandfather is my patient, but I assure you we met here tonight by chance."

"Not entirely," Zina interjected demurely. "I joined Grandpa at his office visit this morning. I overheard a man give tickets to Dr. Ross. I knew he'd be here tonight."

"You planned to run into him on purpose?"

Her lips rounded in a pout. "Perhaps. Perhaps not."

This puzzled Ross. Father Palaeologus's appointment had been at two in the afternoon. Newsome arrived at nine sharp bearing tickets. She did not overhear him.

"Okay. Enough. You're right. It's none of my business. You took our picture just now. Let's see what else is on there."

Zina handed over her iPhone. Detective Leeks fumbled with it a few moments before handing it back.

"Do it for me," he said, adding sheepishly, "I have an Android."

For several moments they examined photos, of Ross as he clumsily descended the stairs and attempted CPR, then of the policemen as they examined the corpse. A final shot of the zippered body bag, and that was that. Zina retrieved and shut off the phone. Other than nude selfies, she teased, pirouetting for emphasis, her gallery was empty.

She then surprised Ross by confirming Leeks' earlier suspicion. She had indeed attended the concert solely to see the good doctor. All of a sudden, there he was and she walked over. What was all the fuss about?

"It's strange you snapped photos of a crime scene."

"I also took pictures of Grandpa's doctor. Did I break a law?"

Toning it down, the detective explained the problem. There were no witnesses to the murder. None of the yawning ushers had seen anything out of the ordinary. Just this young woman taking pictures, perhaps of the entire event. Behavior that as a detective investigating the crime he could hardly overlook.

"I now understand," he said, "You have the hots for the doctor. Too bad you missed the important action. Say goodbye to your boyfriend. He and I have to talk."

Zina waved goodbye with a lacquered hand, treating Ross to quick dose of perfume as she twirled by. She then vanished behind the bank of plastic plants and was gone.

Leeks dragged his gaze back to Ross. "Take a seat, Doc." He gestured to the stairs, "We're going to be a little while."

CHAPTER 3

An usher cracked an aisle door, and the sonata's third movement, *Wiedersehen*, *The Return*, floated out to Ross. Archduke Rudolph, the composer's primary and favorite patron, was back in town, Vienna to be precise, the spirited music of 1809 reflecting energy and heartfelt joy at his return.

For the briefest instant Ross was transported back to happier days of recitals and catered soirees on Boston's Beacon Hill, only to return to the gruesome, surreal present when Father Time closed the auditorium door. A few feet away, Detective Leeks' team was wrapping up their investigation.

"...guy never on a diet, boss," he heard one of them say, "Where you want Big Boy's autopsy?"

"Crushed neck and skull? Take him to Clearwater. We'll do it there."

The detective called down to Ross.

"Hold on, Doc. I'll be right with you."

The audience began filing out at intermission. Ross searched for Signet but saw no sign of the severe security man. In an evening in which his emotions had run the gamut from excitement to fear, lust to crushing disappointment, anger now made its appearance. Why had Signet tracked him down at Eckerd Hall? Why all the angry looks, the sneaky nonsense?

He sprang to his feet. He'd had enough of crushed necks and body bags. He wanted out.

"Will you wrap this up?" he called out to the detective. "I'm leaving."

Taking his time, Leeks ambled down the steps and sat on the bottom, then waved for Ross to join him.

"Will you look at this," he said, unfolding a copy of the concert notes. "Following the break, Furkleboer's will play *Opus 106, The Hammerklavier*, Beethoven's most majestic middle period sonata. If I didn't have to supervise at the post mortem, I'd take your seat in there."

For the second time tonight, someone was regaling him with *program notes.*

"You had questions?"

"I do. Did you see this? The final movement is a fugue. It's said to be his most aesthetic creation. Why would you miss that?"

"Look, Detective. The murder shook me up. Nothing would please me more than to hear the sonata. Now is not that time. What's up?"

Detective Leeks regarded him over the top of bifocals. Glistening orbs. Red-rimmed. Partial stubble. The guy had been interrupted. Probably at dinner.

He flipped open his notepad and scanned pages.

"Let's review what we have. You and Mr. Newsome came for a concert. He received a note, left his seat, and was immediately killed. Any idea who would do this?"

Ross shook his head. "As I said before, I don't have a clue. I hardly knew the man. We met by chance six months ago. We were at Bonefish Grill, sitting at the bar watching baseball on TV. We got to talking. He said he was a journalist on assignment. A cover feature. Medical breakthroughs. That sort of thing. I explained my new surgical device, which impressed him. Said, if his editor agreed, he would include me in his piece for an upcoming Sunday Supplement. I don't see how this implicates me in his murder."

"Didn't say it did."

"Why all the questions then? I'm a glaucoma specialist with an invention to treat glaucoma. He was a journalist. Maybe he made an enemy on a past assignment. He's the one you should be investigating. Not me."

"So you don't think there's a money angle here."

"I don't see one. At least not on my end. Glaucoma is not a high-paying field."

"You're not in it for the money?"

"Definitely not. More for the thrill of discovery."

Detective Leeks re-examined him over the glasses, a perplexed grin playing on his lips, then jotted a few notes.

"If I may make a suggestion," Ross said, "Find the usher who handed in the note. He'll tell you who gave it to him. Case solved."

"Remarkable," the detective replied. "In addition to medicine and music you have a flair for criminal investigation." He pretended to scribble in his pad. "However, your insight brings us to a most curious detail...."

The cop's eyes gave him a mercurial scan.

"We reached the same conclusion. The ushers are the key. Except they *aren't*. It took a while to pry it out of them. It seems the perp handed the note to a sleepy fellow who handed it off to yet another semiconscious comrade who then managed to descend from Eckerd Hall's upper chamber to Tier Nine, step into the auditorium and deliver the message. The perp spoke in a high-pitched voice and wore shaggy, mechanic-type overalls. A perfect disguise. That's all we have and why we need your help to proceed."

Ross shook his head. "I truly want to help. I have nothing else to add. Surely someone saw this person. It's not a busy place."

"Busy enough. Your pal Ludwig is popular these days. Our guy fit right in. No one saw a man in overalls, which, by the way, we found in an upstairs trashcan. Tell me again how you two met—you and Newsome...."

"We already went into this."

"Humor me."

Ross retold the story. Earlier in the year, while enjoying braised salmon at Bonefish Grill as the Red Sox trounced the Rays on the bar TV, Newsome sat down beside him and ordered a bottle of chardonnay. They hit it off. Soon they were cheering on Big Papi who, at the plate in the ninth, hit a home run over the green monster at Fenway in Boston. An exciting game, wine flowing, conversation engaging until they found themselves discussing the distressed state of American medicine and the difficulty of launching new devices. When Ross said he had a way to cure glaucoma, the reporter's eyes lit up. As it so happened, he was working on an article for the New York Times Sunday supplement due out in the autumn. He asked if it was okay to feature Ross's invention as the miracle cure of the decade.

"He just showed up. This journalist from the famous New York Times. An odd coincidence, don't you think?"

"Why is it odd?"

The detective nodded and resumed flipping pages. "You say you work at Arriva."

"Over six years."

"That giant, pastel cube in the middle of farmland."

Ross laughed. "You nailed it. A futuristic building at the edge of a cypress swamp. Not your typical Florida postcard."

"According to the St. Petersburg Gazette, Arriva recently installed a razor wire fence."

"Not my idea. Security strung it overnight."

"To keep out demonstrators." The detective consulted more notes. "In fact, the *specific* group representing that rival company based in India. What's the name?"

A slash of a grin appeared on Leeks' grizzled face. He knew the darn name. Simcoe, Inc., a rival Indian firm, was always in the news. Common knowledge they had, for unknown reasons, placed Arriva in their crosshairs. They were always causing a disturbance at Arriva's gate. A harassment campaign that got them nowhere.

"Simcoe, Inc. They're based in Mumbai."

"What's their problem? Why storm the gates out there on Keystone?"

Ross gave it some thought.

"We think they're trying to delay the debut of my Glaucon device. It's unique but a bit complicated. It depends upon a photon-activated film that propels certain ingredients into a glaucomatous eye. Simcoe wants that film. They've been trying to miniaturize such a device for years."

"That accounts for their placards: 'No more Nano Now,' 'Respect the Ecosystem.' That sort of thing."

They exchanged a look.

"While you were chitchatting with that purple bombshell, my guys at the precinct searched for answers. Who is Dr. Ross? Where does he work? You know, the usual."

"How does this…?

"Relax. You're not a suspect. You work for the government, right?"

"Not exactly. I work for Arriva."

"Which the United States government owns. My team found out it's contracted by DARPA, that super-duper high tech secretive research arm of the Pentagon. The funding of your project comes straight out of a master grant. Which in itself is peculiar. Arriva is a company that makes proteins, not medical devices."

Ross now took a fresh look at this increasingly adversarial officer of the law. Partially disheveled. Rumpled suit. Tiresome manner. But, informed. Amazingly so.

"Then you already know my boss and CEO is Mr. Arturo Campesi."

"So, tell me. Are the demonstrators angry with you or him? Are they fighting the basic science of biological development, or your tube thing? Don't look so surprised. My team called Arriva a few moments ago and got filled in."

Ross's pulse skipped a beat. Mr. Campesi could easily fly off the handle about this. Ross didn't need any embarrassment at such a critical juncture. He decided to see Arturo in the morning. Explain this mess at Eckerd Hall before it became an issue. Update him on Newsome and the planned article. Make him realize an article in The Sunday Supplement could help both Glaucon and Arriva. Certainly Arturo could see that.

"Well, Doctor. What is it?"

"Mr. Campesi and I own the patent to the nano-film material. It's a unique molecular substance that's never been manufactured before."

"In other words, you and Arriva are in competition with this Indian outfit. It explains how corporate espionage can enter the picture."

"No one is competing here, Detective. I have Glaucon, my project. Simcoe has nothing. They haven't published a single paper in an American peer-reviewed journal. I have no idea what they're up to. They don't concern me. I'm a published clinician scientist."

He felt puffed up, challenged, and now slightly embarrassed by the ridiculous response. The detective was just doing his job.

"Sorry," he said lamely. "It's a bit late. It's been a tough few hours."

"Well, don't get your feathers up. I'm on your side. Tell me more about Arriva It seems an odd place for a physician to work."

Ross hesitated, uncertain how much to share.

"Let's say Mr. Campesi continued the assistance his late wife provided."

Because at the beginning of his odyssey it hadn't been easy. All the research labs and big pharma outfits turned him down. Last on his list was Arriva, the only company that produced BDNF, a protein central to his project. He wrote a letter to then-owner Stephanie Campesi; a longshot, to be sure. But the letter sparked her interest, and, after a good deal of prodding, she convinced her husband that it was a project worth pursuing. After all, Mr. Campesi, with the backing of the Pentagon, used the brain-derived nerve factor BDNF to treat PTSD in veterans; Ross used it to treat glaucoma. Nano products were the basis of each delivery system. After his wife passed away, Arturo merely continued the arrangement.

The detective raised a hand.

"Let's summarize. Your boss dreamed up the BDNF vaccine for PTSD. You came up with a glaucoma application."

"That's what I just said."

"It explains why the late Mr. Newsome happened to show up at Bonefish Grill. I remember the game myself. Everyone cheering when Big Papi hit the dinger over the monster."

The detective placed a hand on Ross's shoulder.

"We found an ID card in Newsome's wallet. He was an accountant at Simcoe Enterprises. There's a company photo. Shows him suntanned, a happy fellow. We think that he was after something. Either about the BDNF or your nano motor. Someone found out and took care of business. Except, and this is the hooker, it's not that simple."

Ross kept shaking his head.

"A Simcoe *accountant*? I don't believe it." But, even as he said the words, the truth of it clicked. Newsome knew the lingo. He had specific questions. He had been well coached.

"What exactly did you tell him?"

"I don't know. He took notes. He always took tons of notes." Ross wracked his brain, dredging up the memory. "At one meeting, during the summer, I provided a video of the actual surgery. But it had to have been the motor. He was always asking about it. Tonight he asked again. He seemed a bit pushier than usual. Never once did I share any details about the nano-motor, though."

"Pushy, like in a hurry?"

"I suppose...."

A moment passed. The foyer crowd began filing back into the auditorium. Opus 57 up next. He'd miss that as well.

The detective moved closer, his tone hushed.

"Let's say someone staged the whole thing. He discovers Simcoe has dispatched the accountant again, this time to pump you for information at a concert. Only there's a complication. This other party gets impatient. He's mad. Damn mad, in fact. So, he or she decides to take care of the accountant tonight. Why now? Why here? That's the mystery. Anyway, they send in a note that worries the accountant. He surfaces and is murdered. Now, I have to ask again. Who do you think did this?"

Ross was prepared to fire back, to tell Leeks he knew nothing about any of this, when Signet came to mind.

Had the security guy been staring, not at him, but at Newsome?

Still, he couldn't figure why he'd commit murder in a public place. Signet came across as a person who thought things out, perhaps obsessively so. This was so impulsive. If Signet had done it, Ross had to keep it to himself. He couldn't breathe a word of suspicion to this detective. Campesi would hear of it for sure. Ross would then become a traitor. Goodbye Mr. Innovator of the year. Goodbye job. The possible repercussions sent shockwaves down his spine.

"I have no idea," he said evenly. "It's a complete mystery."

"Think about it, okay? There's one final item. The note Newsome intercepted. It wasn't addressed to him. It was sent to you."

The detective handed him the folded paper. Ross gingerly unfolded it, horrified by the unsigned, printed message.

ROSS, GET YOUR FANNY OUT HERE. YOUR PAL NEWSOME IS A FRAUD.

"Now think, goddamn it. Who could've written this? Who could've been after you?"

Ross refused to think. Because if he did, Glaucon, his special project, would never launch. Not from Arriva, not ever, if his suspicion proved to be true.

"Hey, Doc. We're not finished yet. Come back here!"

CHAPTER 4

He sped past Bonefish Grill, the conceit of celebration. A booth reserved, Cakebread Chardonnay chilling in a bucket, crunchy appetizers on a tray, his name and achievement in the limelight for all to see. Easy times. Or, at least, less frenzied.

Instead, a fraudster lay dead, Ross's humiliation guaranteed.

He hooked left and entered LANSBROOK, a sprawl of subdivisions flanking Lake Tarpon, the inland body of freshwater close to the Gulf. Ross raced down the central tunnel of arcing oaks, passing a dozen bizarre declarations: Water Crest, Wind Hollow, Sneak Aye Ridge and many other developments. Shielded by a stone wall to discourage lake alligators, his neglected duplex in Juniper Cove compared poorly to Melko's tidy Tudor a block south, his current destination.

He slowly backed the Corolla into his pal's driveway, avoiding both the lustrous Mercedes and sedate Jaguar, perks of Melko's thriving bar and grille on the bayou.

Again, his heart flopped. The coveted perk he alone cherished, the infirmary wall portrait, had descended another rung on the ladder to achievement following tonight's Eckerd Hall disaster.

He parked, got settled, gulped a lungful of warm air. Time for another reality fix from the retired, no-nonsense Massachusetts detective, amused always by what he called Ross's episodes of syncopated suffering.

He'd barely emerged from the Corolla when a deep voice shot out of the shadows

"Hey, Danny-boy. Where you been? You're late again."

It was Franklin "Mad Dog" Casio, suddenly in Ross's face.

"Not now," Ross said, edging around the guy. "I'm in a hurry. Later, okay?"

"Wait up, Danny-boy. We have to talk."

Mad Dog extended a smudged paw, followed by a frenzied gush that shook the night and unleashed a swirl of unidentifiable odors.

"Heard the news, yet? I'm talking Eritrea, man. That tiny country in East Africa? The latest lie out of Washington. The manipulation. Staged sound bites. How does State know what's on the ground? Hey, stop. What's the hurry? This is vital."

Franklin had his arm in a vise, forcing him to pay attention. Just ahead lay the front door of the Tudor mansion. So close, but, with Mr. Schizo in control, so far away.

"Sorry, no, I didn't hear the news. I appreciate the update, but I have to get inside."

"What the heck, man. This ain't no *update*. This is the Big Lie again. We're talking civil war. That's what's going down. You have to pay attention." The hovering bulk stood his ground, breathing hard, making escape impossible. "The story is everywhere. You can't miss it. Our boys in Washington, at it again."

"Should I call your father?" Ross said hopefully, as the threat had worked before. "Your dose may need adjustment."

"Shit, man. I'm not medicated. This is real. It's happening!"

Two years earlier, Mr. Casio, head of a major, now defunct, hedge fund, dispatched his nutty son to Florida after NYPD informed him of countless complaints: *Get your boy off the subways, mister. Take away that damn megaphone. He can't be bothering riders with his mumbo jumbo.*

Since then Mad Dog had been living in an expensive house on Lake Tarpon, a quiet neighborhood, corralling captive audiences with wild theories and speculation. One could remove the boy from Manhattan, but, not the fear and paranoia from the boy.

Behind them, at the top of the steps, the front door creaked open. Melko poked his head out, watching the confrontation.

"Don't call my dad. He don't know jack shit. Just remember what I told you. Eritrea, man. We can't go there."

"Got it. Don't worry. Always a pleasure."

"If you repeat the lie often enough, people begin to believe it."

By degree, Ross edged past the obstruction and ascended to the porch, his nemesis tracking every move.

"Don't believe what they say. Terrorists are not crossing the Red Sea to occupy Masara. Another lie, man. We can't wind up in Eritrea. Look what happened in Iraq. I'm talking brutal pigs, man. Hey, did I explain dark matter to you? That's another capitalist lie."

Melko pulled him in, jamming the heavy door shut with a distinct thud.

"Christ, Daniel. You look like crap. How was the concert?"

✱✱✱

Melko got him seated on the silk divan, then uncorked a bottle of red. It was a well-chilled Assyertiko Santorini, and, he proclaimed, his new winner.

"Remember that New York Times reporter I met last summer?"

Melko nodded, pouring two glasses and offering one to Ross.

"The large fellow who rejected fresh sea bass at my grille for, what was it...?"

"Fried shrimp."

"Right. At that place in Clearwater? What of it?"

"Well, Mr. Newsome was an imposter," Ross continued, recounting the tale of woe, from their first of four dinner meetings in Clearwater and culminating in the man's unexpected and brutal death at Eckerd Hall only moments earlier.

"What did you say? The man was actually *killed* during the concert?"

He omitted not a single detail, including the appearance of his patient's crazy granddaughter, who snapped iPhone pictures of the murder scene and was interrogated by the head cop.

"I should have seen it coming. A Times exclusive? Who was I kidding? It was all a joke, man, and, it was on me." Ross paused for breath. "What truly rankles, I thought he was culling nuggets of knowledge and insight. All along, he was simply milking me for information. I fell for it. I'm such a, a...."

He held his head, searching for the word. Naïve. Stupid. Gullible. They all fit. He had needed the recognition. He needed it bad.

Melko paused to take it all in, then gestured to Ross's untouched glass. "Take a sip. I need your opinion. Will it complement the grouper?"

Grouper? What the heck. He was in trouble here.

Disgrace blocked any hope of sampling fine wine. Still,

out of respect, he took a sip anyway, then drained the entire glass. Not bad. Not bad at all.

"Excellent," he agreed. "I'll have another."

Before long, his host uncorked a second bottle. A light buzz intensified. Before he knew it, his thoughts cycled back to square one.

"I can't accept he fooled me. *Me*, the inventor of a terrific eyeball device. Using BDNF, for pity's sake. Plus a photon activated motor. My God. What if I turn it into a solar panel? But, I was conned. Mr. Campesi will have my ass."

"Good. The wine's taking off the edge. Ass. I like the sound of that. A real improvement over your usual, ultra-proper Beacon Hill talk. As fruitcake Franklin might say, chill. I'll prepare dinner. How do Greek leftovers sound?"

"Simply awesome," Ross replied, another quote attributed to Mr. Big Lie himself.

A few minutes later, when Melko fanned souvlaki chicken beneath his nose, he hustled to the dining room and dug in. As expected, Melko wore his improbable Red Sox apron. He served Greek salad and spinach pie, pouring, with a discrete twist and a sly wink, another dollop of the bottomless Assyertiko, the third bottle, but who was counting?

"Eat up," Melko instructed. "We'll return to Beethoven later."

The presentation was vintage Melko: Japanese flatware, pink silk napkins and, what the cultivated cop referred to as his "good luck money trees," twin bonsai plants on the credenza. Completing the décor, twin antique tables graced the side wall, scarlet damask drapes framed a rear window while Kashan carpets bloomed underneath. Parking himself behind a pristine, lakeside park and festive gazebo, the retired detective from Belmont, Massachusetts had done well for himself. He had also refurbished a rundown grill on the bayou and turned it into a prime tourist attraction and local hangout.

Tarpon Springs honored him.

His souvlaki chicken, to die for.

"What do you think?" Melko pointed to the half-consumed bottle. "Hint of cherries after a smooth finish? A superb choice for the daily catch?"

Finally, the dreadful murder caught up with Ross. Despite a full belly, he was cheerless.

"I was so easily fooled," he repeated. "How could I have been sucked in?"

"The simple truth? You're obsessed. When you came in with that long face, I figured Fertile-Burger fumbled a *poco slendando*. That wasn't the case at all. Someone wants you dead. You just can't decide who or why. Lucky he nailed the wrong person."

"Furklebower. That's the pianist. And why 'nail' Newsome if I was the target?"

Melko shrugged. "The note betrays anger. You ask me, rage got the better of the man. Or woman. It's up in the air at this moment. I'll get back to *Ms. Shade of Night* in a minute."

"That article for the Sunday Times was to feature me and Glaucon. Newsome labeled it the advance of the decade. But it was pure fabrication. Franklin would love this. Talk about the Big Lie. Right on the money this time."

He dropped his fork, pushed away from the table.

"This isn't like me."

"It is not. But easy on yourself, amigo. Tonight was unique. In a sense, you dodged one bullet but took a second. I refer to the discovery of this guy's lie. It struck your Achilles heel. Your heart, your very dream. But you cannot let it eat you up. Don't fret. You'll bounce back."

Suddenly, the iconic scene in *On the Waterfront* when Marlon Brando says, "I coulda *been* a contender," flashed through Ross's mind. The accountant's death reminded him that, despite endless sacrifice, his goal of achieving a place in ophthalmology history would remain unattainably distant. That a portrait on the infirmary wall? An illusion clouding his meager judgment.

"Sorry," he said. "I got carried away."

"Is *that* what you call it?"

"Okay. I am obsessed. I need Glaucon to succeed."

Melko's unflinching gaze speared him.

"Let's return to the note. It was directed at you and prepared well in advance. A prearranged drop-off and disguise concealed the attacker's identity. Then, whoever it was, waited for you to come out. Who would go to so much trouble?"

He refused to go there. The implication too awful to consider.

"I still can't accept someone planned to kill me."

"Mark my words. They'll be back. A deranged mind keeps at it."

"It doesn't make sense."

"Get real, son. You know damn well your CEO wrote the note. The imperious ass of Arriva Incorporated, that mysterious orange cube in the middle of a cow pasture at the edge of a swamp. We don't know why Campesi did it. I'm curious why you didn't share your suspicion with this Detective Leeks."

"That's just it. Suspicion. Any Arriva employee could have made that note sound like him."

Melko resumed eating, cogitating as he chewed. He aimed a fork at Ross.

"Whether it was the CEO or a clever imitator doesn't matter. They found out about Newsome and went into action. It might even be Arriva's new security guy. He has access to Arriva's emails. Maybe he picked up a trail online."

"I don't have a trail. Besides, Newsome gave me the ticket this morning. I'm sure he didn't call up either Mr. Signet or my CEO and tell them."

Melko shook his head. "We might be overlooking the obvious. Newsome must have told his boss what he was doing. What the hell's his name...?"

"Ravda. Mr. Ravi Ravda. A frail creature in a Gandhi shirt. I once saw his picture in the newspaper. Even an Eckerd usher would remember him."

"I didn't say it was him. Only that your presence at the concert was no secret. The whole scenario stinks. Why plan an attack in the middle of a concert? Why all the cloak and dagger? Why all the drama?"

"You're referring to Mr. Campesi."

"Wake up, please. You're a damn sight smarter than this. It has to be him. You didn't come out as summoned so your CEO whacked Newsome instead. Believe me, he's certifiable. I still can't see why the government uses his company for that vaccine." Melko kept jabbing the air with his fork. "You're not eating. Want me to rewarm the souvlaki?"

"It's fine."

Ross washed a bite down with the Santorini.

"No mystery there," he said. "The idea came out of Dr. Braun's lab. Out of her mind, I should say. She was one of the original contract scientists out there. DARPA simply expanded her footprint."

"Right. Dr. Chopsticks-in-her-hair. You're fortunate she was assigned to you."

Ross nodded in agreement.

"The one decision Mr. Campesi made in my favor. But it wasn't out of kindness. She was there to show me the ropes. To keep me out of trouble in the lab."

"Yeah. Mr. Generosity. I still don't trust the ass. You're not asking the basic question. Who benefits?"

Reluctantly, Ross arrived at the obvious conclusion.

"I didn't see him at the concert."

"Didn't mean he wasn't there. Regardless, all he needed was a messenger. But, why kill the accountant? He expected you to come out." He chewed some more. "Tell me about this guy Signet. A new hire?"

"Fresh out of special ops. Quiet and intimidating, like he's dealing with suppressed anger. He was brought aboard a few weeks back. He gave me the shudders then. He gives me the creeps now."

Ross would never forget the moment. Two weeks earlier, Mr. Campesi summoned all employees to an urgent session in the cafeteria. Standing stiff as a pair of poles, the CEO introduced the soldier at his side.

Chest layered with medals, anvil chin set high, Corporal Signet had sent a shockwave through what he seemed to consider his recruits. Yet his elite, aloof attitude was misguided, if not outright insulting. He wasn't facing a squad of disheveled youths looking for leadership, but a group of published, highly respected scientists who nevertheless wilted before the serenely confident and quite firm representative of special ops, a branch of the military known to them only in the abstract before that cheerless moment in the Arriva cafeteria.

He had been dispatched on temporary status by DARPA, the Defense Advanced Research Projects Agency, to Arriva to assist and safeguard the upcoming launch of the PTSD—post-traumatic stress disorder—vaccine project. Technically, their company was contracted by and therefore an arm of the Defense Department. Because the vaccine treatment program was of national importance, interference of any sort would not be tolerated. Veterans depended on this new vaccine. And, because disambiguation was the order of the day, he would commence his inspection at once.

"'Disambiguation'." Melko raised an eyebrow. "He actually said that?"

"I googled the word after the meeting. 'To clarify. Remove uncertainty.' Instead, he injected worry."

"Intriguing."

"Before retiring to an assigned office, he conducted a thorough tour of the facility. Dr. Braun told me he logged into the main server to examine financial accounts plus a ton of other reports. He had access to email accounts and calls into and out of the building."

"That's how he must have learned about the concert. He came across Newsome's name in one of the files."

"Why would he be in an Arriva file?"

Melko shrugged as he gathered plates.

"I'm just guessing. Maybe an employee previously saw you

two at that boner restaurant. He told someone at Arriva, who stuck the info in a file. Corporal Signet read the file and, being thorough, did some research. Remember at that time, Newsome claimed he was a reporter. Corporal Signet might have been acting proactively, you know, looking for evidence of breach of confidentiality. As a product of that DARPA outfit, this new vaccine is government property. Your security guy would want to plug any potential adverse publicity."

"I'm out of the vaccine loop. My only concern is Glaucon. What you're saying, this special ops creep murdered Newsome in cold blood, at a Beethoven concert, as you are so kind to remind me."

"All I'm saying, this accountant may have been in an Arriva file."

"We had dinner three times. In a rear booth at Bonefish. Believe me, no one from Arriva saw us."

"Then try this. He discovered the Simcoe demonstrators at Arriva's gate. A potentially worrisome scenario. Vociferous rag-tags interfering with the vaccine launch? Corporal Signet must have told the Simcoe people to back off. He wants to talk with the man in charge. Maybe that's how he found out about Newsome."

"And so, what then? He tails the accountant to Eckerd Hall?"

"No, Daniel. What he does is speak to Simcoe Enterprises. To that Gandhi guy, in fact. And, he talks to Newsome. Assuming he tells Corporal Signet what his accountant is up to."

"And what does Ravda do? Not much of anything, because Newsome was still pumping me for info." Ross took a breath. "Nothing adds up. There has to be another explanation. Signet was sent to control bad news, not make it."

"I agree. He wouldn't risk crushing hyoid bones at a concert, even if it was Beethoven. Just kidding. I love The Fifth Symphony. Da da da dah. You're absolutely right. Has to be some other explanation. Supreme Jerk Campesi wasn't there. Mr. Signet didn't do it. Who else?"

They let out a collective sigh. Took their glasses and the near-empty wine bottle and sank into the cushions of the couch.

"Great detective you are." Ross laughed. "So far, you are batting zero on suspects, motive and timing."

"Point taken. Let's consider other possibilities."

They entered a moment of silence as they sipped and gazed into inky blackness beyond the patio window. In the distance, Lake Tarpon lay as a velvet ribbon between clumps of trees. The vagrant drone of a late-night speedboat filtered in amongst scattered swamp sounds closer at hand. A quiet moment. Peaceful.

Despite being immersed in a tragic murder, an optimistic ray of light peeked through. Only four days remained until the all-important Friday glaucoma symposium. A meeting he had arranged to present data. A coming out party for his new device. The anticipation, overwhelming.

Chieftains from Boston, Miami, and North Carolina, the

newly installed New York Infirmary Chairman, plus a former dean of a California medical school were traveling to Tarpon Springs. Each man an innovator, a small club whose ranks Ross wanted to join. A convincing Power Point presentation, a video of the procedure, and questions from what he hoped to create, an excited audience. Finally, agreement reached on a multi-institutional study set up to gain FDA approval. The near reality of the moment cast Newsome's murder in a new light. A bump in the road, a feature article not required. Ari and Pedro, Chairman and Dean. He couldn't wait to see them.

"Aren't Glaucon and the PTSD vaccine related?"

The sudden question returned him to the gloom of more immediate concern.

"They are," he said. "Both utilize BDNF, a biological protein, but in totally different ways. My Glaucon device injects the molecule into the eye. The PTSD vaccine attaches it to a virus and sprays it inside the nose. Two separate projects."

"Seems similar to me."

"Not at all. The vaccine hones to the amygdala nucleus inside the brain. It rehabilitates overactive neurons, essentially the cause of the disorder. In my case, BDNF rescues dying ganglion, or vision cells. The techniques do not intersect."

Melko downed the final drops of wine, his inebriated eyes misting over.

"I'm looking for answers. You abandon a three-million-dollar practice and for what? To be murdered in Ruth Eckerd Hall?"

"Of course not. Sure, I had a good practice. But think about it. It's a life going in and out of dark rooms. It got to me. I admit the surgery was fun. I was small-time though. There are surgeons who do seventy to one hundred cases a day. That's a repeatable algorithm which, in the future, will become the domain of robots." He shrugged. "No self-contained, repeatable surgical steps exist for glaucoma. I wanted to make a lasting contribution. My practice was my seed money. Coupled with funds from Mrs. Samantha Campesi, my angel investor, I couldn't fail."

Melko snorted.

"'Coupled' is right, ole buddy. The former homecoming queen of Tarpon Springs High School? She took a special interest in you, I'd say. Come into my parlor, kind sir. Please 'cure' me."

He emitted a drunken bark, the evening going into serious overtime. Ross decided to get out quick before Melko coughed up more delirious recollections.

"It wasn't like that, certainly not at the beginning. Almost blind but the cancer was in remission. At the end, well, I just happened to be there."

"Right. The DARPA husband who spent most of his time in Virginia."

"That's where he worked then. We were lucky. At least my device stabilized his wife's glaucoma."

"That's not all you stabilized, my friend."

"My God, Melko. She was dying of lymphoma."

"Yeah, and the loving husband wouldn't bring her to the NIH for the latest treatment."

"She refused to go. The ballgame was over. She knew that."

"Hey, lighten up. I'm only kidding. You never misbehaved. The Boy Scout from Massachusetts? You follow Akela."

Ross had to confess there were opportunities, whenever he showed up to update his patron on the progress of the project or simply to play her Steinway. She in her subtle way had let him know she was available. But cross that boundary? Never.

"Our relationship was platonic. She was always cordial, almost sisterly."

Then came the final afternoon. Springtime, the large shutters open, fragrance in the air, her pale limbs deployed across the settee next to her magnificent Steinway. At her request, he played Chopin. Opus 19, a favorite. A few nocturnes. Then … nothing. She had fallen asleep, too weak to listen. He bid farewell, a sad longing in his heart as the housekeeper led her up the sweeping staircase one last time.

She had made his dual-tube project happen. The ultraviolet activating nano-matrix motor, the biological, savior fluids. Samantha, the initial engine of his success.

Near success. He wasn't quite there yet.

Melko sighed, eyeing the granddaddy clock in the corner.

"What I'm really driving at," he said, mindful of his guest's growing impatience, "is your unhealthy relationship with government-owned Arriva. DARPA is no joking matter. They gave us the stealth airplane and the M-16 rifle. They aren't a forgiving bunch."

"You sound like Franklin."

"What's on his plate these days? You guys were having a cozy chat."

"The Horn of Africa. A place called Eritrea."

"What's the big deal? Send in drones and a Seal extraction team. We don't need the whole fleet."

"According to Franklin, that's the Big Lie. Fool the people. Control what they think."

"Before you go, we have a final item to discuss. The young babe who accosted you at Eckerd."

"Zina? In stiletto heels and skintight dress? She couldn't have killed Newsome."

"Didn't say she did. I'm referring to your empty life. Look her up. She's, ah, ready."

Sensing the change of wind, Ross got to his feet.

"She's all of twenty five. I'm forty two—way too old."

Once again a troubling urge coursed through his bones. He flashed on young Zina, the source of this disturbance, her enveloping scent and beguiling manner. It seemed years since he'd reacted like this. Seven years to be exact. First the desire, then the infatuation, next the wedding and honeymoon, and finally, for him, catastrophe the afternoon she said goodbye and it all came crashing down.

On the other hand, Zina seemed friendly enough. Sort of.

"She was taking pictures," he said, lamely. "We bumped into one another."

"Forgive me, but this detective finds it odd—"

"*Retired* detective."

"...that she snapped pics at the precise moment you administered CPR."

"The cop went over that."

"She was there. That's all I'm saying. Don't take her act so serious, though."

"What does that...?"

"You forget she called Dr. Azzizi's office twenty two times to complain about dear granddad."

A friend, Dr. Azzizi allowed him to see referred glaucoma patients in his Clearwater office, an arrangement counterbalancing Ross's research life at Arriva.

"You think she wrote that note?"

"If I were Detective Leeks, I'd ask Ms. Palaeologus a few more questions."

"I didn't do anything to that old man except save his vision."

"She's convinced otherwise. Father Palaeologus was once a popular and devout priest."

"What of it?"

"Didn't she tell you he's become a playboy with a gold chain around his neck?"

He had indeed told Melko. Zina's accusation was absurd, however. He had merely sutured a pair of tiny plastic tubes to Grandpa's eye and injected three entirely safe and thoroughly vetted biological agents into the chamber. Nothing wrong with that.

"I'd say, you two have been on each other's radar for months."

"For God sake," Ross muttered as the two men moved to the front door. Melko pulled it open for him.

"Describe how she looked again," he said as Ross half-slipped, half-stumbled outside, "That part about Shade of Night, her intoxicating perfume wafting up and out of accessible shadows."

The laughter pursued him all the way to his car in the driveway, that and a parting admonition.

"Better be careful, Danny-boy. You're mixed up in something."

CHAPTER 5

The scooter picked him up at the East Lake intersection. When he turned left, it appeared in the rear view, a menacing red bug with hooded rider on his bumper all the way to Keystone Avenue, aiming east when he did, tracking the early morning sun into flat farmland. The sputtering growl grew fainter as it sped past him, the red insect a vanishing dot that left Ross alone on the highway.

A new experience for him. Or, maybe just his imagination. After a fitful sleep, he'd awakened with a start, dreams loaded with dark alleys and whispering zombies much resembling Eckerd Hall's ancient ushers. Then, fully awake, the dreadful moment returned. The note, the mistaken victim, his conceit a major newspaper would tell his story. And now, more bad news: followed on his trip to work.

The hunched and hooded rider made him wonder. He didn't know anyone that small. Although concerned, going to the police seemed a non-starter. *Let me get this straight, Doc. You were pursued by a red scooter? My advice, adjust. The state is known for bizarre stalkers. Call back if you have a problem.*

51

Definitely a non-starter.

Other than this dissonant note, Tuesday was off to a terrific start. Penetrating deeper into the misted countryside, he buzzed down the window, absorbing the faint, early chill of Florida farmland. For this displaced urbanite, the surrounding scene always proved a welcome sight. Grazing cattle, islands of tufted pines, and swampy wetlands punctuated an endless landscape. Once again he slipped a gear in time, welcoming the curiosity of his adopted homeland, at the very edge of civilization, near the dawn of existence. An adventure he fully embraced.

And then, Arriva, an adventure of an altogether different sort. Where each mental synapse, within the corrugated landscape of his mind, was required to fire past its limit of endurance, a necessity if he hoped his long ascent brought him a painting on the infirmary wall. A pinnacle of achievement. One, he suspected, for all his travail, might forever lie beyond reach.

His reach. Because there was space for other more deserving alumni.

Angling left, he entered Arriva's long approach road, taking yet another step to reach his goal.

Bordered by fishtail palms, the gravel road led straight as an arrow to the guardhouse at the far end. He swiped his pass card through the machine, punched in the required code, and waited. The gate didn't budge. He repeated the security check. Same result.

Signing in was usually an automatic pit stop. He tried the intercom. Static. The glassed-in guard house to his left stood empty, as did the watchtower ten feet above.

An unfamiliar voice now crackled out of the intercom, relaying an instruction to Dr. Ross. He was to park inside near the front walk where Corporal Signet would meet him. Then, after more crackles, Ross overheard a terse conversation between the voice and Corporal Signet.

An alarming disturbance here at the gate, sir.

Wait, came the brief reply. *Let the mob disperse.*

Ross hadn't noticed the protestors on his way in. He saw them now. Materializing from a stand of pines, a throng of beards and weathered jeans stepped onto the gravel road. Their raised placards bore statements he had seen before: No More Brain-Nano; Shut Campesi Down. Others of similar ilk.

Today, the hoard screamed louder as they approached the Corolla. And then he heard the chant and understood why.

"NEWSOME NEWSOME NEWSOME."

They knew about the murder.

His sympathy lay in short supply though. He found the smug appraisal grating. The man's demise had been his own fault. He seized the note and went out to the corridor. Ross had nothing to do with it. He'd been the intended victim. Their man was killed, but it might easily have been him.

As the gate swung open, he saw the razor wire atop the chain-link fence.

Keep them out. Keep them out.

All he could think of as he drove to the designated slot. He pulled in, as he so often had, next to the green Audi, and got out.

Seated behind the wheel of a patrolling golf cart, Corporal Signet came into view. He'd emerged from behind the clutch of Quonset huts housing the ground crew. He bore down on Ross as if magnetized. And now, disembarking, the security man's reptilian gaze found him. Squirming, face to face for the first time, Ross refused to succumb because, whether correct or not, he would not knuckle under any pretense of dominance.

Instead, he turned to marvel at the monolithic, peach cube beside them.

"Will you take a look at that?" he said. "To think, I've been working in this architectural masterpiece for six years. Always takes your breath away. Know what I mean?"

He cared less about Corporal Signet's take on Arriva's geometry, his take on anything at that moment.

Bypassing the ruse, never altering his focus on the unfortunate idiot before him, the corporal laid an inspecting talon on the rusting Corolla. A man in black, head to toe, like a giant raven knocking on Ross's door. Passing some kind of judgment on Ross's graveyard car.

"You are late," he said, softly.

Ross fidgeted.

"I am? You're the one driving out of the shrubs. I've been

waiting on you, Corporal Signet."

"Do not call me that. I am Signet. No title. Understood?"

"I'm Dr. Ross," he replied, weakly. "Call me Daniel. Oh, heck. Call me whatever you want. I don't need a title either."

Met with Signet's piercing stare, Ross returned to the peach cube. Anything to move this guy along. He had to get inside. He had a presentation to prepare.

"Three stories high, and climbing, right up to that vast and cloudless sky. Those are manicured gardens, by the way. The grounds people are much too busy to give you a tour. You're new. Someone should show you around."

"I am not new, only recently assigned. You are here. You will have to do."

He did not appreciate the calm assessment, bemused expression, or the gnarled hands suspended loosely at his side. He was not much liking the guy at all.

"Are you confused why I asked to meet you here, in the parking lot and not in your closet of an office in Ophthalmic Therapeutics, the label Mr. Campesi gratuitously assigned for your efforts?"

Matching baloney with malarkey, Signet signaled he was up to any challenge. A trim, stiff soldier who gave no ground.

"Tiled, interlocking hallways. Keypads to access laboratories. Except for your lab. No secret what goes on there." Signet paused, examining his quarry. "Yes, Doctor.

I am well acquainted with the building, its inhabitants, what decisions were made and why."

"Are you also acquainted with a red scooter?"

"Five foot seven. One hundred and twenty pounds. You will meet her again shortly. Why do you park in the same place every morning?"

The reply threw him.

"A female? Tell her to be more careful next time. She nearly hit me."

In a disturbing shift, the grin changed to a rigid stare.

"I have examined the surveillance tapes." Signet nodded at small cameras anchored to the light posts dotting the area. "They are revealing. As is the employee handbook. No regulations state you must park beside this Audi sedan. Yet, this is where you park every day for three years. Unless Mr. Campesi is out of town. Then his spot is empty. You also run your hand along the fender. You sigh, shake your head, then walk to the side entrance to check into the Rubik's Cube."

The uncanny recital spooled out in a monotone. He had tuned into Ross's ambition, his vulnerable, most inner sanctum. Or, perhaps not. Signet only reviewed tapes. It was he, Ross, jumping to conclusions.

"You've noticed quite a lot in such a short time. You're good, Signet. Very good."

This warranted a near imperceptible nod of approval.

"You work out regularly at the YMCA. You tolerate heat and pain. Join me, Doctor," he added, grasping Ross's elbow. "Let us stroll."

Whereupon, brooking no refusal, he led them down an adjoining walkway.

"To correct any misapprehension," the corporal said, indicating the peach cube to their right. "I am familiar with design details. Eighty meters on a side. Seventy five contract scientists. Not counting you, an anomaly on the premises, the one clinician scientist who chooses fame, not fortune, like so many of your medical colleagues. Your admiration of an Audi sedan, notwithstanding. Obstacles in your path predominate, however. The question of courage arises. What you must conquer for that long path ahead."

"You refer to the FDA?"

In answer, Signet tightened his grip and moved faster.

"Will you please slow down? We're not racing."

"Not much time before your eight o'clock with the CEO. He awaits you in the third floor conference room."

"Good. I have something to tell him."

"It concerns last night's murder."

"I wonder how you two learned about that."

"The newspaper. How else would we find out about Mr. Newsome?"

"You were there. I'm guessing at the exact moment of the murder."

Signet's blank expression didn't alter. He maintained pace. They passed the side door, heading further down the walkway.

"I remained for the first movement. I could not stay longer."

"Did you enjoy the sonata, though? You had better than front row. You were on stage."

"Archduke and Prince Imperial of Austria. Prince Royal of Hungary and Bohemia. And, we must not forget, heir apparent to Franz Joseph I, Emperor of Austria. Do any of these names ring a bell?"

"They all refer to Beethoven's most important patron. Why does musical history interest a special ops veteran?"

The veteran gave him a sidelong glance.

"Mr. Campesi asked me to investigate. Why a Beethoven concert, he asked. Who is Dr. Ross's new friend? I only had a short time to familiarize myself with the basics. Your CEO said I would not enjoy the concert. A program of tiring sonatas, was how he put it. He was wrong. I found The Goodbye movement appropriate. Although, as a simple fellow from the Carolinas, I much prefer country...."

Ross pulled them to a halt.

"You told Mr. Campesi I was attending that concert?"

Signet ignored the question.

"...music. The classical variety, like a meteor, is captivating at a distance, but never close at hand. Newsome was the easy part. The Times never heard of him. Therefore, the man was a fake, conducting a fraud. And, no, I did not kill him."

"Who did then? You were there. You must have seen what happened."

"As I told you, I abandoned ship early. Nor is Mr. Campesi a likely suspect. He left Arriva at supper time to retrieve a colleague at the airport."

"I don't understand. You knew in advance I'd be at the concert. In fact, it seems even before I knew I was attending. Yet, Newsome only gave me the tickets yesterday at my office. Did he tell you? Is that how you found out?"

"As an investigator, I investigate. What you should have done. Quite a coincidence meeting a Times reporter at a restaurant."

Signet turned away, the conversation over.

Yet, the problem wasn't over. Signet and Mr. Campesi somehow knew in advance about the concert. But, if neither man committed the murder, who did?

They soon paused at a fork in the path. Behind them lay the code-locked door to the pastel building; in front, a collection of towering, exuberant palms. A breeze brought the scent of musky flowers, the faint whistling of distant pines, and the constant drone of buzzing insects. Normally an alluring ensemble of sights and sounds. Yet, the day felt alien, sliding fast out of focus.

Signet was studying him again, this time in cool appraisal. Ross bridled at his iron composure, at the implication Ross was somehow involved in Newsome's murder.

"If you actually do investigate," he said. "Who killed the accountant?"

Signet shook his head. "For me and this Detective Leeks, it remains a puzzle. He called Mr. Campesi at his home late last evening. He had questions."

Ross blinked. He'd not expected this.

"'Who is this Dr. Ross?' 'Does he really work at Arriva?' 'What sort of person is he?' 'Please explain his Glaucon project.' 'Is he pulling taffy or what?' He also asked if your CEO ever heard of a J. Lawson Newsome, senior accountant at Simcoe, Incorporated."

"He asked about *me*?"

"As did a reporter for a Tampa newspaper. A verifiable reporter this time. A leak in the police grapevine, we imagine. Mr. Campesi persuaded both to keep your name and Arriva out of it. He had no idea who killed this accountant. I am certain your CEO will discuss this upstairs."

Signet's expression darkened.

"You are not to blame for the accountant," he said with a brief shrug. "But you must move on. Overcome your fear.

That alone detains you. Enough of this morbid subject. I need a favor. A friend requires your assistance."

Caught off guard by Signet's oblique and shifting manner, Ross listened to the story. A mother of a former member of Signet's Iraq unit was going blind from glaucoma. A Philadelphia specialist said there was nothing to be done. Stem cell therapy, a pipedream for the future. He did not advise marijuana. Within a year, her few remaining ganglion cells would die off. Then, it would be service dogs and a white cane. Upon hearing the news, the son became defiant. He refused to accept the verdict. A cure must exist, he insisted. He would find it.

"The son knows I work with DARPA scientists," Signet said. "He asked me to use my contacts to find a better specialist."

"DARPA?" Ross said. "Aren't you a security expert?"

Signet's eyebrows shifted gears.

"To date, you have stabilized twelve such patients, including Mrs. Samantha Campesi. Perhaps, even Father Palaeologus. The late wife trusted you, and so shall my friend's mother."

He'd misjudged Signet. Behind his icy exterior, a heart pumped.

The physician in Ross then asserted itself. Without question, he'd try to help this woman. He'd find an immediate opening in tomorrow's schedule.

"I have already taken the liberty," Signet casually replied.

"You will examine her at eleven. Now, go upstairs. With Mr. Campesi, keep your eye on the ball."

There was a squeal of brakes and a roar of applause at the front gate. A bearded man in a Gandhi shirt and leather sandals emerged from the newly arrived van. His arrival rekindled the demonstrators.

"Ah, Ravi Ravda. He is here." Signet spoke calmly, as if familiar with the spectacle. "A troublemaker, to be sure. We do not discredit him, however. Someday he may well offer you a lifeline. If he does, accept it."

"Now what are you talking about?"

Signet whispered into a walkie-talkie. A moment later, another golf cart appeared from behind the gardens and sprinted for the front gate. A guard jumped out, promptly corralled the disruptive group, and sent them packing. Their leader escaped in the fringed van, roaring off in a U-turn down the gravel drive.

Halfway to Keystone, it skidded to a stop. Leaning out of the driver side window, Ravi Ravda called Signet by name, performed an awkward salute, then continued on to the highway, turned right and disappeared.

"You know that guy?" Ross said.

"It was Mr. Ravda who informed us about the accountant. In exchange, your CEO promised no arrests of his ragged flock if it stood down from the vaccine rollout."

"You knew this *before* the concert? Why didn't you tell me? I was almost murdered, for pity's sake."

"To see you and Mr. Newsome together for myself. Ravi Ravda is deceitful. He might have lied so his protestors gained access to the Arriva compound. The man's death was a complete surprise."

"And, now Mr. Campesi thinks I'm involved. All this could have been avoided."

"Involved with murder, no. Speaking with Newsome, yes. For the last time, I have no idea who did it."

Signet then spun on his heel and led them back to the side door. He punched in the code, and they entered Arriva's main corridor. Cool air washed over them, and, as on so many previous days, not one of the white coats dashing into punch key labs offered a greeting. No surprise there. Ross's work had failed to penetrate DARPA's secret universe. Worse to consider, the Eckerd Hall concert had been a setup.

Signet tapped him on the shoulder.

"Preoccupied with Mr. Newsome?"

"That obvious, huh?"

"You were easily fooled. The reason: fear of failure. You must ask yourself: who benefits?"

"Precisely what I'm thinking. I'm also surprised I'm so easily read."

"Only by me, Doctor. The explanation? Mirror neurons. Mine to yours. Yours to mine. An involuntary connection allowing us to communicate together."

Explanation rendered, then another near imperceptible shrug. A micro twitch, Signet's lone betrayal of emotion.

"Seems a chancy way to go about it."

"Yet opportunity for synaptic delay does not exist."

Ross eyed this human specimen anew. *Synaptic delay?*

"To disambiguate. Isn't that your goal?"

Signet now bored more deeply into him, shaking him down with some invisible marker.

"You pay attention," he said. "A useful talent. Employ it wisely for what lies ahead."

The elevator arrived. They ascended in an upward whoosh of chilled air.

Signet broke the silence.

"Such connections I refer to are involuntary. In time, perhaps for you as well, assuming suitable rearrangements can be made. We shall see about that."

"You lost me."

"Our brain cells, Doctor. Neurons. They discharge to produce a movement or a thought. Identical cells, in a pair of individuals, fire at the same moment. First, a discharge in the originating brain. Second, in that of the receiver. In our case, mirror neurons, yours to mine reflect what you are thinking. Perhaps, later on, a return pathway may be established."

The guy wouldn't stop transmitting these ambiguous,

deceptive outbursts. Talk about a need for disambiguation. Riddles, evasions, a few outright lies. Not much to hold on to.

"The mirror neurons described in the literature," Ross said, "only refer to observed actions, not thought patterns."

"Sensed thoughts broadcast their own wavelengths. Output loud and clear to a receptive person."

"More doubletalk? What's this 'reverse direction' business?"

The mysterious fellow placed a finger to his lips.

"Attend closely to the confrontation. We will speak later."

The elevator slid open on the third floor. Signet led them across the hall to a formidable Redwood door, rocking on its hinges from a heated exchange on the other side.

'You will stop. Do you hear me?'

'Fuck off, Colonel. I said FUCK OFF!'

Signet opened the door.

"Don't be fooled," he said. "They are foxhole buddies from way back. Good luck."

CHAPTER 6

He stood before the rear windows, feigning interest as always in the panorama of subtropical Florida, while his foxhole buddy hovered in the far corner, tight as a sphincter, skull-and-bones shoulder patch an ominous omen, his sharply pinched expression caught midstride by the sudden interruption.

"Yes, Corporal. What is it?"

"Dr. Daniel Ross, sir. The doctor in question."

"Punctual as expected. Very good then. Arturo…" He cast his osprey gaze to the starched white shirt at the window. "Our guest is here. Shall we begin?"

Soldier Sphincter thrust his shoulders back, drawing attention to a thousand elegant medals, ribbons, and colorful commendations that elicited respect, if not a little fear, at least from Ross. Mr. Security, for his part, regarded the evolving scene with a look of benign patience.

Yet, there was no doubt, the fuming soldier wielded power, exceeding in authority that of the CEO, their supposed host.

"Sir, shall we stand or sit?"

"Whatever. Sit. Stand. Crawl. Arturo, are you with us?"

Exhibiting a more passive approach to authority, Mr. Campesi came alive. With languid ease, he shot his cuffs, flashed a confident smile, and sat.

"Daniel. Thanks for coming. Gentlemen, you may not realize the good doctor and I have spent countless hours in this very room. Is that not correct ... Daniel?'

"Ah, yes. That is quite correct."

"Have you filed the consents? Did you chart this week's pathology reports? Review statistics with Dr. Braun? Detail each item for our beloved FDA?" The CEO chuckled. "It was intrusive, I admit. But, as dear Samantha always reminded me, you were a quick study. And, by God, you measured up. An exemplary performance. Until, of course, today. Colonel Bame—Benson—did you bring the newspaper?"

Ross glimpsed the blistering headline in the soldier's hand. It resembled the one Newsome showed him the night before: "DEFENSE DITHERS—To Eritrea or Not?" After folding to an inner section, Sphincter—Colonel Bame—tossed it across the oval table to their host. Mr. Campesi broke out his ceramic grin and gently brushed the offering aside.

"Not that one," he said. "The article about the Beethoven concert."

"Have it your way. We'll forget Eritrea for now. You know

I won't go along with it. I'll work it out with Corporal Signet. What do you plan to do about that goddamn article?"

The CEO chided the soldier to mind his manners. Proper introductions were required first. He bade Colonel Bame to shake Dr. Ross's hand, which he did with icy efficiency.

"Now," Campesi continued with a magnanimous smile, "About the concert article … It's appropriately vague. Let's have a firsthand account. Signet, can you help us?"

Corporal Signet settled into a seat beside Ross.

"Not very much, sir," he said. "I was only at Eckerd Hall a short while. I did not witness the murder. But, may I remind us," he added, giving Ross a genial pat. "This man was the intended target. Had he met the accountant's fate, Arriva, Inc. would suffer investigative scrutiny. This would delay and embarrass the PTSD vaccine launch. As it is, a Simcoe employee, with no known connection to this company, bit the dust. A tragedy, of course, but not for Arriva."

After a quick stretch and a crack of vertebrae, the corporal resumed standing.

"This time we escape," the colonel said. "The Secretary will not tolerate another mishap. Is that understood? Next week's launch must proceed as planned."

"Indeed it shall. I am certain we are all pulling the same oar. Now then, Daniel."

Here, Mr. Campesi swiveled about for a prolonged look

across the mahogany table at its lone occupant. As tanned and fit as the two soldiers, the CEO wore tailored slacks and a snow white, creased shirt, anchored by palm tree cufflinks, snug like a uniform. In manner if not dress, the man was cut from the same military cloth. Attired in a rumpled seersucker shirt and shorts, Ross cut an altogether different figure.

"It is one thing to upset me, your helpful mentor. It is quite another to raise the ire of our very own Special Assistant to the Secretary of Defense. As of this morning, the colonel here is home from a successful sojourn in Mosul, Iraq. His men helped decapitate ISIS insurgents instead of the other way around."

The colonel emitted a strangled cough.

"Cut the bullshit, Arturo. Forget Iraq. Let's deal with the doctor. He's the one in the news."

"I am merely drawing attention to the obvious. You and the Secretary of Defense are not to be fooled with. Something our esteemed glaucomatologist must not forget. Did I say that right? Such an awkward term. Glaucoma specialist then."

"May I remind the colonel?" Signet interrupted. "We possess an antidote to fight terrorists anywhere, including our backyard."

"Not now. One problem at a time. An easy one, if we are to believe our *esteemed* CEO."

The so-named dismissed the implied threat with a flick of his bejeweled hand.

"Alright then. The doctor. As we know, he has developed a cure for glaucoma which, as he is so often reminds me, remains a curable form of blindness. Alas, he is also in today's news. May I ask? How was the concert?"

"Mr. Campesi, may I remind you, he did not hear the concert."

"Thank you, Signet. Very well."

With a heavy sigh, the CEO sat back, shaking his head, fiddling with his cufflinks.

"Such a nasty business," he said. "A surprise for us both. Yet, compared to other rough times we've shared, a minor bump in the road. I'm thinking about dear Samantha's final illness. Her awful, lonely death. Or, passing. I guess that's the polite term for ashes to ashes these days."

He paused, with another shake of his weary head, as he glanced to the portrait of his wife on the side wall. A marvelous oil of a younger Samantha in soft silk and lace, pensively regarding a world she inhabited but a short fifty-three years.

"She's here with us now, you know. Can you sense her presence? You managed to preserve her vision until leukemia ended the story. Yes, we both suffered with that one. It hasn't been all success and glory at Arriva these past years. No, sir. It sure hasn't."

The room dropped into an expectant silence. They had reached the slow, middle movement of Campesi's improvised sonata. Beginning on a lyrical note, it shifted to the subdominant, followed by a reverberating development of a fresh theme pointing now to what they all awaited. The maestro did not disappoint.

In a fit of apparent rage, he banged the hardwood.

"Damnit. This is *one bump* too many."

"I can explain."

"Don't bother. We know what happened. The accountant deceived you and paid the price. Colonel Bame is justified to worry about the fallout from this stupid article. Our Wounded Warrior Program must not be tarnished. It is one of great distinction, perhaps the best veteran centered programs the DOD has ever launched. For god's sake, we're talking the U.S. government here."

"I realize that, sir. The article did not concern me or Arriva, let alone the United States Government. It was solely about a cruel murder at Eckerd Hall. I'd never do a thing to jeopardize the PTSD vaccine project."

Ross turned to Signet, whose attention had shifted. Steering clear of the skirmish, he stood shoulder to shoulder with the colonel, both men examining Samantha's portrait as if it were *George Washington Crossing The Delaware*. An obvious novelty, heads tilted in rapt concentration, eyes glued to silk curves and mysterious folds.

It fell to their host to convey proper dismay with Ross's behavior.

"We are, may I say, disappointed, Daniel."

"And, if I may say, sir, you and these Army stalwarts disappoint me. Where's the due diligence here? Will one of you guys please explain the perfidy I've committed? I've done nothing to compromise DARPA or the PTSD project."

Leaning down, Signet whispered in his ear.

"Stalwarts? Perfidy? You're on a roll, kid. Don't stop now."

Mr. Campesi raised a hand, again corralling focus.

"You are correct. The murder does not relate. Let us pray it remains that way."

"I agree," Colonel Bame added, as an afterthought. "You, an innocent bystander, witnessed a murder, the victim an imposter. No connection whatsoever to Arriva or the vaccine launch. End of story. Next."

Relieved to be off death row, Ross prepared to return to his lab. But the two soldiers pulled back a fraction, acting strange. An awkward pause settled over the room.

Next?

Something else was on the agenda. What had transpired so far, prelude to yet another movement. Then it came to him. From initial introductions, to well-timed comments about Samantha, even Signet's nonchalance, the entire meeting prearranged. And, now a fresh vibration in the air, a kind of coda to a dissonant composition.

"Do you remember Margaret from the FDA?"

"Sure," Ross said, on high alert. "Why do you ask?"

"She finally got back to me about your three agents. As

it stands, your original plan will not be approved by the committee. She suggests, no, she *instructed* me to inform you, to concentrate on just the BDNF factor alone. Forget the other two. BDNF is the way to go. I realize this is quite a blow. Shit happens. The woman changed her mind. Glaucon cannot include that anti-caspase stuff, what do you call it...?"

"The BCL-2 inhibitor," Ross said, appalled this champion of biologics was so ignorant of this agent. "It's a compound that turns off cell death. It saves neurons. It stabilizes glaucoma."

"Please. Not a hissy fit. You also have to jettison that virus mediated gene agent."

"*The extron modification factor?* It reverses a genetic defect. It's vital to the procedure."

"Stop whining. The workaround is simple. Simply load up the three chambers with BDNF. You'll prolong the effect. Patients will only have to refill their chambers every ninety days instead of monthly. I'll have the engineers reprogram the chip."

"You can't do that. Glaucon was designed to both rescue and preserve damaged neurons. That's why it's revolutionary. You have to convince her."

"Sorry. I signed off yesterday."

"BDNF will only preserve—"

"Stop, dammit. The matter is settled. We're dealing with the FDA. The BDNF decision is final."

"Are you forgetting the Phase I and Phase II trials?"

Mr. Campesi gave him a look.

"Each of those twelve patients received three agents."

"I realize that. Take another look at the mouse data. It shows BDNF is the single most potent agent. In theory, your cocktail is pure heaven for injured ganglion cells in a petri dish. In the real world, it's another matter. Remember, we removed the entire retina from those animal eyes with glaucoma and put them in a petri dish. Unlike the separate ganglion cells, the retina as a whole responded best to the BDNF. You didn't need those two other factors. I'm convinced that's why your patients improved. It's a disappointment but you'll adjust. We'll stick with BDNF."

An oversimplification to be sure. The retina "as a whole" did better simply because the ganglion cells were better. And their status was determined by all three factors, not BDNF alone. Yet, it was futile to argue. Change the FDA's mind? Might as well reverse Earth's orbit. One significant issue still had to be addressed though.

How ethical was it to proceed with Friday's symposium? His presentation concerned data about three treatment modalities. All twelve subjects received the original concoction. Data for BDNF alone did not exist, at least, not in human subjects. But it did in animals.

Backpedaling hard, Ross searched for a way out of the dilemma. Maybe he should just consider the animal data.

The CEO was correct about BDNF. All the mice and

the two chimpanzees in the Bethesda complex regained vision in the original BDNF Phase I and Phase II trials. That data was secure. The basic concept established. Both the BCL-inhibitor and the Extron motif also worked but it had been BDNF that provided the required boost. He reconsidered. Everything was in place. As the CEO said, he'd adjust.

"Okay. I'll go with it."

"That's settled. Thought you'd be a bigger pain in the ass about it. Margaret will be pleased. Now, off you go. Work hard. Signet, please show the doctor out. It seems Colonel Bame has a problem to discuss."

CHAPTER 7

He had already gripped the handle when Signet reached over his shoulder and slammed the door shut.

Startled, Ross whirled around.

"Where did you come from? You can't keep me out of my lab. Let me go. I have work to do."

For a brief moment the cold, unwavering gaze immobilized him, but he refused to be intimidated. He had tired of the man's theatrics.

"You are frustrated, irritated, and angry."

"Great observation, Chief. Get out of my way. I have to change the entire presentation."

"For you, an easy alteration to proceed with the symposium."

"And, stop this mirror-neuron mumbo-jumbo. It's obvious how I feel."

"You failed to see me on the elevator. Your mind is distant, preoccupied with failure."

"You're right. I didn't see you. I do now. So, screw off, guy … Hey! What the heck?"

Signet had seized his elbow and was propelling him down the corridor.

"Not yet, Doctor. There are matters to discuss."

He could not escape, the guy's hold ironclad. Thrust through the side door, he stumbled along as they took the encircling walkway to the clump of Quonset huts behind the complex. The grounds were deserted, the Simcoe protestors gone, the air alive with insects and the ever-present aroma of blooming foliage.

Signet released him when they reached a bank of Viburnum shrubs. Edging past the leafy barrier, they entered the bower of Quonset huts, concealed in shadow courtesy of soaring slash pines filtering out the sunlight.

Ross emitted a low whistle.

"So this is what lies behind the curtain of bark and berries. Who selected this spot?" he asked. "You or Mr. Campesi."

Signet didn't respond. As he had with Samantha's portrait, he seemed genuinely taken by the unique setting, as if encountering it for the first time.

Ross angled his gaze in parallel and found himself staring at a pair of Great Blue herons, rare long-legged creatures, oblivious of their audience, just beyond the encircling pines. They were perched upon exposed roots of a cypress tree, one of many stretching up and out of the algae-tinged swamp. Other clusters of the odd appearing trees merged in the near distance. Then his focus widened. He watched a small flock of swooping birds call out a warning as a marauding hawk, weaving amongst the pines, gave them a quick appraisal before flying off.

The scene primitive, tranquil, a natural paradise. Goosebumps erupted beneath the seersucker. Concealed from the front gate and uninvited attention, the grotto a perfect hideaway for Arriva's Chief of Security. But why lead Ross here?

"Unique," was all he could think to say.

"Did you see the sandhill crane?"

"Only the herons."

"How about the boat-tailed grackle?'

"What? No. I missed...."

"In time, you may yet see what is there. Come inside. I have much to show you."

Before unlatching the door to the first hut, Signet glanced back, over his shoulder, at the pastel cube they'd left behind. Seen from this viewpoint through branches and vines, the structure appeared more an abstract blob than a well-financed, DARPA facility.

"Your CEO has a certain charm," Signet said. "Give him that."

"You can't be referring to Mr. Campesi."

"Charitably, I admit. Almost magnanimous, yet arrogant,

devoid of empathy despite the remarks about his late wife. Do not be misled. Manipulative and callous, he entertains few qualms about stepping upon others to further his goal. His favors are but a decoy to the treachery beneath. He smiles for spreadsheets only, his contempt for employees obvious. I have been here a short time only but time enough to know he is untrustworthy no matter the bonhomie. Without DARPA backing, his outfit could not compete. Although it is not my place to give advice, I suggest you leave this dungeon on the next plane out."

"Tell me what you really think."

"Look behind the net he casts. He never spoke to Margaret at the FDA."

Ross shot him an incredulous look. "He lied about that?"

"It is easier for him to manufacture BDNF. His company already has the process up and running. According to estimates, your other two biologicals would cost a fortune. He will charge this growth factor to the government." He paused, chin down, digging into thoughts. "It amounts to quite a windfall. A scam, really, but an arrangement encouraged by the Defense Department to inspire other private companies to follow suit. Do not get more involved with Mr. Campesi."

"Why was Colonel Bame upset? We heard his voice in the corridor."

Signet measured him more closely.

"I was dispatched to oversee the PTSD program. To investigate how Arriva functioned. The colonel has returned home because of the CEO himself. That matter does not concern you. Not yet, at least."

"Clear as swamp water. But that reminds me. Mr. Campesi indicated the colonel arrived this morning."

"What of it?"

"You said earlier Mr. Campesi went to Tampa Airport last night. I assumed it was to fetch this Colonel Bame. But if he didn't actually go to the airport then he just might have been at the concert."

"His office said he went to the airport. I assumed, as you did, it was Tampa Airport. Whom he met then or dropped off does not concern me. Colonel Bame did indeed arrive this morning. Your CEO could not possibly have picked him up at Tampa Airport."

"He arrived by helicopter?"

"Not likely. Important emissaries of the Pentagon, particularly on a flight from the Mideast, fly into MacDill Air Force Base. That is where special ops command is located and where Campesi found him."

"If the colonel flew into MacDill this morning, Mr. Campesi still might have been at the concert last night."

"Again, unlikely. Whether he retrieved someone at Tampa last evening is unimportant. This line of thought leads nowhere. It is a distraction. If you ask me, he never attended Beethoven."

"Why is that?"

"He detests music, his lack of a musical sense, a rare trait." Signet now opened the door to the hut. "Your rods will soon adjust. Take your time. Dr. Braun expects you at eleven thirty."

Cute, his mention of rod photoreceptors. The corporal had no doubt enriched his eyeball vocab after a sojourn in Ross's research files. Good for him. They now possessed a common language. But, not so good, his misleading comments about Mr. Campesi's various trips to airports. It reinforced Ross's suspicion that the CEO, and possibly Signet himself, remained a factor in the murder equation. According to Signet, his boss was manipulative, a liar even, traits the security man also appeared to possess. The question morphed. Was either man capable of murder?

His rods quickly adjusted to the dim light. As he began to inspect the cramped quarters, his host withdrew to the shadows, vanishing for a moment on the other side of a suspended tarp bisecting the curved interior. Alone, swallowed by a creeping silence, he found the place unnervingly dark. Moisture lined his brow. Unaccountably, he felt nervous.

A shadow materialized on the curved dome above. Signet, hovering close.

"Take a moment. Get your bearings. Outside I spoke of a disguised psychopath. In here, there is no disguise. And no one chose this spot. It chose me. What, may I ask, is a gony-scope?"

"*Gonioscope*," he corrected. "It's an outmoded method of examination. A patient lies back in a chair. A pair of special magnifying lenses is then placed on each eye, enabling a simultaneous examination of both."

"You don't do this anymore?"

"There are quicker ways to perform the exam," he said. "More useful for both the patient and cash flow. With all the financial cutbacks, one does not dawdle."

"Tomorrow, will you employ the outmoded or quicker exam?"

"I'll do the *correct* exam. I can't believe you asked that."

To suggest he might skimp on a consultation was insulting. He might have moved out of Boston, but brought his training with him.

"For you, it may not be too late. You may yet take your place on the wall."

This hit dead center, the reference close to his heart, to his entire life.

"What are you saying?"

"The ones you admire. The ones who trained you. Those that trained them. Your idols."

He should have anticipated this. The guy read his file, the stuff Samantha would have known and supplied on his original application. His hope one day to have his portrait on the wall outside the library at the Boston Eye Infirmary. His dream, outlandish as it was, to make a difference, to warrant such recognition.

Signet stepped fully into the cone of light of the hanging bulb. Despite the gloom and his sinister aura, Ross thought he detected a hint of a friendly twinkle in the man's steely expression. Then a butterfly somewhere flicked its wing and the moment clarified. Not a twinkle. Not even a friendly crease. Simply a variation on neutral, the shadowed face obscuring recessed sockets, distant caves on a forbidden landscape.

"Look around, Doctor. You are here to witness and to learn."

Ross moved deeper into the interior.

Twenty yards long and half again as wide, the hut, though sufficiently spacious for a lone dweller, proclaimed a cramped existence. He wandered, first to the heavy curtain then along the near wall greeted, as he progressed, by rows of framed photographs featuring soldiers in foreign lands.

"Is this your former squad?"

He pointed to six men in body armor, rifles at the ready. Surrounded by bombed out buildings, they wore double ammo belts with helmets half concealing grim faces.

Signet lightly fingered one of the pictures.

"This one, the very first to which I was assigned. You may recall Fallujah. We avenged the Blackwater Deaths. Good men, dragged through streets like animals. A terrible tragedy, much like ISIS and current beheadings. I have a book if you desire details."

Ross shook his head. Pictures featuring the stark horror of dying men were unnecessary. He moved on, passing photos of armed vehicle columns, of soldiers pulling the maimed and injured from alleys, of explosions, smoke and bodies in every conceivable position. Scenes of war more graphic than TV coverage he'd seen before.

"I reenlisted. The second time as volunteer. Too many left behind. I had to return."

Ross paused at a gruesome shot of three dead civilians in the dust.

"Insurgents," Signet said. "Show them no pity. I shot them with an M821. My sniper rifle at the time. Please examine the next photo."

This snagged Ross's attention.

"You were a *sniper*?"

"Seal sniper team. The 2nd battalion, assigned to mop up resistance. That was early November, two thousand four."

In his easy monotone, Signet told him about the booby-trapped buildings, the tunnels, the intermixing of civilian and insurgent, the constant cascade of mortar shells and exploding grenades as they searched for a place to hide. In this particular case his men had taken up residence on the second floor of a half-cratered structure. They waited hours for an enemy sniper to show up. When he did, Signet took him out.

"My avenging bullet traveled through a brick wall then two companions before it reached its mark. As a tribute and to lift their spirits, the men laid them out in the dirt."

He snorted, a kind of laugh, one of the few uttered by this seemingly calmest of violent men. Lift spirits. A joke buried inside a recollection? Amazing to imagine what this man endured. Yet, here he was, a survivor.

"It worked. We won the battle."

"You actually shot those men with a single bullet?"

"I tell this story for a reason. As a result of that one brazen shot, my senior officer transferred me to tactical close quarter combat school. That was long ago. A lifetime, really. I was young, eager to excel. Next, I was introduced to Colonel Bame. It was his job to find and train superior warriors. He sent me to a DARPA facility where they erased my fear with a special technique. I was then dispatched to Nuristan in northeast Afghanistan. I conducted solo missions, no longer afraid in the slightest. Three encounters with the enemy. I brought back trophies. There. Examine the knife."

A floor lamp illuminated a picture. Ross read the inscription.

Seal Team Pup Knife, 9.5 inches, Serrated, Black, Kydex Sheath

Signet had turned this section of the hut into a shrine dedicated to war and its weapons. For Ross, the entirety of it was unsettling, yet at the same time ... magnetic. It drew him in, forcing him to see the man before him in a new light.

"What exactly did you mean by trophies?"

Signet held up a hand.

"Enough of the horror. That was then. Here is what came next, why I asked you in."

The former sniper directed him to the partition curtain. He drew it aside revealing an earie, yellow glow that immediately immersed them, an odd experience for Ross's photoreceptors. Swamped in blue after-images, opponent colors battled the altered gloom.

The swirl of blue and yellow caught Signet off guard as well modifying, for the slightest instant, the corporal's military demeanor. Despite the shifting wavelengths, Ross caught a low wattage grin sliding in and out of focus. Then, firmer reality reasserted itself. The man, still an enigma, became Signet again.

He ran a bedazzled eye around the interior.

Beyond shifting shadows lay the fixed contour of a narrow cot, squared off with a green and black military blanket. A reclining chair stood in the middle of a lush green carpet while low tables held incense holders all aglow. Soon, as he became aware of an invisible scent assaulting his olfactory neurons, other senses jumped ship while his nostrils zinged in strange delight.

A Buddha statue occupied an entire corner, its presence explaining the carpet of yin-yang symbols, the incense and cannabinoid, yellow glow. The Enlightened One, witness to it all, sitting to one side maintained eternity as his only goal.

Ross had entered a time warp. Not at all what he expected.

"Land of Oz," he said. "The man behind the curtain?"

"It might well be."

An incomprehensible comment, in tune with the decor.

"Or, your private ashram. A remarkable juxtaposition."

More accurately, a claustrophobic man cave best described it. As the utter silence of the realm descended, he buried the unkind thought.

"Consider this my sanctuary. Before you find your own, consider two countervailing aspects. Most familiar to you, that of the light and the dark. And, also now for you and once for me, the fear, then the courage. Relax, Doctor. No place to hide here."

"I am relaxed. I'm not hiding."

"In your alien environment? Impossible."

In a way, Signet hit the nail. At least for him, this aromatized enclosure was his sacred space, where he found a resolution, a kind of redemption for earlier times. For Ross it simply represented a life of smoke and mirrors.

"If I understand you correctly," he said, "You imply I resemble, in some yet undefined manner, what those photos out there suggest. I am but one of the angry, injured, and scared. But, if I'm lucky, I may learn to meditate past the slaughtered bodies and wind up here. Do I have that right, Corporal Signet?"

The stinging rejoinder sailed right past its target, who waved it off as he might an insect.

"Regard this visit as metaphor. Mr. Campesi elicits fear to coerce you. Find and replace its likeness upon the infirmary wall in Boston. When you do, it will set you free."

Ross motioned to the segment of the hut on the other side of the curtain.

"You found and eliminated your own fear. Is that it?"

"It disappeared down a rat hole. The same can happen for you. If not, I will formally introduce you to Colonel Bame."

"I already met him."

With a gentle shove, Signet moved him through the curtain and back to the other side of the hut.

"Return to your lab," he said. "Go, before I use that knife and claim another trophy."

He nodded at the serrated blade in its glass case across the room. He fingered one of Ross's ears.

"You're kidding. Unreal."

"One final thing to remember. The concert note was addressed to you."

"How did you learn about that?"

"Detective Leeks informed me. Now calm yourself. Doctor Braun expects you."

Chapter 8

Like a locomotive, Dr. Beth Braun barged into the lab, opening and shutting the door with a loud snap. Ross kept focused. Absorbed with the delicate task of assembling the tiny matrix motor, he finally glanced up from the microscope, greeted her, and repositioned the jeweler forceps.

Beth tapped his forehead.

"There's a naked female in the corridor," she said, parking on the adjacent stool.

"No kidding." Familiar ruse. "I better go revive her."

"Calls herself Theodora Palaeologus. Said you fixed her grandfather's eye. Said she's very grateful. Said, if you were willing...."

He laid the forceps aside. Scrutinized her carefully and found the playful twinkle oddly reassuring.

"You look like the proverbial cat that swallowed the canary."

Her matronly chin turned up.

"Merely attempting to bring some cheer after the disappointment."

"You heard."

She nodded.

"Like everyone else. The bio people are upset, big time. They thought, with three agents, Glaucon was a winner. Coupled with the post-traumatic vaccine, a positive double whammy for our returning troops. Can't argue with Margaret at the FDA, though."

"Right. The FDA."

"So, other than that, Mrs. Lincoln, did you enjoy the play?"

Another of her morbid jokes. He laughed anyway.

"I've been thinking," he said. "What if we use private funding for our upcoming, multi-institutional trials? Bypass DARPA and the FDA altogether. That way we can develop Glaucon for the European market. That's out of FDA jurisdiction."

"It won't be easy. Arturo will represent a formidable roadblock. He will never sign away patent rights. And, *he* is DARPA all the way."

She was right, the lord of the manner intolerant of insubordination amongst the serfs. Things were not that bad though because, even with three biologicals reduced to one, the essential concept behind Glaucon stayed the same. That was the true light at the end of the silicone tube-tunnel. Reprogrammed to handle only BDNF, the delivery module would be easier to assemble. It would also deliver three times the dose that stabilized glaucomatous, or injured, cells in culture. Down the road, after they were up and running, he'd rejigger the biologicals back to three. Now all he had to do was redo an already complicated symposium presentation.

Beth tapped his head again.

"Hey, cowboy. Is that a frown behind your frazzled whiskers?"

"I'm rethinking my slides."

"What about your own 'matrix tubes'? How are they holding up?"

Overcome by her own humor, Beth teetered on the brink of a calamitous fall. The sturdy stool held fast as she wiped away tears.

"Sorry about that," she said. "Got carried away. What you got on the platform? Let me have a look."

Adjusting the oculars, she examined the two centimeter device for several moments then grinned in approval.

"It's so small," she said, "How do you suture it to the eye?"

"With an operating microscope, ding dong. And, while we're on the topic, how are your tubes functioning? Are you, ah, giving them a good workout these days?"

They both had a laugh with that one, this back and forth a

familiar routine dating to their first days of collaboration. Samantha had assigned this DARPA research scientist to his project, and he'd been indebted to her ever since. Indispensable from the start, Beth had taught him to use ultra-fast centrifuges, critical microanalysis techniques plus a dozen other lab-related skills including the unique talent required to deal with the FDA.

And now, no little thanks to her, his symposium was on autopilot. After some last minute tweaking, it would be ready to go.

A lighter mood overtook him. He opened a folder and took out his talk.

"I was serious before," he said, crossing out the words "Three Unique Biologicals," adding instead, "The One Most Critical Factor to Halt and Cure Glaucoma: BDNF." "How *are* your tubes holding up? You're only forty-five. If you get lucky, you might still conceive."

"Listen, buster. I could have propagated. I chose science instead."

"Tell me about it." He offered a twinkle of his own for a change. "Aren't you the one who discovered 2-Proton Imaging? A game changer, if there ever was one."

"True, but not as earth-shaking as Z-Femto-Second Microscopy. The idea for that ultrafast technique came straight out of your busy little brain inside *this* lab."

"Hold on a minute. You're the one who nailed Zircon Uranium-Lead Geochronology. A whole new ballgame after that."

"Bet your silicon tubes," she said. "I'm branching out. No longer a bioengineer, I now examine rocks, see what they're made of."

They exchanged high fives, the reference to complicated, cutting edge research tools neither knew a thing about or would ever use always provided a certain decompression, today being no exception.

"I'm also branching out," he said. "I'm now researching mirror neurons and mental teleportation. It seems Signet's got the gift and can read my mind. Or thinks he can. I returned from his hideaway a few moments ago. Can't figure out what he wanted to show me."

"Samsara. Nirvana. The distance he's travelled. Did he show you his disgusting knife? It gave me the shivers."

"Me, too. An ear cutting, Seal Team item." Ross suppressed a shudder. "Beth, do you remember our discussion at Bonefish Friday night after the movies?"

She nodded. "You took me to a zombie flick then eyeballed chicks at dinner. Some outing."

"We were talking shop and wondering if Mr. Campesi would attend my symposium this week."

"And I got the days mixed up. I said he wouldn't be able to go because he was scheduled for a pickup at the airport. Only, the pick-up was last night instead. What of it?"

He shook his head. "Do you happen to know who it was? The colonel arrived this morning. It couldn't have been him."

Beth's eyebrows crunched together. "I have no idea. Family member, maybe, or this colonel fellow? Rumor has it he's commander of Special Ops Iraq. Supposedly, he flew direct to MacDill to problem shoot the PTSD rollout. Except, we were all told Signet was brought in for that. Another rumor says he's here because of our esteemed CEO. It's hush-hush. Keeping us in the dark."

Ross rose from the scope, stretched until his back cracked, then jiggled the chopsticks in Beth's hair. The tidy woman playfully slapped his hand, accustomed to the intrusion. Composed and attractive in a hemmed-skirt, starched-coat sort of way, Beth seemed primed for romance. Aside from quirky Melko, she was the only friend he had.

"If the colonel arrived this morning, where was Mr. Campesi last night?"

"I assume at Tampa Airport. What's bugging you?"

He debated sharing his suspicions but decided against it, aware of how crazy it sounded.

"Oh, I overheard him and the colonel arguing this morning. I'm worried they think I had something to do with that murder."

"You, the micro-gadget guy? That's a laugh. You might kill a palmetto bug. Maybe."

He felt her eyes on him, then she moved back to stand beside him.

"Dear boy. You look intense." She took hold of his shoulders, gave him a good shake. "Are you alright?"

"Just obsessing over the presentation. I have to rearrange and make new slides."

"That's what this is about. The BDNF switcheroo. Well, put your mind at rest. Arturo and the colonel were not arguing about BDNF, or the murder, for that matter. Heck, after Friday, you'll be famous. You'll be able to call your own shots." As Signet had a short time earlier, Beth tugged his right ear. "Who knows, you might get a portrait out of this. Hang it alongside all those hotshots from Boston."

A blast of embarrassment cooked him solid. He had once shared his dream with Beth. He wished he'd kept his mouth shut.

"You're right," he said, eager to change subjects. "That 'switcheroo' is a hard pill to swallow. We spent months developing those two other agents."

"Not to mention all those Saturdays you spent in this very lab." She took a breath. "We're talking twenty five Saturdays last year alone. That's right, amigo. I counted. Right now you're probably torturing yourself wondering why."

"Exactly. But really I can't get Newsome—his murder—out of my mind. Heck, I can't get Mr. Campesi out of my mind. He might have...."

Again, he debated telling Beth about his suspicions that Campesi had either orchestrated the murder or perpetrated it himself, and that he, not Newsome, was the intended target.

"I'm not supposed to do this," she said, interrupting his rumination. "The barrier between your project and Arriva proper is absolute. But I'll tell you this." She retrieved her stool, plopped down beside him and rustled his hair in a familiar fashion. "Signet scheduled a last minute meeting at seven this morning. All senior lab administrators attended. He explained what took place at Eckerd Hall. The idea is to limit any potential fallout."

"I didn't know about that meeting...."

"Why should you? It's Mr. Campesi's job to handle you. Signet will take care of the employees."

The meeting was a short one, she said. Signet brushed over Dr. Ross's involvement with the fake reporter, his behavior foolish and naïve, the accountant's demise unfortunate. The goal was, and is, to contain information. There was to be no discussion outside of Arriva. No media interviews. For now, no phone calls. All police interviews were to go through Signet. Ross was a victim of circumstance, the official cover story if it ever came up. Right now, the CEO was on edge, not only about the concert murder but because he made a wasted trip to MacDill AFB the previous evening. Colonel Bame's flight out of the Middle East was delayed and he had to return to the military airport that morning to get him, the reason he missed that morning's meeting.

"Wait. Back up," Ross said. "Did Signet mention he was at the concert himself?"

"Of course. He stayed to the end. Told us about a Beethoven fugue." Beth shrugged. "Not sure why he told us. But he did."

The HammarKlavier piano sonata. Difficult to believe the security guy actually heard it, including the complex, driving, totally absorbing fugue. But there was more.

"Mr. Campesi drove to MacDill last night?"

"Haven't you been listening?"

"Okay. I got that. Signet said he abandoned ship early, meaning he didn't hear the whole concert. Now you're saying he did."

Signet, then. Not Campesi. The CEO really had been out of the area.

Beth laughed.

"About our new security guy? Take what he says *cum granum sale*. Make that *two* grains of salt. He's a veteran of the clandestine services. He was trained to lie and deceive. Same for Mr. Campesi. They're both experts in that domain."

She stuck her arm out, pulled him over for a stretch hug.

"Let me give you some advice," she said. "You're too focused on the Newsome fiasco. Don't be. Let the police do their job. While you're at it, forget about this Bame character. He's here on a military matter. Both these men work closely with DARPA. The advanced research agency has their own projects. Let them be. Keep your cute head down. That brings me to one final item."

Beth dropped her arm. Rearranged herself in a more serious posture.

"You've got to get laid," she said, quietly. "It's been a while. I can tell."

"My god, Beth. Really?"

"Not me, you goof. A younger female. A ripe, blossoming, available woman. There has to be one out there."

"I can't believe we're having this conversation."

"We're not conversing. I'm directing." She pointed a chopstick at him. "Wavy hair, deep blue, hungry eyes. How could any good girl resist? What about this Paleologus honey?"

"Zina. I operated on her grandfather's eye. What about her?""

"Well, she's called this lab a dozen times since the surgery. She knows where to find you. So, let her. Become available, young man. Have your way with her."

Another bout of smiles, giggles and a few outbursts of laughter.

"Get laid. I can't believe I said that." With a sigh, she patted his head and returned to her corner of the lab. She hit keys on her computer, emitting a chuckle from time to time.

Ross flipped open his laptop. He tried returning to the PowerPoint slides. Instead, images of the young Ms. Palaeologus flooded his mind. Beth was right on target though. His monkish habits were out of control. Like Signet, he had his own foldaway cot, kept in a closet for weekend overnights when analyzing data. But, *Zina*? He just couldn't. Or, could he?

The slide show then showed: <u>Glaucon, a Three-Part Delivery System to Cure Glaucoma.</u> Time to change it.

He erased the three and punched in more data about BDNF. Thanks to the PTSD vaccination program, BDNF research was backed up to the hilt. If the FDA thought inhaling a vaporized concoction of the biological safe for humans, so be it. All the details about the growth factor had been thoroughly vetted. A no-brainer, as Mr. Campesi said.

Beth came up behind him and deposited a piece of paper on his keyboard. She hurried back to her computer, struck a few keys, and left the lab.

He read the note.

SAVE YOUR PRESENTATION TO A FLASH DRIVE. LEAVE THE BUILDING. MEET ME AT HOME. SEVEN PM, TOMORROW NIGHT. YOU ARE NO LONGER SAFE AT ARRIVA.

Ross jumped up to follow but was too late. She had vanished down one of the labyrinthine corridors.

He wasted no time. He located the flash drive, downloaded the Glaucon project in addition to his revised presentation. Moments later, he was looking at the Arriva compound in the review of his tired Corolla as it clunked up the entrance road.

No longer safe.

What the heck did that mean?

CHAPTER 9

Thank God for TV images. They always offered a welcome distraction from self-torture.

While he ground out final calories on the Cybex exercise bicycle a row of news screens on a suspended tier provided endless coverage: torrential storms, abducted teens, hit and runs, plus—a real winner—split screen images depicting, on top, a map of the horn of Africa and, beneath, people scrambling from bombed-out buildings. A running news feed supplied details:

The Eritrean Crisis - Conflicted Administration - HOW TO RESCUE HOSTAGES - Diplomacy a Failure - Ground Force Expedition Risks War - White House Dithers.

And, all brought to you by smiling, tanned men and women, ceaselessly upbeat throughout reportage concerning catastrophes large and small, local and worldwide. Always the mindless, rehearsed coda:

Thank you so much for sharing your evening with us.

Enough.

He stumbled off the exercise bike, winded like other similar-minded masochists in the cavernous chamber. Almost trim at forty two, he kept at it, nodding at fellow crunch mates deployed around the enclosure: Miss Grim, tight-lipped on a nearby treadmill; Mr. Larynx, in another monologue with Back-And-Forth, the ripped bodybuilder wandering up and down aisles between sets. All here, including Mr. Huff-And-Puff himself, the eyeball doctor with his nightly struggle on the machines.

Tonight one variation punctuated this otherwise routine agony of joints and muscles: fresh worries threatening his career and, possibly, his life. First, the botched Newsome murder. It should have been Ross, horrid thought. Next, the looming decapitation of his Glaucon project, the suspicion that both issues might be related.

No longer safe at Arriva.

With an anxious pat, he touched the elongated object in his shorts. Wrapped in cellophane, the flash drive was safe from moisture, but from outright theft? Hence his decision to keep it on his person at all times.

He again tried to reach Beth. Straight to voicemail, same as the other half-dozen times. Why didn't she pick up? Tomorrow night, she said. He'd have to wait until then.

Regrouping, towel in hand, he vacated the exercise hall.

It was a relaxed and much anticipated part of day, an out-of-sync departure from the high-pressure Arriva atmosphere, treasured moments to collect himself and review his life path. Even now, trudging down the back corridor of the YMCA, this journey, ostensibly jagged, seemed preordained.

"The Moving Finger writes; and, having writ, Moves on..."

An apt quatrain, applicable from the outset, beginning with college scholarships, moving through the grind of medical school, then on to ophthalmic specialty training in Boston and Sunfish adventures in The Charles River basin. The whole amazing spectacle culminating in his Florida migration that led to Glaucon, his private universe of hard work and dreams of which he never thought himself capable.

He'd meander home, fix a salad, uncork a twenty-year aged port, and try his hand at Chopin, the Trois nouvelles etudes, the studies in polyrhythms....

A flashing light beamed in through a side window. An annoying strobe flutter he first noticed in the main hall while burning through the 525-calorie mark. Here it was again, a syncopated, intermittent flashing, like Morse code only more erratic.

Curious, he went to the window.

The infuriating light came from across the street. Deep shadows concealed whoever or whatever was responsible, though it was clear the source lay behind the hedges fronting the golf club parking lot.

A quick pair of flashes and, after a short interval, two more, then two more, an irritating, repeating strobe either unnoticed or ignored by others. At eight in the evening, it was too late for golfers. Kids then, pranking the Y.

He picked up his pace, eager to leave.

Magnifying the intrusion, a wave of raucous, thumping reverberations brought him to a stop. The freakish blast of music echoed from an exercise room to his right. The sound an invisible barrier, forcing him to take notice. Between thuds of pounding noise, he recognized popular tunes, all quickly submerged beneath unforgiving shocks to his nervous system.

He approached the door, creaked it open and looked inside.

It was an open space, mats, plastic chairs and large, red and blue exercise balls lining the walls. A bank of mirrors faced a wall of windows looking out on the same parking lot and strobe light he saw earlier. Giant mirrors, reflecting every bounce and curve of the woman in the center of the room.

The woman familiar, someone he'd seen the previous evening. She twirled in his direction....

Zina Palaeologus. He'd almost failed to recognize her. No mistake now, though she was not dressed in skin-hugging silk but in revealing shorts and halter. And, bending in dance maneuvers completely new to him.

Not seen for months, now on consecutive nights. Dear god, what a sight!

He hurriedly ducked away from the door, backpedaling to the safety of the corridor. He couldn't risk being seen. Yet, the apparition was too magnetic. Unable to resist, he inched forward and stole another glance.

Zina.

It was difficult to adjust. First, the tough-kid street urchin, her persona for months on end. Then, last night, a beguiling Byzantine seductress with geologic cleavage. And now, a ferocious karate kid whacking, with roundhouse blows, an anchored, bobbing manikin, that were it some hapless person, would be rendered either unconscious or dead. Probably both.

His pulse lurching, Ross nudged the door open. With trepidation, he poked his head around the corner for a more enhanced inspection.

Synchronized with a blasting boom box on the floor, Zina administered repeated, jabbing cruelty even a suffering manikin didn't deserve. Mesmerized by the girl's balletic athleticism, her provocative, pouncing beauty, he kept his eyes glued, to her black hair pinned in a lopsided bun, to her smooth, glistening skin and arresting yoga shorts....

He froze. She saw him.

Their eyes locked as Zina's extended leg slowly drifted to the floor. His chest went haywire, extra systoles sending thumping beats across the room. What was this, she must be thinking, a peeping Tom paying much too much attention to forbidden curves?

The granddaughter, for pity's sake.

"Doctor Dan ... nee ... ell, is that *you*?" Her mocking, sing-song voice competed with the music. She reached down, a languid flick of finger, and it was gone, his eardrums sighing in relief. "You hesitate. It is only me.

Come here. I won't bite."

Spikes of current sizzled up and down his spine. He struggled for control. Long-dormant emotions began to surface, threatening to take hold, urging him to caress this fantastical apparition, still heaving with the exertions of the moment.

With a hooked finger, Zina drew him on, forcing him to enter uncharted waters. Nerves twitching, he stood face to face, her soft pungency invading his nostrils. Somehow he managed to stifle a sudden ache, the need to touch, to hug, squeeze, and do all manner of things. At the same time, he detested his involuntary decision to hold back. His hand trembled, refusing to budge despite dorsal frontal neurons demanding the precise opposite. Where are you, Beth Braun, when I need you?

Take hold of her, young man. Do not equivocate. Lay down a mat. Lay her while you're at it.

Yet, overridden by fear, by a part of his brain that knew better, he ignored the mats and Beth's naughty invitation. What was he talking about? *His invitations.* But, he remained immobile his eyes soldered on.

"Beethoven versus rap and hip hop. What do you think? Are these not terrific vibrations?"

Lyrics zinged inside his skull: "...like a wrecking ball ... don't know why I'm here ... haven't got a clue ... just the way you are...."

He was speechless.

"I work out like you do. Except I have my own assignment." She fished a book out of a small bag and handed it over.

"'Krav Maga,'" he read aloud, "'The Next Level of Fitness and Self Defense.'" He looked into probing eyes. "Do you compete?"

She shrugged. A thin smile creased pouty lips.

"Once there were four boys walking along the bayou. Not very nice boys. School bullies, who took an unexpected swim. Later, when we have more time, I will finish this story. We must now move on to our scheduled talk." She veered off, bending at the waist to replace the book inside the bag. "Did they catch the murderer? The newspaper said you were friends. You did not tell me that last night. I am sorry for your loss."

The remorse came as an afterthought, though she had managed it well enough.

"Not really friends," he said. "Acquaintances. But, look. What are you doing here? I didn't know they taught Krav Maga at the Y. And, what do you mean, scheduled talk?"

She poked him on the shoulder, detouring past his questions.

"Tonight you wear the black shirt and orange shorts. Last week, a grey pullover and sweatpants. You have a pattern. Oh yes, Doctor. I have noticed."

She looked him over, running her teasing gaze this way and that, as he had done with her.

"You're right," he said. "I am organized. How do you know what I wear?"

"I use the treadmill behind you. You never notice. Not for a moment, this pretty girl watching you. You lost weight this summer. The orange shorts are loose at the waist. Such dedication."

"What? Oh, thank you." Self-consciously, he patted his waist. "I've been preoccupied these past months. Writing up the Phase I and Phase II trials. It's no picnic."

It was true. For a while, he'd even lost his appetite for Melko's souvlaki chicken. But his weight wasn't the issue.

"If you were behind me, why didn't you speak up?"

"Shy, perhaps. I have watched since March when you operated on Grandpa. For six months I have come to learn about the quiet man who saved his vision. Who also changed his life." She rotated a shoulder, slinking away, Ms. Coquette in charge again. "Let us not speak of these matters. Let us talk about us. We are quite special, you and I."

Taking him by surprise, burdening his already overtaxed circuits, Zina guided his yielding paw over her waist, to upper thigh and firm quads then, after a faint nudge, to the very shores of bliss and enchantment.

What on earth?

He retrieved his hand, terminating the excursion.

This girl, any girl, simply could not happen. Other than a few scattered yelps and whistles, his recent dating life remained intentionally inactive. He could ill afford to backtrack or to lose concentration now. Yet, this Zina scenario was decidedly different. And, to his disappointment, objecting neurons still spiked disapproval.

Get a grip!

"Special?" he mumbled. "In what way?"

Her eyes moistened, voice slipping into a firmer register.

"I have concluded, after reading Uncle Stephano's *History of Byzantium*, I descend from the royal purple. From Empress Theodora, in fact. She lived in the fifth century."

She paused to let that sink in.

"I see," he said, not "seeing" at all. "You've had your DNA tested? You are a member of this empress's family tree?"

She shrugged.

"No DNA test is necessary. I know what I feel. There is a strong connection even though Uncle claims I am mistaken to think so. I tell him, as he told me, study that important period of history. It is our heritage. Yours, too, I might add. You, Emperor Justinian, were also famous at that time. But, indecisive. And I, the exact opposite. As you will soon see."

"Hmm," was all he could come up with.

"It is Uncle's goal to educate me and restore my confidence. I dropped out of high school. No major loss, to either Tarpon Springs or to me. Uncle was disappointed, of course. He is a wealthy Greek expatriate. Or, he was. He has only this week returned from Greece. They swiped his yacht and bank accounts."

She hesitated, searching for a reaction. Ross smiled encouragingly. He felt admiration, for precisely what he couldn't say.

"Theodora. Hmm. How do I fit into all of this?"

"You remind me of my emperor. Brainy. Slow to act. And, I am like Theodora, a great and strong-spirited woman."

Moments elapsed before Zina continued the revelation.

"I now refer to myself as Theodora. Not all the time. But a lot."

"I think I get it. An ancient role model."

"Precisely. I have read all three volumes of this history. Byzantium was the eastern Roman Empire. Ever hear of Constantinople? A very exciting and powerful city. Later known as Istanbul. That's where you and I ruled for many important years."

Although endearing if not enchanting, Zina, he was forced to admit, seemed a tad delusional. If she were being medicated, the dose required adjusting.

"Stop the tolerant look," she said, eyes blazing. "I am building self-esteem. By trying on a new identity, I may find my own. You can help me in this project."

"I can? I hardly know you."

"That is exactly what Theodora said when Justinian found her."

A bell sounded deep inside his hippocampal memory circuits. He'd studied history in college. Compared to European Literature and Organic Chemistry, one of his worst subjects. Now, though, he recalled the incredible story, of how a courtesan named Theodora married very far up the social ladder and became an empress. Certainly, a peculiar identity to emulate. Yet, apparently this was where Zina landed in her search, and though with all her provocative gyrations she came off as a master tease, she still seemed too innocent for the precarious street life Theodora must once have lived.

A draft of air reminded him of his un-showered body. He had to go, he said, and started for the door.

"Not yet." She snared him by the arm. "You will become Emperor Justinian to my Theodora."

"I will?"

"Our new identities will serve us well."

"You can't be serious. Why do I have to be some emperor? I'm an eye doctor."

"An emperor is better. In time you will agree. I have been assigned to you. Be patient. I require lots of work to move beyond dropout status."

"Assigned?"

She waved a palm.

"Later, okay? I will explain then. I only mention this particular history now because, by reading it, Uncle hoped I'd also learn more about Grandpa, where his religious beliefs came from. You remember he was once a priest?"

So this was where she was headed: Grandpa's behavior change. It wasn't Ross's fault Father Palaeologus had become fond of plump women.

"In the fourth and fifth centuries, people slaughtered each other for differences of belief. Theological hairsplitting, not basketball or baseball, was the contest of the day. With Grandpa, it was never a contest. His personal knowledge of God was strong. At least, it was. The theological life is now over for him. Perhaps seeing me as Theodora might revive his vows."

Her position hadn't changed but her tone had shifted. No longer accusatory, it hinted at reconciliation, albeit indirectly. Justinian and Theodora. How would he deal with that?

"Please reconsider," she said. "Think of Justinian's achievements. You are both great creators. He built Hagia Sophia, the largest, most elegant church in history. Surely, you're invention rivals that."

"I'm pleased you approve of Glaucon. For a while, I wasn't sure. I want you to know I am sorry your grandpa changed after the operation. I can't explain what happened. I am only happy he can see again."

Zina placed a finger against his lips.

"Apology accepted. You must also accept mine. It was

wrong to call you nasty names at your office. If you don't forgive me I shall apply a Krav Maga maneuver. A reverse bear hug and a kick to vitals should do the trick."

They broke into an easy laughter, the sound a new music in the room. Zina presented more contours than first met the eye. Unfortunately, they were separated by ten, maybe twelve, years in age. But was that really such a big deal? The great composer Verdi propagated at eighty five. Or was it Vivaldi?

Propagating at eighty five.

Whatever was he thinking?

It happened again. The same light behind the hedge began its odd, two on, two off, syncopated flashing.

"Ignore them," Zina said, grabbing his arm. "They watch us all the time. We must leave."

Outside, they turned left to the bicycle rack where an outsized red scooter was chained in place. Zina produced a key, unlocked the scooter and swung a leg into position.

"This PCA 150 is sleek, don't you think? Uncle Stephano sold it to me for borrowed money. He also sold his Cadillac to Aunt Sophia." She faced the distant lot. "I will deal with them. Go home to Jasmine Lane and wait for me."

A black SUV emerged from the parking lot. It nosed to a halt. Then, with a sudden lurch, it swung left and disappeared around the corner.

"Wait. You're not going to follow."

With a rumble and a roar, Zina zoomed off into the night.

CHAPTER 10

He kept the window down to clear his head. Faint drumbeats of worry returned, building soon to a crescendo: *the note was addressed to you; you are not safe at Arriva; they have been watching.* And, the real kicker: *go to Jasmine Lane.* So Zina knew where he lived. She also rode a red scooter, the same vehicle that had pursued him the other morning. At least one mystery solved. Empress Theodora had latched on to him for some reason. *I have been assigned.*

Madness.

He swung into the driveway, parked and hopped the steps to the front door. The key proved unnecessary. The door was ajar, the hall light on inside.

Scaring him to holy hell, a familiar lump of shadow jumped over the porch railing and landed beside him.

"My God, Franklin," he said, recoiling. "I told you never to do that again!" He took a breath, adjusting to yet another intrusion of the neighborhood nut job. "Normal people walk down the sidewalk, depress the doorbell or politely knock. They don't spring out of nowhere like a complete idiot. This is not the New York subway system."

"Hey, man. Cool it. You're right. I'm sorry. I already gave a 'polite knock'. I wanted to discuss Eritrea with you." He slapped a wad of paper into Ross's hand. "Read it. You got to know it's all a fraud. Don't believe the shit they tell you."

Ross began the count to ten. He stopped at three.

"Forget about Eritrea," he said. "Tell me about my open door. Did you pick the lock?"

Franklin shook his head.

"Not me. I promise. It does explain the noise." Head darting side to side, he lowered his voice from baritone to cautious whisper. "I thought it was you at first. Had a bad day. Goddamn rats die on you. Banging stuff around like you usually do. But tossing chairs and smashing glass? Man, that's extreme. So, I gave it a moment, came over and pushed the bell. That's when I saw the open door. Next, I hear the rear patio door slam shut. Someone thrashing out through your back swamp. I didn't even try to follow. Hell, man. You got gators back there."

He paused, winded, still swinging his head about, searching the shadows for whomever had vandalized Ross's house. This sort of stuff wasn't supposed to happen in Lansbrook Development. Upscale community, adjacent to a vast lake, speedboats and laughing bikinis on slapping waves and sunshine. No jewels, loose money or drugs. It made no sense.

A sputtering grumble came down the road. With a screech of brakes, Zina's scooter barged into the driveway, missing his Corolla by an inch before skidding to a stop. She hit the kickstand and bounded up the stairs to join them.

"Hey, Franklin." She slapped a high five with the bemused giant. "What's cooking?"

"You two know each other?"

"Naw, man. She's just a looker with lots of questions. Who wouldn't talk to her?"

"About what?"

Franklin inched to the side railing.

"I don't know. Fake news on Facebook. Investor buyouts. Hell, man. Questions!"

And, he was gone.

"You asked him about *investor buyouts*?"

"Don't be silly. I asked about you."

"Why did you do that?"

Zina snugged her hiked-up shorts, thighs overexposed from the evening joyride.

"Not now. Tell you later."

"Add it to the list, all you plan to explain at a later date. Never mind. I can wait." He pointed to the open door. "Do you see that? Someone broke into my house."

She shrugged, an innocent movement but one setting

loose a chorus of urges Ross struggled to control.

"The door jam," he muttered. "It's shattered."

"No big deal. Signet can find a repairman. Listen to what happened."

In a breathless whisper, reminiscent of paranoid Franklin, she told him about her pursuit of the black SUV. A real bummer of a ride, it turned out. She'd tailed the speeding vehicle for thirty minutes, tracking in and out of neighborhoods behind Publix, going as far as Tarpon Springs on Route 19 before circling back only to lose the crafty SUV behind the crowded Varsity Club restaurant, a local hamburger and karaoke hangout a mile down the road from Jasmine Lane.

"They were quick, with tricky turns," she said. "Uncle Stephano's 150 is too clumsy. Difficult to handle. I couldn't catch them." Her chest heaved with the recollection of the effort, distracting him from the story. "I can't identify the make. It had a yellow ribbon on the grill. Oh. I got the tag. EAG E65. Identical to the one last week when you left the Y."

"You saw it *then*?"

"Eyes up here, my emperor."

She redirected his gaze north, embarrassment flaming his brow.

"Have you already forgotten what I told you? I have been at the Y for months. I watch you and see who follows. How could I miss a dumb vehicle trailing you here in the darkness?"

"It came *here*?"

"Think, Justinian. You came home. It followed. I was right behind."

There were too many pieces to the puzzle. Impossible to assemble. To glimpse even a bare outline of explanation lay beyond him.

"Look," he said, swatting a mosquito. "If you knew someone was tracking my movements why didn't you contact the police? They probably broke in while I was at the Y. This could have been avoided."

"Perhaps. Only if your assumption these incidents are related. I did tell Signet. In these situations, the police are hopeless."

"You have the tag. They could trace it. Hold on. You told Corporal Signet, Arriva's new security chief, I was watched and followed? Why would you do that? How the heck do you even know him? He just arrived from Virginia."

"As with so much else," she said, dismissively, edging past the open door and into his front hall, "An explanation must wait. My, God, Justinian. What a mess. Did you forget to pay the mortgage? Someone is very angry with you."

"You think?" He followed her in, kicking back the torn red Bokhara throw rug. "Maybe it was the same people in the SUV?"

"Or, high school teens searching for dope and money.

What is that in your hand?" she added. "An eviction notice? After this destruction, don't be surprised."

He forgot Franklin gave him a wad of papers. He'd been mindlessly holding on to it. He groaned when he read the title: "Eritrea Analysis – The Big Lie" then tossed it to the floor. He didn't have time.

"No need to explain," she said. "From Crazy Franklin, I bet. He explained a communist plot made up dark matter. Or, dark matter was a capitalistic fraud. I forget which way it went. As if the stuff did not exist on its own."

"How could it be either the result of a plot or fraud?"

She shrugged, voluptuous shoulders once again in motion. Anticipating inner, limbic trouble, he glanced off to keep proper synapses in order.

"Did he see who broke in?"

He wagged his head no.

"Mind giving me a hand here?"

Together, emitting low groans and squeaks of despair, they wandered amidst the wreckage. Zina went to work trying to restore order. After rearranging slashed cushions and broken chairs she lifted shards of pottery off the floor, genuinely disturbed by the total anarchy at her feet.

"For a benign and reclusive eye doctor," she said "you attract bad enemies. I will ask Signet if he can learn who did this. He knows everything."

"I don't get it. Why would you ever consult him? You

haven't yet explained how you know this person."

Zina brushed off the question and crossed into the kitchen.

"What a sight! All your plastic dishes are broken. Not substantial items, thank goodness. Why did you ever buy them?"

"They are not *plastic!* They're delicate pieces of Japanese tableware. I bought them at auction on Beacon Hill, Boston. On Louisburg Square, to be exact."

"So uppity. Well, they are thin and easily cracked. Your cabinets are empty. Your visitor didn't find much to steal in this designer kitchen."

Her sarcasm, irritating as it was, paled in comparison to the pain he felt with his broken home. His Bokhara throw rug, dating to Boston, had been nearly bisected, presumably with a scissors big enough to do the job. His prized Kashan carpet also sliced down the middle, an act of useless destruction. Then came the furniture: dining room table, squashed, as if struck by a ten ton truck; the four Chippendale chairs hacked to pieces; the leather couch sliced into fringes like Buffalo Bill's frontier jacket. Even his fake antique roll top desk lay demolished, the legs torn off, the corrugated top smashed beyond repair. Strangely though, his MacBook computer stood untouched beneath the Steinway, which also appeared unscathed.

The computer, then. Had the burglar come for that? If so, why leave it behind? Maybe they consulted it first, his password Arriva spelled backward, easy enough to hack. Other than innocuous laboratory notes, all they'd find were insulting missives from the IRS. Misunderstandings, really. A few, undocumented deductions. Some unpaid bills, but no delinquent notices about the mortgage. More curious still, his volumes of Beethoven and Chopin lay neatly stacked to one side. Other furnishings, sparse as they were, had been completely ruined.

He could hear Zina yanking drawers open and shut in the kitchen. Then, a peal of merciless laughter.

"Two cans of tuna in the fridge plus a jar of cashew nuts and Cakebread Chardonnay. Great diet, Mr. Doctor. No pictures on the walls. No family shots. Are you certain this is home?"

Another catastrophe greeted him in the bedroom. Mattress slashed, bedside and bureau drawers emptied on the floor. Striped and polka dot socks strewn everywhere. Sporty stretch shorts and muscle shirts crumpled in a corner. Yet, he again found room for hope. Untouched and bizarrely displayed in the middle of a pillow, were his Academy cufflinks, won in a raffle on eBay. Stranger still, his multicolored Brooks Brothers ties hung intact in the closet. His scuffed Italian loafers had escaped, too, as if the intruder, whoever it was, respected a dress code.

He rejoined Zina, now chortling in the living room.

"He was searching for something," she said, wisely, tapping her forehead. "That is clear enough. Did they find the diamonds? Your expensive wristwatch? Maybe a girlfriend's platinum bracelet? Scratch that. In your case, Zirconium."

"I wear an Ironman, thank you. I don't have a girlfriend."
He patted the flash drive in his pocket, secure in the fact
that at least his project was safe. "Other than the Steinway
and my computer, I don't possess anything of value,
including diamonds. There are the cufflinks. No. Forget
them. They're a dime a dozen. I'm confused. What were
they after?"

"It wasn't your sound system. Who would steal a seven-
disc CD player? As your smelly neighbor suggested,
teenagers looking for drugs. After all, you are a doctor.
Signet will find out for us. He will discover the answer."

"I don't have any drugs, other than proton pump
inhibitors. Tell me how you know Signet."

"There." Ignoring yet another question, she pointed to a
bare section of the entrance wall. "That is where you will
hang your first picture. I will bring it to you tomorrow
morning."

In all the confusion, he'd practically forgotten about his
next day's schedule. Zina was bringing Father Palaeologus
in for a post-op examination. There was also that soldier's
mother he'd agreed to see. But, with Zina at his elbow, his
brain a complete cipher.

She now emitted an uncharacteristic sigh, inspecting first
the chaos in which they hardly made a dent, then him
with a look of obvious disappointment.

"This disturbs my plans," she said. "I had hoped to spend
the night. Emperor and his new Empress, together for the
first time. Don't worry. Only a fantasy, at least tonight.

Recall that, once ignited, Justinian and Theodora's passion was absolute. I have fulfilled my assignment. Barren walls and diet. No stains upon kitchen or bathroom counters. Yes, I have learned quite a lot about the good doctor this ravaged evening."

After planting an abrupt kiss on his lips she was out the door. Moments later, the sound of popping scooter faded up the block.

CHAPTER 11

Blurry-eyed and poorly rested, his brain a complete wreck, Ross lumbered off the third floor elevator unprepared for Wednesday clinic. Catching him off guard, Doctor Gamel Azzizzi greeted him with a welcoming smile and a cup of steaming coffee. From Panera Bread, he said, guiding Ross to his office down the hall.

"Please, my friend. I know this is no way to treat a colleague. We have this awkward problem only you can solve."

He got Ross seated in the cushioned chair before his inlaid desk, immaculately neat as always. Smoothing his lab coat, groaning from unidentifiable pain, he sank down in the adjacent seat.

"Such a fine morning, Daniel. Sweet with cool air and autumn. Not so sweet is that man in the waiting room. I tell you, he put the office in an uproar when he arrived."

Catching his breath, Gamel sipped his coffee, black, no sugar or cream. Ross tried to thank him for the fresh brew but his colleague had more complaints to share.

"He calls himself Signet, not *Mister* Signet, thank you. Please, sir, do not make that mistake again. You should hear him talk. So severe and rude. Even more unnerving, he claims he knows you. *Compatriots*, he said. That is what you two are. From Arriva, where you work. And, as if these declarations were insufficient proof, of exactly what he did not say, he had a blind woman in tow. Most certainly a visual wreck. She pokes about with her long cane. Poked him in the—what to call it? Yes, she poked his ass to shut him up. Clear out Doctor Ross's afternoon, he finally said. Doctor Ross will be in surgery instead."

Ross was startled by his older colleague's reaction. A man of fluid grace, European in both elegance and bedside manner, Gamel was also one of Tampa Bay's most illustrious retina surgeons, unflappable in the most trying situations.

They'd been good friends ever since Ross joined the practice shortly after arriving from Boston. A unique partnering, glaucoma and retina embedded in Gamel's thriving practice or "company" as the basement nitwit nightshade called it. A perfect combination, Ross's metamorphosis into research-clinician, a dream come true.

He and Ross also shared a love of the arts. Once, following a Bach concert at the St. Petersburg Consortium, Ross partook of late night dinner with Gamel and his gracious wife. A marvelous evening of Montrachet, braised lamb chops, a disquisition on Egyptian artifacts, even a midnight dip in the nearby Gulf, followed by a three-aspirin morning. To Ross, well worth every pounding throb between earlobes. Gamel had arrived at the office looking as if he had just stepped out of a bandbox.

Now, as he described the security chief's behavior, Ross could well understand his frustration. Not only had Signet ordered the staff to clear out his schedule, he nearly precipitated a heart attack in one of Gamel's patients scheduled for a membrane peel that very morning.

Ross now saw a solution to the mayhem.

"Is Gina working today?" he said, adopting a conspiratorial tone. "She's the high energy sparkplug around here. She'll shock his contrary ass."

"Why, of course. An excellent idea. She commands the troops right down the hall." Gamel leaned forward, eyes ablaze. "She tells me the Yankees reached the playoffs. She is an ardent fan, you know. Always working overtime to pay for all her tickets. In defiance, mind you but with my full approval, of the eyeshade in the basement. He claims, by working overtime, she steals from the company. Can you believe such a person? God knows why I hired the nasty man. Anyway, where was I? Oh, yes. Sparkplug Gina. Definitely assign her to Signet. She will straighten him out. "

He reached across his desk and hit the intercom button.

"Imagine, Daniel. He demanded we place his patient in your 'premier examining suite'. He also insisted you use the proper gony scopes. Can you believe this audacity?" (Definition: gonioscope. A method of using special contact lenses to examine the eye.)

Ross hastily explained the situation. A retired Army

Corporal, Signet was now Arriva Inc.'s temporary Chief of Security. He asked Ross to evaluate the mother of a fellow soldier. Going blind, her problem lay beyond the expertise of Philadelphia's best specialists. Or so, she claimed.

His colleague nodded.

"Lost causes always find your doorstep. Of course you must try and help her. Even vague light perception is worth an effort. Let me surprise the front desk with your suggestion."

Gamel hit the intercom button again. Issued instructions, and sat back, relaxed. Only after meticulously smoothing a nonexistent crease in his hand-tailored trousers did he smile, himself again.

There was a knock at the door and a curly-haired woman stuck her head in: Gina, the wizard of Gamel's hand-picked team.

"Don't worry about that dude," she said, her Bronx tone decisive. "I told him to shape up or ship out. He gave me a hard look so I pointed to the door. He said shipping out wasn't an option so I let him stay. On one condition. He either behaved, or I'd give him the boot. He's now quiet as a mouse with that new patient in Room Three."

Wow, Ross thought, after the technician departed. *A devil wrapped in a cyclone.* Assuming what she said was true, he couldn't wait to see Signet.

"Can you imagine?" Gamel escorted him to the door. "She calls me the Egyptian magician. Only, today, with that man, I possessed no magic at all. Go. Deal with him yourself. Save the eyesight of that poor woman."

Poor she was not, Ross discovered upon reading her history and assembled notes. Blind as the proverbial bat in her right eye, Mrs. H. Ascot Chaneuil hailed from privilege in South Carolina. She had schooled abroad in Paris and Rome then finished the tour in Cambridge, Massachusetts.

Fingering immense pearls, she asked, in a most cultured tone, if the esteemed Dr. Daniel Ross might be of assistance.

"You see, young man. I have no vision."

"Your left eye identifies large objects."

"Indeed. I can see you're a doctor in a white coat and not a refrigerator."

After a thorough exam in the cubbyhole of Room Three, not in some imaginary 'premier examining suite ,' he announced in his most professional manner, that he might well be able to *assist* her left eye retain form vision but that her right eye was kaput, hastening to add that this latter term, though not a medical one, captured the essence of the matter.

"I am in your very capable hands, Doctor. Siggy claims you are the best."

"Siggy," he repeated, shaking his head. "The man from DARPA, also one of the very best."

A soft guffaw drifted out of the rear corner. Dressed in

black as always—turtle neck pullover, military garb, and running shoes—Signet more resembled a disabled raven than retired special ops warrior. Thanks to Gina, a very subdued one at that.

"Please excuse the corporal." Mrs. Chaneuil nodded in the direction of the Security Chief behind her. "He is so military, so cut, dried, and correct. Tell me, Siggy dear. How would you describe my 'kaput' globe that strays to one side?"

"Gone, ma'am. A disembodied self. Perhaps the genius can preserve what remains."

"How very Zen," she said. "Doctor, please understand a few things. This brave man saved my son's life on a barren hilltop in Afghanistan. In similar fashion, he is now determined to save my eyesight. I am afraid this challenge will tax even your expertise."

She was correct about that. A thorough review of the optic nerve photographs, and detailed structure-function measurements, confirmed what she so clearly surmised. The million or more axon fibers of the right optic nerve were gone, having vanished in the devastating process of glaucoma. The optic nerve was white, the vision beyond rescue. It was another matter with her left eye. Clinging to a precipice, it had a fighting chance.

He gave the woman the dismal odds and offered to operate if she was willing to take the risk.

"What risk?" she said, staring off into that small segment of space her tiny keyhole vision provided. "My eye pressure is forty-five. I have less than three degrees of sight. Go ahead. Make my day."

Summoning a hopeful spirit, she allowed Gina to lead her down the hall to the sign-up desk for surgery that afternoon.

Signet then came to life.

"You will need this," he said, handing Ross a small, silver box. "Mr. Campesi had Dr. Braun prep your device for this patient. If you don't mind, I would like to watch the surgery. She will sign the necessary forms."

Ross considered the request and saw no reason to exclude Signet. But, only after he apologized to Dr. Azzizzi and his entire staff.

"Do not lecture me. I have already absorbed quite an earful from this Gina individual. I will apologize later when the opportunity presents."

"Why the hurry with this woman, though? I have an opening next week."

"Doesn't her high pressure require immediate attention?"

"I could have tapped it off with a needle and scheduled surgery for next Monday. She would have kept until then. By the way, how do you know Zina Palaeologus?"

"There is a red flag in the Glaucon file. As you know, it concerns Father Palaeologus. I needed to be reassured by the family he would present no problem. I refer to the PTSD vaccine project. Naturally, I had to speak with the granddaughter who, I believe, sits in the outer waiting room as we speak."

"What sort of problem?"

"The commotion in the Greek Orthodox community. Their priest is not the same."

The security man administered what had to be his hard look. Then, his gaze mysteriously defocused, a peculiar vacillation that disappeared in a mini blink. His vague attention landed on a spot above and beyond Ross's ear.

"Who told you to interfere with my schedule?"

"This woman reminded him of his late wife. You operated upon her when you recognized the problem. You can operate on this woman as well."

Ross was stunned.

"Is Mr. Campesi aware this is a private office? He can't issue orders to these people. Why did you even tell him about this unfortunate woman in the first place?"

Signet returned to his withering look.

"I am reminded of a night in Nuristan. The icy rain, the outpost life, the incoming rockets. You recognize and accept the difficulty. You persist to exist. I had no part in the decision to move so fast. I took an order."

"Which you followed with the subtlety of a hammer."

"And, you, Daniel Ross, are the nail. Accept your destiny. The CEO will rendezvous with you later on."

Chapter 12

Father Palaeologus jumped to his feet when Ross opened the door. Freshly shaven, straggly hair combed back, he bounded across the room and shook Ross's hand, then, in a fit of enthusiasm, hugged him until his spine cracked.

"Thank you, Doctor. I am a new man. I am so very grateful."

He hugged Ross again, smacking his shoulder, old friends reunited, together at last. Except, as Ross suspected, it was all in the old man's head. Of course. How stupid. Where else would behavior come from?

"Grandpa, behave. This is not the Bayou Grille. Have more respect."

The blasé voice issued from behind the door. Closing it, Ross had a look for himself. Again, he went into temporary cardiac standstill. Attired in a revealing, purple tee, legs in tight, tattered jeans, Zina had merged personae. With her hair pinned back, minus even a sprinkle of makeup, she appeared restrained but arresting in a listless, seductive sort of way.

He resisted, however, fighting off this fresh assault on his limbic brain. Fortunately, grandpa broke the spell and guided him to his own chair behind the desk while he, happy as a lark, sank into the examining seat.

"I will tell you a story. I heard it last night at the Grille."

"Grandpa. Please. You are here for a check-up."

Ignoring his granddaughter's protestations, he pushed on.

"There is an old couple, both going on eighty. A genie comes to them and says, to celebrate the old man's birthday, he will grant one wish. The old man says he would like to be married to a woman twenty years younger. Poof. The genie grants the wish and the old man turns one hundred."

"My God! Grandfather!"

"Do you get it?" The priest's eyes sparkled. "I made the opposite wish. Poof. Thanks to you, I am now twenty years younger."

"Will you calm yourself? Apologize to Doctor Ross. Think of what he has done for your vision. Do not waste his time with a silly story."

"It's okay," Ross interjected, sensing strands of an ongoing argument. "Your grandfather is simply grateful about—"

Interrupting him again, the old man came to his feet, hands wide to the air.

"I am grateful for *everything*," he announced. "You have saved me. Because of that operation, I am this new and happy man."

Zina puffed air, a steam engine leaving station.

"I will tell you what he is." She came over and poked her grandfather's sunburnt head. "He is a sassy skirt-chaser who now drinks beer on the bayou. Recommend a brain doctor. He goes downhill fast."

Ross had to admit the priest had undergone a remarkable change. For their early meetings, he wore black from head to toe. Not the sheer military dress Signet favored but baggy trousers and blunt shoes. Today, he featured white linen shorts, tasseled, sockless loafers, and a red striped tee shirt emblazoned with the words "Epi-Genome Now?" Quite a transformation.

"He owns another shirt," Zina said, still on a rampage. "'Higgs Boson Rocks.' It is about physics. Even he cannot explain it."

"Pay no attention to Zineeta. She only sees what came before. Who cares about a Higgs Bosom?"

"*Boson*, grandpa. Not *Bosom*."

Father Palaeologus shook his head. "A simple error. Easy to make with my new life. That is what I want to explain. Here, sit you two. I will tell you both."

As if summoned at school, they gathered around Ross's desk. Zina leaned against an edge, her finger tapping displeasure, while patient and doctor occupied twin guest chairs. A cozy moment and not what Ross had planned. The old man was there to complete an FDA questionnaire while Ross filled out necessary forms. At this pace, he'd be backed up all morning.

"You have changed how I think. What you have done for me is a miracle."

"He believes that gadget you sewed to his left eyeball changed his life. He uses it to justify new and nasty habits."

"Habits." The priest laughed. "That is exactly it, Doctor. I have exchanged old habits for the new. Let me ask you: do you know the purpose of a priest's life?"

"Provide spiritual guidance?" Ross replied. "I've never given it much thought. My morals, if that's what you're driving at, are always on autopilot."

"Morals. Hah. This so-called spiritual man tosses beer cans into the bayou. I caught you, Grandpa. Don't deny it."

The priest shrugged.

"A momentary lapse. Buoyancy. I was experimenting with the here and now. Let me continue. The purpose of such a life is to achieve a spiritual union with God. Well, that is gone. It was all only an *idea* in the first place. Spiritual union? A thought pattern inside my head. That is what I have come to understand, thanks to you. There is no underlying truth to this idea and a tremendous relief it disappeared."

"An *idea* no longer exists. Is that it for you?"

In response, a distant look, very much like Signet's thousand-mile stare, transformed the old man's gaze. It was a glimpse of a reality invisible to others.

"What an idea it was, too," the priest went on.

One that had warped his entire life, ever since his early days at the Massachusetts seminary where grizzled instructors instilled an abiding fear of life. They instilled another, equally insidious notion that to be saved from life's so-called awful abyss, one must believe in God. Their antidote to fear became the creation of fear itself. A crazy, illogical but perfectly religious equation. In order to escape their first false belief, they substituted another. Yet Father Palaeologus required no such antidote because he no longer believed in God. Dr. Ross had erased this concept as he had eliminated the basic fear he would one day die to dust.

"My life was self-delusion," he said. "Why, at one time, I conflated with the Almighty. I was Earth-Jesus himself. Because I read our Bible I was forgiven. I could do or think no wrong. It was okay to acquire property along the lakefront. Charge rent. Be a prosperous landlord. Don't laugh, Zineeta. That notion is gone, and I am the better for it. Besides, where would I have found the money?"

"Call me Zina," his granddaughter replied. "I am a brand new Zina, though. I am becoming more and more like the ancient Empress Theodora."

This brought them to a curious impasse. To the Byzantine Empire, in fact to a time and place central to both grandfather and granddaughter, but for different reasons. To Zina, the time of the Eastern Roman Empire featured the source of her new role model, Empress Theodora. While to the priest, it contained the origin of his former belief system, orthodox Byzantine Christianity that he now rejected.

No question, both had changed since their first meeting six months earlier. Ross also had changed, an alteration of more recent vintage. His former belief system, if he could call it that, once centered upon lab results and people as patients yet to be identified and explored.

Now, being drawn ever deeper into the spiraling Palaeologus vortex, into the absorbing network of emotions young Zineeta unleashed, emotions facing him head on as he listened to the bizarre quarrel before him, he realized an inner tectonic shift was underway. A slow shift of rusted plates, however. He had not, after all, seized hold of the girl when she so much as offered herself to him the previous evening....

He was fantasizing again, an automatic rumbling from neurons too long dormant. Zineeta's magical spell was propelling him forward, at least he hoped that was the intended direction, not backward or, extinguish the thought, downward. Zina, Zineeta, Theodora. Whomever. She had become very real for him very fast.

He cleared his throat.

"I can explain what happened."

He proceeded to point out the obvious. Because his eyesight had improved so dramatically, the priest was no longer depressed, a state common in glaucoma patients. He was experiencing an emotional rebirth, a different kind of spiritual reawakening.

"Utter nonsense," the priest thundered. "No disrespect, but this is not a *spiritual* reawakening. The very opposite.

140

No longer am I burdened by a religious calling. For the first time, I do not fear time, the end of time, the end of *my* time. What concerns me is *here and now*, you and wonderful Zeenee, this very office, the spin of planets, everybody's Higgs Bosom moment. I am very clear about this. Thanks to you, I am a more intelligent and living person."

Zina sprang off the desk, whisking Ross from his chair to sit beside her grandfather.

"It is dumb to lose faith," she said. "Remember those who did. General Belisarius took care of them in the Hippodrome. Their end was bloody."

"Ah, the Nika rebellion," the priest replied, cradling Zina's hand. "You return to the sixth century, to 532 in Constantinople. To the time of Emperor Justinian and Empress Theodora. And, I know why. You wish to remind me of my religious roots. But, you are mistaken about the cause of those terrible riots. The slaughtered thousands lost faith in their rulers, not God. I have simply lost faith in the latter, and," he added gleefully, "faith in a hereafter."

He turned to Ross, eyes moist in recollection.

"Forgive us both. To some degree, my excitable granddaughter and I are each trapped in ancient time. When, if you can believe it, men argued and killed one another over debates about Jesus. Was he part man and part godlike, or just one or the other? I descend from the Monotheists, the one-aspect wing. Reminding me about them, no matter how well intended, will not change who I am now. The people she refers to were killed for other reasons."

For Ross's benefit, he briefly explained the Nika rebellion. An enormous horde of people, well over ten thousand by scholar's recent count, had ceased believing in the sacred right of their emperor to rule. Hence, they rebelled. Order was restored when generals were dispatched to decimate the unruly mobs. Thousands were butchered but not for any religious belief but because they opposed their rulers.

"That time does not relate," he concluded. "There is no uprising here. Nothing to quell. My change is permanent."

"The rebellion matters to me, though. Theodora took command of the court. Justinian was unable to act. It was she who dispatched General Signet to the crowds. It was she who reclaimed the royal court. She was strong, as I will be." She tossed a glance at Ross. "For our days ahead."

With that, the curious confrontation ended. Zina returned to her corner seat while Ross examined his patient, carefully charting his findings on the computer. Then, with Zina's assistance, the priest, or former priest, filled out a form about his postoperative recovery. Afterward, Ross escorted them out.

In the waiting room, he held Zina back, asking her to explain the odd remark about "our days ahead." He also pointed out she had confused Signet with a Byzantine General.

"I called him that?" Her eyelids fluttered. "It doesn't matter. Both he and Theodora were in command." Without fanfare, she thrust a wrapped package into his hands. "Take this, brave emperor. Hang it in that bare spot near the front door. Our days ahead? We shall see about that. Come, Grandpa. Aunt Sophia is waiting in the Cadillac."

When they were gone, Ross opened the package in his office. It contained a framed photograph of an ancient mosaic icon depicting Empress Theodora herself, the caption stating the original lay in the Basilica of San Vitale, Ravenna, Italy.

He found the flat, wide-eyed expression baffling. Aquiline, flaring nose, red lips, hair concealed beneath a jeweled crown. This then, the tantalizing female with whom Zina now identified, her puzzling comment about days ahead still unexplained.

Ahead of what?

Monotheism. Lost faith. Icons from a Basilica. Empress Theodora and the Nika Rebellion. So bewildering, this bubbling cauldron from the sixth century. And, in some inexplicable way, it involved him.

All he had done was suture a tiny gizmo to the man's eyeball.

CHAPTER 13

It was three o'clock when Ross finally attained a sliver of peace and silence. Seated at the operating microscope, oculars adjusted, he was home again, surgery his true calling, the operating room the ultimate domain. If any lasting cure existed for the dreaded glaucoma it lay in Glaucon, a device capable of achieving ganglion cell rescue and survival. With Mrs. Chaneuil draped and sedated, he set to work.

After placing the eyelid speculum and the twelve o'clock stay suture, he rotated the globe down to expose the superior temporal quadrant, his worksite, and made the first incision. Signet, with a rude nudge, moved him aside so he could have a look himself.

"The surgery is easy," he whispered. "Enlarged to a billiard ball, anyone can perform the operation."

Ross surrendered his chair, calling the man's bluff.

"Go ahead. Make her day."

After a pause, Mr. Security, *Siggy*, relinquished his position.

"A hypothetical, Doctor. I am here to witness the miracle. Please, maestro. Proceed."

To prepare the security chief for a trip to the OR, Gamel dispatched Gina, most querulous of technicians, to instruct the dude herself. Speaking quickly, ignoring questions, she lathered it on thick: *Sit to one side. Do not talk. Do not touch instruments. Put on mask and gown. Sterility is paramount. Now go. Behave, nasty man. You might learn something.*

The girl, loving her work.

Playing his part, Signet acted genuinely engaged, especially with her mini-lecture on the tube implant device. Looking on intently through the assistant's oculars, he sat rigid as a pipe while Ross sutured the twin-tubular appliance to the globe. Moving deftly, he angled the first tube into the vitreous, the middle cavity of the eye, then inserted the second tube into the front part, the anterior chamber, to control pressure. He finally anchored the motor.

Surprising Ross, Mr. Security provided, sotto voce, a running commentary as he worked. A recital of Gina's mini lecture, repeated word for word, conveying either a splendid memory, or a twig of comprehension, perhaps both.

"The first tube conveys BDNF," he softly intoned. "The nutrient factor for ganglion cells. The second tube drains fluid to control pressure. May I interrupt? Please explain the black box. Your bossy technician did not get to that."

Ross filled him in about the "black box". It contained the

unique motor that drove neuron rescue elements inside the eye. Then, using jeweler's forceps, he removed the tiny nano-motor from the box and held it beneath the oculars for close inspection. This incredible device, he explained, created the energy required to activate cylinders that moved BDNF down the thin tube to the vitreous cavity, the first tube he just inserted.

"I am interested in that glassy, satin layer." The security peered intently through his oculars. "Is that the patented cesium-selenium pyrite?"

Ross glanced over his mask at this highly informed emissary from DARPA.

"You've done your homework."

"I found it all on classified Arriva servers. Except details are sketchy. What Newsome was after at your Bonefish dinner meetings. I, too, am curious. I need to see for myself. So, the recorded patent states that photons of light activate the pyrite material."

"That's correct. What happens next?"

"Again, sketchy. The best I can deduce, that after photons strike the strip of pyrite, a stream of expanding hydrogen gas is released to push tiny pistons. They, in turn, move the liquid BDNF into the vitreous where it diffuses to reach the underlying retina. Ganglion cells, the first messenger of sight, are thereby nourished. Like a vitamin, only better."

"Very good, professor," Ross replied, "Tell me about the canisters."

"They are difficult to see."

"They lie concealed beneath the pyrite layer."

"I knew that." Signet's eyes, visible above the mask, briefly narrowed. A thin smile. Then, in a nano-mini-micro second, it was gone. "They number three," he continued. "Each a centimeter long, preloaded, thanks to Dr. Braun, with thousands of highly concentrated BDNF molecules. Of course, only because the FDA reconfigured the equation."

A line of perspiration dampened Ross's face mask.

"Right," he bit off. "You mean before Master Campesi cut two agents out of the system."

"He did not 'cut' your project, though. It is still on track. And now, thanks to your device, Ms. Chaneuil, who lies in la la land beneath the drape, may retain some eyesight."

They exchanged a sideways glance.

"You sure are a font of knowledge."

"Your Arriva file contains the story. It is unfortunate the vital liaison Dr. Braun has so long provided is disbanded. A temporary arrangement, we hope. For her own safety, Campesi sent her home. He may have another plan for you."

"What the heck does that mean?"

"...hey, boys ... stop arguing ... I hear you down here."

His patient's groggy voice filtered out from the drapes.

She was coming to. Not a concern because the operation was almost over. Lowering the decibel level, Ross asked why either Dr. Braun's or his safety was an issue.

"I will deal with this," Signet said. "It is not yet your concern. Stick to Glaucon. Make that your single focus. Who knows," he said, more genially, "perhaps it will land you a portrait. I hear there is an empty space between two former chieftains."

Ross pulled away from the scope.

"You mock my aspirations?"

"Not at all. I admire them, particularly after going through the complete file."

"*Complete* file?"

"Mrs. Campesi closely followed your progress. She kept notes, both personal and professional. About you both, in fact. Those afternoons at the piano. Her fevered desires. Then, after the second round of chemo, the fading impulse. She kept a diary and entered it, along with results on mouse amygdala dissections, for a while on a weekly basis. Although I do not comprehend her choice, she more than once volunteered herself as mistress."

His throat tightened. Hands shook.

A diary?

"This is all in my Glaucon file?" He felt the tide of energy slip away. "The file Mr. Campesi read to monitor my progress?"

The security man nodded, a transitory, nearly imperceptible glance of sympathy.

"...are you boys ... still arguing...?"

"We're not arguing, dear." Siggy reached down to pat Mrs. Chaneuil's shoulder. "The doctor is nearly finished. A perfect job."

Wrestling control over trembling fingers, Ross finished suturing hardware to the globe. He then closed the wound, removed the speculum, and instilled antibiotic ointment. Moments later, his patient was wheeled to the recovery area, chirping away, delighted the surgery was over.

"Why did she keep a diary?" he said. "Her husband was bound to read it."

"My conclusion? Her intent. To reveal her lonely heart and with whom she'd rather share it." He raised an eyebrow. "From her standpoint, there was nothing to lose. She was dying, their relationship, in her heart, already dead. All she left behind was guilt. She tagged him with that."

"She tagged me as well. What was she thinking? She must've known her husband would mistrust me. He never really liked having a young clinician-scientist at Arriva."

"That does raise an awkward question."

"I, we, never once...."

"But, what if you had?"

He shrugged.

"It crossed my mind at the beginning, but...."

"Had you succumbed, she might well have shared the moment."

"A kind of revenge on her part?"

"Perhaps. She did confess great admiration for her 'youngish' friend."

"Why then make such a diary entry?"

"More disappointment with Arturo than admiration for you."

"Why are you telling me this?"

Signet's impassive voice filled his ear. "Let us turn to a thought experiment. It may prove rewarding."

"Something Zen, I hope. But, sure. Go ahead."

"You employ special properties of BDNF to cure glaucoma. It is also the basis of Mr. Campesi's vaccine to cure post-traumatic stress. What if one were to reverse the equation? What would you make of that?"

"What do you mean, reverse?"

"Instead of reviving malfunctioning amygdala cells with a vaccine, you kill them."

"You mean, eliminate the amygdala altogether?" He shook his head. "Why would you do that?"

"Was there not once such a situation? A stroke victim. Your Dr. Braun referenced the article herself."

"You're right. I remember now. A very rare kind of stroke. A bilateral wipeout of the man's amygdala nucleus. A remarkable case study, in fact."

"How so? What was this person like after the 'wipeout'?"

"Is this important?"

"Humor me."

He shut his eyes, digging into memory. When he came aboard, Beth handed him a stack of articles that explained her work on the mouse brain. He'd last seen the paper six years earlier.

"Well, I think the man had been an office manager. A totally rule-driven bean counter. Not much personality. It's what made the outcome so noteworthy. He became a completely different person. His wife immediately got pregnant, even the housekeeper. I mean, he turned into a risk taker. A daredevil...."

Signet pointed to the clock on the OR wall.

"Please, Doctor. Tie this together. I can always read Dr. Braun's summary."

"Okay. Let's see. I seem to remember a lot of dangerous activities. Rock climbing without ropes. Bungie jumping off bridges. Skydiving. He handled snakes. Shot rapids in a kayak. Things like that."

"You describe a fearless individual. Have you ever met such a person?"

Signet did not wait for a reply. He tore off the gown and

strolled out of the OR, leaving a perplexed Ross staring after him.

Had they been discussing another DARPA project? A new vaccine to destroy this area of the brain? And, what relevance to Samantha's diary? Her amygdalae weren't obliterated. Worse. She was scared to death. Why bring such a wipeout idea up at all? Unless it had to do with Ross, instead. Reverse the equation. Was Signet suggesting were it not for fear of reprisal he might have taken a position between Samantha's flaccid knees?

Crazy. A lunatic idea.

Mystified, he went to his locker, changed, dictated an operative report and scaled the rear steps to his office.

Turning a corner, he bumped into Mr. Thought Experiment, who was just then emerging from Ross's office. A surprise encounter, the back area of the office deserted by the professional staff at this hour.

"I heard a noise and went inside." Signet continued through the door and up the hall. "As you can see, the suite is empty."

He glanced in for a look. The "suite" was empty but a complete mess. Books lay scattered over the floor. The contents of desk drawers strewn across the rug. His lab coat ripped from the hanger, pockets turned inside out. The ransacked office was similar to his burgled home the night before.

"What sort of noise?" he said. "Except for a few desk clerks, the office is closed. Who do think was in there?"

"No idea. That is precisely why I checked. Dr. Azzizzi should install a better security system."

He turned abruptly, aiming up the corridor.

Ross got a clearer picture of the day. Mr. Campesi arranged for the sudden surgery to allow Signet to conduct the search. What was he looking for, the flash drive? That still lay secure in Ross's pocket. Moreover, the Glaucon project was on Arriva's main server.

What had he been looking for?

"I now understand the urgency for the surgery."

Signet stopped, paused a beat then turned to face him.

"A blind eye. An elevated pressure."

"It provided a window of time to scramble my office."

"I did not mislead this woman. I was honoring a former commitment."

"You Seals are a loyal bunch."

"I also wished to see the great surgeon at work. You are indeed worthy of a spot on that Infirmary wall."

Signet retraced his path to Ross. Although no acrimony existed between them, the soldier saw fit to apply a withering stare. At close range a variety of scars became visible. A ragged line descended behind the left jaw line. Another curved up and over a buzz haircut. Yet a third wiggled over the collar of his turtleneck, to disappear around the occiput in back. Given the gruesome injuries on display in his Quonset hut, Ross was certain additional disfiguring memories of war existed beneath the black cammies.

A discomforting thought surfaced. That this killer elite, a surviving, carved up and decorated veteran of Afghan mountains, had for some reason been assigned to him. And, Signet, in turn, enlisted Zina's assistance. But, to what end? Who was doing all this assigning in the first place?

"Her nine o'clock post-op is at Arriva tomorrow morning. Don't be late."

"I see post-ops in this office."

"Tomorrow is an exception. Mr. Campesi arranged the visit. Do the right thing and comply with instruction."

"But, am I safe at Arriva? Dr. Braun warned me to stay away."

Signet nodded, a flicker of surprise. Then, gone.

"I see. Yes. You are safe. See your patient then leave. I will try to be there. "

Message tendered, Signet swept back to the front door and left the office. In his wake of departure, Ross sensed a menacing vacuum in the hallway. Because, whether intended or not, the security man buried a knife deep inside the very fabric of Ross's being. Not the Seal pup knife but a different one. Sharper. More deadly.

Do the right thing.

The remark, so offensive. The guy read his file. Knew his credentials, that from childhood on, covering more than ten years of post-graduate education, he had always done the right thing. Punctual, reliable, honest.

The implied threat unleashed a more immediate concern. He rushed back to his office, found the phone under the desk and dialed Manhattan. He found his friend, Jose Catalan, M.D., in the middle of Grand Rounds. A former colleague and friend, the Chief of Ophthalmology and Glaucoma at the university, broke free of his duties to take the call.

"I hope this isn't another diagnostic dilemma, Daniel. We have enough of them up here."

"No, nothing like that. The reason I'm calling—"

"After you nailed that case of tunnel vision," Jose interrupted, "I'm surprised you require assistance. Cancer Associated Retinopathy. Great call. The patient survived her surgery."

"Thanks. We were all lucky. Listen, the reason I'm calling—"

"Did you get that flyer I sent you?"

"Yes. Inspiring. All your new residents are magnificent."

"I haven't seen a better crop of applicants since our Boston days. I'm currently interviewing a Kenyan woman with three degrees. I'll send you a copy of her thesis: 'Meuller Cells And The Ganglion Cell Environment.' You'll love it."

"I can't wait."

"What's on your mind? Shoot."

"I, I'm going over final details about this Friday's symposium. Are you still coming?"

"Are you kidding? I spoke with Maren Kulifabo yesterday. He's bringing his best bio-molecular engineers from California. Don is coming from North Carolina. Brad from Boston. They'll all be there. We're rooting for you."

Ross signed off and sat back. Great. The best players will be there. No one, not Signet or Mr. Campesi, could stop him now.

He removed the flash drive from his pocket.

You're on, buddy. Let's go for it.

CHAPTER 14

After a lazy forty minutes on his faithful Cybex 750, Ross pulled the plug. The magic wasn't there, his legs heavy, body tired. Not finding Zina on the treadmills or in the karate parlor, he aimed home.

It was dusk, the sun low, the air clear along Lansbrook Parkway. That time of day again, the evening stretching out like a battle plan. After a cool shower, he'd pop a can of iced tea, then invite Melko over for a stroll along his dock. If lucky, they'd encounter a gator taking a meal, maybe an unfortunate fish, a dog even, owners unaware of the danger always lurking in their midst, like East Lake cops waiting behind cover to pick off unsuspecting prey with laser-like precision.

His headlights now poked a tunnel through the canopy of flanking trees, his private wormhole through space and time. The passageway increasingly took on this aspect, transporting him from pain and reckoning at one end to a vague space of peace and achievement at the other.

Jose, from New York. Maren, from California. Roberta

from New Hampshire. She may bellow at abandoning her fly rod. But, she'd show up. Everything was in place. He couldn't wait to tell Melko.

They were waiting for him in the porch shadows. Franklin, he recognized as the vast bulge occupying the suspended swing. When his high beams swept the Escort in the driveway, he identified Franklin's companion. Had to be Detective Leeks paying him a visit.

Ascending the front steps, he pondered the proper etiquette. Was he obliged to invite this duo into his so recently demolished house? Before heading to the Y, he managed to repair most of the damage. Still, various eyesores remained. Littering the floor, tiny puffs of pillow stuffing shared space with tinier shards of ceramic splinters plus wood shavings from his now absent roll top desk. Also impossible to ignore, Zina's icon on the wall behind the front door, a constant reminder of the girl's rude comments: *Tuna fish, cashews and chardonnay. Have you even moved in yet?* Zina, for all her appealing weirdness, spot on.

Squeezing his nostrils, he dropped into the tilting seat beside the goliath,

"East Lake pharmacy has a sale on body wash," he said, off hand.

"We should both go." In good form, Franklin returned the gibe. "Hey, Leeks. Get a whiff. This man's a dump."

"I came from the Y. What's your excuse?"

"Seems you two know one another."

He shook hands with the detective. Emitting a low chuckle, Leeks sank back to his haphazard deployment on the top step.

"Has he updated you with his latest conspiracy?" Ross said. "Don't be surprised if he unloads a ton of useless data."

"Man, there you go again. We were talking income disparity. No amount of health care reform will change that." Franklin shook his head, the swing's ceiling chains creaking imminent disaster. "I suppose you don't care about that either."

"Have you told the detective about dark matter?"

"We were only getting started."

Detective Leeks looked over at them in the swing. The porch light revealed his bemused expression.

"No disrespect for either you or your neighbor, Doctor Ross. But if Mr. Franklin is representative, I'd say you're surrounded by fruitcakes. He operates under the delusion everything is interconnected. I fail to see how our invasion of Eritrea, as he chooses to call this imaginary event, and the lunatic assertion the United States is underwriting the ISIS terror organization, another, wild completely unfounded assertion, mind you, how any of that is possibly related to NASA's so-called manufactured story about dark matter."

"That's cool, Mr. Leeks. I see where you're going. Hell, what you two still don't appreciate, it all starts with income disparity. This led to the collapse of my father's hedge fund. He was into home surveillance drones and laser guided missiles. Off the grid shit like that. And, don't for a moment accept the hands-off reports on Eritrea. We invade over there, all bets are off. Father's hedge fund will be up and running in no time."

"It's *Detective* Leeks. And, Franklin, do me a favor before you go."

"Sure, dude. Whatever."

"Explain the underling thread connecting these various narratives."

"Hey, Doc. I thought I told you. It's the one percenters. They control astrophysics, man. What we know about particle interactions. The negative heat of evaporation. Higgs Boson. Stuff like that. Man, you guys don't know the half of it."

The big guy had gone tangential yet again. And, to judge by his chuckle of acceptance, Detective Leeks wasn't put out by the "fruitcake". As he always did when his sanity came up for review, the compliant giant made his departure, the mermaid arm tattoo shimmying as he hurtled the railing and thumped off through the shrubs.

Ross unlocked the front door and invited the detective in.

"My working diagnosis," he said. "Ambulatory paranoid schizophrenia. Franklin accommodates an assortment of warped belief systems."

"Don't we all? You, for example, entertain teleological fantasies life aims towards a greater purpose."

"Say again?"

"Teasing, old man. Paraphrasing our friend out there. Actually, he's quite entertaining. One thing he didn't get into or have time for, religion. This is not why I'm here. Mind if I sit?"

With a sigh of relief, he removed a torn cushion from the couch. Abandoned belief systems, a self-defrocked priest metamorphosing into a bayou playboy. Ross was delighted no time existed for venturing into religion.

After getting his visitor situated, he took off for the shower.

"There's chardonnay in the fridge," he said. "Be back in a minute."

When he reappeared a short time later in a Brooks Brothers pullover and khaki shorts, he found Detective Leeks, hands clasped behind his back, reading the inscription on Zina's icon. No sign of uncorked wine or plastic cups, the shattered remnants of his fine crystal glasses buried with the other rubbish in the kitchen garbage.

"'Detail of Byzantine Mosaic, The Basilica of San Vitale, Ravenna.'" The detective stepped back a fraction, head cocked at a contemplative angle. "On the opposite wall is an icon of Emperor Justinian, the two of them, Justinian and Theodora, locked in an eternal, visual embrace."

"Poetic. How do you know about the opposite wall of the basilica?"

"My wife's interpretation, not mine. We were art history

majors in college. After Reed, we traveled all over Europe. Spent a lot of time in Italy. We particularly liked this basilica in Ravenna. An instructive trip for a lot of reasons. It taught us true love didn't pay the bills. She went on to earn a doctorate in social work. I chose forensics." He stole another glance of the icon. "Old habits never die."

Without further preamble, the detective returned to the couch. He was there to discuss Newsome's murder, he said, although by the looks of the furniture, a good deal of "murder" took place here, on Jasmine Lane.

"I had a break-in."

"You don't say."

Ross relayed the details.

"Anything important missing?"

Ross shook his head.

"Kids, probably. Looking for drugs."

Or, Signet on a search for Mr. Campesi. Ross kept the suspicion to himself, plus the security guy's break-in at his Clearwater office earlier in the day. Any discussion of Signet led back to Arriva and, eventually, to the volatile CEO.

"Your burglar might have done you a favor. Not to be critical, but this house needs a makeover ... though it's obvious you have good taste. Those fake Chippendale chairs a good example. Even discounting the, ah, chipped veneer. Wonderful pieces. The same for that tub of plastic flowers." He chortled, stabbing Ross in the shoulder.

"Teasing again, Doc. You're such an easy target. At least you own one authentic item. I'm referring to that bottle of Cakebread Chardonnay in the fridge. I didn't have the heart to uncork it or open that dusty jar of cashews. I gather you don't get out much, do you?"

A homicide cop with attitude. Ross hadn't picked up on it Monday night. It now required a closer appraisal. The guy was educated to be sure but much too cocky. Who else would notice a veneered fake antique, unless the legs were cracked off? Also, a weirdly dressed individual. Scruffy, mismatched argyles and a rumpled, undersized plaid jacket. Hopefully not the norm down at headquarters.

It was the probing, teasing sarcasm that got to Ross though. Pulling the plug on the rude dude, to quote Franklin, he pointed to the front door.

"This conversation will wait," he said. "I'm exhausted. By the way, you missed the vase. Another example of refined taste. My Mayan masterpiece features a made-in-China label on the bottom."

He rose from his chair. The detective didn't budge.

"I find curious your lack of concern with the accountant's recent demise. That note had your name on it, not his."

"I'm well aware of that," he said. "Repeatedly reminded, in fact. Don't misinterpret. I am concerned. Sorry to disconnect like this, but you're leaving."

"It's clear your life is in jeopardy. Yet, you're blasé. Detached. Not a care in the world. If it were me, I'd lock myself in the upstairs bathroom with my wife's shotgun.

Hell. I'd arm myself with her buzz saw. Maybe I didn't tell you. She dismembers trees. Doc, something's off here. Help me."

What was not "off," Leeks position on the ripped couch. But, he chided himself, where were his Beacon Hill manners?

"I'm aware I was the intended target, though the reason eludes me. But, I've had no choice but to move on. I'm preparing a critical symposium for Friday. It's already Wednesday. That doesn't leave much time. That's why I seem detached. I simply assume you'll catch your man."

Leeks' eyebrows shot up.

"So certain of the gender?"

Zina. He was still preoccupied with the timing of her appearance at the concert. An absurd suggestion though. Minutes after the murder, she was fully costumed. Not a strand out of place or ripple in her purple eyeliner. She also seemed too small and physically ill-equipped to punch a man to death. A bobbing manikins perhaps, but an adult male? Besides, what was her motive?

"You are right about one thing," Leeks said. "My job is to find the perp. And, yours is to give me a few minutes before you hit the sack. I want to summarize what we have. See if you can add anything useful."

One of his first stops after Eckerd Hall was to visit Mr. Ravi Ravda in his Clearwater estate on Tampa Bay. The CEO of Simcoe Incorporated had money up the kazoo, mahogany window sills, imported Italian marble, an

Olympic-size swimming pool in the basement. What he did not possess, however, was a motive to kill his favorite accountant. He admitted to dispatching Newsome on a special assignment. To that he would freely admit. The illicit hunt for secrets. The fraud. That was the extent of his involvement. As far as he knew, Newey had no enemies.

"He thought Newey might pry open the nerd from Boston. His words. Not mine. But, the accountant got squat, the 'nerd' unwilling to share details about, what he called, your secret photon motor."

The detective paused, trying to gauge Ross's blank expression.

"I asked why your 'motor' was so important. Know what he said?"

Ross offered the blankest stare in his arsenal.

"To get a leg up on the competition."

"Which means he planned to steal it."

The detective shrugged.

"Corporate espionage. Theft. Happens all the time. Like that inventor who took his special sensor device with him when he changed employer."

"Driverless cars," Ross said. "I read Google is suing Uber for stealing the patent."

The detective's grin shifted out of neutral. It bore into Ross, implied accusation gathering steam.

"You aren't thinking of jumping ship?" he said. "You know, leaving Arriva to hook up with Ravda's outfit. If so, it provides a tidy motive to hold on to your motor."

He shook his head. A tireless, stupid comparison.

"Unlike the Google-Uber business, I am not switching sides."

"Don't get your feathers up. I'm only asking. You sure this Ravda character never made you an offer?"

"And, when I refused, he killed his accountant?"

"Okay. Forget that scenario. Consider this one. You turned his offer down. Miffed, he wrote you a note to take revenge."

"Ravi Ravda was not at the concert."

"How do we know that?"

"Newsome said he first offered the ticket to his boss. Ravda rejected the invite. Said he hated Beethoven. I mean, how could I 'hook up' with such a person?"

Their gaze locked.

"Neither Ravda or his accountant made me any sort of offer. Heck, I thought he was a reporter at the time. No. I'm wrong. Newsome did once make me a generous offer. I wanted some forty-year-old port. He saw a bottle of vintage Graham on the top shelf. He snapped his fingers. It was mine. Anything else is a farfetched, baseless speculation."

Leeks nodded with a look of disappointment.

"Sorry. Just had to mention it. Besides, killing is not Ravda's style. A gust of wind and he's gone. Same for you, too. You may pump pedals at the Y, but you don't pump weights. You're too weak to take a life. You also don't possess a motive. Why steal what you already own? And, should you go elsewhere, you'd lose control over a patent. You can't start from scratch."

"Do I always make such a favorable impression?"

"What? No. I mean, yes. Very, ah, favorable. Actually, from all I've heard, you are one terrifically capable individual. No. It's true. Everyone I talked to. Well, maybe one equivocator. Your Mr. Campesi, God strike me down if I lie, is a prodigious jerk."

Their eyes met again. A grin crinkled the detective's orbicularis oculi muscles, a smile that deepened. A genuine kind of apology.

Ross grinned as well. Apology accepted.

Switching gears, the detective opened his notepad and checked notes.

"Did anyone know you and Newsome would be at that concert?"

"You asked me that at Eckerd Hall. I couldn't think of anyone then. I can't now."

"Think harder. This person had to know beforehand."

He maintained a tight control over both limb and voice. He had no desire to implicate anyone at Arriva.

"I spoke with a Mr. Signet," the detective said, eyes on the notepad.

"What did he say?"

"He checked the logs, both going in and out of the compound Monday night. He was able to account for everyone's whereabouts. Other than you, no one from Arriva went to the concert. To the movies, perhaps. A whodunit on a train is everyone's favorite these days. But not a Beethoven concert." He shot a questioning look at Ross. Squinted briefly. Returned to his notes. "Your CEO signed out to the airport at six to pick up a military hot shot. Beth, the lab coordinator, was at her station working on a project, as was Signet, researching expense reports. All solid alibis. That's the problem. I have no leads at the moment."

"Did Signet mention which airport?"

"Come again?"

"Tampa. St. Pete. MacDill. There are several in the area."

The detective gave him his full attention.

"The latter, again according to Mr. Signet. He left Arriva to meet some hotshot colonel. Signed him in at the Marriott at seven and went home to Odessa."

"Seven, huh? I didn't know that."

A disturbing fact because both Dr. Braun and Signet agreed the colonel had flown in yesterday morning, not the previous evening. Therefore, Signet lied twice to the detective. Ross was not the only Arriva employee at the concert, and the CEO picked Colonel Bame up Tuesday morning, not Monday night. By establishing, thereby controlling, the fictitious seven o'clock timeline, Signet left open the possibility Campesi had an opportunity to kill Newsome. To frame him, perhaps, or to establish an alibi. Either way, it directed attention away from Signet himself, who most likely was on scene when Newsome had his trachea crushed. Clearly an accomplished liar, for all his denials, Signet might indeed be the murderer.

The special-ops guy then. The killer with a ragged scar along the jawline.

The detective pocketed his pad and pen.

"Don't worry," he said. "We'll catch this guy. He's one nasty number. The smashed hyoid did the job. Yet, the perp delivered a stunning blow to the back of the neck, fracturing the third and fourth cervical vertebrae. Annihilation, not murder, was the name of this guy's game."

"You've determined the gender then.""

Leeks shook his head. "It had to be a male, someone strong and well-trained. The blow came at a right angle. A pair of take-out shots. A man, for certain."

He came to his feet. Had to be going, he said. Other fish to fry. At the door he glanced at the framed icon, sighed, then continued out to the front porch.

"We think Newsome's was a rage attack, but this person wanted you first. That's the tricky part. As far as we can determine, you're well-liked by everyone we talked to."

"What did the jerk equivocator say about me?"

"Your CEO?"

Wearing a thin smile, Leeks descended to his car.

"Not much. He thought you worked hard. He referred me to Dr. Braun, your ongoing mentor."

"Okay. I'll bite. What was her opinion?"

The detective wagged his head from side to side.

"You were a great lab rat. Smart, over dedicated. One negative only. She wished she was fifteen years younger." The detective had to laugh. "Who would have guessed? But, back to business," he added, sliding in behind the wheel. "In my experience, someone always lies. To establish an alibi. To implicate others. To misdirect the investigation. I sure hope it isn't you."

CHAPTER 15

It was well after eight when his Maps app took him down Wood Terrace Lane to his destination, Beth Braun's Northlake Condominium complex.

He parked amongst flourishing shrubs and regarded the fading sun sparkling off the water. He lived a mile down the eastern shore, their proximity to Tarpon Lake making them almost neighbors. But, they were not neighbors. Friendly, dedicated collaborators. Not even friends.

Ever since she handed him that note, their relationship seemed ill-defined, possibly strained. Still, chopsticks Beth, matronly and accomplished, was a favorite. Fifteen years. He chuckled at what the detective said. Who would have guessed? Indeed.

And now a second note, almost as fun as the first:

YOU ARE NO LONGER SAFE AT ARRIVA.

If unsafe inside a razor wire fence, what about outside? He wondered again of the wisdom of returning for a post-op visit. A problem for tomorrow, however. Tonight,

Beth had to explain the altered landscape, why he sensed his career shutting down around him.

She would lay it out for him. She had to. As a distinguished DARPA contract scientist, her professional life exhibited integrity, honesty, ideals with which he identified, a role model this woman of numerous awards, including the coveted Cooter Medal for lab excellence, the Belcher Career Award, plus many honorariums, obligatory book chapters and two books of her own. She'd won the prized Gilly Certificate for accomplishing a rarity in science these days. She and many others could replicate her work. An astonishing career.

All of which made Beth the consummate insider, loyal to the academy, to Arriva, and most of all, to DARPA and the Department of Defense. Where did his own niche lie, he the marginalized semi-scientist, in all this? He was here now, honoring her request—command, really—for answers.

He rang the bell. The door promptly flew open.

"Ninety minutes late," she said, crisply, examining the nearby vegetation. "I've been waiting."

"I, I had a visitor," he stammered. "The detective working Newsome's murder. He paid an unexpected visit."

"Leeks. Hmm. He stopped by earlier. An annoying, unkempt fellow. I had nothing to tell him. I prepared paella, with shrimp. That is, if you're not allergic. Crispy chicken and cashews, if you are."

She led him down a hallway resplendent with wall coverings.

To his left, a tapestry of a bloody bullfight faced, across the hall to his right, a brilliant Toledo Sunset. A mural-sized portrait snared his attention. A regal gentleman, draped by a burgundy cape, gazed out across expansive pastures. Jet black horses, lumpy cattle, and stately brick buildings stood off to one side, all enclosed by a white board fence, the color matching his ornamental vest and neck ruffles.

"My great-great-great granddaddy," Beth said, identifying the lord of the manner. "Maybe a few more 'greats' tossed in. I really don't know. He lived a very long time ago. A prosperous landowner before Queen Isabella possessed his farm and deported him."

She ushered him into the rear study, an antique parlor, actually, with period pieces from her long-dead family who once lived, she added, as a footnote, in a faraway Andalusia, Spain.

"These upholstered, high backs?" She tut-tutted, patting the moldy chairs. "Not what you would call very, ah, millennial, modern. However one labels current fashion. Make yourself comfortable. We have a lot of ground to cover."

"I didn't know you're Spanish."

"From time immemorial. That portrait out there? Painted at the height of his glory. Before Isabella and Ferdinand got rid of him. Expelled quite a huge number of Jews. The Alhambra Decree. Fourteen Ninety Two. You remember the date, Columbus set sail for the Americas? Great beginnings. We've all had them. No escaping our past. Anyway, back to the present so we can plot your future."

"When did your family 'set sail'?"

"I'd love to chase down old memories...."

"Do you have family here?"

She drew up a fraction.

"Never married, if that's what you mean. Never saw a use for it. There's a philosopher brother in Colorado Springs. Look. We have to get going here. Time's a-ticking."

Off to the side, a teak table had been set for two. Twin bowls of paella, a pair of goblets with a half consumed bottle of scarlet wine. He'd been late but in time to interrupt somebody's dinner.

"If you're wondering, it's a vintage Bodegas Rioja. Don't worry. He's long gone." Beth got him seated on a couch, facing a Dell Inspiron on the coffee table. "Did you bring your flash drive?"

He patted his pocket.

She nodded approval then hit the keyboard.

"Here's the current list of Arriva projects. It still includes Glaucon, a relief. But, you're not out of the water. Not by a long shot."

Beth continued tapping keys, consumed, while Ross sneaked a peek at her obvious makeover. Not one to notice her coiffure, the pageboy style was new. Darker as well, the bushy bun straightened out. What a difference a day makes. She still found room for lacquered chopsticks, their bright red stripes of a piece with carefully etched lipstick and plaid skirt cut provocatively close to the knees revealing, for the first time, vertical scars of prior surgery. A sparkling woman of a certain age, Dr. Braun had gone full throttle for her dinner companion.

She'd also gone full throttle at a file now displayed for his review.

"What do you think?" she asked. "Meet with your approval?"

He peered closer at the monitor.

"I haven't had a chance to—"

"Not that, dummy. Me. I caught you looking. I'm, ah, tired of staid wisdom. So, your verdict?"

"The new you. I'm impressed, but I'm probably not the only one." She turned as scarlet as the Rioja. "Terrific, Dr. Braun. Really."

"Thanks." She pointed to the monitor, getting back to it. "See here. Good news and bad."

The former being her firm alibi. For some odd reason, Mr. Campesi questioned her whereabouts at the time of the theft. Detective Leeks reviewed the same question, his concern with the time of the murder. The sign-in ledger clearly established her alibi on both counts. She was out of the lab. Period. Arturo suspended her anyway. She was not to return to the research campus until the theft was resolved.

"Now for the bad news," she said. "It appears you—"

"Hold it. Why did he suspend you? You had nothing to do with that man's murder."

Beth paused, taking a breath.

"I'm going too fast," she said. "This has nothing to do with that horrible murder. It concerns something far more important, at least for our esteemed Arturo. He claims you possess a flash drive copy of certain classified DOD-DARPA projects. That's Department of Defense, Daniel. It's a federal crime, punishable as a breach of national security, to steal Defense secrets."

"What did you say?"

"Arturo's IT people tracked the unauthorized entry site to my computer in our shared lab. I received notification of the theft and that you are the prime suspect. That's why I told you to copy your project and leave Arriva. Other than me, you alone have access to that lab and my computer."

"Unauthorized? I never stole anything."

Alarm bells rang up and down his spine. Perspiration rimmed his brow.

"IT is very specific about the time. The entry took place right after you left the meeting with Arturo in the conference room. It was close to twelve fifteen, the time I joined you in the lab."

"That can't be right. I was with Signet for a good twenty, maybe thirty minutes."

Beth nodded.

"Maybe I'm off with the exact time. I spoke with Signet. I'm sure he will vouch for you. I know you would never do this. That's what makes the accusation so peculiar."

"You spoke with Signet about this?"

"Soon as I came home yesterday. I fired off an email. He emailed me back. Said, not to worry. He was on top of the problem."

"He never mentioned any of this to me. He brought a patient to the office today." Blindsided, chest pounding, he sat back against the cushions. "I can't use your lab computer. I don't know the password."

"Exactly what I told Arturo. I wasn't there. You weren't there. Yet, according to IT, at that precise moment someone downloaded the entirety of certain documents."

Ross came to his feet. The whole thing was outlandish.

"Every Arriva employee has access to that lab," he said. "As I understand it, that's the way Arriva works. Free flow of information. Shared ideas. But, each employee has their own password-protected account on Arriva's servers. I was never a full-fledged DARPA employee, though, so I was never granted a private account. My project was kept separate. I don't have access to any of Arriva files. Period."

She shrugged, a partial, almost noncommittal response. "The Glaucon project is on an Arriva server. So, in essence, a pathway in. What IT calls, a hacker's dream."

"What the heck? I didn't 'hack' these darn documents. I wouldn't even know how to go about it if I wanted. Look,

Beth. You know I have access to one single file. How could I somehow sneak into the main DARPA data base? I would need a special password you once told me changes week to week. You know that. Mr. Campesi knows that. What the heck is going on here?"

Dr. Braun patted his trembling hand.

"Arturo is ripped about your contact with this Newsome person. He thinks the Simcoe accountant was involved."

"I had no idea he was a Simcoe spy."

"Arturo believes the opposite. He's convinced himself you're colluding with Ravda. He's paranoid. We all know that. Now, with Colonel Bame looking over his shoulder, the post-traumatic vaccine on the launch pad..." Beth paused, her eyes searching his. "You can appreciate his concern."

"How about *my* concern. If he thinks I betrayed him or Arriva, he could ruin me. He's ultimately in charge of Glaucon." He raked his hair, trying to make sense of it. "He can't accuse me like this. Without proof, he's denying me my rights. My God. Maybe I need a lawyer."

"Hush now. You're jumping to conclusions. There's a rumor about some kind of timeline evidence. Let's see how it plays out. Arturo would not risk an unwarranted accusation. He doesn't want some government inspector general coming down on him. So, calm down."

"This is simply crazy."

"Sounds that way to me, too. If it's any help, to Signet

as well. Remember, he was assigned to Arriva by a very high authority at Defense. If he's on your side, you have nothing to worry about. Well, less to worry you."

"But, wait…."

"Arturo knows Newsome, as an accountant, is familiar with computers. The man could easily have taught you to access the system."

"That's a joke, right? Newsome would have to know your password."

"These guys work around passwords."

"But, why would I steal anything that belongs to Arriva? That place is my lifeblood. Besides, how would Newsome gain access to the building itself let alone our lab or your computer? Arriva has security cameras. If Newsome were on the compound they would have caught him." He sighed. "I would have to be a fool to steal classified DOD-DARPA projects."

He paced, overwhelmed by the enormity of the alleged crime.

Beth patted the couch. He plopped down, strung out.

"I very much doubt your project is in jeopardy." She struck a key and another image filled the screen. "I need to explain what's in those files. You have to understand what you're up against."

"Unreal."

"Pay attention. You have to make the right decisions in the days ahead."

"Now you sound like Signet and Zina Palaeologus. What's this about 'days ahead'?"

"Those before your Friday symposium. It's Wednesday night. You don't have a lot of time."

"I know. I should be home preparing slides."

"I'm not talking about that. I'm talking about this."

The walls were closing in, a frightening force squeezing him tighter. Signet had searched his office and most certainly his home. A stalking SUV was on his trail. And, now he was charged with a theft he did not commit. Worse, his project was on the line.

Careful, Danny-boy. You're mixed up in something.

"Go on," he said, "Enlighten me."

Chapter 16

It all began with DARPA. Years earlier, the Department of Defense tasked the research agency to discover ways to improve the capabilities of the modern soldier. The resulting project was based upon research that revealed human error to be the common denominator accounting for poor battlefield performance. Not faulty weaponry, communication failure, the terrain or weather conditions. In all cases, human error was at fault. The DOD concluded if a soldier were impervious to stress he'd be able to make better executive decisions. The same applied to drone-attack personnel, all the way up the ladder of command. In the modern era, with the constant threat of terror activity not to mention violence in both the far and Mideast arenas, the need was urgent.

"That is the thinking. It's what got the ball rolling. Not surprisingly, DARPA researchers focused on the amygdala nucleus deep inside the brain."

Ross scoffed.

"Why didn't I think of that?"

"Don't be a smart ass." Beth pointed to the monitor. "I'll review some neuroanatomy for you. Take a look.""

They were viewing a coronal section of the human brain. Like a slice through parallel loaves of bread face-on, one loaf, or cerebral hemisphere, to each side. The outer crust of the loaves represented the frontal, dorsolateral and temporal cortices of the brain. Much deeper lay the hippocampal or memory cortices that housed, adjacent to its convoluted curves, the twin, almond shaped amygdalae nuclei, one to each side of the brain.

"Piece of cake." Ross tapped the screen. "There's the interstitial nucleus of Cajal. Just lateral to the nucleus of Darkschewitsch. What of it?"

"You're referring to a microscopic structures not even on the screen. Think amygdala, Daniel. That's where the action is."

"I remember," he said, finally tuning in. "Your rodent work. You worked it out with mice. You erased their fear avoidance by injecting BDNF into the amygdala nucleus. The little sniffers were unafraid of an electrical shock to reach their food. You put the nerve factor, BDNF, on the map."

"Correct. And, clever lads that they are, recognizing a potential bench-to-clinic application, DARPA latched on to it in a flash. It was astounding what their further research revealed."

"In healthy individuals," she continued, "the amygdala generates appropriate fear responses. It kept our ancestors safe from lurking tigers. It also keeps soldiers out of trouble. When it overreacts, however, PTSD develops. Simply stated, the amygdala is out of control and hyper-reactive to minor stimuli—a backfiring car, the rustling wind, a baby's cry, an otherwise simple memory—long after the soldier leaves the battle field and returns home. The result, unexpected behavior like rage or suicide. Hence, the importance of DARPA's new vaccine. Properly inhaled, the BDNF molecule is able to correct the persistence of battle induced stress. The amygdala returns to a homeostatic threshold. The soldier doesn't hit his wife or take his life."

"Very commendable. But, I don't get it. As soon as the vaccine program gets under way, this will become common knowledge. Where does the theft fit in?"

"The production details are top secret. They will never become 'common knowledge'. They include the exact biochemical method used to attach the BDNF gene to a unique virus capable of penetrating the olfactory nucleus, what the vaccine first encounters when inhaled. More than that, the documents reveal how this highly classified nano-chitosan, multi-gene construct ferries itself out of the olfactory nucleus inside the nose, down the olfactory nerve to the amygdala inside the brain." Beth took a breath, dialing back her enthusiasm. "Those are only a few of the secrets. Think about it. Each olfactory nerve, right and left, is connected to each amygdala. It's like a direct tube, a conduit, to places deep inside the brain. DARPA merely takes advantage of this arrangement nature has so neatly evolved."

"How does this involve Mr. Campesi? It's DARPA's loss, not his."

For a few moments Beth stared at the monitor. In a huff, she went to the side table, snatched a pair of fresh goblets, poured the Rioja to half-mast, and returned to the couch.

"Better have a shot," she said, "It will soften the blow."

He took the advice and emptied the goblet in a single gulp.

"Mind if I refill?"

"Better not. You need to be relaxed, not fogged out."

She tapped the keyboard.

"The CEO has a lot riding on the PTSD vaccine," she went on. "In exchange for developing it at Arriva, he was allowed to sell it back to the US government for a huge profit.

"It sounds iffy. Yet, in this case, the arrangement fit. When you consider the thousands of returning soldiers requiring treatment, you can imagine Arriva's financial shortfall if any of this became public. It might result in an embarrassing scandal, like a dagger through the heart of this icon of secrecy." She paused as this new aspect sank in. "Consider an even worse scenario. What if these documents fell into Mr. Ravi Ravda's hands at Simcoe, Inc.? The fallout would be horrific. Your career might very well be over. The US government takes corporate espionage very seriously."

"*Espionage?* You've got to be joking."

"Afraid not. It's for real. It could happen. Now, this PTSD project goes by the code name, GENESIS I. Let's move on to Genesis II. Another secret project, also based at Arriva."

After their success with the PTSD vaccine, certain creative folks in DARPA's Neuro-Behavioral Unit decided to eliminate the amygdala all together. In PTSD the nuclei merely misfired. They wondered what would happen if these nuclei were permanently put out of action.

"A 'thought experiment,'" Ross said.

"Come again."

"How Signet described it yesterday. What if, instead of reviving the amygdala, you destroyed it?"

"No doubt you remember that famous case. A heart attack. A stroke, leaving the man with the fenestrated amygdalae. A risk taker. A former coward who then climbed Mt. Everest."

Ross nodded. "I mentioned it to Signet. The patient rode motorcycles down cliffs...."

He stopped. Beth had gone silent. Her pupils dilated, furrowed crow lines more pronounced.

"You see where this is leading?" she said.

"Not exactly."

She struck a key. Another coronal section of the brain appeared on the monitor. This slice was different though. At the base of the section, at the location usually occupied by the amygdalae nuclei, were two honeycomb areas of absent tissue.

"You're looking at a fearless soldier. Genesis II. The intentional destruction of a man's brain. A chopper in Helmand province took a hit. Trapped in his seat, this soldier rode it down. His charred corpse was sent home. Colonel Bame demanded an autopsy. This is the soldier's brain."

"Colonel Bame demanded it? But why?"

"Later."

"How did they do *that* to him?" Ross thumped the screen. "This is crazy."

"Guess. Never mind. I'll cut to the chase. Rather, to the soldier's absent amygdalae. Imagine an ordinary, well trained soldier who becomes, through dint of hard work and incredible suffering, an Army Ranger. Then, without warning, decides to become a SEAL. A man tough as nails but also conditioned to handle fear."

"Tough as nails? I can think of at least a dozen. They became brain surgeons. What of it?"

Beth inhaled again.

"Just this. DARPA's neuro-behavioral unit sought volunteers for their new project. A man, the soldier in the chopper, was the first, the reason DARPA and Colonel Bame wanted a postmortem on the brain. The soldier I'm now referring to had offered no reason why he wanted to volunteer. Curious, was all he said, signing the consents.

Upon receiving the experimental, intra nasal vaccine, he changed. On every conceivable measure of performance, his numbers were off the chart. He was suddenly able to analyze pivotal battle situations with rapid and keen precision. An unexpected advantage also emerged as the months passed. He became impervious to pain. Physical. Psychological. Any method of torture possible. Water boarding. Ice bath immersion. He was incredible."

"You're describing a robot!"

"Far from it. We're talking about a transformed human brain. This person did not experience conflicting emotions. Oh, he recognized them, in others and within himself. He just did not *respond* to them. Anger also did not interfere. He was aware a switch had been thrown and, the amazing part, had no desire to return to his former self."

"No wonder DARPA wants to keep the lid on this one. Mercenary, fearless soldiers. DARPA must be pleased."

"Not exactly, for a number of reasons. A group of vaccinated soldiers went overboard in a certain experiment."

It took place in Nuristan, Afghanistan. In the coldest, most forsaken mountains on the border of Pakistan. A squad was tasked to take out a group of insurgents. The odd and added piece of the experiment involved returning to base camp with a body part to prove they completed their mission. What these ruthless men brought back was entirely unexpected.

"They trooped single file into camp, silently grinning before handing over their trophies."

"Trophies?"

"A bag of severed ears. Amazing, huh?"

"You're kidding. *Ears*?"

"Colonel Bame, the man in charge, was horrified. That was his official reaction. Off camera, he and his superiors were overjoyed with the outcome. The worry at the time was this pet project might be placed on hold. After all, his men had turned into raging assassins. Then, after several months, something surprising happened. The men changed again, another switch thrown. All but one became peaceful, tree-hugger types. They soon quit the army and rejoined society. For example, Signet went into security work. And, by doing so, they became exemplary citizens."

"Signet? My God. He was one of those soldiers?"

"You saw his SEAL pup knife. I bet he fingered your ear."

Ross shook his head, the memory of the peculiar moment still vivid.

"That's precisely what he did. But a tree-hugger? I'm surprised that's part of his resume."

"It's not. Consider it a metaphor for change."

"But an ear slicer? Holy mama."

"Want a peek at Corporal Signet's MRI?" Beth called up another image. An exact replica of the helicopter pilot who couldn't bail when hit. "This is him six months following the inhalation. Quite a package, don't you think?"

Another pair of fenestrated amygdalae nuclei, the sight incredible. It accounted for a lot about Arriva's new Chief of Security. Yet, as Beth indicated, the man had changed since this six month image acquired years ago. On one level, quiet and perceptive. On another, particularly when his black marble stare punctured your composure, disruptive, controlling in the extreme, his behavior anything but normal. He felt your pain. He simply didn't give a damn.

Beth reconfigured the images on the monitor.

"What do you see here?" she said. "Remember, the red parts indicate increased blood flow, the color code for ongoing mental or brain activity. Yellow is the opposite."

What he saw surprised him. Three regions were lit up like Christmas lights: the medial frontal, posterior parietal and dorsolateral prefrontal cortices. He knew a little about the function of all three. Dorsolateral proved easy. It was the area of the brain that became active when decisions were required. The parietal, where all the senses were unified to orient the individual in time and space to the external world. And, the medial frontal, where social and emotional interactions came together to ensure appropriate behavior. What was strange, all three were functioning together in total isolation from the remainder of the brain, which remained yellow or inactive.

"We obtained this configuration whenever we tasked him with a special project."

For the measurements, Signet lay in a special MRI scanner. Colonel Bame then asked him to imagine cordoning off a certain landscape. His mission was to isolate insurgents and plan their removal. A plan he later used to great success in Nuristan province.

"Was he instructed to slice off ears?"

"He most certainly was not. The ears were the work of Signet's most uncontrollable soldier, a reconfigured bad guy named Sauer, one I hope you never meet." Beth hesitated, stole a sideways glance in his direction, then resumed the story. "On a bloody rampage, Sauer sliced right and left. At one point, holding up an ear, he invited Signet to share the glory. To his credit, the corporal refrained from maiming a single insurgent even though they were already dead."

She sighed, and with a quick look at the table set for two, polished off her wine.

"A strong moral code," he said. "Good to remember. For the days ahead. Do I have that right?"

Beth colored, ignoring the sarcasm.

"Back to the blood flow monitor," she said. "I hope you appreciate how astonishing this is. Three areas, not normally co-active, were networked together, functioning simultaneously as one unit, at least as far as can be determined. I was unable to find a single reference in the research literature describing such a phenomenon. No input from the orbital frontal or insular cortices, no emotional processing or confusion whatsoever. What was even more unbelievable and it definitely had not been anticipated, Signet's brain began to undergo what neuroscientists call neuroplasticity, a remodeling of both connection and function between additional areas of the brain. After a period of ten months Signet's MRI resembled, in many respects, that of a Zen monk."

"Right. Mr. Zen. Former ear man. I'm impressed."

"Your sarcasm is way off base. You saw his Yin Yang rug. You inhaled the incense. Take a look at his brain now."

She summoned a split screen image of two brains. The MRI on the left displayed a coronal section labeled "Signet"; the one on the right, a coronal section labeled "Zen master". According to the subtitle, the latter was obtained from the Journal of Introspective Science and Psychology. The two MRIs were identical in color distribution.

"We tasked him to attend to the surrounding environment. The clanking MRI magnet, the sight of the cylindrical tube around him, even the Beethoven sonata striking his eardrums. He was to remain calm, alert, and totally focused. The most significant additional parts of his brain to light up were the precuneus and cingulate cortices, areas that we know, from many Zen studies, come online when a person finds himself in an unfamiliar situation. Total alertness," she added. "A mental state Zen masters call 'Satori', or the state of seeing into one's true nature of non-duality, whatever *that* means. It was how Signet described it. By eliminating his amygdala, active neuroplasticity was set in motion. This unleashed process turned him into a calm and introspective individual. Remarkable, don't you think?"

"If it's true, yes."

"To intentionally realize this unusual state, DARPA's molecular scientists had altered the original PTSD vaccine. Instead of loading the penetrating virus-chitosan nano-particle with a BDNF enhancing gene, Colonel Bame authorized one that coded for neuron death."

"*Death?* Why would he do that?" He was appalled. In medicine a doctor takes an oath to do no harm, *primum non nocere.* Colonel Bame was undertaking the opposite. "Did DARPA develop another vaccine to do this?"

She nodded again, vigorously this time, jiggling her chopsticks.

"You have to agree it's elegant. They've created a completely different person. Like setting neuro-evolution on steroids. Such a transformed personality is truly revolutionary."

He found her admiration of Signet's mysteriously rewired brain compelling. They were ranging far afield, though. He had been accused of stealing copies of these documents. Another even more threatening problem now arose.

"Haven't you just proved the accusation?" he said. "You've shown me the essence of this Genesis II project. In fact, that makes us both guilty of stealing state secrets."

Beth wagged her head, a creepy smile on her thin lips.

"I have access. Where do you think the password came from? Yet, technically you're correct. This is what they want to hide. Why they need the copies of these files returned."

"But, you've made me an accomplice."

He tried to get off the couch, felt her hand on his arm.

"This is only between us, Daniel. I promise. I had to educate you about the significance of those documents. It's anyone's guess what Genesis III is all about."

"There's *more*?" He rubbed his head, sensing the enormity of the issue. "Aren't you worried this neuroplasticity business might get out of hand? How many 'Signets' are there?"

"As far as I know, just one. Remember, Bame had an entire platoon to experiment with. So, yes, I am alarmed. These transformed soldiers may present a major problem to Colonel Bame and his immediate superiors. Neuroplasticity turned Signet into a terrific assassin. Stage one, you might say. Stage two, when he became this calm person. Stage three, assuming there is one, currently undecided. He claims he isn't morphing any more, just becoming better at who he now is. But, therein lies the problem. Stage two has made him untrustworthy as a Special Forces operative. He completely ignores orders he finds disagreeable. Which to Colonel Bame means he has rejected the military point of view, or as Signet put it, their 'belief system'."

A bell sounded for Ross. *Rejected their belief system.* A situation reminiscent of Father Palaeologus, a priest who'd lost his faith. Another similarity, both underwent a change in personality. Except, as far as Ross knew, Zina's grandfather was not the subject of a vaccine program.

Beth left the couch, refilled her goblet and resumed her place at the monitor.

"Signet considers himself a free man," she said. "He only obeys self-generated orders."

"That's a problem?"

"To the military, yes. We're getting off track. You now know why Colonel Bame is frantic about this theft. Forget Campesi. The colonel is your real problem. Not only can he shut down the Glaucon project, he could land your fanny in federal prison. He's terrified this will go viral, that people might discover once highly skilled killers are loose in society. An exposure of this magnitude could damage DARPA. These projects have to remain secret. That is why, if you have any idea where those copied documents are, you must return them."

He remained calm. Beth knew he didn't have any DARPA files. He repeated his innocence. She waved him aside.

"This is a serious matter," she said. "So much so, Arturo brought the FBI on board. Together, they can not only ruin your reputation. They can also kill you. Don't put it past them. At this juncture, my advice, go into hiding. You might even consider moving on. You know, set up shop elsewhere."

"*Move on?*" He was stunned. "How can I do that? My entire project is at Arriva."

"You have that flash drive in your pocket."

"Where would I go?"

"You're always talking Manhattan. Take Glaucon to your friend. He'll help you."

"I can't do that. I'm registered with the FDA at Arriva. I've done all the work there. We're practically partners."

Beth closed her Inspiron, then took him by the arm and led him, as gently as possible, to the front door.

"I tell you this for your own good. Arturo knows you are weak, that you are vulnerable. He can read you exactly as Signet does. Except, and you should carefully mull this over, unlike the CEO, Signet cares for your wellbeing."

With that, she pushed him out the door and snapped it shut behind him.

CHAPTER 17

Thursday morning he was tailed again, this time not by a red scooter but a black SUV. It rode the Corolla's belching exhaust pipe down the long approach road to the very end where, at the last second, it hit the brakes, spraying Ross with pebbles large and small before veering right toward the Simcoe protestors just getting started with angry chants and jeers.

Another morning in paradise.

At the gate, he tried the intercom. The metal bars refused to move. High above, the glassed-in booth appeared empty. After a short interval, Signet's disembodied voice crackled out of the box.

"Do not move. I want to see this."

The protestors, always loud, were going ballistic.

Scattering the horde, the SUV had also struck them with pebbles as it crunched to a stop. Disembarking to catcalls and worse, a large belly pair was attempting to corral the disruptive band while a shorter individual patrolled the periphery barking orders. Were it not for their FBI-emblazoned jackets, they might have passed as protestors, missing only spitfire-dragon and lightning tattoos.

He caught sight of Ravi Ravda, the tall president and CEO of Simcoe, Inc., employer of the late Mr. Newsome and instigator of the street characters now being dispersed from the property. With his loopy, buck-tooth grin and backwards baseball cap, he looked positively goofy.

"Hey there, Mr. Danny Ross," he called out, his voice high-pitched and singsong. "You and I, we will get together someday soon, okay?"

The unexpected comment stilled the air. All heads turned to Ross. After a brief moment, a second round of activity erupted. The short FBI guy shoved Ravda out of the way, then summoned two of his men, who circled Ross's idling Corolla. Startled, he fumbled for the door handle, thought better of escape and flipped the lock.

With a whoosh of air, a body landed with a resounding thud on the roof of the Corolla. Signet slid over the hood to emerge standing before the three men. FBI had to tilt their heads back to take the corporal's measure.

"Nice jump, big boy," the smaller of three said. "Out of the way. This is official business."

Big boy stood his ground. Undeterred, the rude spokesman tried an end run around the giant blocking his path.

"Hey, mister. Can you read the letters?" Pointing to his jacket. "You don't want to mess with us."

"Exit your vehicle," Signet said to Ross. "Go inside and wait for me."

Fingers shaking, he clumsily unlocked the door and hustled through the gate.

"I said, out of the way, bozo. That guy's coming with me."

"You are mistaken, Agent Zalin. The doctor is here to see a patient."

He glanced back to catch the action. The man Signet identified as Agent Zalin was dangling in midair, held aloft at the waist as he kicked frantically to get free.

"...listen to me, buddy—"

"Signet. That's what to call me."

"Got it … now put me down. I have to arrest that man."

Mr. Zen put the FBI man down, not on the pavement, but behind the wheel of his SUV. He politely held the rear door for his scuttling companions then ordered the team off property. After the black vehicle disappeared down Keystone, he gathered Ross and entered the building. Greeting them was a blast of cool air, a tumble of late, oblivious employees and their usual rude dismissal before scurrying into keypunch labs.

"Whew!" Ross mopped his brow. "Where did they come from?"

Signet depressed the elevator button.

"The FBI? Mr. Campesi's decision. Following the theft of top-secret files, he thought it best."

"Dr. Braun told me our beloved leader believes I stole them."

"His thoughts. Always a difficult matter."

"I need you to explain I was at your Quonset hut when the server was breached."

His outrage failed to register. Aloof from further discussion, Signet effected a calm demeanor while waiting for the elevator. But, thanks to Beth, he understood this detached attitude came from the man's reconfigured nervous system. Anyone's guess what thoughts churned away inside his brain.

At the same time, Ross was all too aware of his own churning worries to stay silent.

"You know damn well the FBI didn't just arrive. They've been watching me for weeks. I saw them at the Y."

The blank asteroids did not waver.

"Did you hear me? Damn it, man. I'm being set up. Dr. Braun said the documents were stolen yesterday, but these FBI characters were on point two days earlier."

The elevator arrived. They slowly ascended to the second floor. Only when they angled down the tiled hallway did Signet find his voice.

"Mr. Campesi is unhappy with your uncharted conversations with Newsome. For him, that is when this episode began. According to your contract, you were to clear all such interactions with the CEO. When I arrived, I was asked to investigate. The reporter turned out to be a Simcoe IT expert. Naturally, your CEO was displeased."

"Forget Newsome. We're talking frame-up here. I am innocent and damn it, man, you know that. Talk to him. Clear this up, for Christ's sake. My project—my whole career—is on the line."

"Do not swear. For you, inappropriate. It does not fit. Never forget facts do not matter to him. It is only critical what Mr. Campesi thinks. I have no influence there."

Ross shook his head. More insane by the moment.

"It's not a matter of 'think' but a matter of *fact*. I was with you. I could not have downloaded any files. Someone else broke into Beth's computer."

"I agree. Someone possessed the password."

"You see. I'm right. I didn't do it. Will you explain that to Mr. Campesi?"

"Perhaps he copied the files himself."

"Why on earth would he do that?"

An eyebrow twitched. A barely noticeable upward flick, a first for the impervious Chief of Security.

"To reinforce suspicion. He does not trust you. He is also devious. I told Beth to explain all of this to you."

It took a second. Then, he understood.

"How was the paella? Sorry to barge in like that."

"We thought you forgot the invitation. The paella was

excellent. I had no time for the Rioja." He swiftly guided Ross around the next corner. "You are late. Your patient awaits you in the exam room."

"Why didn't you tell Detective Leeks you were at Eckerd Hall Monday night?"

"And, join his investigation? Unwise. Like you, my participation is innocent."

Ross paused, struck by Signet's ambiguous reply. "When you say participation, are you referring to the computer theft nonsense or the murder? If the former, of course, you're uninvolved. You were with me when it occurred. IF you're referring to Newsome, that's still an open question."

"To some. Not to others."

Having a reasonable conversation here was proving difficult. Signet tossed curveballs when straight answers were required. According to Beth, neuroplasticity was at fault, that is, if emotional blunting and straight-up cognitive function were more a liability than neural gain. In some fashion, being detached from and subservient to cognitive thinking, emotions took a back seat in Signet's stripped down, super-analytical universe.

But, it got Ross to wondering about music. After all the guy, willingly or not, attended a Beethoven piano concert featuring Opus 106, arguably one of the most noteworthy sonatas in the entire repertoire. For a vast potion of mankind music, most likely not that of the great master, was the emotional cathartic, the ultimate, pervasive release from mental captivity to regions undefined. Did

Signet's bizarre detachment apply to music?

So, to toss his own curveball for a change, he put the question to Mr. Neuroplasticity.

"Ah, Signet. Dude. My man. This may come as a non sequitur, but did you enjoy the Beethoven concert the other night?"

Signet hesitated a few beats before answering.

"Your tone has changed. Perhaps our mirror neurons are engaged. You know, like Einstein's term, spooky action at a distance, for two particles in quantum entanglement."

Talk about non sequitur.

"No diversions please. Will you address the single question?"

Less than a hint of a twinkle sparkled from deep within Signet's recessed sockets. Then he was back, probably even before his eyes changed gears.

"If by 'enjoy' you mean was I affected or not? Yes, I was, but not in the manner you may expect. I detected deep structure. Such fine musical turmoil, that impossible fugue, underscoring, if you will, a constant surface tension. Indeed, I was overjoyed by form defining substance. I sensed the struggle of the individual, of his long goodbye."

And, to supply his own final cadenza, Signet winked. Briefly, to be sure, but it was there.

"You mean Beethoven?"

"Whom else? The Les Adieux, the first offering of that night, a masterpiece. While you dallied with dead Newsome, I joined the composer for his energetic Return. Which, I might add, may someday be your fate. Either to applause or ignominy. We shall see."

Their gaze locked. A view across the Grand Canyon, the inseparable distance of two minds.

"What did you think of it? I mean, did you actually like the sonata?"

"All metrical deployments intrigue me. Including those that constitute music and others that guaranteed successful missions in the Nuristan border region. Need I remind you? You are late, Doctor."

✳✳✳

Mrs. Chaneuil's line of gaze shifted in his direction when he entered the room. Hopefully, not to the sound but to his actual visual presence. He wanted his device to work. Dropping the pressure from forty-five would restore ganglion cells on the brink. For the majority of the rest, however, the ghost had long fled the corpse of its axon.

He got her seated behind the slit lamp, supported her upper lid, and inspected his handiwork.

The twin tubes lay correctly aligned against the globe, each snaking to its appointed destination. The cornea, lustrous. The chamber, deep and clear. The pressure, a perfect ten. And, when he actually tested her vision found, to their mutual surprise, her eye correctly perceived his hand moving before her smiling face. Not yet count fingers, but a small achievement over shadow vision of the day before. With luck, more improvement might occur in the days to come. He still had to activate the growth factor unit.

"I can see again. You have long black hair and a firm chin. My goodness. This is wonderful. I can see objects."

A tad incorrectly, though. He had short, brown hair and a regular, hardly "firm" chin. It was a start.

"Let's wait until the eye fully recovers," he reassured.

"Oh, my. Yes. You're so handsome, doctor."

He swung the arc lamp into position at the side of her head and depressed a switch. A bright strobe came on for ten seconds then switched off. He repeated the maneuver three more times. Afterward, he informed his patient the device was activated, her prolonged treatment regimen underway.

"Is that it? Am I finally cured?"

Only time will tell, he cautioned. Her glaucoma was already far advanced. Optic nerve pale white, saying goodbye, the latter reflection kept to himself, however. Meanwhile, until their visit the following week, she was to apply the antibiotic and steroid eye drops as instructed. Then, after a handshake and a quick hug, they parted ways as a technician led her down to the cab at the gate.

On cue, a bemused Signet came to life. With a secure grip, he led Ross to the door.

"Congratulations," he said. "Upstairs it will be another story. Your luck may not hold."

CHAPTER 18

"Come in, Daniel, and do us the honor of joining the discussion. Corporal, pour the man some water. Colonel Bame won't be here today. He's off to MacDill on a return to Iraq. Special Ops needs its commander."

And thus, with his engineered smile, Campesi invited them in. As always, he loomed immaculate at the distant end of the table. Blue seer sucker, both pants and jacket, plus the obligatory half blinding, snow white shirt and damnable onyx cufflinks clinking on the hardwood.

Ross assumed a seat opposite the false bon homie. As always, particularly today, he resisted the tug of their asymmetric relationship. A close call, however, his foot planted squarely on the brakes, wheels spinning at the cliffs edge, fending off the manipulative baloney concocted for their meetings.

"I didn't do it," he announced, not waiting for accusation. "Ask Signet. He knows where I was. He'll vouch for my innocence."

"Do you ever think about the distance?"

"*Distance?*" For a moment he floundered, the CEO doing a job on his concentration. "I thought I was here to discuss this absurd claim I stole important documents. I absolutely deny...."

Mr. Campesi summoned his most disconcerting smile. Tossed it to Ross, leaned out across the mahogany.

"From the time you first joined us. You know, me and Samantha. The distance you've come."

His foot lifted from the brakes. An involuntary error. Once again, the poor relative at the back door.

"Sure. I remember. Your wife introduced us. She sold you on the idea. We were a natural fit."

Mr. Campesi turned to the side window, slowly, with a barely suppressed sigh, as if the mention of his wife's name was almost too much to bear. A well-worn gesture. Ross experienced variations on the theme at various times over the years.

Following a few measures of silence, a sigh of resignation, he swiveled about. A fresh grin. Reloaded.

"I remember it that way, too. And, now your future awaits you." Another vivid smile, cufflinks clinking as he leaned further over the hardwood. "A promising one, I might add."

"I have you to thank for that. We've co-authored a half-dozen papers. Seminal, ground breaking ideas with supporting, replicable data. We enjoy a terrific collaboration."

Standing behind him, Signet cleared his throat.

"Yet, I must remind you. Though prospects seem bright, there is no guarantee."

"Of course. Understood. Yet, I detect a note of concern. Let me reassure you. I was with Signet when the theft was said to have occurred."

The CEO shot a quick glance over Ross's shoulder, nodded.

"Good. You've been brought up to date. Let's review the situation. See what's at stake."

Mr. Campesi drummed fingers as he summarized the problem.

There had indeed been an unauthorized entry into the main server. An extremely bold and untimely penetration. The stolen material contained vital details about their PTSD project, specifically about the highly secret technique used to prepare the viral vector. Because this was patented material it was mandatory that it be returned ASAP. There were other projects stolen as well. Items concerning innumerable DARPA projects, licensing agreements, and most importantly, memos to the Secretary of Defense.

"I am confident you appreciate the significance here. We're talking matters of national security, material for which you do not possess the required clearance. You have committed a criminal offense prosecutable by both Justice and Homeland Security. You can go to prison, for God's sake."

Ross squirmed, the drumbeat roll of accusation impaling him like an insect on a board. What really stung, Campesi's smug arrogance, his condescension, the assumption this outlandish accusation was true. Signet, on the money, had warned him facts did not matter. Yet, Ross kept a lid on it. He refused to succumb to such a mean spirited attitude.

"I never stole or copied anything. Signet can vouch for me. I was with him at the time. Arriva is my home. Why would I jeopardize that?"

"Again, you mention our Chief of Security. I believe he has established the important timeline." He motioned to Signet to take over, but he demurred.

"You have the gist of it, sir. Keep rolling."

"Listen closely, Daniel. Your lawyer, should you choose to engage one, will require these details."

"Do I need one now?"

"That remains to be seen. Hear me out first."

To his credit, Signet emitted a guttural cough Ross took to be a sign of support. Meanwhile, the star-chamber prosecutor hammered his case home.

Dr. Braun had quit her private Neuro-Diagnostic Laboratory precisely at eleven forty-six a.m. the previous morning. She proceeded to the lunchroom, where she remained until twelve thirty p.m. She then joined Dr. Ross in the laboratory on the first floor. While Dr. Braun was eating lunch Dr. Ross returned to his lab at approximately eleven fifty-five a.m. after his meeting with Mr. Campesi.

Signet then invited him to his quarters behind the main complex where he remained for twenty minutes, until approximately twelve fifteen when he returned to his lab.

"Does that sound right to you?" he said in conclusion.

Ross had been taking notes, charting the timeline, and saw no discrepancy. Still, something didn't click. He was vague about the precise minutes spent with Signet except when the meeting ended. *Dr. Braun expects you.* What he now realized was at twelve thirty, when he reentered his lab.

How did Signet know when Beth expected him? Had the time away from his lab been intentionally arranged?

"I spent a good thirty minutes with the corporal," he said. "Not twenty. Also, Dr. Braun, came in a few minutes after I did. An insignificant issue. I do not know the password to her computer, only the code to access my separate project. I wouldn't have had time to enter the Arriva server or down load files without that passcode."

"Untrue, Daniel. The reconstructed timeline does not lie."

"Excuse me, sir. Your 'timeline' means nothing if I do not know her password."

Still, he played with the inexorable timeline laid out plain as day. Maybe he was off a few minutes off leaving the Quonset hut. They were talking at cross purposes, the CEO uninterested with what he said.

"Okay," he said. "Let's see where you're going with this."

"Very well. I'll proceed."

It all indicated, the CEO said, that from twelve eighteen or so, when Dr. Ross might have been expected to enter his lab, until twelve thirty when Dr. Braun joined him, there were twelve minutes when he was alone. Plenty of time, with Mr. Newsome's prior assistance, to break into the computer, download files to a flash drive and return to his desk before she joined him.

"Dr. Braun volunteered you kept a flash drive in your desk drawer. It is now missing."

Campesi's porcelain complexion turned grey. Blood drained out of his skin, most likely uneven flow to his brain. Ross removed his Samsung debating to call 911.

"In summary, you possessed opportunity, means, and most conclusive of all, a motive to commit this invasion."

Ross turned to face the corporal, this newly hatched Zen master with a fenestrated brain.

"You know this is wrong. I was with you for a good half hour. During the exact time when the Campesi theft occurred...."

"Don't call it that, doctor. You are the one accused, not I."

"Duly noted...."

"Sarcasm," the Zen master whispered, "wins few hearts."

"Look. Will you please straighten out this timeline business? I was with you for what, twenty five, thirty minutes. Dr. Braun joined me in the lab only a few minutes later. Will you tell him I would never commit this horrible crime?"

"The timeline is well documented," Signet allowed. "In all details, correct. There was an intrusion."

"But there is no conceivable way I could have done it."

"Another detail must be considered," the CEO said. "Last week, in pursuing the Newsome nonsense, Mr. Ravda confided in Signet. He indicated you and Simcoe were contemplating a licensing agreement. Motive, Dr. Ross. *Motive*."

Ross shot to his feet. His chair scooted backwards, bouncing off Signet's boot. Rigid as a statue, the man who just stabbed him in the back stared into the middle distance, rejecting his appeal, avoiding interaction altogether.

"Excuse me, sir, but that is a goddamn lie. I have never spoken with that goofball in my life. I would never betray you, Arturo. You must believe me."

"This brings us to our final item. I have arranged for one of our techs to present your talk tomorrow morning. That is, she will be *prepared* to do so. And, will do so If, for some reason, you are indisposed and unable to proceed yourself."

Ross banged the table. The water pitcher jumped.

"*That* is completely unacceptable," he said. "Glaucon is *my* project. I came up with the idea. I did the research. I made the slides. I prepared all the videos. I wrote the entire talk. I sent out the personal invitations. You *cannot* do this."

"Signet, please fetch Myla."

"No need, sir. I took the liberty of copying the Glaucon project to flash. She can prepare at her convenience."

Ross circled the table, pushed chairs aside, and approached Mr. Campesi, who suddenly had renewed his interest in the side window.

"Listen, Arturo," he said. "A technician with a room temperature IQ is unqualified to deliver a comprehensive, scientific, medical talk. You have to know that. Would you allow Myla to present PTSD data to DARPA officials? Of course you wouldn't. She can't be expected to field questions about glaucoma, let alone ganglion cell rescue, or about the intricacies of tube surgery. I know these physicians. It's fundamental I convince them. She's out of her depth. She's a technician. A water carrier. For pity's sake, Arturo."

"You exaggerate," the CEO countered. "True, she lacks a scientific background. She is, however, capable of reading from a script and delivering a power point presentation. Any idiot can show slides on a computer and recite the captions. Besides, these physician-scientists have read your published articles. They'll know exactly what the technician will be saying. Power Point slides speak for themselves."

"They have to be presented, though. She will not know how to do this."

It was all so wrong, so unfair. So *stupid*.

"Look, Arturo. I recognize this as punishment. That in

itself is bizarre. Your treatment of me might easily, in some less professional an employee, trigger unbelievable legal repercussions. An unpleasant work environment? Harassment. Unfair accusations. Jesus. Come on."

He was crossing a boundary here, addressing Campesi in this fashion. His cold, blue-eyed narcissistic boss. No private pictures of Samantha on the walls. Just the portrait of Arriva's founder. Impersonal, not a family shot. *Nada.* Only a photo of him alone scaling some snow-capped mountain. Or, the one directly behind him, atop the Great Wall, the photo snapped with him standing beside a magnificent stone soldier, his arrogant hand on the Chinese soldier's helmet. And, talk about his anger management issues....

He had to slow down. This review of the man's psychopathology got him nowhere. Ross was in the crosshairs. That was the salient issue here.

Get a grip, man. *Focus.*

"These nationally renowned scientists did not travel to the Arriva campus to hear an ill-equipped technician deliver a critical talk. They will be insulted. *Myla*, Arturo? Think of the consequences. Doesn't she deliver the mail?"

"It can be done. It will be done. Signet, please escort Daniel to his car. When he returns what he has stolen he may resume his position at Arriva. Get with this tech. Explain the plan. Help her prepare."

Signet held the door, opened the front gate at the curb. Like with Dr. Braun, not a word in goodbye or in explanation. Crushed by the massive lie, by Signet's inexplicable betrayal, he made the lonely drive down East Lsake, severed from his dream, devastated.

Lost in a deepening gloom, he had at first not seen the piece of paper taped to his tiger head door knocker. He parked, hauled defeated fanny up the steps then saw the scrawled message:

First the Goodbye, now the Absence. Come find me at the Tarpon Springs Aquarium.

I swim with the fishes.

Zina

The Beethoven sonata again?

Much too early for the treadmill. An appetite for lunch, non-existent. And so, he cranked it into gear, veered out of the development and aimed his ancient Corolla north to Tarpon Springs.

CHAPTER 19

Feeding time in the giant tank.

Attached to an undulating air hose snaking to the surface, a diver distributed chunks of food to hungry fish in the 120,000-gallon tank. Snook, nurse, and bonnet sharks plus schools of tiny tarpon swarmed for their midday meal.

Meanwhile, squealing in delight, hordes of children crowded the tank, craning their necks over the restraining cord for a closer look. With a sudden whoop, they jumped back as a magnificent tiger shark darted into view, brushing the double plated plastic wall, the sole protection from its crushing maw. Any child, or adult, a quick lunch in a single bite for this formidable predator from the deep.

An amusing milieu that, as Ross's scotopic vision readjusted, came into sharper view.

An all-purpose aquarium, other delights abounded for those curious about life in the ocean. Glassed-in cubbyhole enclosures housed crabs of all shapes and sizes, twisty eels, plus colorful fishes on a spectrum from tiny to gigantic. For those so inclined, a sting ray petting pool invited old and young alike. Marvelous treasures of the deep but it was the huge reservoir that drew the most attention.

Nudging him aside, additional kids pressed against the cord. There was a sudden commotion near the diver.

Descending in the water, a fish-tailed creature slowly emerged. A mermaid, a child exclaimed, pointing to the strange, new occupant of the feeding zone. Moving in gentle loops and turns, the new addition fed a hovering shark before turning to the audience. In what seemed a languid departure from script, it angled toward the glass, black, flowing seaweed hair, framing the goggled face.

With a jolt, Ross recognized the mermaid, and she, him. Magnified by goggle and glass, expanded globes ensnared him. She floated closer, her suspended form a fresh mutation of the former girl with purple eyes, the glimmering demolisher of manikins, the tantalizing Byzantine empress, Zina Palaeologus a.k.a. Empress Theodora.

In this, her most provocative costume to date, she secured his attention and, in a manner, before that moment, unimaginable. A few children also took notice of the mesmerizing mermaid, squealing for the strange beastie to feed more sharks.

After a quick wave in greeting, she hooked a finger over her left shoulder, and with a ferocious kick shot to the surface to disappear in a flurry of bubbles.

Pulse surging, Ross shrank away from the amused kids. Freshly energized by the aquatic encounter, he went in search of the mysterious Zina. She indicated left so he turned right and moved further into the aquarium.

He found her beyond a roped-off corridor in a narrow locker room. Emerging from a shower in a snug bikini, unfazed by his awkward presence, she glided deeper into the steamy enclosure, Ross in tow. She found a locker adjacent to a row of benches. Again, natural as you please, she removed the bikini and donned a purple tee and spray-on shorts pausing at crucial junctures, as if inviting him to unglue and lend a helping hand.

"Do you like the mermaid?" she said. "Was she convincing?"

"Yes to both questions." Embarrassed, he tightened his hold on errant thoughts. "Aren't you worried the sharks might bite?"

"The aquarium permits one feeding at midday. They are not so hungry then. What do you know about mermaids?"

"You're my first."

With a beckoning wink, she bent down to fasten her sandals. A revealing perspective, purple stretched delightfully taut. He fought desire. Forced himself to glance off.

"No reason to fear me, Justinian. The shark may bite. I will only nibble. But, I worry this mermaid might have glaucoma. Would you care to examine?"

In a flurry of motion, she laid her towel over the bench and sat, legs akimbo, on top. Sensing his hesitation, she abruptly stood, flung open the locker door, and finished dressing. Again, welcoming an audience, she tore off her tee and snuggled into a lavender bra. He realized the more often he saw this rare beauty, the more of her he saw.

He caught sight of the book in her locker: *Krav Maga: Advanced Lessons.*

"Still practicing?" He mimed a chop and a kick. "Met any manikins lately?"

She shook her head.

"I progress with lessons anyway. I am on page seventy four: 'Disarm The Attacker. Make Him Suffer.' Tell me, Doctor," she said. "Why are you here?"

An hour earlier his future lay punctuated by lies and evasion. It now considerably brightened. Here he was, conversing with a lovely denizen from some dark lagoon, inviting him in.

"You left a note. A polite request to meet you here."

"Still, I am surprised you came. You have a job."

"On leave of absence." He tapped her book. "My lucky day."

"Exactly how it was explained to me."

"What does that mean?" As if he required an explanation. This guy Signet, always looming nearby in the background.

"Up to now, the sad farewell, the Lebewohl section. Now comes Abwesenheit, your absence. Do you not recall the program notes from Monday night? They are in German, thank God, with translation."

The great master, once again. Why, he wondered, did she feel it necessary to keep referring to that particular piano sonata? Her attempt to communicate in a familiar language, perhaps? So unnecessary because she was already a great communicator in accomplished non-musical skills. Her varied visual presentations, for example. Coupled with an active imagination and, he increasingly realized, an array of exceptional, native smarts, Zina conveyed a unique package of delights. Plus a good dose of trouble tossed in. Deciphering its dimension now his immediate challenge.

"Finally, Wiedersehn," she said. "Your return, and the way it looks now, unlikely to occur. It is your absence that concerns us, though. The emotional solitude will be difficult. You must be prepared, my Justinian, to do the right thing."

Her remarks echoed those of Corporal Zen, the betrayer. If by "goodbye," she meant his leaving Arriva, she was correct. If by "absence," his banishment from Glaucon, she was again on the mark. It was the "return," however, that remained problematic. He had no clue how to achieve that. The irony struck him. Das Wiedersehn depended upon him returning what he did not possess.

Doing the right thing. The heck was *that* all about?

"Please call me Theodora."

"And Corporal Signet is simply *Signet*. What is it with you two?"

"So impatient. Exactly like Emperor Justinian. That is, before Empress Theodora took charge. Do you recall the Nika rebellion? Loss of faith became mortal failure. Come," she added, taking his hand, her palm moist and welcoming. "Let us stroll the docks to find answers.

✱✱✱

Like a Yorkie on a leash, or emperor on a cord, she led him up the sidewalk. Swarmed by tourists, he submitted to her will.

Despite embarrassment, traveling incognito with the mermaid-empress seemed acceptable, however. Besides, numerous diversions in the milling crowd kept his gaze otherwise preoccupied. Considering Zina's proximity, this was wisest.

Still, her physical presence allowed him to disregard the scorching sun. Less easy to ignore, reckless cyclists and skateboarders required full attention. On occasion, she bumped against his arm, at first to avoid collisions, but then, for no apparent reason, the bump as prelude to a sudden embrace as she encircled his waist with a demanding arm. She disengaged when he snuggled closer, nudging him aside as he bumped again in search for more.

A tease. Like poison ivy, best to look at, risky to touch.

They wandered, first up Dodecanese Street, the main thoroughfare, to the very end. Reversing direction, they crossed the road, passing Melko's Bajou Bar and Grille, his sparkling Lexus at the curb, then Nicko's Souvenirs and, further on, Theopolous Hair Salon. Boutiques, outdoor cafes and souvenir shops, all tourist traps, abounded. A typical weekday afternoon on the famed sponge dock.

Their tour ended abreast a row of rusted fishing vessels. They ducked under an umbrella, accepted menus from a bespangled youth, and sat.

"Thirsty?" Zina asked, her gaze down the dock. "The lemonade here is good."

They agreed to raspberry flavor then waited for their server to reappear.

Zina took advantage of her captive audience. Due to the distraction of the surging crowd, he absorbed little of the Greek history lesson. A polite nod here, a suitable exclamation there proved sufficient to guide him through the rough spots. Difficulty with popes, barbarian tribes, Goths, and Persian invaders. Nothing escaped Zina's zealous regard, though not very much sank in. More local highpoints were another matter.

Tarpon Springs, he learned, was home to the largest group of American Greeks. Drawn to this spot on the Gulf of Mexico by the flourishing sponge beds, they turned this natural resource into a flourishing industry. Until, that is, the red algae ruined the beds and hence the sponge trade. Undeterred, the spongers veered from deep sea harvesting to tourism, the nearby Gulf and adjacent bayous easily accessible, easy to fish and also easy to exploit.

"We also have a vital theological community," she said. "Nearby is the famous weeping virgin. An icon you must not miss."

"An actual, crying statue?"

She nodded, steering clear of two Japanese posing for a selfie.

"Real tears," she added. "Only for the devout. You must pray to see them."

He let it slide. Misinterpreting his silence, she ventured into more history.

"To better understand the theology, let me tell you about the Ecumenical Council of 451. After that, I'll tell you how Justinian met Theodora. She came from a poor family—"

Requesting a time out, he held up a hand.

"How about a Greek salad or a pita sandwich?" he said. "Later, we'll go for a walk and continue our discussion."

"We already walked. We are not 'discussing.' I am explaining. You are listening. I am also not hungry. Mermaids are fed before the sharks. Where was I?"

He took a breath. The girl did not stop.

"Very well. You win. Something about a council...."

"Thank you. Signet said you are stubborn. On a narrow corridor down life's river." She shrugged. "Did I remember that right? Signet spoke fast when he told me."

She shrugged again, eyes darting down the dock. "Did you know in Theodora's day, great arguments erupted over faith?"

"I don't doubt it. Why are you so obsessed with all this?"

"Blame Uncle Stephano. He worried when I dropped out of high school. For me, it was boring and dangerous. This past summer, after he returned from a trip to Salonica, he insisted I read Greek history. To tap into my roots, he called it. And, to help grandpa. He learned of grandpa's behavior from Aunt Sophia. Perhaps if I showed interest in ancient Byzantium, he might become reinfected. Next came a three-volume set on Byzantine history. Did I not tell you this at the YMCA?"

"Some of it. You were supposed to reinvigorate grandfather's religious calling."

She grimaced. "You see how that turned out. He now bows before skirts not the sacred altar. Let me tell you more about your namesake."

"Can this wait? I really need to unwind. I didn't tell you before. I'm having trouble at work. Let's take a short intermission."

Annoyed, she tapped the table.

"What terrible service. We should go to the Bayou Grill. Mr. Melko will find us a table."

"How do you know him? He's my best friend."

"A retired detective. That is all I know. Wait." Her gaze shot over his shoulder. "That silly girl dropped her doll.

I'll be right back."

She was gone in a flash, covering the expanse of wooden planks in seconds. Instead of halting at the edge, she sprang into the air between a pair of fishing vessels, heading for the water below. Ross didn't hear a splash, though. A moment later, she reappeared, pulling herself to a seated position with the doll wedged between her teeth. After returning it to the awestruck girl, she ambled back to the table.

"So careless, dropping Snoopy over the side. Her momma should pay more attention."

"Why did you jump? You might have hurt yourself."

"I landed on a walkway. He is here," she said, pointing to the distant street. "Time for answers, my Justinian doctor friend."

CHAPTER 20

With a spring to his step, Signet made a quick beeline to their table. Darkly dressed as usual—black shirt, trousers, cross trainers—he scanned the motley throng on the dock searching, no doubt, for concealed enemy, snipers, whatever a retired Seals warrior might encounter in the unfiltered public on a lazy, sunny afternoon.

Mr. Security slapped a newspaper down on the table, the block print headline screaming its message:

ERITREA: ANOTHER BEACHHEAD?

"Do either of you understand the meaning?"

Equally dumbfounded, they shook their heads.

"Is this important?" Zina said. "We came for another discussion."

"The message reflects indecision. It reflects *fear*."

Despite the supposed urgency, Ross barely suppressed a yawn. The unrelenting sun, an unpredictable, semi-clad mermaid, and now Signet coming on strong. The sum total weighed on him. He needed rest not unrelenting pressure. Signet sounded a lot like Franklin. The unwashed, paranoid who also discerned "meaning" difficult for others to detect.

"Bored, Doctor?" the security guy asked, examining him closely. "Not for long, I assure you. I will soon capture a response. From both you and Colonel Bame including his superiors. At the moment, they cannot chew straight. Eritrea is a simple matter. Hostages are in peril. They must be saved. An emergency mission is required."

He brushed them with icy contempt, as if they and not the military decided military affairs.

"Not bored," Ross clarified, "Relaxed, or at least I was until you showed up. I don't see how Eritrea is relevant, not to us anyway. May I suggest another? How about, 'Wanted for Questioning. Chief of Security, Chief of Lies and Deception'?"

"Dr. Danny-boy is right. Take your battle elsewhere. We came as requested. Unexplained is why you chose this location for our meeting."

"You took a big jump back there. A remarkable achievement."

Zina shrugged.

"The whimpering child," she said. "A lost toy. It was automatic."

"Now it is. But, not always." Again Signet thumped the newspaper. "*This* decision should be automatic. Only courage will change that."

Their server sauntered over, and Zina placed the order. Ms. Tattoo then wandered to another customer before disappearing inside the bar. Moments passed, Signet erect as an Easter Island statue.

"You are correct," he finally allowed. "Eritrea can wait. First we must address the timeline."

Ross sat up straight, fully alert.

"That timeline is a complete lie," he said. "I was with you when that smug ass Campesi claimed the theft took place. Speaking of this so-called theft, you arranged for Dr. Braun to show me what was taken. Classified documents, in fact, making me an accessory to the crime. And, why did she go to all that trouble? To prepare me, she said. Only she neglected to say for what. Next thing I know, Campesi blindsides me, and I lose the symposium, maybe my entire project. What I don't get is why you went along with this. You're complicit as heck. You probably helped set it up."

He was out of breath, perspiring like a leaky faucet. Meanwhile, dry as a bone, Signet remained unmoved by the outburst as he followed a fishing trawler sputtering up the river.

The server returned, set down the pitcher of lemonade, quickly assessed the silent discord, and vanished amongst the busy crowd. An ominous silence shrouded the table. Quicksand, Ross concluded, as Zina poured three glasses. Mired to his waist and sinking fast.

He poked Signet's shoulder. "Tell me what's going on. You created this problem. You have to help me out."

"Beth's role was indeed to prepare you. If you don't do the right thing, Glaucon will blow to smoke. Your career may be tarnished beyond repair. With Myla on board for tomorrow, your time is running out. You must return the flash drive."

Zina nudged Ross. "Who is this *Myla* person?"

"A lab tech," Signet said. "She will deliver Doctor Ross's key address to a symposium tomorrow morning. She will screw it up. He must not accept that."

Signet now brought Zina into the picture. Mr. Campesi, the CEO of Arriva, accused the doctor of downloading secret, government projects from the company computer. If he wants to maintain control of his project it is his duty to return what he took.

"That's ridiculous. I didn't take anything."

Signet raised a finger.

"Wait," he said, suddenly surveilling the noisy boulevard.

After a thorough vetting of boutiques and clip joints, he returned to the conversation, lowering his voice, drawing them in.

"Let us discuss why you are here."

"I am confused," Zina interrupted. "Dr. Daniel claims he is innocent. Are you involved with this false accusation?"

Signet gave her a piercing glance.

"Not now, Ms. Palaeologus. We must move on while there is time."

"Why the formality, *Corporal* Signet? My name is Zina. Or, better yet, Theodora. Call me that. Why do you whisper? We are nobodies in a shifting crowd."

The corporal covered her hand with a gnarled paw. A moment passed. He moved on.

"We will begin with a simple question. Six months ago, would you have jumped off a pier?"

She shook her head. "I am different now."

"Tell me."

"Back then, I was a high school dropout. Thanks to Uncle Stephano, I read Byzantine history. I will now finish high school, college after that. If Empress Theodora rose from a humble start, so can I."

Signet nodded, his apparent pleasure a departure from his habitual reserve.

"I am certain of it. Do you ever wonder about Grandpa Palaeologus? The newspaper claims he, as priest, will lead the Epiphany Parade. Yet, I am told Father Palaeologus does not exist."

"The 'priest' in Grandpa is on sabbatical. The church fathers fool themselves. He will never toss a holy cross into the bayou. He is much too fond of female supplicants. My uncle and aunt voice constant disapproval. What is wrong with him?"

To Ross, that was harsh. Grandfather Palaeologus was still a man, and he'd always be a priest. Zina's aunt and uncle should be more accepting. At least Grandpa confined his activities to *female* supplicants.

"Your grandfather feels rejuvenated," he said. "He abandoned what, for him, was an outmoded faith. There's no harm in moving on with life."

"I agree," Signet said. "No harm at all. From his perspective, a welcome alteration. I will show you what happened."

Signet withdrew a slender box from a hip pocket and with solemn fanfare laid it on the table. He paused before opening the box. Then, in the same curious manner, unveiled the contents: a small piece of a grey material, no larger than a postage stamp and just as thin.

Ross identified it at once.

"The pyrite, nano-crystal!" he said. "It's the photo layer that drives my Glaucon motor. What are you doing with it?"

"Keep your voice down. Probing ears might listen."

A ludicrous notion. They were a tiny atoll in a giant ocean. Nevertheless, Signet swiveled about to examine, in rapid but exquisite detail, every conceivable person in the vicinity of their inconspicuous table. When all appeared to be in order, he continued on.

"Doctor Ross is correct. This is the device that drives Glaucon. Yet, it is more than that. This film contains the equivalent of the nasal vaccine Beth described."

"Incorrect," Ross said. "The nano-crystal is designed to absorb light, to transform photons into energy. There is nothing 'bio' about it."

"Vaccine?" Zina asked, suspiciously. "This is news to me."

It required another glance around the dock before Signet summarized Ross's visit with Dr. Braun the previous evening. He outlined DARPA'S plan to develop a perfect soldier, one immune to the mayhem of war with enhanced cognitive capacity. They accomplished this feat employing a unique, intranasal substance. He himself received a double dose, one whiff of vaccine to each nostril. This highly classified program was named Genesis II, its predecessor, the PTSD program, Genesis I. All of it copied to a flash drive in Ross's possession.

"That is complete nonsense. I have no such flash drive."

"You vaccinated your *nose*? Why do that?"

"Curious. I have no regrets."

"I want to return to this so-called flash drive I don't have."

Signet placed a finger to his lips. "Listen to me. Your ingenious nano-film has been reengineered. If you look closely, you will notice the slight shimmer to its under surface. That is the biofilm. It conveys an incredible ability to enhance performance."

"Like your 'performance' that night in Nuristan? Tell Zina about the patrol. Go on. Tell her about the ears."

"Not enough time or I would gladly share the story."

"Tell her anyway."

"You are so much like Emperor Justinian," Zina breathed, "The parallels are incredible."

Signet's eyebrow furrowed.

"Why do you call him that?"

"Her uncle assigned three volumes of Byzantine history for reading," Ross said. "Now she's a minor expert. She's been regaling me with her new, obscure knowledge. You get used to it."

"There is nothing *obscure* about Emperor Justinian and Empress Theodora. Consider our parallels."

Ross laughed. "Now, it's 'our'."

"Hmm," Signet muttered. "Theodora. I understand. I think."

"The empress lived for action and quick decision, exactly as I do now. Like Justinian, you, Dr. Danny-boy, live inside your head. Recall it was she who defied the men of the court. She alone arranged the bloody fate of those foolish enough to join the Nika Rebellion."

A vast silence gripped the table. Ross refused to intervene. Byzantium. The Nika rebellion. His imagined resemblance to a long forgotten emperor. Zina, the strong-willed empress. He had to keep on point, to focus, if he ever hoped to wade through this dense thicket of confusion.

"The crowds destroyed churches and icons." Zina continued. "They nearly tore down the palace. The imperial court was lucky to have such a wise woman to save them."

Signet gave her a look. "You are indeed brave," he

observed. "You jump today. Before, you might have watched from the sideline."

"Empress Theodora was even more impressive. She singlehandedly kept the eastern empire securely linked to the western. Same for her solution of The Nika rebellion. Tell me more about this new vaccine. Why inhale it?"

Reconstituted, the royal court turned to Signet for details.

"To explain, I, too, must return to history," he said. "To Iraq to be exact, years ago, when I was ordered to join patrols. We were young, all of us eager but terrified, I the worst of the bunch. Trembling in my boots, paralyzed with fear, I always remained the very last in the column. One night, Colonel Bame took me and other feeble cowards aside. He told us the latest scientific research about a place inside our brains called the amygdala. This, he said, was a paired structure that caused fear to happen. For us soldiers, it was far too active. It sent out far too many fear signals, signals compelling us to retreat. To not think straight. It was now possible to silence the amygdala and become strong. Stronger than ever, the colonel promised. Brave. Not careless. All we had to do was inhale a liquid vaccine. I volunteered first. I never looked back."

Zina scoffed. "You became a human guinea pig? Is that legal?"

"I signed a consent. We all did. After the horror of Fallujah, the massacre of soldiers in Nuristan, it was for us a no-brainer."

Signet's eyes softened. Dark caves beamed pools of black.

Then, in an instant, the hardness resurfaced, the control of emotion always close at hand.

"At the time, even now, I believed it best to live without fear."

"He neglects to mention that prehistoric man would have never survived without his amygdala. Because of its fear signals, society and religion evolved. I am amazed someone decided to destroy the amygdala with a vaccine."

"Destruction is only partial," Signet said. "Though small, the nucleus has over a dozen separate compartments. The vaccine, Doctor Braun assures me, only hits a central basal portion. That is a topic for another day. We now reach the critical part of our meeting."

"Are you planning to tell us about the ears?"

Signet sighed, what to Ross, seemed a practiced hyperventilation.

"I sense we will not proceed unless I tell you. You must remember, dear Theodora, this was wartime. Atrocities rampant. In this case, it involved the external ears of Pakistani insurgents. The incident occurred in the dead of night in Nuristan province. Suddenly, our patrol was surrounded. Excellent warriors by that time, thanks to the vaccine, we quickly dispatched the insurgents. Colonel Bame's favorite soldier then harvested ears and returned them as trophies. It was quite an event."

"Signet kept the man's knife. It is coated with dried blood."

"Waste no pity on insurgents. They were savages who

crept over mountains to slaughter American soldiers. We rebalanced the equation."

Signet wore a fleeting gleam of triumph.

"None of us remained lethal soldiers, however. Neuroplasticity set in. As a result of nasal vaccination, new nerve fiber circuits developed. This is a well-known phenomenon after brain injury. In our case, the rerouted circuits altered our behavior. This rewiring was not what the colonel or Dr. Braun expected or desired. We became calm, self-aware and capable of unflinching focus."

Signet shifted his gaze once more to the dock and its meandering herd of sun-soaked customers, all oblivious to the staggering revelations shared in their midst. Mr. Neuroplasticity broke into a thin smile, yet another slash of emotion, quick to appear, gone in a nano-nanosecond. A fleeting wrinkle in his unrelenting composure.

"You remind me of Belisarius," Zina said. "He was Justinian's and Theodora's most skilled and trusted general. He also balanced equations, first annihilating invading Persians at Dara, what is now the Iranian plain, and then at the Hippodrome to end the Nika Rebellion. Shall I tell you the story?"

Signet shook his head.

"Sorry, my dear. This story will have to do. You see, Grandpa, you, and I have all been vaccinated. In your case, I had no advance warning. Time to tell you how that happened."

CHAPTER 21

Their host of ceremonies next removed from his other hip pocket a flattened plastic water bottle. He set it beside the nano-crystal box.

"Do either of you recognize this?"

"A squashed Zonder Springs water bottle," Ross said, pointing to the green label.

"Theodora, did someone ever hand you and Grandpa a bottle of this water?"

She shook her head.

"Not that I remember."

"Think back to Grandpa's postoperative visit at Dr. Ross's Arriva lab."

Zina squinted in recollection.

"Hmm. We did meet there once. Mr. Campesi arranged the visit. He wanted to witness the great success for himself. Doctor Braun came in for the same reason. I remember now. She brought water for both of us. It was a hot afternoon. Grandpa emptied his bottle in one gulp."

"That is how it happened."

"How did you learn about the visit?" Ross said. "You arrived many months later."

"Dr. Braun informed me. Let's move on."

He now returned them to that very day. Two months had elapsed since the operation. Grandpa had recovered a patch of peripheral vision. Mr. Campesi was pleased. Yet, he invited Father Palaeologus and Zina in for another reason.

"He secretly inoculated you two with the GENESIS II vaccine. The very same one used for me and my unit."

The CEO was well aware of the results of that earlier inoculation. Neuroplasticity turned one soldier into a successful businessman. Another into a politician. And, in Signet's case, an intelligent agent. Still, the CEO remained curious.

"He wondered about someone of strong religious faith. What sort of neuro-plastic change would such a person undergo after an inoculation?"

Signet sighed again. The same exaggerated intake of air. The head shake. All artifice. The proof? A sly, rapid wink aimed at Ross that Zina missed.

"Therein lies the problem," he said. "Colonel Bame, the man in charge of GENESIS II, did not learn of this departure from protocol until much later. An anonymous letter alerted him to this problem. It is what brought him here from Iraq. Your CEO has gone off the reservation. We must bring him back."

"Not 'we'," Ross said. "You. This is a military matter. Let them take care of it."

Signet glanced off, distracted by a squad of screeching seagulls. They fluttered away. Mr. Security did not reply.

"Let me speak with this CEO," Zina said. "I will tell him about grandfather. He has become a seventy-five-year-old neuro-plastic playboy."

"While you have become a neuro-plastic Theodora." Signet gave her a decisive nod. "A no-nonsense woman capable of leaping off a dock. Think how much your attitude has improved."

Another silence engulfed them. They seemed to have reached a conclusion of sorts, but they really hadn't. Signet was omitting a crucial detail.

Ross fingered the flattened bottle.

"What aren't you telling us?"

Zina also focused on the plastic bottle.

"What exactly is *this*? How does a flat bottle relate to me or Grandpa?"

"Excellent. The central issue at last. Return again to that day in the lab. While Mr. Campesi stayed in the examining alcove, Dr. Braun provided you and Father Palaeologus with bottles of chilled water. Please inspect the inside label. I brought this one to illustrate the method."

A brilliant scientist and schemer, Mr. Campesi figured out how to inoculate the unwary. He first severed a similar bottle half way down. Then, he annealed a piece of nano-crystal to the inner side of the label. Next, he bonded the GENESIS II vaccine to the reverse side of the crystal. This was the side that faced the water. Finally, he glued the severed halves of the bottle back together.

"And, a unique delivery mechanism is born. He called the invention and its intended application Genesis III. A bold but immoral way to inoculate various members of the public. You and grandpa, for starters. We are sure there will be others."

"I don't get it. You need a strobe light to activate Glaucon."

"GENESIS III is different. Any light source will do. Daylight, for example. Indirect illumination inside a restaurant or at a party. The vaccine particles enter solution where carbonated bubbles carry them to the top, there to be inhaled by exposed nostrils as a person drinks. A remarkable achievement but off protocol and forbidden. His secret program must be stopped."

"But this is Colonel Bame's responsibility. Who the devil sent him some 'anonymous' letter? It doesn't matter. He's here now. Have him arrest Mr. Campesi. End of problem."

"The colonel is worried about the bad publicity that will result. This cannot be allowed to happen."

"Then hand him over to Homeland Security. The Department of Justice will have a field day with him."

"Indeed. A neat solution. Still, it would be impossible to prevent a leak. News of his transgression or of DARPA's clandestine projects must never see the light of day. It is for this reason you must return what you have taken."

"Not *this* again." Ross jolted upright, stung by the incredible suggestion he had actually broken into secure servers and stolen secret documents. "I already went over this. I simply could not have downloaded or stolen any of these projects. My god. You have to be kidding."

He heard the desperation in his voice. He grabbed his lemonade, the cup unsteady in his hands.

"This is crazy. You have to find who hacked Dr. Braun's computer. I did not do it."

Zina slapped the table, startling them both. Their server appeared at her elbow. Incensed, brow a coruscated sheet of anger, Zina waved her off.

"You *poisoned* me and Grandpa with a sliced bottle?"

"I prefer 'inoculate,' and I had no part in it."

"But why did you not tell me before?" She seized the crumpled plastic, examined the inside label, then tossed it into Signet's lap. "What other secrets are you holding back?"

"None. I promise. Your reaction explains why we must stop this immoral behavior. If exposed, it might ignite a firestorm of objection. Worse, imagine if unpredictable Mr. Ravda gained possession of these projects. His company might construct their own PTSD vaccine. And, what if he ever uncovered details of GENESIS IV or other top secret projects? Catastrophe. Bet on it." Signet impaled Ross with his cold gaze. "This entire problem is now yours, Dr. Ross. Your ingenious Glaucon project remains at stake the longer you hold out. Locate that missing flash drive. I insist you bring it to the party tonight. Mr. Campesi expects nothing less."

"*Party*?'" The speed, the complexity of events, baffled Ross. Every minute a new reality rained down on him. "No one mentioned that before. Why should I go? I haven't stolen anything from Arriva."

"Look harder. You will find it. You have always done the right thing before. Make no exception now."

"Stop!" he burst out. "Tell me what the hell is going on."

With dainty fingers, Signet returned the bottle to the table, dark eyes darting up and down the dock as if expecting a threat to Seal Team Six.

"We are in crisis mode," he said, tone solemn. "The mob will soon descend. Before that happens, I make this confession. I hacked into your former life."

"You did *what*?"

"He contacted your former Boston professors."

"Why would you do that?" More reality. More downfall. "Doesn't Arriva have my resume on file?"

"Your academic background, yes," Signet said, dryly. "I required more personal info."

"What the hell for?"

Signet sat back a fraction, distancing himself, ever so slightly, from his disclosures.

"Listen to him, my Justinian. He brings wisdom and guidance."

"Stop calling me that."

"Enough, you two. Time runs short. I chose you for a reason."

"*Chose*?" Ross held his head, irritation settling in. "None of this makes any sense."

"But, it does. Think of what I learned. After establishing credentials in the Boston area, you traveled south to the Cape, deciding no matter what the storm, patients came first. No excessive testing or photographs. What your eye shade administrators call up-coding, padding the insurance bill. Then, in an abrupt reversal, you quit the Cape. Although envious of a Lexus sedan, of Mrs. Campesi's magnificent house and Steinway you, in six short years, reversed course again. This time you turned inward to create a human-centered device, but one you cannot lose at any cost. In this reverse-course process, you blossomed into the individual I require for my own project."

"You lost me," Ross said, but not really.

Blossomed.

A heart-stopper. Like a key to the inner vault. Because, for all his annoying attributes, the guy was on the mark, although what he meant by *my own project* remained obscure. But, his burrowing into Ross's past ended with a poignant memory emblematic of his current state.

A concluding image, in fact, of his former benefactor during a lazy afternoon when, following introductory etudes, she collapsed upon the cushions. Offering encouragement, she guided him to Opus 57, their favorite. Beethoven competed with sighs and groans from the couch behind him. Yet, he played it through, too aware of Samantha's translucent skeleton languishing nearby, nearly blind, in pain and at death's door, while he bravely obeyed her wishes. Then, as the nurse led her off, a murmur of approval, a thank you and her departing coda the whispered reminder:

Stay on track. Resist fame's allure and all its trappings.

She had understood the dream. The overwhelming fantasy of driving a sleek Mercedes to the awards ceremony, of accepting honorariums and grant monies, perhaps even an invitation to Dr. Oz and a grand demonstration of glaucoma, loss of vision, the miracle of the Glaucon cure.

The allure did not end there, however. It rested secure only with the penultimate achievement, his portrait on the wall, standing or seated, take your pick, but a framed oil canvas, some modest inscription. Yes, this dream eclipsed the others, the painting his own small footprint on the journey into the annals of eye medicine history.

Was this the blossomed man Signet spoke of? Would he ever follow Samantha's injunctions?

At this moment, sitting on a sun-soaked dock, an enchanting seductress at one elbow, a self-contained trickster at the other, with evidence of malfeasance on the rickety table before him, he wondered about any actual achievement. He stood an accused criminal, adrift with no direction home. Not some portrait on the wall either, but a thumbtacked likeness down at City Hall. Forget the oil-on-canvas. A mugshot would do.

Vanity of vanities. Simply awful.

"Are you back yet?"

Signet, probing eye on fast alert, examined Ross, the boulevard and sidewalk, his paranoia on fast forward once again.

"Your vulnerability concerns me," he said to Ross, a suspicious eye on the Snoopy doll now in the bayou current. "You identify with Glaucon. You need your portrait on that library wall. This is your new and controlling belief system."

"I get it. Shades of Father Palaeologus. You plan to inoculate me into a different person."

"First, concentrate on Mr. Campesi. He will use your weakness as leverage with Glaucon. That is why you must find and return those stolen files."

"I already told you...."

"They are in your possession. Find them."

Zina jumped to her feet as a squeal of breaks shattered the serenity of the dock.

"They are here. Exactly as predicted."

They rose to confront the familiar black SUV swerving to a halt at the curb twenty feet behind them. People jumped out of way. Howls of outrage and anger filled the air. Abandoning Ross, Signet and Zina fanned out to greet Zalin and his two men now spilling on to the sidewalk. No FBI-emblazoned jackets this time, just plain shirts and chinos.

"Do you recall *Krav Maga,* page seventy four?" Signet approached the threesome, as if welcoming the enfolding confrontation. "Lead with a feint. Engage with a kick."

"To the letter," Zina replied, facing one of the agents. "This morning, four former high school punks took a bath in the bayou. I used the maneuvers on them."

The ear slicer and this delicate girl settled into a low crouch, preparing for battle. Taking on the FBI before a sweltering crowd, quiet as a funeral. The Sponge Docks. Snoopy drifting out to sea.

Madness.

"The four punks who teased about your mermaid?"

"Who also overturned crippled kids in wheelchairs. Stamos, their leader, retrieved the cross from the bayou this year. Where Father Palaeologus, replaced by church elders at the last moment, planned to toss it, a man of God no longer, thanks to you."

Zalin pointed at Ross standing stiff as a post several yards from the front line.

"You, buster, are coming with us."

"What the hell for?"

"You're guilty of espionage. Get him, Sergio. Take him into custody."

An absurd order that the unfortunate agent soon discovered. With sudden speed, Signet stepped forward, seized the man's arm, and wrenched it backward with an audible snap. Recoiling in pain, the damaged agent dropped to a knee. When Zalin reissued the order, Sergio nodded. Cradling his arm, he gamely regrouped, a decision greeted by low applause from the tourists now forming a semicircle around the action.

Zina now shifted into gear. Sliding to her left, she felled the second agent with a stunning blow that sent the unsuspecting man to the deck. She felt for a pulse and moved on. Shifting weight, she next delivered a round house surprise to the already damaged and shell-shocked Sergio. Like a sack of rocks, he dropped again to the boards with a distinct thud. Impressed, Ross almost applauded. This dainty but deadly tornado of a ballerina had just immobilized two hefty men.

Exercising better judgment, Zalin backpedaled to the safety of the SUV. After his rattled agents stumbled to their seats, he revved the engine and zoomed off. A mighty boom of approval erupted from the audience and, with a sweeping bow, Zina acknowledged the acclaim.

A moment later the crowd dispersed and the three, make that two, stalwarts returned to their table.

"Masterful," Signet said. "Turn to Chapter Eight. You are ready."

"I am already on Chapter Ten: 'The Attack of Five'. All I need are victims."

"Perhaps at the party tonight. Zalin's team will revive. He will bring reinforcements."

Ross banged the flimsy table, catching the lemonade pitcher before it fell.

"You guys are too much," he said. "The FBI wants to arrest me, and all you can think about is the 'attack of five' Unreal. No, it's surreal. What's this party all about?"

Signet dusted off his hands, the cool commander down from the mountains after a dangerous mission severing auricular appendages.

"A celebration in your honor," he said. "Don't act surprised. This is your vital moment. Important colleagues suggested such a gathering to your CEO. He agreed."

"Are you saying Mr. Campesi invited my glaucoma colleagues to a *party*?"

"Does brain derived growth factor revive dying neurons? OF course he invited important colleagues. Think of it as an inauguration. Your new life awaits you."

"Colleagues from Boston, Miami, and New York? You invited *them*?"

"At the CEO's house, tonight in Odessa. Look for them there."

Preparing to leave, the security man straightened his wrinkle-free pullover. A mysterious gesture, as Zina had done most of the fighting. She tidied her tee shirt, the sight riveting. His earlier conclusion stood firm. From slithering mermaid to FBI fandango, this new reality too easily edged aside his own.

"And, bring the flash drive," Signet said. "It will satisfy Campesi and neutralize Zalin. You may well avoid prosecution."

There it was again, the reminder of his possible fate.

"But, how did he know where to find me? I came here on impulse. Zina invited me."

"Zalin received an anonymous tip. If he came here at five, he would find Dr. Ross. Now go. Prepare. The party starts at seven. Don't be late."

Signet sprinted across the sidewalk to the distant parking lot. Zina took off in the opposite direction. After a brief hesitation, Ross followed her.

Anonymous tip?

Was this anything like Colonel Bame's *anonymous letter?*

A bizarre but plausible idea crossed his mind. The entire afternoon had been scripted. From Zina's note tacked to his front door, to the mermaid's naked body on the locker room bench, to Signet's then Zalin's well-timed arrival. All of it orchestrated, including this party tonight, to which he seemingly in afterthought had been invited.

He'd been manipulated all right. His role as central

character in an unfolding drama. A hidden script to pursue, plot hazy, his lines unclear. And, then Zina, his chief supporting actor, like Signet, a person bearing secrets.

He caught up with her rounding a corner.

"Wait. Stop," he said. "Tell me about this party."

"Do not worry about Campesi," she said. "Soon he will have more than stolen files to deal with."

"What is Signet up to? He knows I'm innocent. How can I find what I did not steal?"

"Do not trust him," she said. "He is devious. No matter what he tells you, think the opposite. You were supposed to be an easy target. 'Find the doctor,' he said. Disrobe. Do whatever he wants. Gain his confidence. And, please. Only a few lectures on Byzantium. Well, Justinian. I have done as he asked. Except he forgot to tell me about the Zonder Springs water poisoning...."

"He said to consider it...."

"I know. An inoculation. Well, a rose by any name is still a prick in the finger." She paused, stretching her back, drawing him in. "I tell you, my emperor. We will not accept this."

"Accept what?" he said, eyes in caress mode.

"This is like the Nika Rebellion. Remember how that turned out?"

"People were slaughtered. It was horrible."

"Exactly. Now go. As the man said, prepare."

Before he could utter another word she vanished in the crowd.

CHAPTER 22

Prepare he did, weaving past swirling thoughts vying for attention.

First, the enigma of Odessa, a forty-minute drive east to the middle of farmland. An easy shot. He'd make it on time. He knew the locale by heart. Cypress swamps, a pine forest, the adjacent wilderness of a preserve. *Samantha's* preserve, where he was now invited. His pulse lurched. Was such a visit proper?

Second, the party itself. A planned tribute to both him and his invention? An incredible achievement to be so honored. Unexpected good fortune, difficult to believe. Had his time actually arrived?

Third, the ill-advised nature of the event itself. Imperfect timing, particularly when a mere lab technician would deliver the grand presentation the following morning. There was no chance he'd ever meet Campesi's deadline. Missing files? As far as he knew, in the wind.

Fourth, and more disquieting, the FBI. If they showed up, distinguished professors of ophthalmology would learn of the accusation. Who cared if it were off the wall? A charge of corporate, if not national, espionage was a career ender.

What *then*?

Abandon ship, as Beth suggested?

For the moment, he sailed past this raft of worries. He had to dress. Dripping wet before the bedroom mirror, he debated: Florida formal or black tie. As the man of honor, in the Boston tradition, he should underdress for the occasion. Or, maybe that only pertained to the host. Ralph Lauren, he finally decided, taking a middle ground with fashion.

Signet was on point about his preference for name brands. As if it mattered. For all he knew, his grey slacks and cream-white Oxford broad cloth were Chinese knock-offs. After a final glance in the mirror, he was ready. Pursuant to Beth's instruction, he stuffed the Glaucon flash drive deep into his pocket where even the stealthy Signet wouldn't find it.

Finally retrieving his chirping cell from the front hall table, he noticed two missed calls, one from Melko, the other from Dr. Azzizi, both placed during his Sponge Dock afternoon. He took them in order and dialed his friend at the Grille. Breathless, shouting orders, Melko was just rushing out the door.

"Why didn't you mention the Odessa shindig before?"

"What are you talking about?"

"I'm catering your boss's party. Your security honcho, Mr. Signet called this morning. Fifty people, he said. At least."

"He called you *this morning*?"

"Strange, huh? I remember what you said Monday night. Just wanted to give you a heads up. Hold on a sec. Have to get this last tray loaded."

He broke away. Loud voices. A slammed door. He was back.

"He said make it Greek. Look. We'll talk later. I have to drive the van myself. Someone tossed my usual driver and his pals into the bayou."

Greek? A party in Samantha's honor, not his. It was her favorite cuisine. He suddenly remembered. She'd died six years ago this week. Whatever was he thinking?

"Wait. I almost forgot the best part. This security fellow said I'd need extra help to serve the guests. He specified that if one Zina Palaeologus showed up looking for work I was to hire her. The strange part, the girl herself sauntered in an hour after his call. She was desperate for temporary work, she claimed, so I hired her on the spot. The only hitch, as I discreetly pointed out, she'd have to exchange her tee for a real dress. Not to worry, she said. Friend Signet had already bought her a dress for just the occasion. That's what I found curious. A dress, in advance. Something odd going on here, partner. I'd keep my distance. Got a bad premonition about these two. Well, have to run."

They disconnected, Ross in a fresh daze.

He'd been right all along. Scripted, the entire day. Even the idea to offend important physicians with back-closet Myla. Also, my God, he couldn't forget the allegedly stolen Arriva, read DARPA, documents.

And, now this party. So much arranged beforehand. Astonishing. Most disarming of all, both karate choppers were in on it, whatever *it* turned out to be. So, why warn him Signet was devious?

Next, he called Gamel. After an interminable delay, the retina surgeon came on the line.

"Ah, Daniel. Good of you to call." The gravelly voice sounded unnaturally aggrieved. "I despaired you might not receive my message."

Ross apologized for not getting back earlier. They exchanged chit chat about patients they treated in common. The conversation then turned south.

"The reason I called was to tell you what he said. Such a nasty request. I swear, I nearly pushed the off button."

Gamel paused to catch his breath and a giant door swooshed open in the background. Ross visualized a view he'd witnessed before: a vast panorama of Tampa Bay, the sound of distant bells, the aroma of bayside air. An inviting paradise fitting for a person of the man's style and temperament.

"In better temper, I recalled he was your nominal employer."

"You're referring to Mr. Campesi?"

"Alas, yes. That is the man."

"What did he want?"

Gamel sighed.

"This is difficult but I must tell you. He said, on the possibility of your being indisposed—a very vague term if you ask me—he asked if I might do your Glaucon operation on scheduled patients next week. Perhaps into the future if it came to that." Gamel paused. "I tell you, I did not like the sound of 'indisposed'."

A deep flutter sent Ross's system reeling.

Indisposed. If it came to that.

Mr. Campesi was indeed out to destroy him.

"Daniel, friend. You are there?"

"How did you respond?"

"Can there ever be a doubt? I said, no. Absolutely not. It is Doctor Ross's operation. In no way whatsoever would I comply with such a wish. Well, I was upset as you may imagine. That I freely admit. This man is obscene. Oh, something else. It nearly slipped my mind. A man named Signet rang me up this afternoon."

More flutter. He'd change shirts if this kept up.

"What did *he* want?"

"Ahah. From the sound of your reaction I was correct about him. He was the spooky fellow who searched my office the other day. I never told you about that. He attempted to be sincere. It was obvious he was faking. Yet, today I believed him. He said I should prepare for your arrival."

"My *what*?"

"You and others will visit later tonight. Leave the lights on, he said. He will come. Well, I reassured him, I shall look forward to that."

"He actually said tonight?"

"Anytime, my friend. I have a new statue of Pharaoh Amenhotep. It is quite sensational. You will see."

Ross didn't have the heart to bring Gamel up to date. Besides, he had other things on his mind. That afternoon, he relayed with a light heart, upon depositing wife and daughters on a jet to Miami—"I tell you, Daniel, the quiet is marvelous here when they travel"—his pal planned to ride his bicycle along the beach, shower, translate Amenhotep's hieroglyphs and get ready.

"Come when you must," he said before disconnecting. "My pharaoh and I await your arrival."

After the call, Ross stepped out on the front porch and breathed deeply. A lovely evening. Cool breeze. Dusky sunshine. A lot of information to digest.

Then, a dark cloud descending, his neighborhood nemesis rushed up.

"Sorry, Franklin. Can't talk now. Maybe tomorrow."

He did a double take. Make that a triple. Franklin had

found a new wardrobe. Quite a step up from the pigpen look in the New York subway system or, for that, transplanted to Jasmine Lane. He wore a tailored jacket, an immaculate button down, open at the neck, pressed trousers and leather sandals on sockless feet. He'd also shaved and splashed cologne, perhaps a first for this dweller of the dark and dirty. A makeover of miracle proportion. The guy looked surprisingly normal. A pleasant shock.

Ross whistled.

"Wow," he said. "You must have a date."

"Nope. Going to a party. A big one, out in Odessa. The invite came in today's mail. Actually, it was tacked to my front door. From your boss at Arriva."

"Mr. Campesi invited *you* to the party?"

Franklin handed over the invitation.

"Take a look. It's embossed. Real fancy. Like a debutant invite to Park Avenue."

A pink card with filigree pine cones and a bold message printed green:

CELEBRATE WITH US. RIVER ROW. ODESSA.

The genuine article. Mr. Campesi's initials indented the lower corner. Fresh ink, not a printed facsimile. Where was Ross's invitation, though? One hadn't been tacked to his front door although maybe it had and Zina filched it when she tacked on the mermaid note.

"I figured it out." The wattage of Franklin's smile dimmed a fraction. "Has to be my dad. Who else could reach this far? His hedge fund had clients connected to DARPA. He lost his alpha when the hedge fund tanked. He didn't lose his contacts. Hey, who cares? I'm going to a real party."

Ross slid into his Corolla and buzzed down the window.

"Need a ride?" he asked. "We're going to the same place."

Makeover man declined. He rented a BMW for the occasion. No Uber for him. Maybe his luck was changing. Other than Melko and Ross, all he had were three cats when his girlfriend split for Vermont. Who knows? Tonight, he might get lucky. His Eritrea Big Lie paper had to wait. Damn place was turning out like Benghazi. Now Eritrea's turn to be on the front burner. Rumor had it the Joint Chiefs might forget the hostages. Talk about a mess.

"Can you believe it? The big brass plans to leave them in that godforsaken hole. Too afraid to snatch them out. Ta-ta, doc. See you on the flip side!"

CHAPTER 23

Like a 737 at Tampa Airport, Signet guided him from River Row to the majestic driveway with a pair of red flashlights.

His ragged Corolla wobbled over the cobblestones, beggar at the rear door, his rust heap misplaced amongst the much grander vehicles lining the driveway. Sensing trouble, the red lights found an inconspicuous spot behind a Bentley. Not wishing to linger, he got out, joined the wing walker and together traversed the driveway, gaze forward, neither commenting on the show of money, the display of power.

They passed sedans, svelte and inviting and, further on, a fleet of sleek convertibles, the mark of exclusivity and attainment. In spite of himself, Ross let out a low whistle, regretting at once the revealed envy, hearing as rebuke the reverberating echo within the pines. True to form, Arriva's security chief took notice. Chuckling, shaking his polished head, much as a friend might react except this man was no friend. What he was remained to be discovered. Ross also accepted his response as rebuke. Almost an accusation.

"What you're thinking is wrong," he said. "I may admire but no longer crave automotive distinction."

"So you say. Still, one can be impressed. The government, via our beloved DARPA, pays well."

In a grand gesture, he swept his arm to include every leaf and frond fronting the mansion behind them.

"Make your peace, Doctor. Accept these longleaf pines, the designer pool in back, the shuttered eaves and elegance of the interior. Regard Mrs. Campesi's success but a magnet to trap you. A magnet to resist, however. Permit a minor congratulation. I read her entries. You acted with restraint. Again, the right thing."

"And you, the grand arbiter, know exactly what that is."

"With the late wife? She begged. You stayed the course. As you will now when you realize what's at stake."

Ross laughed.

"I always listen closely but afterward I have no idea what you said. Aren't you at Arriva to disambiguate, Mr. Zen?"

"A long process, I assure you." He indicated the front door. "The porte cochere. We are here. Let us see who drives up."

Over half a dozen limousines and SUVs had already come and gone, delivering guests but no familiar faces to the mahogany door. Ross pulled red lights aside to ask him.

"Where are they?" he said. "I thought this was a celebratory occasion. I don't see any of my colleagues."

"I said, you may look for, not that you would find, these comrades." He tilted his chin to starboard. A few degrees. Less than a nano-arc. Almost imperceptible. "I confess to a misleading statement. Is it important? You are here now and soon you will be famous."

"But only if I do the right thing."

"Now you're catching on."

"More deception. I should have known."

"Again, does it matter? Look at this house. Perhaps you deserve a similar Tuscan mansion. To attain such a goal, certain minor obstacles must be hurtled. Such as those arriving now."

He nodded toward a limo just then slithering to a stop to disgorge two occupants. From the front passenger seat, a hunched man in a dark suit and wingtips; from the rear compartment, a portly woman in pearls and pantsuit.

"Do you recognize either?"

Ross nodded. Paul Scofield, a senior administrator at the FDA, took a personal interest in Glaucon, helping Ross navigate regulations and various legal issues involving new medical devices. As for Margaret Twitcher, Commissioner of the FDA, she was the one who limited his Premarket Application to BDNF, a crucial decision he had no choice but to accept. Should he ever regain control of his project, that is.

"Bureaucrats and administrators? They aren't minor to me."

"Later, extend respects inside. Time to join the party." Holding the door, he then escorted Ross inside the swarming foyer awash in a tsunami of noise. "Thanks to Mr. Melko," he said, shouting above the din. "The food is superb. He prepared well. Let us hope you did the same."

Mr. Zen moved fast. He snagged two champagne flutes from a side table, drained both in twin gulps then snagged another pair, this time sharing one with Ross.

Shoulder to shoulder, they drank companionably while Ross, buffeted by the crowd, fell prey to melancholy reminiscence. On a zillion, prior occasions he'd stood beneath the same glittering chandelier waiting for delicate Samantha to pick her way down the sweeping staircase. Tonight, the empty staircase, the oblivious horde made the house feel alien.

Ignorant of the realm's fervid history, the raucous Arriva clan thundered on. When poolside drums boomed to life, signaling an end of the combo's break, feet began to shuffle and a few venturesome couples sashayed to the exits.

The Jamaican riff worked its spell on all alike. Nano-Biologics, Nano-Neuro and Nano-Diagnostics swayed with the music. Missing only were departmental chieftains, Ross the lone ophthalmologist in the crowd.

Signet nudged his arm.

"Do not, under any circumstances, accept a bottle of Zonder Springs water...."

"You must be joking."

"...or journey to the study at the back of the house. Are we clear on this? Will you remember?"

"If this party is clearly not for me," Ross said. "Why would our CEO invite the most persona non grata person of all?"

"A sub-rosa invitation. Think of it that way."

Ross wandered.

He turned left, passing into the dining room through a pair of ornate French doors. Here he encountered guests sampling Melko's finger food laid out on the maple credenza. While they gobbled, he again savored the splendid Yannis Stavrou paintings Samantha collected for the side walls.

Opulent stills of fruit, Greek island countryside, peasants and idle fishing boats surrounded the room. He was particularly fond of a dreamy water color of the Parthenon. But more ensnaring memories surfaced, and suddenly besieged by a deep longing, he quit the room and entered the kitchen.

And there, in the middle of the marble floor, dwarfed by oversized cabinets and a gleaming fridge, stood Myla. They exchanged a glance before she looked away. Teetering on elevator pumps, flute aloft, the woman regained balance and let him pass. Too embarrassed for apology, even for a question about Glaucon—surely there were items in the presentation difficult to fully comprehend—she went her separate way and he, obligingly, went his.

Outside, on the travertine patio, he encountered a few of Dr. Braun's lab rats but none he wished to speak with.

Zina, he decided, glancing about. He needed a dose of the Byzantium empress, but she was nowhere to be found.

In time, the combo took another break, and Vivaldi filled the air, emanating from concealed speakers in the vegetation. With a stunning flash of blue, the underwater pool lights came on. Applause and shrieks of inebriated appreciation greeted the Disney-like spectacle.

It quickly dawned on him: he was postponing the inevitable, circulating within a clique where he did not belong. Squaring his shoulders, he decided to beard the beast in his own domain.

A hand pulled him aside. Paul Scofield maneuvered into view, face flushed, eyes alert.

"Are we okay about this?" the FDA man said. "No hard feelings about the decision?"

Ross readjusted. Nothing to be gained by antagonizing a key player.

"Not at all. Approval will be quicker this way."

Scofield sighed in relief.

"Glad you understand. Your other biologicals will eventually gain traction. As you point out, approval will be fast tracked by sticking with BDNF."

Scofield pointed out the obvious. Thanks to the thorough vetting for the PTSD project, BDNF already possessed a green light. Effective and nearly harmless in numerous animal systems, it enjoyed a favorable risk/benefit ratio offering both pharmacodynamic and pharmacokinetic muster. Facts of which Ross was well aware thanks to Beth.

"That only leaves the multicenter PMA program. Once you set it up, you'll be off to the races." Scofield hesitated, glancing over Ross's shoulder. "Isn't that right, Mr. Campesi?"

As if on cue, the CEO had materialized from a side door between plantation shutters. Tipping his flute to flushed employees, he nudged Ross aside to get at Scofield.

"Are you aware how *asinine* your request is?"

The FDA man colored.

"I, I meant to discuss this...."

"Why do you require more toxicology studies? It makes no sense."

"Not toxicology, Arturo. Slides of the olfactory bulbs. We need more of them to guarantee the virus didn't infect any of those animals' brains."

"Utter crap, Paul. It's a goddamn carrier antigen, not the whole fucking virus. It retains zero infectivity potential. Zilch. Nada. What the hell is wrong with you?"

Wasted. Hair moist and matted, the CEO a complete mess. Escape beckoned from the sorry confrontation. Yet, Ross reconsidered. Why not use the moment to demonstrate loyalty to the tipsy ass. Or, at least, pretend to.

"I agree," he blurted. "Zero infectivity. If you examine the literature...."

The tipsy ass shouldered him into the holly shrubs as if he weren't there.

"You know what this reminds me of?"

"No, Arturo. I do not."

"That new pacemaker, what was it called, Arythmostatic? Your regulatory demons sat on it for years, dithering while patients died. Don't you people ever consider the consequences of these delays?"

"Let's turn this around. Have you ever considered the lives we saved? The reason grandma flipped an embolus to her lungs was because a wire came loose. We forced the company to return to the drawing board...."

"Lame, Paul. Pure bullshit. We can't afford to wait on the PTSD vaccine. If you screw this up we'll take it abroad. Can you imagine how that will look: 'FDA Denies Cure For American Veterans.' Your butt will be on the line."

Scofield gulped but held his ground.

"You're absolutely correct. Products reach the market more quickly overseas. It doesn't guarantee safety, though. You have to remember that."

"Hell I do. We're not just talking pacemakers and vaccines here." With exaggerated deference, the CEO beckoned to Ross. "Tell him, Daniel. Aren't there a dozen or more excellent IOLs only available in Europe, thanks to the FDA?"

"Well. Sure. At last count, the FDA keeps thirteen intraocular lenses in limbo." He paused, debating if this really were the correct moment. He made a snap decision. "In fact, the FDA is disregarding our two biologicals...."

"A perfect example. Why are you people holding up Glaucon?"

"Blame Margaret for that. But we agree about one thing. She's right to demand a multicenter approach. Dr. Ross cannot launch unproven biologicals until his work is replicated. Proof of concept, Arturo. Surely, you've heard—"

"I got that. A simple problem. Easy to solve. But, what if your imposed delay drives that project offshore?" He now directed his vodka gaze at Ross. "India has little respect for intellectual property. I'm certain Simcoe Research in Mumbai could easily ignore our patents and develop this device themselves."

The discussion froze. Mr. Campesi's glower turned savage. The previous interchange hadn't been about additional nasal pathology sections or outdated FDA protocols. The irate CEO was only concerned with the stolen server files.

"Look, sir. We have to talk. I'm loyal and productive. You and I also share patents. I would never—"

"Cut the crap. Did you bring the flash drive?"

In a reflex manner, Ross touched his pocket, a stupid gesture he instantly regretted. He had the flash drive but it was the wrong one.

"No, sir. I don't have what you want."

"What the hell is that in your pocket?"

Campesi motioned to the foliage. Like the damn rabbit in a hat, Agent Zalin popped out of the shrubs.

"Amazing. The idiot actually brought it with him. He's a thief all right. What I've been telling Bame all along. Search his pocket," he said, "but watch the rough stuff. Don't want him suing for molestation or, God forbid, a hostile work environment."

Ross yanked the inquisitive hand out of his pocket. Aiming for a side door, the FBI agent vanished amongst the shrubs.

"That thumb drive is not what you think," he said. "It contains my Glaucon project, not any stolen documents."

"We shall find out soon enough." He turned to Scofield, who was following the action. "Please disregard this unfortunate incident. Dr. Ross forgets he's dealing with the Department of Defense. Fortunate for him, he returned what he, let us say, *borrowed*. We hope none of this affects his project. Now, what's this about the olfactory bulb?"

Affects his project.

What on earth had he just done? Stupid. Stupid.

When Campesi realized what the drive contained, he was doomed. Worse, the CEO now possessed the only copy of his project. Outside the Arriva server, one did not exist. If he were forever banned from the lab, he'd need a copy to continue on. Locked out of her own lab, Beth could not help. Which left only Signet. He possessed the required clearance to access Arriva's computers. A risky proposition, however. The man was untrustworthy.

He distinctly told Ross the chieftains would be....

A hand shot out of the maelstrom and spun him around.

"My missing emperor. At last." With provocative ease, balancing a tray of flutes, Zina glided to his side. "I have been looking high and wide, then I find your sad face. I identified the man behind you, put two and two together. How did he upset you?"

"Not a big deal."

"If Justinian is displeased, so is Theodora. *That* is a big deal."

Zina had morphed again. No longer the mermaid or bayou brawler in scuffed jeans or even Empress Theodora in purple eyeliner and painted lips. Tonight, she aimed for a more stylish look. In black chiffon and pearl earrings, she stepped right out of Vogue. A runway model, poised and lovely, Empress Theodora blithely served a besotted throng impervious to this gem in their midst.

Signet had chosen well, the gown a perfect fit.

"You, ah, look great," he said, as that damnable tingle returned to plague him. "Your pearls. Those loop earrings. All of you. Simply stunning."

"Ahah. My emperor takes notice. Come with me," she said. "I am on break."

Yorkie on a leash. Emperor on a cord. He fell in step once more.

They skirted the bulging dining room, slugged a path beneath a glittering chandelier, maneuvered around a mob of teetering guests finally to enter a roped off corridor, reaching at the end, Samantha's private parlor at the front of the house.

And, there, gleaming and magnificent, stood the concert grand in a distant corner. The familiar loveseat, reupholstered a Christmas green, ceased to beckon as it did in times past. The Stavrou prints remained the same. Greek islands and empty carafes faced the piano while a pair of Victorian chairs guarded the corridor door. A mini-cavern of thick carpets and heavy drapes designed for sound alone.

Samantha's space. And, once his as well.

"We are alone," she said, spinning in a circle of raised, balletic limbs. "Tell me again how I look."

"Terrific. I like the dress, the way you, ah, fit into it."

Poured, actually. Every dimple through the fabric.

"Hmm. Your eyes scan closely. You also eye the keyboard. Both magnificent creatures. That is what we are. No, not you, my emperor. The Steinway."

She laughed gaily, swinging her arm through his. Together they traversed the plain of Kashan carpets until, with a sharp shove, she deposited him upon the padded seat. Thoughts of nasty Arturo vanished now as Zina idly thumbed the Beethoven on the rack.

She snagged the dog-eared page and opened to the

abandoned spot. Dare he enter this torrid jungle, dare he attempt the dangerous immersion?

He arched his back, cracked fingers.

"First, a performance," she said. "Signet indicated if I were patient, you might play. Make it quick. Fifteen minutes. Tops."

He turned to Opus 57 and, in his mind, temporal lobes began to zing.

"Not so fast, Mr. Piano-man. Tell me about his Beloved Immortal. In your travels, did you find one yourself?"

He withdrew his hands, plopped them in his lap.

"Come again?"

"Do you have your own 'beloved'? If not, is there room for me?"

CHAPTER 24

Moments musicaux skidded to a stop.

Zina's question, so out of the blue, and obviously rehearsed. The Eckerd Hall program notes failed to mention the Great Master's posthumously published letter. Any reference to such a woman. Signet went deep to find it. But to what purpose, planting this buried secret in Zina's mind? To kindle a romance? Still, the manipulative undertow snared him and, the wonder, he did not resist.

The reference itself fascinated him, however. It presented him with a parallel to consider, a kind of similarity between scholars, long debating the identity of this Beloved, and Zina, searching the Byzantium archives for her own. Antonie Brentano and Josephine Brunsvik dueled for the historians' namesake while notorious Empress Theodora alone secured hers. Yet Zina took it a step further.

Immortal Beloved: Zina. Also Empress Theodora. Identities had merged. Or, was this, too, another manipulation?

Is there room for me?

The inquiry sounded genuine. But with Signet's guiding paw in the background, its actual meaning lay obscure. Like so many others of his spinning problems, the resolution of this one had to wait. The only clarity, Opus 57 on the rack before him.

Immortal Beloved. Do you have your own?

"Please hold the page, Empress Beloved. Turn only when I nod. This won't take long."

The mournful allegro assai emerged from the magnificent instrument. His musical temporal lobes then resumed control, receiving, analyzing, and parsing the notes, fusing him to the absolute.

With an unanticipated jolt, his hippocampus suddenly squeaked a warning, igniting a distant echo from the frontal lobes, his sentient brain looking on from afar, from Samantha herself: *If you must, abandon your invention, Daniel, not the music. Do not follow Arturo's footsteps. Science must never displace art.* The message, like Zina's query, so unexpected. Yet, he took heed and, for these next few minutes, as the music soared, he honored his dear benefactor's request, playing with fury and abandon until, in a fading whisper, it was over.

His hands lifted off the keys. The parlor draped his shoulders. He was back, the adventure over but not the promise to return.

"Splendid." Zina grasped a suspended wrist. "Signet spoke the truth. A momentary lapse for him, I am sure. He was right. You can play a recital."

He recomposed himself and rose from the seat. Pursuing appreciation, Zina begrudged him a kiss.

"So powerful," she said. "Only a few missed notes."

"Well, sure." Damnation. She caught the fumbled trill in the tranquillo section. "It's been awhile. I'm a bit rusty."

"What you are is a perfectionist. Exactly like Justinian. He compiled all the Roman briefs to write his Corpus Juris. A very famous piece of jurisprudence. Quoted to this day, in fact."

"Signet, again?'

She shrugged. "Well sure." And, laughed merrily as if all were some gigantic joke.

Ross retrieved his fatigued wrist. Roman briefs? Any semblance of a Beethoven glow, fast receded.

"Forget Byzantium," he said. "Did you like...."

"Forget? Impossible. Can you imagine Justinian's effort?"

"I only want to know if you liked the sonata."

"Very much. I enjoyed the vigorous triplet chords at the end. The disappearing pianissimo was terrific."

His heart skipped a beat. She had paid attention. She listened.

"Truthfully? The idea of 'triplets' is confusing. Signet helped, of course. He provided a primer. He said I must not sound, what was his word, 'ambiguous.'"

"But, if you did, I would 'disambiguate' for you."

"Yes. Just what he said. You two are on a similar wavelength."

"I suppose he also mentioned 'mirror neurons.'"

"He did. You two seem to know a lot about each other."

A subdued applause erupted from a distant corner. Two well-dressed Arriva employees now occupied the Victorian chairs. Having wandered in by mistake, they nodded at Ross before departing. They opened and shut the French doors on waves of fun-filled laughter filtering in from the foyer.

"May I ask a question?" she said when they were alone again.

"When does an empress need permission?"

"Was this Samantha person your unknown lover?"

"My patron," he said, shaking his head. "A very sick woman. We became friends. She encouraged my return to the keyboard. She also liked Chopin."

"The position must remain open. Is that a correct assumption?"

Words failed him. In their absence, she administered a prolonged hug with all the trimmings. Nibbled ear. Gentle hip caress. More adventurous excursions until poolside drums brought them to a halt. Adding to the decibel distraction, a bracing aroma of fresh kebabs wafted into the room. But, nearer to hand and far more disturbing, eliminating any pleasure a combo, Theodora's warmth or the hint of evening kebabs might offer, Mr. Campesi's familiar bark invaded the parlor.

A sound from hell.

"Your CEO speaks." She pulled away, cocked an ear. "He asks his guests to join him. He plans a toast. Go to him, my emperor. He beckons."

"Ignore the man. Let's find Melko."

In an abrupt surprise, Zina brushed him off like so much lint. She gave him a strange look then bolted across the field of carpets to vanish through a door in the far corner.

Gone. No departing whisper of Immortal Beloved. No threats of another Nika Riot. Only the vacuum of departure and regret.

He regrouped. The whiff of scripted events seemed too strong. The aroma of kebabs, the inviting Bob Marley riffs. Even the proffered intimacy of fondling, the slow unzip. All of it, somehow rehearsed. Until the might-have-been was over. Campesi's voice triggered the next scene. Perfect timing thanks to Signet. Only he could make it happen.

For once, Ross welcomed the interrupting yowl beyond the doors. While his hands groped hills and valleys, he nearly jettisoned precaution. A fly trap, this beguiling female. Still, he managed to escape. For that he remained grateful. The reprieve was temporary, though. Empress and emperor were scripted in. Zina wasn't done with him yet.

His next move? Join the employees.

Quitting the dream parlor, Ross went out to the marble foyer. There, holding court from the bottom step of the staircase, the imperious man implored one and all to continue their quest of excellence. First, the PTSD vaccine. There would be others. New contracts were coming....

The blow to his gut came fast and hard. He doubled over, falling backward, but caught before he struck the floor. The second of Zalin's agents held his arms while the first delivered a follow-up blast knocking air from his burning lungs.

They half-dragged him out of the foyer, past the oblivious throng and through the parlor to the same door Zina used to make her exit. Exploding with phosphenes of sparkling lights, his brain found the answer. The thumb drive. Not what they wanted. He warned them.

They led him down a corridor to a room at the rear of the house. To the one place Signet had warned him to avoid at all cost. The study.

CHAPTER 25

Barry "Hard Knuckles" Bisco thrust him into a padded chair before a desk. Before slamming the shutters closed, he rapped him across the head; back and forth, it snapped, after each set of blows. The guy enjoying his work. Getting into it. Slap and jab. Doling out the pain.

Meanwhile, as sparkles settled, observations trickled in.

Empty bookshelves surrounded the room. Smothering the air, a strong pungent leather buried body odor of the two jailors. The paneling of dark wood, similar to the imposing desk. Mahogany, he decided, as if the type of wood made a difference.

He searched for klieg lights, a side table of chisels and knives. Finding none turned the sour space from a torture chamber to a man cave. A corner refrigerator stood beside a credenza stocked with liquor bottles and a pitcher of water. Completing the décor, a tangle of yellow wires connected twin mounted flat screens to gargantuan speakers.

Samantha's influence never touched this sterile backside

of her graceful mansion. An add-on by the husband, strictly out of sync with subdued elegance, as were the FBI thugs standing guard at each elbow. Arturo knew how to pick them.

A trembling took hold of both hands. Then, fine jitters difficult to control. Streams of fear discolored his shirt. He doubted any Beloved Immortal would ever claim him.

Rockets of fresh pain sprang from his arm. Using wrist cast as bat, Sergio struck to maim, not to break. To leaven the monotony, he delivered several head butts, calibrated to briefly stun, unworried about concussing either himself or defenseless victim.

"...hey ... guys ..." he spluttered, "...don't want ... a concussion...."

"Stop whining, asshole. You broke the law. You have to pay."

"...but ... I did ... nothing...."

He lost the thought. A knuckle jab found its mark, the second agent joining in. When the chair tilted backward, Sergio saved him. A knee jammed his torso. He slumped like a ragdoll, mind reeling.

The agents had a single goal: make him talk. Beat the crap out of him. Smash his brains. Rupture a kidney. His spleen. Whatever it took. Except he hadn't stolen the damn files. How to convince them?

Long moments passed. The second agent loped over to the door to stand guard. Sergio raised his cast, warning

Ross to remain seated. Not an issue, buddy. No place to go.

The taciturn duo communicated with head nods and hand signals reminding Ross of TV dramas. A cop would storm a building, disarm and cuff four perps, then parade his quarry before a shapely blond....

He was rambling. Dumb thoughts. Pointless.

Stop. Think. Escape. Find a way.

He managed to sit up. Forced his back against the chair. Struggled to clear his mind. Images crossed his line of sight. The desk, the moronic agents, bookshelves and pictures on the wall. His eye landed on a bank of framed photos behind the desk. Gruesome images, like the ones in Signet's hut. Injured soldiers, gutted roads, giant craters. A gold-framed photograph stood out from the rest.

A group shot, not of dying and injured soldiers, but of three men inside a Quonset hut. Smiling for the camera, champions it appeared, the occasion noted by a large print caption: "The Mid-Range Black Belt Kick-Off." Ross easily recognized Signet's angular form. Younger then as were his two companions. Grinning ear to ear, Mr. Campesi kneeled beside Colonel Bame, wearing his trademark, stern expression. Six hands extended from white karate outfits to embrace a sizable trophy.

Ross squinted, read the date: Desert Storm 1990. The first Gulf War. These guys went way back, accounting for the camaraderie.

The corridor door flew open. Followed by Agent Zalin,

Colonel Bame swept into the study. Together with Sergio and his pal, they formed a semi-circle and peered down at the miserable slob. Bruised, bleeding from a drooling lip, he tried to think.

Reason with these guys. Make them understand. It was all the result of ridiculous misunderstanding.

Straighten this out.

"I, I'm really on your side," he said, voice weak. "I want to help. I just don't know how. I don't have any stolen documents."

He searched for any sign of sympathy, any indication he'd gotten through to them. Predatory hawks, they hadn't heard. Not even listening.

Taut as a wire, grin contorted, Colonel Bame now crouched before him. He slowly bunched a fist, held it high above Ross's head.

"We, or I should say, you, have a problem, Doctor."

He plunged his fist into Ross's leg with an audible *whomp*.

"Ow! What the hell?"

The chair shook. Sergio held it still.

Pausing for sadistic pleasure, the colonel struck the other leg, twice repeating the attack, eyes like chiseled stones, bizarre grin hard, fixed.

"This ... it's so ... unnecessary."

"You fooled Campesi. Nice trick, in fact, bringing the

wrong thumb drive. But, stupid to stay at the party. Now you're mine."

"...not ... a trick. I don't have—"

Sergio boxed his ear. He shut up.

"The reconstructed timeline points directly at you. We don't know the exact projects you stole. For some reason, neither Campesi nor Corporal Signet will tell me. The corporal claims he doesn't have the code for the private server. As if I believe him. But, I don't need the goddamn code. What I need are the files you downloaded. I need them now."

Agent Zalin reached to help the colonel to his feet but badly misjudged. Irritated, Bame swatted the agent off like a mosquito and sprang up on his own.

"Call me when you've got the documents. Do not call Campesi. Keep him out of the loop."

"He's the one who hired me. He's paying the bill."

"I realize that, jerk. I'm the one who authorizes his funds. Now, get busy. The party won't last all night."

The door banged shut. The colonel was gone leaving Ross with the three men.

Assuming command, Agent Zalin ordered Sergio and Hard Knuckles, the second agent, to take a position behind Ross. Then he poured himself a generous dollop of whiskey from the credenza, retrieved a TV wingchair and set it down, face to face, for what came next.

"Okay, lads," he said, genially. "Soften him up."

Bisco held him by the shoulders and Sergio, cast aloft, went to work.

"Wait. You don't have to do this...."

Yet, they did and with relish. The men exchanged roles after a series of knuckle-skull jabs and Bisco took over. His method of softening up, the swift slap, each blow sharp and jarring. Finally, they backed off and Zalin inched closer. Ross recoiled, not in anticipation of fresh injury, but from the smell of stale trousers.

"Prepared to talk, are we?"

He let the question slide.

"Very well. I'll outline the situation. First, we know why you stole—"

"I already told—"

Agent Zalin nodded and Bisco popped him with a knuckle jab.

"As I started to say, we all know the difficulties you encountered these past years. Animal tests, the monotonous reports, not to mention tedious conferences. You're wiped out, exhausted. You ask yourself, when will it end? Sure, you want to cure blindness and become famous. Yet—and here's the rub—we're talking small gizmo for a tiny glaucoma population. There's no real pay out. Unlike the juicy return on over-priced lifestyle intraocular lens surgery. Or, the sky's-the-limit reward your plastic pals earn lifting lids and tucking tummies.

So, you begin to think millions, and I mean dollars, not patients. You want to be like the big shots who really count. It's natural to want more. You take a look at this big house, the crown moldings and marble floors. The idea finally dawns. Your gizmo won't cut it."

He took a breather while his men went to the credenza. Bisco handed their insightful leader a glass of amber fluid. Zalin held it to the light, chuckling.

"Glenfiddich, doc. One of the perks. By the way, did you sample the man's imported Dumol? Flew in a dozen cases from California last week. What about it, Bisco? Did you get a glass?"

Ross endured the guzzling trio. An empty bottle of chardonnay stood next to the Glenfiddich. No, wait. The man got his scotch wrong. He was gulping a rare single malt, Glenmorangie Scotch. None of them touched the Zonder Springs water. Three bottles still tightly sealed.

"So you're slaving away, and for what? You think about the PTSD program and realize Mr. Campesi's brilliant vaccine might also work for you. The sticking point, you don't know how to cook up a batch yourself. What you need is the formula. And that is where Mr. Ravi Ravda fits in. He wants the same thing and dispatches his man Newsome to convince you to steal the necessary documents. Now, this accountant is shrewd. He's into computers big time. So, after some training, he guides you inside the Arriva mainframe and, all of a sudden, it's a new ballgame."

Ross didn't bite on the deranged fabrication, actually a

belief system embraced by both Campesi and Bame, and now by the FBI. He was defenseless, involved in a still undefined mess.

"We finally figured you out. I should say, Mr. Campesi deduced your motivation."

"Enlighten me."

"It concerns your fear of failure. A lifetime affliction. Same for lots of people, it turns out. Mr. Campesi did a lot of digging."

"He read my file," Ross replied. "It's all there. He and I had a long talk at the beginning."

"Don't get touchy. The point is, you've always dreamed of becoming one of the big boys. You held back though, wondering if you really measured up. You looked into the Boston academic scene, saw it wasn't you, and sidestepped into eyeball practice instead."

He held up a hand, took a healthy swig of Glenmorangie and smacked his lips. "Whew. That slides down real smooth. If you behave, Sergio will pour you a glass. To continue. It was then you turned to different role models. I'm talking highly productive cataract surgeons here. We both know the type, the guy who buys radio stations or invests real estate for outsized profits. The kind of busy doc who trades stocks while operating on patients, the broker in the operating room, issuing buy and sell orders, while he closes up. Hey, you can't blame him. Making a bundle is the American way. Even a doctor can be super-rich. Fee for service or, as I view it, seed money for more lucrative ventures. You want this for yourself. To be a success."

The FBI man stretched, rose, and went to the credenza for a refill. Back in the wingchair, he proceeded with more wisdom.

"Let's consider the consequences of your action."

"My 'action' being what?"

"The theft. What do you think? And, your dumb ass lying about it. Plus your likely collusion with this bad apple, Ravda. This doesn't even include the real kicker, possible espionage. Jesus, guy. Get a brain."

"Thanks for the clarification."

The FBI man sighed.

"I have to agree with your boss. You're an idiot. No wonder he wants to dump you."

"Okay. Got it. Where does your 'script' lead now?"

"So, feeling betrayed, Mr. Campesi takes control of your cutesy project. Worse, to inflict further damage, he hands your talk to a lab grunt. Finally, for real punishment, he brings in the FBI. Remember, you hacked a government computer network."

It was pointless to argue. Yet, he had to try. And, lab grunt? Harsh depiction of a room temperature IQ. At least, without electric shock, Myla had figured out the maze of the building's interior.

"You know this is all nonsense. If I magically find whatever you think I've taken, Campesi will never return my project."

"Who knows what will happen. Bisco, hit the son of a bitch. Knock some sense into him."

Bisco went to work, knocking the 'sense' out of him instead.

The corridor door slammed open, and Mr. Campesi stormed into the study, the also fuming colonel on his heel.

"Did he talk?" the CEO demanded. "Did he tell you where he's hiding the damn thing?"

CHAPTER 26

Agent Zalin may have been FBI but Campesi, backed by the DOD, had seniority. Ross enjoyed watching him squirm as he made excuses. The doctor was stubborn. A hard nut to crack. But he, Zalin, was almost there. With a little more time, he'd break. He'd pulp him if necessary.

"Hard nut to crack?" The colonel shook his head. "Maybe I should 'pulp' you instead."

Campesi edged between agent and soldier, now nose to nose.

"Relax, men," he said. "No one's pulping anyone here, including this remarkable physician."

Adopting a friendlier tone, the CEO patted Ross on the shoulder and dropped into Zalin's abandoned wingchair. He got settled in, as if cozying up for a sporting event on TV, apparently nothing amiss with the pummeled physician-employee half falling off a chair beside him. Hey men, that's why it's called a study. A study in pain and misery.

"My gosh, Daniel. You look horrible. Have these goons been rough on you?"

Bisco and Sergio exchanged high fives, mission accomplished.

"We need a different approach here," he said, turning to the brutes, "No more Torture Memos for my boy here."

He motioned for Agent Zalin to pour him a scotch. Cradling the snifter, he again faced his 'boy.'

"We can't forget Dr. Ross is a respected physician and, of this week, famous innovator. The local press will be there tomorrow morning. We can't disappoint them."

"Come on, Arturo. You've banished me from the campus. Myla will conduct the presentation in the auditorium."

"You have paid attention. However, if you return the copied documents, we'll return to your original schedule."

From deep within his aching body, Ross found a laugh.

"You know I didn't download a single scrap from the Arriva server. This is all about Glaucon. That's what you're after. You're committing kind of justified theft."

"Save it, Ross. I guess the lads here had the right approach all along."

He motioned to the goons. Happily reengaged, they picked Ross up by the shoulders and repositioned him in the chair. Bisco drew his arm back to begin anew. At the last moment, Campesi told him to wait. There were a few items to discuss first.

"Let me start off," Ross said, finding his voice.

"I'd prefer you shut up."

"If I were you, sir, I'd pay close attention. Because, if I don't present the Glaucon talk as originally planned, the press will find it odd. If a nosy reporter looks into it, he or she will mention the Simcoe protestors outside the Arriva gates. And, that will lead to a mention of the PTSD vaccine rollout." He tried to turn to the colonel. In a spasm, his neck remained fixed and tilted to port. "Do you see where this is going? Before you know it, DARPA comes into the picture." He forced a laugh. It came out as a breathless gurgle. "As Zalin here said to me only moments ago, think of the consequences. DARPA may well boot your clipped ass back to Iraq."

"Fuck off, Ross. You're the screw up. Not Arturo."

The soldier's commanding bark settled the issue. The strange part, Bame had to know the theft was bogus. Yet for some reason he wanted Ross to take the fall for this fictitious crime.

With a sigh, the CEO now sat back and steadily reexamined his quarry, his perusal punctuated by disapproving shakes of his head and slow sips of scotch.

"What's it like?" he said. "You know, returning to the scene. Six long years since Beethoven rattled the rafters." The CEO dropped his chin, a note of melancholy invading the study. "Vivaldi used to be her favorite. Mine, too. We listened a lot in those days. The Four Seasons. Concertos. Dozens of them. Then, *you* showed up and all we heard were those damn sonatas. Hell, Ross. *Beethoven?*"

Ross opened his mouth to speak but a mandibular knuckle rap changed his mind.

"Christ, man. Don't you miss her? Can't you see her gliding down that staircase? Today is her birthday. Hell, we used to canoe down the stream out back. Through that damn cypress swamp all the way to the race track. It all ended the day you arrived. A day of catastrophe."

"...too sick ... to paddle...."

Campesi halted Bisco's poised knuckles then waved him off, content to bask in remembrance of the way things were.

Still, his comments touched a nerve. Yes, Ross missed her more than Arturo could ever imagine. In another life, were he not her eye doctor and she not so ill, he might very well have accepted the proffered embrace, one of many offered upon the divan in front of her concert grand. In another life.

He took hold of himself. The CEO was playing at his heartstrings. Trying another manipulation. Today, whipped senseless, the trick did not work.

"Blind and dying of cancer. That was the catastrophe. Not my arrival and certainly not Beethoven."

The blunt comment sailed over the CEO's head. Possessed and stupidly angry, the man was on a roll.

"She asked for you at the end," Mr. Campesi added. "As she floated off, she looked at me and said, 'Tell Daniel, thank you.' Can you believe that? Thinking of you during her final seconds."

"I'm certain you were on her mind. Where is he, she must have thought, there on her bed, alone, skin and bones, as you flew back from Bethesda at the very last possible moment, arriving after her spirit had already reached the pearly gates."

"Asshole. I tried to get here. A violent rainstorm delayed my flight. All I'm saying, we both miss her, each in our own way. I'm also saying if you don't return those files your career will be over. I'm sure Agent Zalin has explained you'll be facing federal prison—"

Another interruption from the outside corridor. This time Corporal Signet entered the study. After a quick survey of the layout, he got Ross on his shaky feet.

"The doctor is coming with me."

"The hell he is. He stays put. You, Bisco, Sergio. Escort Mr. Signet back to the party."

The two agents exchanged a glance then backed off, no doubt recalling their afternoon encounter on the sponge dock.

But Ross didn't want to leave before making another effort to clear his name. He pushed, unsuccessfully, away from his rescuer.

"Time for you to go," Mr. Security said.

"Will you please tell these men I was with you when the supposed hack occurred?"

Ignoring his plea, Signet moved him toward the door.

"Stop. Let me go. Why won't you help me?"

Agent Zalin now stepped into their path. Unwisely, he placed a hand on a far stronger arm.

"You can leave," he said. "This fool stays with us."

His memory of the fiasco in Tarpon Springs did not serve him. With a flick of the wrist, Signet bounced him off the wall.

The Colonel then decided it was his turn. After a hasty reassessment, however, like the two agents, Bame backed away, fresh rivulets of moisture on his chin.

"No one wants a confrontation," he said, a catch in his voice. "But, I order you to leave the study at once. This doctor committed a crime. He stole government property."

"Think closely, Colonel. The documents are not on his person or in his home or office. Therefore, and please note the logic, if the doctor has indeed stolen what you claim, he must first retrieve the files before he can return them."

A stand-off, each firm in his opinion. Then, suddenly, Colonel Bame capitulated. Following a most curious bow, he stood aside.

"If I may ask, corporal, where are you taking him?"

"We will discover destination when we arrive."

"More Zen?" Ross said. "For God sake. Tell Mr. Campesi I didn't steal anything."

Ross continued struggling to get free. Useless effort. The security man's grip too strong. Ross was locked into place.

"How can I possibly find what I didn't take?"

"These men think you stole. That, not denial, is what matters."

"What the heck does *that* mean?"

Mr. Campesi then attempted to prevent their exit from the study. He stepped up to Signet but quickly reassessed. Maybe it was the need to look up at the man. Or, the two cowering agents shrinking deeper into the study. Whatever. He quickly shifted to a position near the credenza thus avoiding injury.

"If you give these files to Ravda," the CEO said. "Your career will be finished. I promise you'll go to prison. I'll hand Glaucon to another glaucomatologist, whatever you people call yourselves. Hell, Ross. You'll always drive that crappy car. Come on, man. Grow up."

"You forget, sir. The doctor does not think like you."

"Wait. This is crazy. How do you know what I think?"

"The success you seek," Signet said. "Is not monetary. It lies in a different realm."

Different realm.

"I don't believe this. You don't know a darn thing about me."

"You forget. I backgrounded you. I learned, despite being an excellent physician, you feel deficient. You alone must deal with this problem. The meeting for tonight is over."

"Deficient? What the hell are you talking about?"

Taking them by surprise, a panel door in the wall behind the desk banged open. It caught the Agent Zalin off guard, propelling him forward across the desk. Balancing a tray of champagne flutes in one hand, Zina's torso appeared in the panel opening. Negotiating the small aperture, she guided, first her legs then hips and, with a beguiling twist, her rear end into the room. She had changed wardrobe again. Clinging tee, torn shorts, hair pinned back. Once more the urchin but one now capable of rattling Ross's emotions even in his bruised and bloody state.

"Thirsty anyone? Don't be shy. So much talk and commotion. Everyone simmer down."

Chin high, shoulders set, the transformed cocktail waitress circled the men, offering each a flute, pirouetting past Ross to reach Mr. Campesi.

"I have tasted your excellent chardonnay, sir. Very clever to ship across the Rockies. I have a shipment for you. I bring it in person."

"Very cute, young lady. I prefer the black dress." The host inspected the inscription emblazoned across her chest. "'Boson Rocks'. What the hell? Will you please sashay your lovely ass out the way you came in?"

Waving off the command, she laid the tray down on the desk. Assuming a stealthy crouch, she surveyed the unsuspecting ensemble, laying the groundwork for what Ross recalled would be The Attack Of Five. Adversaries met the proper number. Zina's "lovely ass" prepared for battle.

Here we go again.

Zina then retrieved a bottle of Zonder Springs water from the credenza and flipped it to Mr. Campesi. He snagged it midair.

"Straight from the aquafer spring," she said. "Except, that one contains carbonated bubbles. It tickles the nose. You will enjoy the sensation."

"You are way out of bounds, missy. I hired you to serve my guests. Get out there and do your job."

"*Job*, is it?" She wagged a finger. "What exactly is *your* job, mister? Does it include poisoning me and grandpa?"

Silence, the study tense, Boson Rocks the center of attention.

Signet eased his grip and circulation returned to Ross's forearm. A finger to his lips, Signet cautioned restraint. Then, he nodded at Colonel Bame and the study came to life.

In a blur of motion, the colonel yanked Mr. Campesi to his feet, slapped him hard, shook him like a blanket. Stunned, the CEO spluttered in confusion.

"What the hell, Bennet?"

"You said, 'proof of principle'. Instead, you went too far."

"It was a harmless, goddamn experiment. A strictly 'what if'. No one was hurt."

"Not *hurt*?" Zina tossed him a second water bottle. It bounced off his shoulder. "Grandpa ignores the crying icon. He forgets her tears."

Mr. Campesi finally pried his jacket loose. His hands visibly shaking, he flattened wrinkles, ran stubby fingers through tousled hair, fought for composure. Flushed, angry, he pointed at Zina.

"Enough about grandpa," he said. "I never poisoned that old fart. Far from it. Remember the Quality of Life form he completed after surgery? He went on record with the FDA. He's pleased with the eye surgery. He's a new person. Completely transformed. Don't ask me to explain it, but he claims Dr. Ross cured him of fraudulent beliefs. I swear. That's exactly what he said. Phony, painful religious notions forced down his innocent gullet before he knew better. They're gone. He couldn't be happier. So stop whining, honey. No one's poisoned anyone here."

"Old *fart*, is it? I am *whining*? Look here, Mr. Nasty man. One is never *cured* of a religious calling. You turned him into a seventy-year-old playboy."

"We should all be so lucky."

"Against his will, you damaged his brain. That is crime against humanity."

"A hot ticket, Ross. She's a keeper. That is, if you ever get out of prison to enjoy her charms."

Verdict rendered, Zina turned next to punishment. She darted past Agent Zalin to confront the CEO. With a horrific scream, she planted a powerful kick in his midsection. The flaps of his jacket flew apart as air gushed out, the blow sending him backward into the wingchair where, holding his gut, drool on his lips, he slid off the cushion to the floor.

Only Agent Zalin felt a need to help out. He knelt and felt for a pulse, but the CEO, gaining an ounce of strength, pushed him away and began clawing a path toward Zina. His attempt for revenge ended abruptly when his nose cracked upon impact with Zina's hand. The sort of karate blow that cracked bricks. Again he slumped to the rug as blood streamed out of both nostrils and down his shirt.

Taking their cue, the three FBI agents backed well away from the fury searching for her next victim.

Signet eventually stepped forward.

"Prepare to leave, Ms. Palaeologus. Before we go, I will search for identification."

Stooping, he rummaged through the CEO's pockets.

"How did I perform?" she said.

"Splendid. As always. See what I have found." Adroitly avoiding the blood, he held up a laminated card. "'Blackwatch Security and Protection'. I suspected as much. Mr. CEO hired out. Overweight FBI agents do not exist. Look at these two. No. Do not be offended Mr. Sergio and friend. You must cut back on fast food."

"I don't get it. These guys really aren't FBI?"

Signet shook his head.

"Mr. Campesi's idea. To frighten you into giving them the stolen documents. Colonel Bame is the real deal, and the one to fear. He has other plans if you do not cooperate."

Maintaining his distance, the colonel nodded.

"For once, Corporal Signet speaks the truth. He refers to his former colleague, a ghoulish individual named Sauer. I'm certain you've heard about that soldier's earlobe harvest. Well, he's here, at the front gate so to speak, eager to be released."

Gathering his troop, Signet ushered Ross and Zina to the panel door.

"Keep him chained, Colonel. That is, unless I fail to convince the doctor to do the right thing."

With that, he forcefully pushed Ross through the opening and into a narrow, musty passage. Zina was next, Signet last to leave.

The security man called out to Ross.

"I must caution you," he said. "At all costs, avoid ear-man Sauer."

"In the same way I was to avoid the study?"

"It may not come to that. Ms. Palaeologus, Theodora. Kindly hold the light."

CHAPTER 27

Single file, they worked their way down a dark and narrow passageway. A spelunker's dream, Ross surmised, wiping away cobwebs as he stumbled over blocks of wood following Zina on point. From time to time she flicked a flashlight on and off, illuminating their path while burrowing deeper into this unknown region within the house.

"Sorry for so little light," Zina whispered. "To avoid alerting guests we are here."

Smothering a laugh, she pointed to tiny, drill holes in the wall to their right.

Peepholes, Ross discovered, glancing in as he moved along. First up, a view of revelers in the cavernous dining room. Then, after a few more steps down the winding passage, a magnetic glimpse of a computer geek pawing a willing female behind a rustling curtain. More couples, more fondling in the busy foyer.

Next up, a too-quick glimpse of activity in the parlor. A biology post-doc and an IT tech were coupling behind the

Steinway, busy hands beneath a cocktail dress. Zina pulled him further along, cutting off his view. Signet, however, witnessed the final act, apparent from his lingering stare at the same peep sight a moment later.

The party had fast progressed downhill, eager lab rats in every corner. Meanwhile, smoky riffs from the patio combo provided background motivation. Sweet tendrils of fading drums now nudged the groping threesome down their bumpy path.

"Fraternity life," Signet pronounced, bringing up the rear. "Similar parties have occurred before. Incriminating photos choke the main server. Think blackmail, Hoover style. Stop your peep-tom and keep moving. We are not there yet."

They pushed onward, to the extreme south of the mansion where Signet's shoulder and Zina's foot opened a side door to an overgrown veranda. After creeping through stale and cramped quarters, the night air comforted multiple aches plus the pain of an injured leg, courtesy of Colonel Bame. With Signet's support, Ross managed the final yards.

"How'd you guys know about that passage?" he said. "Where'd you find the flashlight?"

Zina shrugged.

"Signet explained about this door. He bought the flashlight and my dress. He prefers to think ahead."

He limped over to their master of ceremonies standing at the veranda railing. Nose to the evening air, he looked preoccupied with the scents wafting out of the adjacent preserves. It was hard to miss the dank, earthy aroma, but he appeared to detect another presence. Flaring nostrils, head at an angle, concerned but not saying why as he parsed jumbled odors.

"What about you?" Ross said, staring into trees, shrubs and vines draped over swampy water. "How did you discover that narrow walkway between the walls?"

"Your boss informed me."

"You mean, he called you into his office to tell you? Why would he do that?"

"His office, yes. The one here at his estate. He told me when I came for drinks."

The invitation occurred shortly after he joined Arriva. Signet surmised an ulterior motive, and he was right. It had to do with one of the employees, an irregular fellow, hardworking but never one of the team. An arrangement set up by his wife, one he legally was forced to honor after her death. And, to make matters worse, he suspected hanky-panky between said wife and this unusual person, Dr. Daniel Ross.

"He said 'hanky panky', not me. I do not speak that way. As you now know, he is a paranoid person."

And, Signet further surmised, the man's paranoia led him to task his new security man with several missions. First, to investigate certain clandestine meetings Dr. Ross had with an equally quirky individual named Newsome. Second, to look into certain clandestine piano days with his wife in the parlor.

"Clandestine, my foot. He knew about those afternoon visits. The housekeeper knew, and she reported to him on his wife's daily situation."

"Hmm. Touchy, aren't we?"

"Not in the least. Anyway, go on."

Signet averted his gaze from the shadows. Ran it up and down Ross. Tilted his chin in mock concentration, then resumed the story.

"One summer, when his wife was in Europe, after consulting blueprints, he hastily had that inside passage created. At the time, she was CEO of Arriva, he second in command. He wished to eavesdrop and, like you, peep tom. He listened in on her business meetings conducted in the study. Also, on various trysts in the parlor. Again, his term, 'trysts'. Not mine. It was his misfortunate, none of the peep holes provided a clear view of the loveseat. Or so he claimed."

"A devious beast," Zina said. "I am not yet done with him."

Ross fought to remain calm, wrestling with images of the incriminating loveseat. Of tentative but partial exploits. There were always obstacles to prevent him from obeying her beckoning finger. For one, the narrow love seat. Never sufficient room for two. More important, his own scruples. The descent into such moral turpitude not to his liking. Even though, in her time, Samantha's beauty would've tempted even a saint.

Collecting themselves, they aimed for the front of this side of the mansion.

"Why did he share this secret with you?"

"A way to evacuate your body," Signet said. "Should you have not cooperated, Bisco and Sergio were to finish the task. Lucky for you, I saw them escort you to the study."

"Why didn't you *intervene*? Those idiots...."

"The answer is obvious. I, too, needed to learn your replies."

No doubt existed now. From the outset, his entire itinerary was a scripted score. From the opening trumpets hailing Newsome's death, to the fake bassoon performance of FBI goons, to their own stumbling oboe escape. A mystery wrapped in a Signet puzzle, under his baton, the accompanying chorus, vivace non tranquillo.

They were on the run.

At the end of the veranda, they turned a corner to find Melko waiting for them behind the wheel of his parked van. He reached back, opened the sliding panel, and told Ross to join crates and crushed boxes in the rear compartment. Zina, he directed to sit up front while Signet slammed the door shut behind her.

Before departing, the maestro raised the baton and issued fresh instructions.

They were first to make their way to Dr. Azzizzi's house on Clearwater Beach. After that another destination would further guide them.

"No cell phones, please. You must remain under Colonel Bame's radar."

311

"Why go to Clearwater Beach?" Ross said. "And, would you stop with the right thing business?"

"What is now right for you is brand new. To discover this, you will have to unlearn the old."

Ross shook his head. Mr. Zen again?

"What exactly am I supposed to learn?"

"That which lies within. That which lies without."

"Why didn't you say so? I think I get it now. If I don't discover something *within*, somebody at the gate *without*, this Sauer person, will be released to kill me. I don't have a good feeling about this."

"Find the thumb drive. Keep Sauer on his leash."

Before Signet shut him in, he snatched his cell from his hand.

"No calls. Not even to Detective Leeks. Trust me. It is up to you."

Zina stifled a laugh.

"How did you know he dialed the detective?"

"Mirror neurons. Right, Signet?"

"In your position, I would do the same. Summon the National Guard. A few tanks. A missile may help. However, if Sauer has been tasked, all hopeless. He represents the deadliest of psychopathic killers. In addition to amputated ears, he delivered a bagged heart to the colonel. I tell you this to clear your mind."

"And this is the soldier you saved? Incredible."

"Even a predator deserves protection."

"I get it now. This Sauer guy is Mrs. Chaneuill's son."

"I offered a quid pro quo. To save his mother's sight, leave the doctor alone. My ploy to placate did not work. Sauer knows no kindness. He may kill us all."

The side panel slammed shut. Melko jammed the van into gear. Spitting from the rear tires, gravel showered holly shrubs and parked fenders. They were off down the cobblestones.

✳✳✳

"A bagged heart!" Uber Melko banged the wheel. "Like Brad Pitt in that movie, what the devil's the name...?"

"*Legend of The Fall*," Zina said. "A great flick. Real passion."

"He stole behind enemy lines. Killed the guy. Cut the heart out. As Sauer did in, what's that place...?"

"Nuristan province. Afghanistan. The border region with Pakistan. It was nighttime. Like now."

"Cheery thought, partner. Way to light up our mood."

At the end of the driveway, he crawled to a stop. When he veered right to enter the lane, a group of Simcoe demonstrators came into view. Not agitating and screaming chants, they sat companionably beneath a pineapple palm quietly munching slices of pizza. Green chopsticks a jiggle, a white apron cinched tight, the good doctor distributed pizza from a low table perched beneath another pineapple palm, the pair oddly reminiscent of hand grenades but with fronds. With each slice she also passed out water bottles bearing an all too familiar logo: Zonder Springs.

"Do you see *that*?" Alarmed, Zina buzzed the window. "I must warn them."

Melko held her back.

"Don't bother. It's not our battle."

"Whether it is or not," Ross said. "Their first amendment rights entitle them to an alternative message."

"You're trying to zing that Campesi fellow. Pay him back, what he's doing to you."

Ross sighed.

"Still, you just can't poison the messenger. We know their fate. We have a moral duty to speak up."

Zina turned back to pat his head.

"She might be serving real water, Dr. Danny-boy. Ever think of that? I have changed my mind. Drive on, sir. It is a long trip to Clearwater Beach. Hold on." She pointed to a lone figure at the fringe of the crowd. "What is Mr. Franklin doing here?"

"He received an invitation. My God. He drained that bottle in a single gulp."

"Another playboy in the making."

"Maybe even a Signet. A Big-Lie Zen Master down the block. Terrific."

"He might also become another Sauer who rips out hearts."

"Good to know," Melko said. "Hold on, folks. We'll make this fast."

He floored it sending Ross back across the crates. The van lurched left propelling him forward against the right hand metal door, then back across more crates as Melko killed another curve. Finally, the designated driver reached the main road and the ride smoothed out, the groaning vehicle pushing sixty through moonlit countryside.

"Sorry for the rough ride," Melko said.

"Why the big hurry?"

"My mood, Danny-boy. I'm irritated like hell with your pal Signet and his peremptory requests. He calls, at the last minute, to have me cater his friggin' party, also to bring Ms. Palaeologus here to assist with guests. Not that I mind taking a look-see now and then. Then later, I'm preparing crab cakes, mind you, he saunters into the barbecue pit and tells me to park in the shadows by the southern porch. Where, in twenty minutes give or take, I'm to pick you up for an emergency ride home. He never mentions this psychopathic assassin and nary a word about a trip to Clearwater Beach." He twisted around in the seat. "Do you have the faintest idea what this is all about?"

Ross paused debating how much to reveal. He really owed his friend something, After all, he did try to warn Ross. And, he was here now in the getaway car. So as not to incriminate his own bad luck, stupidity really, he jumped to the bottom line: Mr. Campesi's wrongful accusation about stolen documents, taking care to bypass the mermaid-aquarium dust up, his sponge dock encounter with charlatan FBI dudes, and revelations about the GENESIS projects.

The primary issue, the CEO's accusation. It was a killer.

"If I don't return what I don't have," he said. "This pompous, horse's ass will assume control of my special project."

"Did he not also threaten jail time?"

Thank you, Zina, for the helpful reminder. As helpful as pointing out the messed up triplets in the piano sonata.

He gave her a sideways look. "Thanks. Can't forget that."

"Can he actually seize control of Glaucon?"

Ross nodded.

"He already has."

"But the Zalin creep is imposter FBI. He has no power to arrest you."

"What's this about an imposter?" Melko said. "Masquerading as a federal law official is illegal. I don't get it."

Ross was compelled to cough up more details. Mr. Campesi, he said, had hired private security and decked them out as FBI to intimidate Ross into returning stolen material he knew Ross didn't possess. Moments ago, back at the mansion, these same FBI guys had tried beating fake information out of him. He was lucky Signet and Zina arrived in time to save him.

"That explains the big hurry. You're right. This Campesi is an ass."

"There's more. Signet claims Colonel Bame is my real worry. Because Campesi's goons screwed up, I'm positive he's enlisted this Sauer person to find and torture me. A few shattered teeth. Some broken bones. Whatever it takes. Sauer's an indiscriminate assassin who, in the famous words of our security chief, may well kill us all."

"Is Bame a real military *colonel*?"

"He flew in from Iraq earlier this week. He's convinced I stole incriminating documents, one of which incriminates Campesi. It clearly reveals he administered a vaccine to Zina and her grandfather that changed their personalities. Public disclosure could well derail the PTSD vaccine rollout."

"Why vaccinate them? What was he trying to achieve?"

"When I tell you, you'll say I'm crazy."

Melko snorted.

"Don't need a vaccine for that."

The idea was to destroy the amygdala, the part of the brain responsible for generating fear when its cells over reacted. The PTSD vaccine had been designed to return the cells to normal. Campesi's idea: eliminate the amygdala altogether to change behavior.

"So, let me understand this. Unless you return documents you did not steal, an assassin will kill you. Why didn't you tell me? Now it makes perfect sense." Melko shook his scraggly head. "I told you not to get mixed up like this, amigo. I hope you got a plan B. I sure do."

When they reached the intersection at East Lake Road, instead of turning left for the forty-minute excursion to Clearwater Beach, Melko went straight on Keystone Road. At the Route 19 intersection, instead of heading left to Clearwater, he continued straight for two lights then hooked a right, and stopped at his restaurant, the Bayou Bar and Grille on Dodecanese Boulevard. They exchanged the van for his Lexus sedan and resumed the trip.

"My Lexus will make better time."

As they did a U-turn, Zina scanned the milling crowd for Grandpa. Dozens of buzzing tourists mingled beneath the neon lights, but no reformed priest in sockless sandals.

"Probably inside," Melko said, maneuvering into traffic. "He found a girlfriend. A giggling cutie, all of fifty five. I should've mentioned this before. Don't worry. He's in expert hands. Literally."

He laughed, merriment confined to one.

"Is she clean?"

"As soap suds. They light up the downstairs bar. Hold on, guys. We'll be there in a jiffy."

✷✷✷

They backtracked the way they'd come. At East Lake, they turned right towards Clearwater. Once again, Melko pulled a detour his passengers didn't at first notice. Dozing off, they had settled in for the coffin-quiet luxury of padded seats and soft music. Zina detected the right hand turn and opened her eyes. She punched Ross awake and they both sat up. They were zipping down Lansbrook Parkway, the mega complex of subdivisions, home to both Ross and Melko.

She pointed to sprawling oaks lining the road right and left.

"This is not the way to Clearwater. Are we changing cars again?"

"Turn around," Ross said. "Dr. Azzizi expects us. Signet told him to wait up."

Melko glanced at his two companions.

"Sorry, folks. This is as far as I go."

"But, we must go. Signet claims we have to show up."

"Not me, Theodora. Did I get that right? I'm not following any more orders. This is end of the line."

"Then can I borrow your car?"

"This 450 Sedan?" Melko shook his head. "Sorry, 'ol buddy. I have to say no. It's Tarzan to your Mickey Mouse rust heap. Neither you nor it would be safe."

He pulled into his driveway and parked.

"Besides, this entire escapade is half-cocked. Dashing off merely on Signet's say-so? You might be driving into a trap. I'm talking about this new player suddenly in the picture. Where in hell did Sauer come from? As far as I'm concerned, Signet is a weasel. He's probably setting you up. He invited you to his damn hut. He invented the timeline. Why the devil would you listen to a thing he tells you?"

"How did you learn all that?"

"Tonight he told me in while I was cooking kebabs. Don't ask me why. I looked up and he was there. Something about bringing a friend into the picture. Anyway he said a timeline placed you at Dr. Braun's computer at the specified time. He said he helped assemble, not create, the damn thing. Also that you'd be questioned about it in the rear study. And, that Ms. Palaeologus would save you. But, as I said before, nothing about this Azzizzi fellow or your new pal, assassin Sauer."

It took a moment. The evening then came into sharp focus.

"I cannot believe you guys knew I'd wind up in the study."

"He said you would be treated with respect."

Zina squeezed his hand.

"He suggested you might experience trouble, but I would arrive in time to help. He promised me The Attack of Five. Yet, I only had time for one."

She paused, gaze shifting to the house. Ross followed her line of sight, to Melko's front door at the top of the steps and the open crack in the hinge which emitted a sliver of light knifing the darkness.

"You've been burgled, Mr. Melko." Zina, again pointing out the obvious.

They got out of the car and stared at the wrecked door of the dark timbered Tudor.

"What the hell. Why me?"

CHAPTER 28

Despite the aggrieved tone, Melko took the devastation in stride.

"Zalin's men," he said, calmly, ushering them into the damaged foyer. "Signet told me this might happen. He promised Arriva would cover the repairs. I regret calling him a weasel. I mean, what wild animal offers to repair the nest of another?"

"The 'weasel' *warned* you in advance?"

Arriva hadn't said anything about covering his home repair expenses. Of course, his Italian loafers and academy cufflinks were unscathed. Still, his roll top desk. The knock off Ming vase....

"Don't freak out. This damage is no big deal."

"But still...."

"This home invasion was no guarantee. Only, that if it happened, not to overreact. Signet had no way to recall the imposters."

Sergio and Bosco. Ross might have guessed.

They started to clean up. Feathers from slit pillows floated like snowflakes as they traversed the mess. Yet, both Melko and Zina moved about with a perplexing nonchalance, as if bored with torn silk cushions, shredded medical mystery novels and a shattered flat screen TV. The owner gave it all a blasé inspection. Neither the shattered Cloisonné Chinese vase nor torn Knotted Tabriz carpet fazed him. Prized knockoffs to be sure, but sentimental pieces lugged all the way from Belmont. Now gone.

"Doesn't this bother you?"

His friend shrugged. "I'll call The Hustling Cook, that novel nuisance store on Beacon Hill. They'll be glad to send replacements."

"Weren't they robbing you blind?"

The reference to Boston, returned the detective to a previous lifetime, lit a fresh sparkle in his eye. Ross felt the same jolt, riding a similar wavelength as memories surfaced of a happier, saner, existence.

"Do you remember that July afternoon at Fenway?"

"The time I squirted mustard over that woman with the large tattoo?"

Ross smiled at the scene.

"Yeah. The mustard shot three rows down in front. Boy, was she surprised."

"And pissed. She called an usher. No one gave us up. How

was I to know those packets were under pressure?"

"Like the pressure of two beer-soaked fingers?"

They laughed, immersed in the mustard-splattered tattoo of entwined hearts.

"What about the foul ball that nearly capped you?"

"No. That was later. The day Big Papi hit the three bagger. Totally capsized The Yankees."

"Speaking of capsize." Melko said, half bent over with laughter. "How about that time we copped a sunfish and sailed in the basin. Man, what a moment, except for that lanky dude out of Cambridge Boat Club. What was his name?"

"McIntyre. Two miles downriver, claimed he was off course, the reason he almost clipped us."

"Off course from his austere wife. Recall, I introduced you three at The Head Of The Charles Regatta."

"Oh yeah. That was a good one. Almost as great as our messy tomato fight at Lidia's Cabbage and Carrot farm."

Their bout of nostalgia proved tiresome to Zina. During the sunfish story, a pair of too audible yawns accompanied her journey to the rear window. There, she made the most of a view that Ross, from all the evening dinners, knew too well.

If she looked close, she might pick out from the inky blackness the twin algae pools separating Melko's Tudor from the lake. The full moon should help, he mused, still chortling with his friend as they continued to reminisce. Her mind lay elsewhere though, swatting imaginary bugs, sighing with displeasure, all the while casting the men pleading glances to terminate the discussion.

Ross caught the whole act. One eye on Melko, the other on the bedazzling silhouette in the picture window.

Finally, she confronted the merriment within the sea of feathers.

"I listen to your chatter. The monster you speak of at Fenway, sailboats in the river, even the museum gift store where you, Danny-boy, found Patriot neckties. But this is no time for memories. Signet has brought us together. To survive, we must figure out why to avoid more tricks."

For emphasis, she booted a pile of trash across the floor.

"We were talking baseball. Big Papi, the famous Red Sox slugger, now retired. The Red Sox are a big deal."

Melko's voice faltered as she reigned them in.

"Sauer," Ross said. "A 'trick' waiting on the horizon."

"Possibly closer. We have no way of knowing where he's at."

"Exactly. But, why unleash this terror at all? Mr. Campesi's concern for stolen documents is phony. We know that. By this time you could have already sent them to this Ravi Ravda fellow, or to anyone else. It is puzzling he wants them back."

The scrape of wood across the kitchen floor ended the

discussion. A familiar voice then boomed out of the shadows.

"Not Campesi, my dear. It is Colonel Bame who wants the documents returned."

And there he was. In battlefield regalia, camouflage pullover to lace up boots, Colonel Signet stepped into the wrecked room. His bleak ensemble soon became sprinkled by a swirl of feathers his feet kicked up. A comical black and white apparition yet his unexpected appearance alarmed Ross. Eavesdropping and unannounced, the man was not supposed to be there.

Again, he sniffed pre-planning. Like the sudden arrival of Zalin at the sponge dock. Trouble when least expected at your doorstep.

"Do you wonder how I found you?"

After maneuvering around debris, he chose an unsliced cushion, and alighted upon the couch.

"You came for the Lexus, an anticipated move, particularly after a phone call to your restaurant revealed the vehicle to be missing. You simply traded in the van. Not a surprise decision for a gentleman of your discretion." He retrieved a shard of pottery from the torn Tabriz. Read the inscription. "'Made in Mexico'. The Zalin dolts said they 'whacked' an original Ming vase. Wouldn't they be surprised? Wise to buy a fake. Unwise, to return home. An unanticipated detour that may invite sudden turmoil any second."

Ross was right to be suspicious. Trouble indeed lay around the corner.

Snapping to attention, stating absurdly he was the nominal host of this ad hoc assembly, Melko nudged past his cracked Noguchi table, another Boston relic, and asked if any might accept a goblet of wine. Though not a vintage offering, at eighteen ninety-nine a liter, the Boutari Nemea was an irresistible acquisition. He went to the front closet and removed the bottle from its Zalin-proof niche.

"A sumptuous Greek red," he said, uncorking the Boutari. "It offers a delightful, lasting finish."

Signet waved him off.

"Not for me," he said. "Not for any of you. You must all depart for Dr. Azzizzi at once."

"To avoid this turmoil you refer to?"

"Your distrust is accepted. What is the expression? The genie of suspicion, once free of the bottle, is difficult to return."

"You might assist the genie, though. Assemble this puzzle for us. I'll list the pieces you've created."

"Sarcasm is unappealing, doctor. We should now leave this house. I suggest allegretto. A very fast exit."

"First, there's me, a neurotic, easily led physician. Who, as a pretend thief, almost became a dead man thanks to you. Next, we have Zina, or Theodora, a lovely and mysterious, strong willed woman as intoxicating as her exotic scent, but involved in a secret mission that, for some inexplicable reason, concerns me. Then, friend Melko, a retired, portly detective, entrusted with tidbits of information Mr. Security feels fit, on occasion, to divulge. And, we must not forget mean spirited Mr. Campesi, irate CEO of Arriva, anxious to co-opt my project and, again for unclear reasons, ruin my career. Lastly, I can't forget our mentally rearranged priest or, or for that matter, my pal, Gamel Azzizzi. Have I got them all? Oh yeah. Sauer...."

Signet greeted his recital with a troubling nonresponse.

"*Portly* Daniel? That's hardly fair. I use a treadmill. I lift weights."

"You think me 'lovely' and mysterious?" Zina's face turned crimson. "I complement you as well, my emperor. I am pleased you approve of Shade of Night, my new perfume."

"Okay, maybe I got carried away. I did not mean to offend or embarrass either one of you."

"Tonight, think of me as Empress Theodora."

"I will, but don't be distracted. I'm merely laying out pieces of the puzzle Signet created but has yet to assemble."

"There is one item you omitted," Signet said, rising from the couch. "Eritrea, the key to this 'puzzle' you refer to. It's assembly I shall postpone to a future opportunity. There is a reason I now intercept you here at Mr. Melko's. You, Dr. Ross, are poised at the beginning of a race against time. A race you must finish by tomorrow morning, promptly at ten o'clock in Odessa, where you will present the stolen documents to your chief executive. If you fail to make the deadline, your lives will be at stake."

After a quick glance at his watch, he launched a hurried explanation about Colonel Bame, the impetus behind Ross's race against time. As current commander of Special Operations Afghanistan and Iraq, he had been assigned the task of retrieving hostages seized by Rawdadi Fazuki, the leader of Houthi insurgents in Yemen, and smuggled across the straits of Bab el Mandeb to Eritrea. Unfortunately, the colonel developed cold feet and cancelled the rescue.

"This is now *your* problem, Doctor. Solve it and both Glaucon and that Infirmary portrait will be yours."

Eritrea? Not again. And, why bring up his quest for a portrait at this exact moment?

"This is not my problem." Ross said. "It's a military matter. Why am I mixed up in any of this?" He paced, tripped on the torn carpet, got his bearings, his thoughts straight. "Please explain how this Rawdadi person relates to Newsome's murder at Eckerd Hall. That's what got this crazy ball rolling. While you're at it, tell me how my almost murder relates to my almost theft and Colonel Bame."

"Your 'almost murder' made you the solution to other problems." Signet almost sighed. A rehearsed, unnatural emotional display. "Later, when there is time, I will fill in the gaps. For now, it is imperative the colonel change his mind. Only you can do it for him."

"How can I do that? He's a hardened soldier. I'm only a doctor."

Without providing an explanation, Signet hurried on and

briefly outlined the nature of the Yemen civil war, a proxy skirmish the United States did not wish to join.

"That is why the intended rescue operation must remain secret. If Campesi's illicit inoculation project is exposed, the operation will never fly. The Joint Chiefs would crush it. The PTSD project may stall as well. Worse, the colonel will lose a promotion to the Joint Chiefs, a position he's desired for years and now, like your infirmary portrait, almost within grasp. In my opinion, the imagined loss of this huge promotion is his biggest fear. It is that which you must change."

"His fear? But, how...."

"Bame also worries about the media. What if they learn about this Sauer person?"

Signet nodded then consulted his Luminox wristwatch.

"Correct, Theodora. A perilous situation because of Sauer. That brings me to the final segment to tell you."

Like Signet, a product of an Army Ranger background, the SEALS and counterintelligence work, Sauer volunteered for the colonel's nostril inoculation program. Except, and the most critical part, his preliminary MRI revealed a different picture from the other soldiers.

"From birth, his brain lacked a fiber pathway called the uncus fasciculus. In normal people, this pathway connects the emotional brain with critical parts of the central nervous system. Stranded, Sauer's emotions have been rendered useless. If he really ever had them to begin with."

They functioned in complete isolation from the man's coldly calculating frontal lobes. Untouched by controlling emotions, these frontal areas always operated at full tilt. The result: a man with a total lack of conscience and an appetite for violence.

"His MRI was that of most psychopaths. It explained his lifelong, ruthless behavior."

Without an amygdala, Signet continued, only anger is disconnected. Minus this special fasciculus, remorse and guilt never occupy the man's behavior. After Bame's inoculation, this ordinary psychopath became a psychopathic elite *assassin*, enabled to perform whatever atrocities Bame cooked up for him.

"Should Mr. Campesi inadvertently inoculate a citizen, for example an outwardly normal functioning psychopath without this uncus fasciculus, and let me tell you there are lots of those in society, well, the risk is too much to accept. Therefore, Dr. Ross, by returning the purloined documents, you will eliminate this distraction for Colonel Bame and get the Eritrea mission back on track."

"The documents, not Campesi, are the *distraction*? Why not simply stop the CEO and his damn project? And, while you're at it, lock up this maniac assassin."

"Such an outcome will also depend upon you."

"I get it. When I do the right thing."

"He is correct about the nasty CEO," Zina said. "You must stop what he is doing. Like Justinian, I also wonder why this man Sauer goes free."

"He is not easy to corral. Besides, we, I depend upon him. In fact, the entire Eritrea mission depends upon a squad of such men." Signet turned to the kitchen. "All this talking, I am parched. Thirsty anyone?"

He left the room. The fridge door banged open and shut. After a clatter of metallic popping he returned with a tray of opened soda cans.

"We owe this refreshment to Mr. Melko. A note of caution, though. The fluid is caffeinated. You will require energy for the trip."

"What trip?"

"To friend Gamel. Where else?"

"Why do I have to disturb a retina surgeon in the dead of night?"

"That will soon become apparent." Signet again checked his Luminox. "It is early. Only nine thirty. Also, his family is in Miami. Drink up. We are all together on this.'"

A car door slammed shut up the block. A low thud, clearly audible. They stopped drinking the sparkling soda, looking to Signet for instruction.

"He is here," he said. "Allegretto is now prestissimo. Move very fast. Outside. All of you."

CHAPTER 29

Taking care to avoid debris, Signet led them through the kitchen and out the door to the screened-in patio. Herded into a tight group, they stood by the pool, engulfed once more by musky scents from another patch of wild preserve. Nose to the breeze, Signet again sampled the night air.

"Anything?" Ross whispered.

Signet raised a hand, listening hard. Then, finger to his lips, he silently unlatched the patio door and ushered them to the asphalt walkway. Encircling the two algae infested pools, the walkway wound a path through the shadows, ending fifty yards away at the dock bordering the lake.

Zina's squeezed Ross's hand.

"This does not feel good."

"I know," he said, fresh perspiration on his brow. "Watch Signet. He'll know what to do."

"Think so?" Melko barked. "If we're talking Sauer here, I'm unconvinced."

"For God's sake, keep your voice down."

"Okay, okay. I'm just saying this is a bit melodramatic."

Still, he joined the tight huddle, each humbled by the sheer weight of the unknown, by the heavy clunk of a slammed car door resonating in their ears.

The odd part, despite the gravity of their situation, the October evening felt perfect. A balmy breeze, Lake Tarpon shimmering under the stars, the moon on the far horizon. Yet, a dark and malevolent force lurked nearby, a psychopathic evil, if they were to believe Signet, hovering in the same breeze that their fearless leader continued to explore for alien scents and sounds, scanning shadows right and left but definitely on edge.

Not a good sign, Ross thought as he watched him closely.

"To the dock," Signet whispered. "You will find a tethered boat, fuel tank full to reach the northern shore. Hurry."

With a hand planted against the small of Ross's back, he pushed hard. Huddling together, the others started to follow him down the path.

"Why take a boat?" he asked, "We'll make a better escape in Melko's Lexus."

"Bad idea. Sauer parked in front of the house. We cannot risk an encounter."

"Why run at all?" Zina dropped to a familiar crouch. "We

are both skilled Krav Maga warriors. I say we take this man together."

"You are a beginner. What you know of Krav Maga will not help you. I trained this person. I will handle him. Go with Dr. Ross. He needs you more."

"Do you have the Seal Pup knife? That would even odds. There is no shame to slice his neck. Better yet, to remove his ears."

"Zina! This is so unlike you."

"A knife is unnecessary." Signet refocused on the shadows directly behind them. "I can take care of Sauer myself."

"With your bare hands? Two against one is always better. I will stay and fight."

"Listen to the man. We have to go."

"I have done this sort of thing before, my emperor. Four boys into the bayou. Don't you remember?"

Their steadfast commander put an end to the chit chat. He grasped obstreperous Theodora by the shoulders.

"Have you read Chapter 15, 'Superior Odds Against a Foe'?" he asked. "I thought not. Here, together, we remain the foe. Your safety will preoccupy me. I prefer you go with Dr. Ross and his friend."

While they dithered, Melko drew Ross aside.

"Did you see what was in the sink?" he asked.

"What sink?"

He could scarcely focus. They should be leaving. According to Signet, they were in jeopardy. And, all this talk about cutting a throat? Zina's crazy attitude. That damn Nika Rebellion. That's how she imbibed these violent notions. Maybe she should get an MRI, look for here uncus fasciculus. Empress Theodora took charge and had her generals decapitate rioting citizens. But that was then. Now, tonight, here she was no match against the likes of Sauer.

"Back in the kitchen. Did you see the empty soda cans?"

"Soda cans? No. I was too busy avoiding broken glass."

"Tell me you didn't swallow...."

A loud noise erupted from the side yard.

"Holy crap," Melko said, pointing. "Do you see *that*?"

Silhouetted against the faded light, a figure rose from a row of shrubs adjoining the house. First the head and shoulders, then the elongated block of a torso sprouted upward, inch by inch, until it loomed as a dark and hovering statue amongst the shadows.

Not a statue but a hungry raptor from the Pleistocene. What began as a swell of dread soon transformed into a tsunami of paralyzing fear. Ross's imagination went ballistic. He visualized a feeding monster on a return trip to the nest.

Eat up, little babies. There is more where this came from.

Either perspiration or another sort of dribble moistened his trousers.

"Holy crap," Melko said. "This thing can't be real."

The 'thing' came to life. Effortlessly, first one limb then the other elevated to full height before the whole creature lifted from its perch, jumping with eerie grace to alight with a soft thump on the walkway beside them, a flight of ten, perhaps fifteen feet. It brushed against a much smaller Signet who, true to Zen form, leaned aside to let him pass. He did not flinch.

"It is you, after all."

"Who'd you expect, Siggy baby? Momma Chaneuill?"

Exactly as Signet explained: mother and son.

Ross had seen enough.

Seizing hold of Zina's hand, he shoved Melko further down the asphalt. A boat already at the dock? He was YMCA fit. He would sprint for it.

"Stop!" Signet called out to them. "That is not a log in the path ahead."

Ross had not given the elongated obstacle a moment's thought. He'd been prepared to hurtle it but Signet got there first. With a sudden kick, he prodded a hissing alligator to life. Having crept in from either lake or preserve, it was looking for dinner and dessert.

In a blur of motion, Sauer rushed forward. Straddling the beast from behind, he bear-hugged the belly. Like a hammer toss in track and field, he spun twice and tossed the creature into the swamp where it slashed through the undergrowth and disappeared.

"Holy crap!" Melko said. "Did you see *that*?"

"Get your portly butt moving. We can't stay here."

"Hey, Siggy," Sauer said, "It's time we settled up."

"In a minute," Signet said, calmly. "You three have to leave. Trust me. It is not safe. Super prestissimo. Move!"

As they half-ran, half-stumbled to the dock, each glanced back to follow the bizarre standoff fast fading in the enveloping twilight. Signet and his giant opponent circled one another, snippets of their voices carrying on the wind.

"...promised ... not ... to kill..."

"...gone ... can't see..."

"...do ... with the heart..."

"...which ... one...."

A touching reunion between wartime buddies. Sliced body parts. Broken promises. Friends catching up.

At one point Sauer stopped the endless circling to stare over Mr. Zen, a half-foot shorter, a third again as wide, to examine the escaping threesome. An unhurried look as they clambered up the steps to the dock. Ross caught the head nod, a movement of acceptance, apparently satisfied with the progress of those desperate to get away. Then, he poked his diminutive adversary in the belly and commenced sparring. Words, not so good-hearted slapping, the man's hand a baseball mitt to Signet's gnarled paw.

Hustling now, they stumbled down the narrow planks leading out over the water. Ross stayed behind to help his puffing friend as Zina rushed on ahead. As she had done on the sponge docks, she leaped into the void, heedless of any danger.

Instead of a splash, Ross caught a muffled thump then, seconds later, yelps of frustration. Yelps that propelled them faster down the planks to Zina, struggling with the motor of a small chipped and flaking outboard bobbing a yard below them in the water.

What was *this?*

Anticipation concocted a different vessel. A large, aesthetic craft with padded seats, tapered bow, even a minibar, not this tiny, ill-begotten termite of a contraption. A single, rusted outboard with hardened arteries, three horizontal, arthritic seat planks and stale lake water, like so much abdominal drainage fluid, sloshing over the floorboards. Additional worries lurked within the sea grass along the shoreline. Cousins of Sauer's hammer toss but impossible to see. Mobile homes across the lake provided limited visibility as did the moon behind high clouds. The water black as Ross's unfiltered mood.

This was their escape?

He jumped in then edged Melko over the side. They sat together in a dangerously low, sagging seat that, in absorbing extra weight, groaned in pain.

Zina finally got the hang of it, and the Miocene motor sputtered to life. She guided the craft around to the front of the dock. Standing in the swaying craft, they peeked above the planks in search of Signet.

Zina gasped. He saw it, too. Sauer had managed to secure his prey in the familiar belly grip.

"If only he brought the serrated blade," she cried. "My God. He just flung Signet into the swamp. The psycho now looks our way. Oh, no. He is running directly at us. We have to get out of here."

It was painful to process. Signet gone, maniacal Sauer covering the distance like a greyhound. He'd be upon them in seconds.

Zina hit the throttle. The damn thing died.

"What happened?"

"Quiet!" She kicked the engine. Slammed it twice. "I am working on it."

She hit the starter button another time. The motor turned over. She then swiveled the craft about and aimed for deeper water. Behind them the sound of cracking planks got closer. Just in time, their miserable boat found a higher gear, chugging out of reach as the psychopath launched a giant, McDonald's arc of a lunging dive directly at them.

Thankfully, the boat responded to full throttle, Sauer's grasping fingers missing by inches. The man vanished beneath the surging wake, his thrusting leap an incredible trampoline bounce off the edge of the dock. A seemingly inhuman power surge, as inhuman as his sizzling eyes that, for a microsecond, devoured Ross before disappearing, along with his whooshing, huge claw hands, beneath the waves.

The creature, swallowed by the lake, left them shaken. Ross fell back against Melko while Zina slapped the gasping motor, cried out "attagirl", and headed for the middle of roiling Lake Tarpon.

Ross finally came to his senses.

"Did you see that? He nearly landed on top of me."

"But he did not," Zina said, then whacked him as well. "Thanks to Theodora, empress saved her emperor again."

"Hey, why hit me?"

"That guy is enormous. Holy effing mama."

"Calm yourself, Mr. Melko." Zina now yelled to be heard in the whistling wind. "We are safe. Mr. Sauer cannot catch us."

Nor could Mr. Security, Ross thought. So difficult to imagine. Signet, no longer able to save them, to adjust his scrip to account for this superseding glitch of a monster set loose either to help Ross locate what he did not take or to silence him. And, permanently, the latter the more likely explanation. But, a pointless act if Colonel Bame was truly interested recovering....

He stopped. He was driving himself nuts with fear. Tons of it.

Extending distance from the assassin, their new captain weaved and wobbled over the slimy lake. In time, she cut back on the throttle, their general direction north, towards an unknown destination determined by their former captain before being hurled, like a sack of rubbish, into the muck. He had looked so pitiful spinning out of Sauer's grip, doing a helicopter nosedive, a terrible loss. Lost also was Glaucon. Without the security man's help, Ross would never clear his name now.

Puffing, quietly retching, his buddy lurched against him.

"I don't feel so hot. Motion sickness. Forgot my suppositories."

Ross exchanged seats, leaving Melko room to heave over the gunwale. Inches above the water, he conquered the urge though. He sat back, gulping the night air.

"A close one. I'm better now. How much longer, Zina?"

She indicated a large house far to their right.

"Myrtle Point," she said. "Neighborhood of snobs. Halfway. Not long now."

"How do you know Myrtle Point?"

"Signet. How else?"

Sense of loss migrated to annoyance. Why was it always *him*? Even with his demise, the man continued to intervene from the grave, or from the swampy filth of snakes and gators. A twinge of guilt then intruded. He tried to think better of Signet, of his hatchet chin and all-knowing, mirror-neuron gaze. To give the trickster some slack.

He gave but not much.

"For someone always brimming with ideas," he said. "Mr. Krav Maga, I-trained-him-myself, didn't have a chance with Sauer."

"Such a smartass, my emperor. Show more compassion. It is not every day royalty loses its most treasured general."

He ignored the reprimand but not the young woman herself. Catching him by surprise, as if annexed to an unexpected force field, his energy seemed to unite with the twisting torso working the engine. His spirit, practically snuffed moments earlier by sea monster Sauer, now rekindled to life, fusing him with this luminous silhouette in the night.

Zina.

How do I love thee? Let me count the ways. To the depth and breadth and—

No. No. Not yet anyway. Too extreme. Yet, what the blazes was going on?

In the floating darkness, in the middle of this vast ocean of waves and seagrass and beer can flotsam he, for an instant, felt becalmed beneath the soft moon, immersed in his own ocean of seething urges and emotions. His cingulate cortex quickly became overloaded unable, for that same instant, to process intersecting highways of nerve impulses flooding his sensate mind.

He shut his eyes. Waited in trembling expectation for the moment to pass.

A seizure, he wondered. Saul on the way to Damascus. A bright light?

No. No. Nothing of the kind. Like love itself, another perilous journey.

Where had his befuddled brain wandered?

He sensed the boat caressing them both, pushing them together. What, he speculated, would her limbs feel like wrapped around his own?

Such overactive imagination. Such confusion. On the other hand, what else should he expect? Faced with Signet's ignominious death, then Sauer's coffin-ready grin? And, Zina. His fate's answer to refuge and release? All of this but new cobwebs sprouting amongst his sulci. Like gravel in the carburetor, screwing everything up.

"You are aggrieved," she said. "You make funny faces. Signet said to expect this. He also said you must look deeper. The answer lies within. Or, somewhere. I was never certain. He enjoyed being vague, I think."

Ross found an ounce of reserve, the sound coming out of his throat more croak than laugh.

"Zen instruction from the swamp?" He said. "I sure hope The Master explained how we escape this mess."

Zina batted at the air, pretending not to hear. "Say again."

"Never mind," he said. "Later."

"*Gator*? We left that one behind."

The same unbidden thought arose. That they were pursuing a script after all. The brief battle with Sauer. The waiting boat. This improbable escape. On the other hand, the assassin's dive and near collision seemed awfully real to him.

He leaned forward to speak directly into Zina's ear.

"It's a much shorter distance to go straight across the lake."

Her lip twitched.

"He said the reason we head north will be clear once we arrive."

"You know an empress should not deceive her emperor."

"I do not deceive. Well, perhaps at times. Quiet now. I am navigating."

It was pointless to press her. Even if gasping a final breath, Signet still pulled all the strings. Yet, maybe he wasn't gasping at all. Chortling more like it. As a former SEAL, survival instincts could easily prevail. They might not have seen the last of Corporal Signet.

Pursuing a path to the north shore, the outboard now chugged along at half-speed. They were alone on the water, the only sound, other than the burbling motor, the constant splashing against the hull. That, and Melko's hurried whisper.

"I have to explain about those cans of soda," he said, edging closer on the narrow seat.

"What cans?"

"The ones Signet brought out of the kitchen. They were never there to begin with."

Ross turned away from the black and empty lake.

"I don't get it."

"He left the empties in the sink. The same place he put the empty water bottles. Think empty Zonder Springs water bottles. Ring any bells?"

It required a moment but the bells eventually sounded. He recalled Signet's sliced water bottle on the dock, Zina's and her grandpa's secret inoculation and Dr. Braun handing out similar bottles in Odessa. And now Signet's cola fizzing up and down the inside of his nostrils.

"He wouldn't do that. Not to *me*. Don't I have enough problems?"

Yet, Signet had indeed inoculated him. The fizzy virus concoction was already inside his brain, wreaking changes to his feelings, items always so neatly tucked away, like inside neuron rescue potions or underneath a photon activating energy system. Out of sight. Hidden. It accounted for the sudden bewildering rush of emotions, the sense he was out of control. Dear God. He almost seized hold of Zina's long, tanned, and very naked legs.

The virus. Eating away at him.

A mysterious pressure began to build at the base of his nose, setting loose a shock of anxiety and outrage. He actually felt the nano-creatures creeping through his skull to the olfactory nerve, an open conduit that led directly from nose to amygdala inside his brain. There was no way to stop them.

"He inoculated *me*?"

The sound of his distress reached Zina. She eased off the throttle and took a seat forward of the two men.

"Why do you rub your nose? What is wrong with it?"

"Accept the possibility, amigo. He snuck in through the kitchen. You keep wine and cashews in the fridge. I keep wine and veggies. No soda cans. Never."

"How can you take this so calmly?"

"I didn't drink the soda. I only tipped the can."

"You're saying I was *poisoned*?"

"*Inoculated*. Your Mr. Signet pointed out the difference. I tried to get your attention, to warn you."

"Will one of you explain this tipping business?"

"Mr. Signet put the vaccine into the soda he served us. Daniel swallowed a huge dose."

"Is that all?" Zina laughed. "I imagined a heart attack or worse. For a doctor, you make a big fuss over very little."

He massaged his temples, the area overlying the location of the amygdalae nuclei deep within.

"What should I expect? Will it hurt? Will I have a fever or terrible headaches?"

At that moment, another pair of hands lay claim to his aching head. Like a giant serpent exploding from the lake, Sauer shot above the gunwale, grabbed Ross and lifted him up and out of the boat and into the water. After issuing a command to take a full breath, he dragged Ross down to the bottom of the lake where his kicking feet failed to find purchase amidst the soft and insubstantial silt. At that spot in the shallow lake, the distance from the surface no more than eight feet.

He started to panic.

Visibility zero. Sauer had him in a neck lock, impossible to break, his arms like steel cables, dead weight. Ross was trapped, flailing limbs useless. He felt the chill of death, the icy certainty he was about to drown.

At the last possible moment, Sauer dragged him to the surface. Once there, the huge man continued to hold him under, prolonging the agony, keeping his nose inches from fresh air. He gurgled amusement as Ross, in a final effort, frantically tried to break free. When his arms finally went slack, the serpent relaxed his grip and yanked his gasping head above water. With a crackle of mirth, the guy slapped his face, three times until he began to suck in air.

"Strike three, Doc," he said. "You're out. Not your ball game anymore."

"…whaaa.…"

He fought the fire burning inside his chest. The need for air to breathe.

"Relax. Save your strength. I'll swim you home."

When Sauer refastened the neck lock, he resisted with a feeble gesture that earned him more scorn, more submerged, sadistic torture.

"No ... not again ... please...."

Instead of keeping him under, Sauer assumed a lifeguard's position. With one hand under his chin, titanium arm taut, the lifeguard churned up lake. Between strokes, Ross caught more chuckles, the guy having sport of it, out for a bit of fun.

Without warning, a frightening sensation swept back behind his nose. A superficial itch that intensified. Then it began to move, burrowing deeper and deeper until he could feel it wriggle about within the confines of his defenseless amygdalae nuclei. Each of them now sending out rays of blowtorch heat, twin pinpoints that burst into a fireworks display of sharp and painful colors, a magnificent cascade of swirling rainbows that became a high voltage electric spark terminating as abruptly as the episode began.

He tried to grasp his head but the lifeguard held on tight.

My dear brain, what is happening to you?

His first suspicion, after jumbled thoughts realigned, turned to an absorbed lake toxin, so much water going through his gills. But, he discarded this reason aware the sudden nose-to-brain experience had a more plausible explanation.

Signet's vaccine spiked soda.

The latency period was right. The exposure took place an hour earlier, enough time for altered, tiny viral beasts to dine upon his amygdalae. Then, these malfunctioning neurons dispersed currents of messed up brain signals to the cingulate, frontal and, yes, his limbic female hungry cortices, cortex unused to being thrown into what he dearly hoped was temporary disarray.

Cognitive abilities seemed intact. He remained fully conscious. Oriented times four. No fever or apparent encephalitis. No doubt now. He was still alive, spitting water, saved by Sauer, at least for the time being.

The lifeguard stopped his crawl. Holding Ross on extended arms, he sloshed a low voice into his water logged eardrums.

"Catch your breath. Kick your legs. You are on your own."

"…got it…."

He began to kick and tread water, he the minnow to Sauer's shark, the assassin barely moving to remain afloat.

"We almost there yet?" Ross wiped debris off his lips. "Last time we meet like this."

Sauer chuckled.

"Signet said you were humorless. Not the first time satori Zen made a mistake."

"Was that before or after you tossed him to the gator?"

"Do you watch baseball?"

The question surprised him. It was the darkest night. Alone in the middle of Lake Tarpon, the shore beyond reach and Sauer was asking about *baseball*?

"Well, sure. The Rays are local. Better talent this year. Rumor has it, going to trade their third baseman." He coughed, snared by the nutty conversation. "Price is with the Red Sox. Archer on the auction block. I mean, that's newspaper talk."

He gulped an accidental mouthful. Spat it out. Started coughing.

"Boston is in town tonight," Sauer remarked. "Ortiz retired. One of the greats."

Ross was getting cold and dizzy. Still, he persisted, curious about the bad guy.

"The Sox are still great. I, I'd like to see tonight's game at Tropicana."

Sauer lifted him out of the water with one of his steel cables.

"You know the concept of closer?"

"...sure ... end of the game ... to finish off the opponent...."

"Think of me as closer. Colonel Bame's *dark* closer. Remember that one fact and you won't sample any more silt under scratching toe nails."

He dropped Ross. They treaded water.

"Closer? I don't understand."

"Return the lifted documents tomorrow morning, ten o'clock sharp, at Campesi's home in Odessa, and I disappear."

"I do not have any...."

Sauer swatted water into his mouth.

"No excuses. Only you can make this happen. Think hard, Doctor. *Dark closer.* It won't be pretty."

He spun Ross around. Fifty yards away, the dingy outboard bobbed amidst the waves. Melko and Zina stood at the bow, snippets of an argument carried on the chilly wind.

"One day, Doc. That is all you have."

The man sank beneath the surface and, after a burst of bubbles, it was the last Ross saw of him.

CHAPTER 30

Moments later, Melko and Zina hauled his dripping carcass over the side of boat. He accepted Melko's shirt to dry off and warm up.

"My God, Justinian. You are freezing. Tell us what happened out there."

After he concluded the story, they puttered on, each digesting the import of his strange adventure. Head zinging, emotions muddled, he settled in above the slippery floorboards. Even in this remote, inaccessible location, he was not safe. So hard to accept the guy found them.

And what sort of name was *Sauer* anyway?

A *sour* nine-month pregnancy and labor, perhaps with a mother, the now nearly blind Mrs. Ascot Chaneuill, with a sense of humor? And, afterwards came what was certain to have been a rocky, mischief strewn adolescence, the psychopathia, at last obvious. Sauer fit. A perfect name.

Then, came his encounter with two bad actors: the obdurate Colonel Bame, and the incorrigible Arturo

Campesi, both responsible for turning him into an intense and very convincing assassin. The spinning, splashing Mr. Security-Zen-master-Signet made it believable. Inconceivable the man managed to follow them up lake to emerge from the hellish water to snatch Ross out of the damn boat. But, he had done just that. Swoosh. Up in the air. Into the lake.

He now considered Zina's role in this lunacy. His prior admiration of the spirited cuckoo had also undergone a metamorphosis. Suspicion and disbelief, the result. But, as she reached back to give his damp leg a healthy squeeze, trains of excited sparks tickled his limbic zone informing him attraction still ruled the realm.

"Poor, Justinian. General Belisarius said you did not swim."

The general. Goddamn. Here we go again.

"Are we referring to Signet?'

"Did I make that mistake again? Sorry."

With that, she bore down harder at the helm.

Yet, the real kicker, what now stoked what was left of his amygdala anger engine, what provoked Bame's interest in this entire matter: Eritrea, a back-of-the-moon desert of despair and desolation. Thanks to a crazed terrorist, that country was now home to hostages wafted out of a collapsing, bomb demolished embassy in Sana'a, Yemen to Wadi-Daba's—whatever the bozo's actual name—quarters in Abbas, across the shark-infested waters of Bab-el-Mandeb.

Simply off Ross's map of comprehension.

For him, however, one additional hostage existed: Glaucon, his revolutionary cure of glaucoma, a preventable form of blindness afflicting millions worldwide. Serving as connecting thread to the drama, this pet project had been snatched from his hands by Campesi, who once actually called it a fantastic notion. But, to its inventor, the gizmo represented a path to a celebratory and immortalizing oil-on-canvas, Ross the deluded prince of double tube, photon activated perfection.

A dumb, naïve and, if Sauer had his way, doomed doobie soon to be closed out darkly, whatever that precisely meant.

Still trembling from his tortuous swim, he peered out into utter darkness. At the waves slapping the sides of their sputtering craft, at the human refuse idly bumping the bow at their passage. Where, he miserably pondered, were they really headed?

"Hey, Danny boy," Melko said, sitting beside him. "Cheer up. By the time we reach shore, you'll be bone dry."

"I'll keep that in mind. Are we close, yet?" he added, directing the query to their engine slapping boss. "I'm shivering my butt back here."

"So rude. Justinian never spoke to his empress that way."

"How do you know? Or, is it written in one of your uncle's Byzantium history books? Never mind. Forget it. When do we arrive?"

"More sarcasm. *You* never mind and forget it. But, now that you ask, ten minutes. Tops. Maybe sooner. I'll add speed." She hit the throttle. The bow poked above the water. "There. A cigar boat. Laugh, my emperor. Why so glum?"

"I thought Signet planned a safe escape. Instead, Sauer nearly killed me."

She shrugged, a voluptuous movement visible in the approaching shoreline.

"He only said the bad guy would present no problem."

"When did he tell you that, dearest empress?"

"Okay, you two. Enough. I'm motion sick again. Why so damn fast?"

"Because I am leaving that man far behind. He remained submerged for a mile. How did he do this? How did he find us?"

Ross had no immediate reply. He tightened his arms about the abdomen. He was cold, damp, his Italian loafers ruined. He should never have worn them to that awful party.

"I have no idea," he said, "but unless I produce those files he'll close me out."

"You said this 'closer' business came from baseball. Why a closer if the game is already won?"

"The game is not already won," Melko said. "Far from it. You see, a closer is a pitcher called in to finish the job. I admit I'm Boston all the way, but I found Mariano Rivera's retirement a heartbreak."

He sighed, fortunately not a sound of imminent retch.

"Baseball's greatest closer. That sinking slider? Unbeatable. Too bad he was a Yankee."

"Boston has Kembrel. Fast ball, a hundred miles per."

"Right." Melko sighed again. "The starched turkey on the mound."

Several minutes later, Zina jerked the craft to port, lining it up against a crumbling dock. As she coasted to a stop, Ross confronted an alternative scenario to the assassin's directive.

Why show up in Odessa at all?

His clothes were soaked, shoes and party clothes ruined, his body contaminated by filthy lake water. Yet, despite this discomfort and just maybe because the vaccine was actually taking hold, he considered jettisoning Arriva, Inc. altogether. Colleagues in either North Carolina or New York would welcome Glaucon with open arms.

A cure for glaucoma, Daniel? How much lab space do you require? Grant money? Name your price.

But, despite the appeal, the beckoning of a completely different avenue to, admittedly somewhat fanciful, immortality achieved, this burst of energy fell flat. Reality squashed the ridiculous notion as quickly as it arose. He wasn't thinking clearly, cognitive functions affected after all. His outlandish idea the result of chaos in rearranged synaptic networks in his vaccine treated brain.

Damn that fizzy cola.

And, damn Mr. Zen for flying into the swamp and pulling the rug out.

First one direction then another. A constant inner struggle, from a sense of dread, to the reality of loss, a situation similar to the existential dismay he studied in a college European literature class. Who was waiting for Godot anyway? What indeed, was the purpose of laboring so hard? Why do anything? His experience, up to this point, looking down the long track of despair? Nothing was coming. Nothing at all.

Synaptic turmoil. That alone forced these wild worries to the surface, all secondary to a vaccine with him the unwitting culprit.

With an abrupt lurch, he seized Zina by the hand. He yanked her backwards. They collided in an embrace. He kissed the gnarled bumps along her palm, desire on the move, groping madly. *Such a lovely mermaid.* He was dumbstruck, venturing a grab of which he should not be touching. That intoxicating scent. He was going crazy.

"Ah, Justinian. You want me now? I had hoped this might happen. Only, and please my emperor, take no offense. Not now."

She immobilized his hands, diverting their excursion. Once more clarity, delayed a half beat, returned. Even his inner metronome was thrown off kilter. Signet's fizzy cola. Her darn perfume....

"Listen to me, Justinian. One is unsteady after inoculation. Strange ideas and behavior. Calm yourself. It will pass."

"You mean, he really did spike the cola?"

"Watch out," Melko said. "We're going to crash!"

Materializing from the gloom, a wood railing was aimed directly at them.

Recognizing the problem, Zina resumed steering. She slowed to a crawl and guided them to a tiny slip. After cutting the engine, she tossed a rope around an adjacent mooring and tied up. Above them, a two story, dilapidated structure loomed hazily against the stars.

"Where are we?" Ross asked.

"An abandoned restaurant." She climbed over the railing and skipped down the sagging porch. "The phone booth is in front. Hurry. We will leave this smelly place."

CHAPTER 31

Smelly all right, Ross's olfactory sense overburdened. Wood rot, dead fish beneath the dock, other flooding aromas. All competed for analysis by an olfactory nucleus, thanks to fizzy cola, no longer in business.

To escape the deluge, he took off after Zina. But, his pal's winded condition pulled him back. He had assisted Melko's transference out of the boat, but there he sat. Hauling him up, the sixty-two-year-old regrouped. Shoulders back, arm in arm, they followed the creaking planks to the front of the structure. Were it not for adherent, moist chinos and squishy loafers, they would've made better time.

The moon, directly overhead, offered a rough outline of a dusty lot bordering the nailed entrance. In the distance, over a low hill, headlights flashed between trees, and it was then Ross finally got his bearings.

They had docked a quarter mile south of Keystone Avenue. Running east and west, the road interconnected Odessa and Campesi's ill-fated party to his right and, another mile west, to Tarpon Springs and Melko's Bayou Grill. Closer at hand, directly east beyond several rows of new developments, stood Doctor Braun's condo, earth movers, tractor trailers dotting the landscape.

And, at the edge of lot, buried in shadow, lay a Leaning Tower of Pisa phone booth. Zina, scuttling fast, was already halfway there.

"Why are we here?" he called after her. "How are we getting to Clearwater Beach?"

"Signet left instructions. Let's find them."

Breathing hard, Melko found his voice. He asked the same question.

"Why lead us all way out here?" he added. "Before the evening went sour … get it, Sauer…?"

Ross let out a labored breath of his own.

"Yes, we get it. You were saying.…"

"Well, why didn't he provide these instructions while we were at my place?"

"He did explain. Earlier, in fact. He said find the cell. The rest will be obvious."

Shattering the night, an all too familiar black SUV roared over the rise and skidded to a stop. Like startled mice, they froze in the glare of supernova high beams. Before the dust settled, pretend Agent Zalin sprang out of the vehicle followed by the two hulking idiots spilling from the back seat. Covered by a small bandage, Zalin's misshapen nose looked bruised, his raccoon eyelids swollen, while Sergio's forearm bore a cracked, plastic cast. Nothing different about Bisco, their intellectually challenged partner, his foul grimace firmly set.

"Gotcha. Deer in the headlights," Zalin barked. "A bunch of frightened rabbits, if you ask me. What are you dimwits doing out here?"

"What is it, big guy," Zina said. "Deer or rabbits?"

Unintimidated by the returning menace, she tossed a rock at the fearless fool. He ducked, the rock sailing over his shoulder to smash a side mirror on the mud caked SUV. As Ross feared, Zina next assumed a fighting stance, fanning away from the phone booth to confront the foe.

"That will cost you, honey. I like the crouch. Makes you an easier target."

"Where are Campesi and Bame?" she snarled. "That would make it a perfect Attack of Five. You three will have to do.'"

"Ah, Zina," Melko said. "That's already too many."

She scoffed.

"Leave them to me."

Her opponents fanned out as well, Sergio and Bisco to her left, Zalin to her right. The shootout at the old corral, the scene almost comical.

The cowboys were better equipped this time around. Using his intact hand, Sergio produced a handgun he calmly aimed at Zina. She came to an abrupt halt.

"Signet said you might bring a weapon. There is time to reconsider."

"So do you, little lady. No more gymnastics. You've delivered your last kick."

He'd exchanged his island shirt for a black pullover. He clearly had the upper hand but appeared ridiculous. Ross wondered what section of Krav Maga dealt with handguns at close range. Oblivious to the danger, Zina sneered, pointing to his scrawny neck, the black and orange tattoo, his incongruous gold earring.

"Fake FBI. Dumb tattoo. The lightning bolts point down, your new direction. When did you last check in with your parole officer?"

She sure didn't sugarcoat it. But, Zalin only laughed.

"I admit. You pegged me. Haven't checked with her for quite a while. Now, move away from the doctor. If we shoot, the bullet might nail you both. You're both coming with me. Not Grandpa. He stays behind."

Zina shifted position, sliding between Sergio and Melko.

"Doc, you and your girlfriend get over here. Sergio, take care of the old fart."

Sergio attempted an end run around Zina. She moved in sync, the man in the cast unable to get a clear shot at his target.

"Aim for a leg. Don't kill him."

Sergio suddenly howled in pain, the scream a detonated grenade in the quiet parking lot. Clutching his hand, he dropped to one knee as his handgun skittered away in the dirt. He kept moaning, fighting off tears.

"What the hell? Where did *this* come from?"

Replacing the Glock, a gleaming black knife now skewered the palm. Blood spurted into the air, covering his shirt as he struggled to remove his belt. The minor gusher intensified when he yanked the knife free, tapering off only after he cinched his forearm with the improvised tourniquet. Meanwhile, on full alert, his pals retreated to their vehicle scouring the shadows for an explanation.

Zalin stepped forward, arms out stretched, hands wide and empty.

"God damn, Signet. I'm unarmed. Stupid Sergio had to bring his gun. Now, look. This isn't part of our plan. What the hell's wrong with you?"

Silence, his outburst greeted by a circle of gently rustling shrubs. Long moments passed, forcing even Zalin to join his frightened men. All three went for the doors.

Finally, a raspy voice floated out from behind the phone booth.

"Sorry, asshole. You're dealing with me now. I should say, with me and my Blackhawk Gideon knife collection. Want to see another?"

"No. One's enough. Who the hell are you?"

Disengaging from bushes and vines, psychopathic Sauer

emerged from his dusty concealment to enter the lot. With his emotions more tightly tethered, Ross noticed what he hadn't before: Sauer's black wetsuit. Anchored securely to a waist harness, a row of sheathed knives shared space with other items, including, what appeared to be a holstered, well-wrapped handgun.

He had found them again.

The fleet-footed assassin wasted no time retrieving the bloody weapon and two strides later stood face to face with Zalin. He wiped the Blackhawk Gideon clean on the pseudo-agent's shirt then, with deliberate ease, placed the blade behind his left ear and started to slice.

"What the *hell?*"

Crying out, hand to his bloody auricle, a look of horror on his face, Zalin stumbled back, banging against Sergio and his damaged hand.

"Relax. I barely nicked you. Hey, *you.*" He hurled a menacing glance at Boscoe. "Want to see what it feels like?"

The man already had his hands up in full surrender.

"Wise decision. You fellows are done here. ¿*Comprende?*"

A pitiful sight, three supposedly invincible men, cowering in the dust. Yet Ross appreciated their fear of this specimen of unrestrained threat, his explosive violence a new experience even for them. For the three bystanders as well, who, though on the outskirts of trouble, warily moved away in unison. Any outburst seemed possible from this vaccine-altered man.

"I know who you are," Zalin said. "Campesi alerted me one of Bame's SEALS might show up. Great job over there in Nuristan, by the way."

"Did he also 'alert' you to the special trophy I bagged?"

Zalin's hands covered his chest. "You wouldn't."

"Since Afghanistan, I only do peacetime work. On a piece by piece basis. Get it?"

He snorted in self-approval, a smiling assassin into his work.

"Did the SEALS teach you to hold your breath like that?" Ross, emboldened, perhaps by the futility of his predicament, challenged him. "I'd guess a mile and a half. How'd you do it?"

"The only thing I held was the dented siding of your crappy boat. Keeping my head half submerged was difficult. That's what the SEALS taught. The skill of concealment."

"So, brave you hitched a ride?" Zina said.

The big guy nodded.

"I overheard your conversation. The chubby guy is right about Rivera. He once had eight straight Ks at Fenway. Saw the game myself. Saw a lot of games over the years. Back when Bame trusted me more with people. What a stadium. That towering left field wall, the green monster. Those sausage sandwiches. Yeah. Great place. Lots of history."

For the briefest instant following this odd oration, his fierce expression softened. Deeply etched, Grand Canyon crevices smoothed to a mere rocky landscape. The reverie soon over, he swept them with a frigid look, the killer instinct again in charge.

Much like Signet, Ross thought. Mannerisms similar. Facial contours ragged. Minus the Zen baloney, nearly a duplicate.

But, the puzzling aspect. Sauer appeared to have accessed an emotional memory. Rivera's Fenway performance occurred years before his vaccination. Despite the congenital absence of an uncus fasciculus, the experience took root, the engendered feelings of pleasure, the very registration of similar outings, but found other pathways to be recalled later and, most critically, relived inside the deranged guy's brain.

Was he still undergoing neuroplasticity? It seemed a distinct possibility. Zalin still had his ear.

Zina poked his arm.

"So serious, Justinian. Your mind lies elsewhere."

"She's right, Doc. Staring at me like that. Don't get other ideas about where you're headed." Sauer took a step towards Ross, stared him down with high power laser beams boring through like hot metal. "Oh yeah. You remind me what Doc Braun said after my inoculation. How did she put it...? That I looked 'lost in a lagoon of reflection.' But don't you worry, Doc. Won't last. Do what you're told and avoid the dark closer. I'm not talking

Kembrel either. In Austin last week, his first pitch landed over centerfield. No one tops Rivera. No one."

The fact finally settled, he went over to Zalin, dropped to a knee and calmly knocked him out. A swift punch, decisive, like Rivera's slider, the fake FBI goon now limp as a rag, head face down in the dust.

Serenely detached, Sauer dragged his unwitting victim to the SUV, chucked him into the back seat and headed for the others. Cradling his hand, Sergio tumbled in next. Disinclined to argue, Bisco took the passenger seat while their new boss assumed the wheel.

He buzzed down the window before driving off.

"Did you watch what I did? Did you learn the lesson?"

"Come again?"

"When the lights go out, it happens fast. Don't see it coming."

"Like with the Yankee's slider?"

"Talking Rivera, man. But, yeah. Like him. A strike out is permanent. It's not personal. Remember that. It just happens."

"It's sure personal to these goons in the car."

"Don't worry about them. They don't count."

He laughed. And, damn if a twinkle flitted about his hard gaze, a millisecond of private mirth. Then it was gone, again like Signet. What was it about a brain without its amygdala? Holy crap. He now had one himself.

"Was it that way with Newsome?"

"Ah. The screw up at Eckerd Hall Monday Night. Signet told me about it."

"You weren't there at the time?"

"I don't know where Eckerd is. Besides, that's not my mode of exodus."

"If you weren't there, where were you?"

Another flicker of amusement.

"Goddamn. I'm beginning to like you. Not so easy for the closeout."

"How comforting. We sure don't want a stressed out closer."

"There you go again. That sarcastic tone of voice. Exactly like Mom used to talk. Except, darling Ascot is blind now and lost her sass. Oh, she tried, all right. Did what any mother would do to keep me out of reform school. Instead, she drove me to the Army, then on to the SEALS and, finally, to Colonel Bame and his vaccine. Here I am now on special assignment. Got to tell you, though, a doctor closeout will be a first for me and for the colonel, expensive. It all depends upon you showing up at Odessa."

Short bio concluded, his arm shot out of the window, seized Ross by the neck, and held him aloft.

"We both like the game, but good closers are hard to find.

Rivera closed out the great David Ortega with a single pitch. Same thing will happen here. Think bullet and you'll show up tomorrow. You'll do fine."

Ross's arms flopped about. He saw stars, brain going hypoxic, shutting down.

David Ortega? The magnificent Big Papi ... comparison off ... Ross never hit a homer in high school....

His brain ceased with the stars and smudgy fog. He tasted dust on his lips. Writhing in the dirt, he heard harsh laughter fading in the night. Saw red lights of the SUV vanish beyond the rise. Fast, loud, the way it arrived.

Melko rushed over, helped him to his feet and dusted him off, then administered a series of painful slaps that finally brought him around. Spluttering, spitting out filth, thanks to the snarky assassin.

"...almost choked to death ... never saw it coming...."

"What? The Ortega Remark? I agree. That was really strange."

Meanwhile, Zina had dashed ahead to the phone booth. She emerged with a dated clamshell device and a folded note, which she held up.

"A computer message. Come here, you two. See what it says."

The message, addressed to Ross, bore a single name and number. He clumsily dialed and within moments found himself speaking with Dr. Keresti, a referring ophthalmologist in New Port Richey who'd been expecting the call.

Twenty minutes later, securely belted into a sage green KIA Sorento with twin kayaks on the roof, they were cruising south on Route 19, the forty-five minute trip dialed into the GPS, a smiling Dr. Keresti at the wheel.

"Everyone happy?" he chirped, merrily. "Mr. Signet said he was your best friend. He asked, when you called, to come fetch you. Do not fret. We will go in fast, jiffy time."

CHAPTER 32

Even at night, immersed in shadow, a trip on Route 19 did not disappoint.

Always on display, the jarring spectacle of disrepair could not be ignored. A variable tangle of orange cones, barricades of construction, dilapidated store fronts, mystery shops and closed mini-malls passed them by on each side of the highway. And, always brightly lit, insistent billboards beckoned with bewildering appeal:

DIVORCE, MEN ONLY

EXPECT THE BEST REAL ESTATE CHEAP

POPULIST FOR THE PUBLIC, RIORDAN LAW

WOMAN-STYLE DIVORCE FOR THE LADY

And Ross's very favorite:

NO-TOUCH WHILE-YOU-WAIT VASECTOMY

Once more a patient searched the curbside for the anxious partner on hold until the no-touch was completed. What a hoot, the quivering victim walking out, nagging stitches in his privates. Some date that night.

This Disney of delights never failed to amuse, igniting both wonder and dismay to the smorgasbord of mindless motorists careening by the windows. Prone to speeding, accidents and general mayhem, it was bumper cars every time. Tonight proved no exception. At eleven forty-five the Friday traffic was horrific.

Oblivious of the maelstrom, Dr. Keresti maintained a pleasing monologue at the wheel. Gesticulating for emphasis, he relayed the numerous challenges a young father faced with twin adolescent girls on the go. Up to the task, he recently volunteered as softball coach, adding it on to duties as neighborhood tutor plus teaching teenage pregnancy classes.

"Yes, Daniel. At times, a nightmarish life, a very busy existence. Would I ever abandon my girls to strange coaches or boyfriends? Not a chance. You may ask, why do I do so much and spread myself so thin? Well, my specialist referral man, because it is rewarding. Yes, yes. Ever so much reward to keep the pretty things on my leash."

In addition, he loved kayaking in Weeki Wachee, the fresh spring river forty minutes north. Well, now maybe fifty because they were going south. Especially so appealing, the mermaid show one might visit after hours of paddling. Also, not to forget, the weekend at Disney, particularly at Epcot, the new exhibits. And, to pay for this rewarding life, he doubled down on his big practice, even coming in nights to drain lid infections.

"May I offer one caution?" He swung about to address Ross. "Do not rush into marriage. Not much freedom after that. Oh, excuse me, miss," he said, as if suddenly noticing the tight-lipped Zina sitting beside him. "Not to offend if you guys are already hooked up."

"No worry there, sir. A 'hook' does not exist between us."

Dr. Keresti slapped his head.

"How silly. You are friends, not lovers."

He offered a sympathetic sound and patted both their knees. Fortunately copilot Melko kept his eye on the asphalt, one hand steadying the wheel.

"What she means," Ross said, clarifying the matter. "We are still getting acquainted. I think that's what's happening. It's early. Plenty of time to hook up."

"Ah, yes. Very funny. I understand. So happy to hear it."

Ross and Zina exchanged a puzzled glance. Melko chortled, and the pilot resumed transporting the threesome to Clearwater Beach.

Attired in a white Gandhi shirt, hand waving, he continued his infectious reportage until, almost by accident, he mentioned Mr. Campesi's name. The prevailing levity quickly vanished.

"He called your office?" Ross asked.

"He pulled me away from patients. Actually, it was Nancy, my senior tech, who yanked my arm. Have I told you? She owns a shotgun and fights bears in the North Carolina woods."

"What did he want?"

"A matter of life and death, Ms. Nancy said. I took the call."

Alarm bells went off. Ross sat forward.

"He implied you might be indisposed in the days ahead. He offered no reason, nor did he respond when I asked why this might be."

"He actually used that word, 'indisposed'?"

Dr. Keresti nodded.

"Then came the zinger. He asked if, for good money, I might continue your Glaucon Project. Part-time, of course. What do you make of that?"

"How were you to do that?"

Their driver paused to change lanes, maneuvering around a stalled truck in the middle of the highway.

"Crazy monkeys. Why do they always stop on the dime? He asked if I would do the surgery. Not the research. That was his domain."

This horrified Ross. The double tube shunt operation was a tricky procedure for even the most facile eye surgeon. Dr. Keresti wrestled with cataracts. Glaucoma definitely not his 'domain' And, glaucoma research? What the heck did Campesi know about that?

"I firmly declined the offer," Keresti continued as if reading his thoughts, "Not only have I not performed a shunt in many years, I would never assume your position. I made that clear to him. His request was so upsetting. What is going on at Arriva? Everything okay?"

Nothing was wrong, Ross said. The CEO thought Ross needed assistance to complete his project, but of course he was mistaken. The project was on track. Full steam ahead.

"Perhaps being indisposed is only temporary."

"Not ever. Tonight is an exception. We're visiting friends."

"Not this morning either. Instead of you, the girl gave the Glaucon talk but in your name. Mr. Signet said it might happen."

"You went to Arriva today?"

Dr. Keresti kept nodding.

"On your friend's kind invitation. In order to update you tonight, he said. It was so embarrassing. This Myla person was unable to answer questions. An illuminati from Manhattan politely stepped in for her."

Once again he felt the pull of marionette strings from the security man's grave. He left nothing left to chance. Involving Dr. Keresti as link to both Myla's inadequate performance and to this trip to Dr. Azzizzi on Clearwater Beach. Nothing left to chance except one vital detail. Informing the chief puppet what the devil was going on.

Sensing a darker mood from the backseat, Dr. Keresti sped on in silence. After a while he turned on the radio.

Keeping beat with each song, Zina edged out of her corner position and slid across the seat. Their thighs touched, the sudden transfer of heat coaxing a thermodynamic, visceral urge to reawaken. Thoughts of hooks rattled his mind, the image of sharp impaling, the resulting attachment.

Sensing his turmoil, Zina hooked a finger, hooking one of his own in the process and placed it on her inner thigh.

"Will you have me?" she cooed. "This mermaid is ready."

Caught off guard, he nodded by mistake. Yes, yes. He wished very much to proceed but knew he should not. Still, she persisted, aware he was incapable of stopping. The finger having hooked, moved on, mischievously pursuing its intrepid journey north.

With things nearly out of control, his wits finally returned. He detaching the 'hook' and pulled away.

"Can this wait?" he whispered. "I, I'm ready. I think. But, here? In the *backseat* of Dr. Keresti's car?"

What the heck was she thinking?

He glanced at the front seat. A pair of tilted heads paid close attention. Not a good sign. Not at all.

"I only tease, Justinian. Your empress should never do this. Please forgive me."

She disengaged yet her proximity kept the heat flowing.

"Nothing to forgive," he said, smoothing his trousers. "Let's hug. A good compromise. Maybe even a beginning."

No doubt about it. He was far from his comfort zone. On the other hand, what harm existed in a hug between compatriots? That didn't sound quite right. He tried "friends." That wasn't it either. They were more than that. Nascent hookups?

Just go for it.

He reached out grasping, it turned out, only air. To his surprise, she pushed him away. The rebuff sent him haywire. One second, a joint project up her leg. Next, nothing for wanting but a block of ice.

"Let's take a raincheck. An emperor should never reach."

"I'll hold you to it."

Despite the putdown, numerous after images remained. Vivid scenes again furrowed his sulci. Vague but also real, they shuttled between over stimulated lobes, up and down the neural axis, making hemispheres reverberate desire, lurid images swerving past chambers of spinal fluid lakes, where his sexed up river ran, through mental caverns, measureless to this man, down to his own sunless sea.

His overworked, insular cortex rocked without restraint. As did his olfactory cortex, under constant impact with her exotic scent, which joined the breakneck ride. Shade Of Night, the remembered name of this shimmering perfume, descended about his head like a shawl.

Quietly, not to draw attention, he took stock.

Yes, he enjoyed the bumpy, emotional ride. Yet, it was

veering from control, like his feelings for this strange, young seductive woman.

This was *so* unlike him. He sensed an inner unraveling, immersed in perfume, mental landscape in shambles. As he concluded before, it resembled a prolonged seizure of his limbic brain. And now, a post epileptic revelation? His bright flash illuminated but a single and very primitive impulse ... that of mating behavior.

With a sudden jolt, the other explanation barged through. The vaccine. Of course. It had altered his amygdala, morphing its customary message into an entirely new communique, tormenting his temporal lobes, jolting them with imaginings untenable:

Girl on seat. Beautiful and sexy. Rip-off jeans. Ignore front seat audience.

He grasped his beleaguered skull.

Insane.

"I can't believe I drank that soda. I'm such an idiot."

Talons at bay, frigid retreat fast receding, Zina collapsed against his shoulder.

"Calm yourself, my frazzled emperor. Listen to the lyrics. Dr. Keresti, please adjust the volume."

As instructed, their driver fiddled with the dial. The KIA then reverberated with gushing teenage heart throbs. Enthralled, he listened to musical emanations a far cry from Opus 57 or was it 56?

How can I breathe without you...?

I love you just the way you are....

Falling into a curious, offshoot mood, he accepted, albeit with surprise, what happened next. Zina leaned up and laid her lips against his. They lingered, neither one pressing hard. He returned the kiss, tentatively, all too aware of her torso against his own.

"Boyfriend and girlfriend," Dr. Keresti said, breaking the spell. "I had no idea."

Melko chuckled.

"Ms. Palaeologus, ah, Empress Theodora, is good for him. I've never seen him blush before."

The front seat burst out laughing. The backseat remained at ease.

Definitely not your average trip down Route 19.

In time, Zina broke free of their embrace and slid to the far corner of the seat. She played with her iPhone, once again distant. He looked on anyway, entranced by her rapid fingers as blurred text and photos passed by in quick succession.

"Who are you texting?"

"Uncle Stephano. He just returned from Greece. The government took away his yacht. We might meet him later on tonight."

"More of Signet's puzzle? I guess he already arranged a visit with your uncle."

She ignored him so they drove on in silence.

Minutes later, the vehicle hung a right on Gulf to Bay Boulevard and not long after crested the Bay Bridge, a view of the resplendent inlet hazy in the distance. They nosed down the causeway and, at the turn-around, swung north up Mandalay. At first, a street of nondescript swim shops and shuttered bistros, it soon became a showcase of single level homes. A final turn brought them to their destination.

"Wow. Take a look at that."

Having never been there before, Melko was impressed.

Gamel Azzizi's stylish, three-story home was indeed a monument to modern architecture and good taste. From the towering hardwood stairs climbing to the front door, to the multitude of suspended foliage along the railing, the home exuded grace and matchless beauty.

"We should all be retina surgeons," the restaurateur noted. "Truly a masterpiece."

"Gamel is also one of Tampa Bay's most talented," Dr. Keresti added, bringing the KIA to a halt. "He designed it himself."

"I am lucky he is my best friend."

"Don't you mean, only? Always in the lab, you do not get out much."

"Now there is you, miss. Maybe you can change him."

"I suppose Signet scripted that. Why don't we get out?

You guys haven't seen the beachfront pool on the other side. It's immense."

Gawking on the cobblestones, they peered through hedges to the beach beyond. Captivating, a too mild description.

"I had no idea retinas were so rewarding."

"Or, cataracts," Ross replied, fortunately no longer envious. "Even plastic surgeons."

Melko laughed.

"They say, gold lies in them thar lids, folks. Charge what the market will bear."

"Do anything but glaucoma. Unless you insert one of the new glaucoma gizmos when you remove the cataract. Heck, why labor through a fellowship? Cataract surgeons are now a surrogate for the real thing."

"You invented a gizmo, Dr. Danny-boy. Don't be the hypocrite."

"It's not the same thing. Not even close."

"Medicine is not all about money," Dr. Keresti said. "True. It has become mainly business. But, I myself do general. I earn sufficient for my twins."

Changing subjects, the general ophthalmologist amongst them pointed to the top floor picture windows.

"I imagine from up there your friend views both the Gulf and Tampa Bay at the same time. Very amazing, this design."

"It is that and more, Karum Keresti." A deep growl of a voice boomed from the shadowed garage behind them. "To visualize both, you must swing your head back and forth to take it in."

Emerging straight from a *GQ* ad, Gamel Azzizzi now made his entrance. He wore a starched white shirt, razor sharp pressed slacks and a pair of trademark Florentine wingtips. And, of course, the trim goatee.

"You have come after all, Daniel Ross. Who, may I ask, are your companions?"

CHAPTER 33

Born and raised abroad but trained in the United States, Gamel Azzizi was the preeminent European gentleman on native soil. Tonight, offsetting his usual regal demeanor, he sported an clean oil cloth in one hand. Polishing his car, he explained, either the Jeep Cherokee or sapphire BMW X5. He didn't say which.

"You may choose either one. Take your pick," he said to Ross. "Both are tiptop. My favorite, the X5. The jeep has more room, though. Perhaps that is a better choice."

Ross raised an eyebrow at him. "For what?"

"Why, your return trip to Tarpon Springs. Mr. Signet indicated four would be going back."

Ross concealed annoyance with the mention, yet again, of the late security man's name. He couldn't figure four, however. Dr. Keresti had his own wheels. That left three unless Gamel joined them. But, he offered a car to Ross. Puzzling.

"Very thoughtful. Thank you," he said. "We are here.

Now what?"

"Ah, yes. There is more to this visit than the mere pleasure of your presence. The box. It is upstairs."

"What box?"

"Patience, my friend. First we finish introductions. Dr. Karum Keresti I already know from the Florida Academy meetings plus his many kind referrals."

"I'd like to stay," Dr. Keresti interrupted, "But, tomorrow is a return visit to Disney. I promised the twins."

After a round of farewells, the KIA vanished down Mandalay. The introductions continued.

"Ah, Mr. Melko," Gamel said. "Daniel's Massachusetts friend. It is nice to finally meet you. But, this one," he added, gracefully delivering a half bow before Zina, "is the remarkable granddaughter. I assume, as you are here together, the animosity over grandpa has resolved."

Unintimidated by old world charm, Zina offered her own hand in greeting, Empress Theodora confronting the lowly pagan at court.

"I am known as Theodora," she said with a twitch of an eyebrow. "There was never animosity. Merely, a disagreement. As for Justinian, he and I are more than *friends*." Her hand slithered over Ross's arm. "A genie whispered 'boyfriend.' That is progress, don't you think?"

Aware he had stumbled into alien territory, their host nodded with equable poise then guided them toward the front steps. No doubt anxious for more amenable conversation, he allowed Zina to lead the way up. Head thrust back, she began to climb.

"You may call him Justinian," she added. "We are united in a common quest."

"Emperor and Empress. I should have known." Never one to miss a beat, Dr. Azzizzi rolled on. "I am well familiar with Byzantium. Justinian rebuilt Hagia Sophia, Church of the Holy Wisdom, one of Christendom's most celebrated churches. Empress Theodora kept the empire united to the east against Persia, while Emperor Justinian patched up theology with Rome in the west. The Age of Justinian. Transition from antiquity to medievalism. It appears we are both students of history."

Melko exchanged a look with Ross. Holding back, they allowed the unlikely historians to ascend together. On the top landing, Gamel graciously unlatched the door and invited them in. They crossed a spacious entranceway, passing beneath a gilded arch of hieroglyphs, to face an Egyptian statue in a near corner. Seated, polished to a high gleam, a thousand-year stare.

"Imhotep. My latest prize," Gamel announced. "Chancellor to the great pharaoh, Djoser. Men of considerable achievement. This way, please. I have much to show you."

Following an appreciative pause, they ascended a few steps to enter what Gamel deprecatingly referred to as his 'time chamber,' a vast space, more museum than living area. The size of a small handball court, it was dimly lit by shaded wall sconces. But, it was the vaulting ceiling of dark wood that established the reigning tone. Sepulchral, if Ross had to choose a word.

And, a tad scary. A vertical mummy stood guard over a central couch, where their host got them settled. Unraveling for effect, the head bent as if contemplating its new companions.

"I remember now." Melko indicated the mummy. "Wasn't your pal Imhotep the mummy that came to life in that movie?"

"Next you will inform me, as all my guests do, that spooky Boris Karloff had the starring role."

Silence. A shiver along the spine. Even the mummy seemed contrite.

"Well then. Now that we are all together, please enjoy coffee. Those cups, they are replicas of those found in a Cairo museum."

Each filled cups ornate with miniature hieroglyphs, the fluid black, strongly aromatic.

"The same for your coffee, Dr. Azzizzi?"

Composure intact, Gamel disregarded the insult. He simply raised the cream container, discreetly sniffed, then allotted his querulous guest a small portion.

"Did you folks like my new statue?"

"We did. Now tell me about this box you mentioned."

"In a moment. Plenty of time for that."

"Although not many indisputable facts are known for certain, over the past three thousand years a great deal has been learned about thus multitalented person. Imhotep was the architect of the famous Step Pyramid. A poet. Many things. May I now introduce old friends to you?" he added, sweeping the room with his arm. "A remarkable assembly as you shall see."

He drew their attention to various statues distributed about the room, as if his guests had journeyed, far into the evening, to this particular home for such a diversion.

First, he identified the tiny figurines in the wall. There was Anubi and Seth, he said, pausing to relish certain memories the objects recalled. With a brief shake of his shaggy mane, he moved on to proud Osiris upon his own pedestal and, in an adjacent illuminated black cubbyhole, to Horus, adding quickly, an apology.

"The god of Death," he murmured softly. "He presides over all the others. My wife disagreed, yet I had to include him."

He next introduced enlarged photographs of pyramids, numerous cartouches, and, finally, the lugubrious mummy, who having already joined them for coffee, seemed the ideal inhabitant of the tomblike room.

"A perfect solution for Mr. Campesi," Ross said. "Mummify the jerk."

"Daniel, please." Concluding his excursion, Gamel offered a brief discussion of a bust of Nefertiti that occupied a distant corner of the museum-room. A prized possession, he confessed, a detailed replica constructed for him alone in a dusty shop behind the museum in Philadelphia. Its unusual provenance, the reason he saved it for last.

"I must confess," he added, now seated with them for coffee. "It was only after a prolonged disagreement with my first wife, may her spirit rest with Osiris in The Land of Two Fields, that I was able to assemble all of this. Incidentally, I am a Copt, a Christian born in a strange land. Still, I am drawn to the heritage, these statuettes but a sad homage to that former day. Though representing but a brief mist of time, these friends, if I may call them that, live on forever as another of mankind's remarkable triumphs. Opus 57 for Daniel. The Age of Justinian for dear Zina. And, for Mr. Melko ... well, I do not know you well enough. What is your image of excellence achieved?"

"The Bayou Bar and Grill. Tarpon Springs," Melko said proudly. "On the water near Dodecanese. You can't miss it."

"Very well. I shall seek it out. Is there a specialty?"

"Spanakopita," Zina said. "Also crabs, when they are in season."

"Excellent," he said, coming to his feet. "To the box and letter. This will take but a second."

With characteristic flourish, he vanished into a side room. He soon reappeared bearing a purple, gift wrapped tiny box and an envelope that, with exaggerated ceremony, he handed to Ross.

"This arrived with a covering letter addressed to me. It asked that I participate in the ploy, that your life depended upon such cooperation. It is why," he added sheepishly, "I did not tell you before. Here. Read for yourself."

Ross opened the letter. He immediately recognized the font as that of the note at Eckerd Hall. Large, block letters, unsigned, the tone slightly awkward but familiar:

THIS IS FOR YOUR EYES ONLY. DR. ROSS AND FRIENDS WILL ARRIVE FRIDAY NITE. ONLY THEN MAY HE READ THIS LETTER. AFTER THAT HE IS TO OPEN THE BOX. HIS LIFE MAY VANISH IF YOU TELL HIM ABOUT THE LETTER AND BOX BEFORE THIS TIME.

"I assumed the worst, my friend. Please explain what this is about."

Ross ripped open the wrapped cigar box. The flash drive was taped to the bottom. He tore it free and held it up.

"Where's your computer?"

Gamel led them to his Inspiron 14R down a rear hallway in a modified office. The computer sat on a plain wooden desk, the nearby walls lined with more photographs of Egyptian artifacts. A view of the distant Gulf and moored sailboats would have been visible through the huge window were it daytime. But, it was past midnight, the only thing on Ross's mind the contents of the mysterious thumb drive.

He sat at the desk, turned on the computer, and anxiously waited for it to boot up, then slipped the flash drive into a side slot and depressed a series of keys to unlock the contents. Another endless moment as he waited for electric circuits to kick in.

"It is quite an old one," Gamel said, seeing his impatience. "On her trip to Miami, my daughter took the laptop. Ah, my dear," he added, observing Zina's interest in various pedestals around the room. "I see you have found a bust and picture of Hatsheput. Is she not something?"

The perfect host, he joined her.

"This pharaoh is a *woman*?" Zina tapped the framed drawing on the wall. "It is hard to accept a female pharaoh."

"That is the fact. Hatsheput, the fifth pharaoh of the eighteenth dynasty, was a very noble lady."

"I never knew pharaohs could be female."

"I assure you she was not the first. Or Last. Her reign turned out peaceful and prosperous, a period of history witnessing the development of an entirely new form of architecture. Do you see that picture?"

She stepped to her right and inspected the photograph. "It is similar to our own Parthenon."

"You are looking at Hatsheput's Mortuary Temple. Located in the Valley of Kings, its precise position remains an enigma to this very day. Notice the rows of perfectly sloped pillars supporting a low roof. It represented an enormous aesthetic achievement at the time."

She let out a low whistle and read the inscription: "'A colonnaded structure of perfect harmony.' Exactly like the Parthenon. This is where it came from."

"Superb deduction. I am delighted you find pleasure in

the temple. Based on what Daniel has told me, I'm not surprised at all."

The console was flickering to life. Yet, Ross lingered on Zina's hesitation with Gamel's inventive comment.

"He told you about me?"

The storyteller nodded.

"We have discussed you on several occasions. I am certain he would agree you much resemble Pharaoh Hatsheput, this lovely intermediary between the gods and man. Both you and she, beauty and power that spans the centuries."

"He said *that* about me?"

The grand prevaricator stole a glance across the room.

"Perhaps not the same words. However, his depiction of your grace and charm hit the mark. As you already know, the doctor is a precise and selective individual."

Out of the corner of his eye he caught the slight shift of posture. She moved so as to shield her nod from the computer, Ross's initial but incorrect assessment. A semi-retired pianist, his still acute hearing picked up the drop in volume then realized the movement's intent lay elsewhere. To conceal her whispered question, which she directed at the minstrel of mischief himself.

"Ah, Dr. Azzizzi. Did he ever … I mean to ask.…"

She faltered but, always to the rescue, Gamel whispered encouragement.

"Go ahead, my dear. Theodora. You were saying?"

"Did he ever mention a beloved to you? Maybe, of the immortal kind?"

Now, it was his turn to falter.

"Ah, now I do seem to recall...."

"You do?"

Nodding vigorously, he mumbled near inaudible phrases.

"...once ... a practice session ... Mrs. Campesi...."

"Samantha. Was that her name?"

More mumbled words. Ross snared a few of these choice verbal escape routes.

"...nothing ... concern yourself ... only ... the empress...."

"He really referred to me? Maybe as one of those immortal beloveds?"

"Ah, now I see where you are going. Beethoven's letter. The posthumously discovered declaration."

"Yes. Did he ever speak of me like that?"

It was way past time to intervene.

"Hey, guys," he said, pointing to the screen. "We have a problem here. You might want to see this."

More conversant with computers than Ross and breathing his own sigh of relief, Melko elbowed him aside. He, too, a party to the not-so-inaudible exchange before The Mortuary Temple. He punched keys, and lines of symbols streamed by. Nothing recognizable, the code seemingly impenetrable to him as well. In time, stymied by the thumb drive, he sat back. Except for the first file, they were all encrypted.

He opened to the page of contents:

GLAUCON

GENESIS I - Encrypted

GENESIS II - Encrypted

GENESIS III - Encrypted

Property of DARPA and the United States Government

Arriva, Inc. Tarpon Springs, Florida.

Gamel donned his readers to peer more closely.

"DARPA would be displeased to find us snooping. You must return this."

"We are not returning anything."

"I agree," Melko said. "We need to examine the contents of these GENESIS files."

"Unless we have the precise encryption key, we're locked out."

"Mr. Campesi must have known the files were encrypted. What the hell's the big deal?"

"There is another possibility, my emperor."

"You have to stop calling me that."

What the heck happened to the "beloved" obsession? Her return to the 5th century, quite strong in comparison. Her identity trumped "beloved"? He put the query aside. More pressing issues loomed.

"Perhaps Signet stole the files and encrypted them himself."

"Did he tell you that?"

Melko thumped the table.

"She may be on to something," he said. "From my experience with the 'dude,' thank you, Franklin, he could easily have done just that. I wouldn't put it past the duplicitous bastard."

Zina began to chew a knuckle. "Signet only said you would know what to do when you find them."

"That means he knew I did not 'steal' anything."

Melko nodded. "Bottom line, 'ol buddy. You have to give this flash drive to Mr. Campesi."

"I concur, Daniel," Gamel added. "DARPA is part Pentagon. It is unlawful to keep them."

Ross grumbled. Of course it was unlawful, but he refused to return the only complete copy of his project. It would ruin his career as an innovator. He would not do it. No matter what Signet had implied, surrender was not the way to go.

He pushed his pal out of the chair and sat.

"I mean, guys, this took an incredible amount of work. Years, literally years, of lab overnights. It's a brand new concept. Soon, I'll include stem cells. I simply will not part with this document."

He opened the unencrypted file and watched as his life's work populated the screen before him. Data sheets, reams of charts, graphs, and statistics too numerous to count. A near impossible achievement and without Dr. Braun's assistance at the outset, a nonstarter. The section headings themselves brought goosebumps: "Proposal: A New Double Tube Drainage and Treatment Device for Glaucoma, the Second Leading Cause of Blindness Worldwide"; "Three Biological Agents to Stabilize and Cure Glaucoma"; "FDA Safety Trials"; "Human Clinical Phase I and II Recruitment". He reread that magical first letter: "Dear Mrs. Campesi, I would like to interest you in the cure of a lifetime...."

A triumph he would not relinquish, at least, not voluntarily.

Then again, did it really make a difference? Glaucon was gone unless he handed over the thumb drive Signet stole in the first place—*this thumb drive, it's copied DARPA files*—and prayed Campesi relented. As if there were any likelihood of that.

For the first time, he welcomed the fizzy cola inoculation. If it had indeed dismantled his amygdalae-driven fear, his priorities might straighten themselves out except, again, where would this leave him? He'd still have to decide about returning illicit projects to a morally compromised person in order to secure his project.

"Genesis I," Melko read. "Is this the PTSD project?"

Ross nodded.

"It began at DARPA. Thanks to Mr. Campesi, it metastasized and took root here in Tarpon Springs."

"No matter the location," Gamel observed. "Encryption is necessary. To guarantee veteran's anonymity. Also to protect the secret method of vaccine production."

Melko reached over his shoulder to scroll down the next encrypted file. The title GENESIS II filled the screen.

"What's this about?"

"The Reverse Amygdala Project. Instead of restoring amygdala function, DARPA plans to destroy it, the idea being to create a fearless, perfect soldier."

"What's wrong with that? Soon ISIS will be destroyed in the Middle East, but it's rampant in the Horn of Africa. Our military will always be needed. A perfect soldier is a great idea."

"But, perfect not for long," Zina pointed out. "They change. It happened to Signet. Once a deadly soldier with a knife, he became a crafty man with a plan. Most of his inoculated pals also changed. Neuroplasticity sets in. Unanticipated results occur because the brain is rearranged."

Ross tapped the monitor, incredulous at the scope of DARPA's imagination.

"Sauer is another product of Genesis II," he said. "But,

he's different. He was an unknown psychopath to begin with. I'm speculating here, but that may explain GENESIS III. They may now be screening trained recruits for psychopaths."

"Signet said he has a squad of men just like him."

"His Eritrea mission?"

Gamel's eyebrows shot up.

"I am in the dark. How do these GENESIS programs relate to you? Why send this flash drive in a box?"

For the benefit of his colleague, but omitting any mention of assassin Sauer who might well have already tracked him to Clearwater Beach, Ross provided a brief summary of what he knew about the GENESIS projects. He began with the PTSD program then moved on to GENESIS II. Originally a purely military program to produce better soldiers, a problem arose when Arriva's CEO, Mr. Campesi secretly inoculated innocent civilians like Zina and her grandfather. A clandestine, potentially dangerous program that had to be stopped. However, he did not reveal he himself had been fizzed with an identical inoculant. No reason to burden Gamel with such a fact.

Zina interrupted.

"Tell him about Grandpa," she said. "How he is no longer a priest and entertains young females on his lap."

Ross patted her hand.

"He knows about Father Palaeologus. Remember, we share the same office. Everyone there heard your, ah, complaints about his unusual transformation. Let me finish with Dr. Azzizzi. For reasons of his own, Signet downloaded these classified documents then arranged for Mr. Campesi to blame me for the theft. The odd part and also for unknown reasons, he sent this thumb drive to you. All I have to do is return it."

The retina surgeon slowly digested the story. Then, he broke into a wide, rear molar grin.

"A priest entertains young ladies?" he asked. "Do you have any extra vaccine?"

Zina snorted.

"He failed to mention his own vaccination."

"You refer to Daniel? How is such a thing possible?

"Because the emperor's royal nostril is quite sensitive," Zina said, thumping the bridge of his nose for emphasis. "The vaccine travels from here to this area behind his ear, three inches inside the skull, to the 'ameegala nuklayus' that it destroys. But, the vaccine takes time to act. First, the mischievous thought. Next, the new behavior. Soon, an altered 'you' appears. I cannot wait until that happens."

"Ah, hold on Theodora. You say he inhaled—"

There was a loud knock on the downstairs door. Then another. Insistent, angry sounds.

Ross shot to his feet. He yanked the thumb drive free of the computer and stuffed it in his pocket.

"How the devil did he find us?"

CHAPTER 34

No one moved. For Ross, a long anticipated moment. Ever since Dr. Keresti had loaded them into the KIA Sorento, he expected the assassin to pop up at any juncture. Even to spring out of the mummy during their host's recital. Now the crazed lunatic was at the front door. No avenue of escape. He would have to make a stand.

"Do you have any weapons?" he whispered.

"Living here, where marauders invade homes? Of course, I have weapons."

"Get them."

"Should we not see who it is first? I shall go down, peer through the peephole and see who it is."

Meticulous and proper, Gamel squared his shoulders, shot his cuffs and descended to the foyer. He was back a half-minute later, a relaxed grin on his grizzled face.

"Whom do you know wears plaid?" he said. "With black sandals and a firearm holstered on his hip?"

Ross thought hard.

"How tall?" he asked.

Hand to chin, Gamel pondered.

"A small man."

"Car at the curb?"

"Ford Focus."

"Has to be Detective Leeks. What the heck does he want?"

They trekked down to the front door to find out. After a cursory glance through the peephole, Ross threw the lock, and the detective stepped into the foyer.

Dr. Azzizzi did not extend a hand.

"What brings a policeman to my home at such an hour?" he demanded.

Deadpan, the cop ran an inquisitive eye over the foursome. He paused to ogle Zina's snug tee shirt then moved on.

"I might as well ask Dr. Ross the same question."

"I was invited. We all were."

"So was I, in a manner of speaking. Your Mr. Signet gave me a call. He discovered the Eckerd Hall murderer is hiding in Dr. Azzizzi's third floor loft. Mind if I take a look?"

The request elicited a unanimous groan.

"This is absurd. I have no such loft. We are the only ones in the house."

"You certain Mr. Ravi Ravda isn't here? He was last seen munching pizza at that Odessa party tonight. According to Mr. Campesi, he's disappeared."

Gamel appeared genuinely distressed.

"Why would such a person come to my house?"

"He didn't come here," Ross said. "Ravda was also not at that party. I was there and never saw the man. Another thing," he added. "Signet is most likely dead. When did he call you?"

"An hour ago. He sounded very alive to me."

"How did you know it was him?"

"Because that's what he said. I never met the man myself."

Distracted, the detective dragged his gaze along the side walls, whistling softly at the ornate furnishings.

"You do pretty well by yourself, Doc. These artifacts look real."

"They are real. All but Imhotep in the corner. He is a fine, bronze replica. The original lies in the Louvre. That's in Paris, France, by the way."

"No need for attitude. I was complimenting you."

Gamel administered a disapproving nod as his unwelcome guest stepped across the foyer. All but Imhotep looked on with disgust when Leeks ran a hand over the statue's gleaming leg. Unfazed by the familiarity, the chancellor to Pharaoh Djoser kept his gaze glued on infinity.

"Better change fields, Ross. Glaucoma will never get you this."

"*This,*" Gamel said, edging between man and statue. "Is one of the most vital individuals in all of Egyptian history. He requires, no, he *demands* respect."

Chastised, the detective shrank back. Meanwhile, taking his cue, their tour guide filled them in about the bronze figure. Considered as probably the very first architect and engineer in recorded time, Imhotep was also a noted physician predating if not superseding Asklepsios, the Greek God of medicine. If that were not enough, he added, sighing with appreciation as he pointed out the papyrus firmly clasped in the statue's hand, this man was also a patron of writing and, most amazing of all, the creator of the first monumental stone pyramid.

"An outstanding individual," he concluded. "From the twenty-seventh century BC. We owe so very much to this wise individual."

Zina now positioned herself near the statue, daring to stroke the serene Imhotep's tapered thigh.

"There is another famous Egyptian person in the room above," she said, demurely. "She is almost a goddess. Am I correct, Dr. Azzizzi?"

"You most certainly are. You refer to Pharaoh Hatsheput, an elegant and dynamic lady from the eighteenth dynasty. If you wish to see them, detective, I have artifacts from her period in the upstairs study."

"A lady pharaoh. That's a first."

"She also built the best ever mortuary temple."

"Again, Theodora is right. Her temple lay at the mouth of what became the Valley of The Kings. To this day, its precise location remains a mystery to archeology."

"My, my. Aren't we the history buffs."

"Forged in the past, our identities always unfold, Detective."

"Like the good doctor here." Melko at last found his voice. "He's consumed by the past. In his case, eye medicine. Did he ever tell you about the portrait wall up in Boston? He sees himself in a line of succession, from a pioneering and revered eye pathologist to the glaucoma greats of the last century, all the way down to a modern day honcho, a cornea specialist known as an okay pro, whose portrait also adorns that infirmary wall. He's knows all their names. Their contributions. The names of their pets. Right, pal?"

He was venturing on to thin ice here. Ross kept his cool, hoping he might fall through.

"Okay, that's enough," he finally said. "We all have dreams."

To Zina's credit, she changed topic, launching into a familiar, tummy lurching rendition of her favorite story: the Nika revolt of 532 A.D. Occurring during the reign of Justinian I, this devastating rebellion saw severed heads and limbs of men, women and unlucky children by the thousands covering the bloodied Hippodrome steps on that fateful day. A terrible slaughter. But, thanks to Empress Theodora who ordered the massacre, the upheaval ended. A steep price to pay but necessary. It saved Constantinople, the royal couple's control over the entire empire, perhaps the empire itself.

"All due to her, my friends. Theodora, The Great."

Not one for restraint, she got into the act. To the surprise of assembled guests, she relived the shrieks and gurgles of the spectacle. During the resulting, faint applause, not up to the thunderous reception received on the Tarpon docks, Ross found himself immersed in the second troubling experience since imbibing fizzy cola.

His brain slid sideways, sulci jolted by a bewildering storm of sensory intrusions. What began as a delicate tickle, grew to a burning desire to process every signal assaulting his neural systems.

First, brightly lit, a myriad of tiny hieroglyphs on Gamel's silk robe, like a string of supernovae bursts, beamed out at him. Coming to life, they spoke in tongues, relaying secrets about Imhotep's long ago realm, about his imagined, disrobing mistress also pulsating to life. Next, the distant hiss of water sprinklers became symphonic, an orchestra of sprayed delight upon his eardrums; a squirt to the pachysandras now a delicate oboe, and irrigation of prickly oleander shrubs a distant rumble of percussion bells and whistles, sounds reminiscent of younger, carefree excursions with a girlfriend to a dense wood. Then, a difficult string section of water pipes inside the walls. A wild conglomeration of augmented but mismatched percolations amongst the ossicles and their auditory connections.

And, finally, an olfactory coda.

His nostrils twitched from the scent of lamb chops on Leeks' breath and then, from Zina's intoxicating perfume, a more invasive scent zooming him back to Monday night at Eckerd Hall when, in full Byzantium regalia, Zina smothered him with perfume, to their conversation on the sponge docks and, just that evening to Samantha's parlor in Odessa and, at last, to the back seat of the Sorento.

A flood of sensations and memories traceable to the sizzling soda he stupidly consumed when Signet handed it to him.

Massaging his temples, he visualized the hoard of dying neurons.

A jarring noise then caught their combined attention. A metallic sound of garbage cans striking the pavement outside the house.

Ross rushed to the hall window, parted the curtain, and looked out.

"Two cats," he said. "Scampering to the bushes."

"I have told Mr. Sousa to cover his cans. Feral beasts. They always leave a mess."

"I don't see any garbage, though, just a pair of empty cans."

Zina had a look herself.

"He is right. No garbage. Maybe the cats were scared."

Ross shot Leeks a worried glance.

"Did you bring backup?" he said. "Do you have a man out there?"

"I'm here by myself."

Gamel opened the door, stepped out to the deck, and peered into the shadows far below.

"You are correct," he said. "Garbage receptacles line the walkway. I will speak with Elmo again about his cats."

While he continued to examine the side lot, the detective drew Zina aside. With his ear cocked, Ross's enhanced hearing brought him the entire conversation. He had been calmly eating a late summer dinner, Leeks said, when he glanced at his vibrating iPhone. Why, he asked himself, had Zina Palaeologus forwarded a set of pictures at that precise moment when she took them Monday night? To which Zina replied, apparently with a tinge of resentment, that if the so-called detective were a true professional, the meaning would be clear enough.

"I did not intend to insult you," Leeks said louder, but the hour was late. "Tell me again why you—"

They were interrupted by another yet much different sound, that of exploding glass in the floor above.

Gamel rushed back inside to inform his startled guests of the obvious. "A gunshot," he announced, leading them up the stairs to his time chamber. There they witnessed two more shots, the first shattering a blue glazed vase, the second demolishing a wide screen TV beside their heads.

"Duck!" Dr. Azzizi cried out as they scuttled for the protection of the sofa.

"We can't stay here. We'll get hit."

Detective Leeks astutely herded them in the opposite direction, where they filed back down to the foyer.

"The shooter is on the rear porch," he said. "I'll be right back."

As he slid out the front door, the adjacent window exploded. Imhotep's head dropped to the floor and rolled to a stop at Melko's feet. He picked it up.

"I thought you said this was cast bronze."

"Bronzed plaster is what I meant." The curator grabbed the ruined head, cradling it like an injured pet. "My most prized statue. I will have to secure a replacement."

Leeks now hustled to the outside landing, keeping his head down, obviously disinclined to have his head join Imhotep's. He paused to peek over the railing. Seeing nothing amiss, he slowly descended, reaching the main walkway without incident.

Zina rushed to the door.

"I will assist the dumb detective."

The three men in tow, she led them down without trouble. By then, the detective was deep amongst the shrubs, gun in hand, carefully exploring the foliage. Announcing all was clear, he ushered the quartet into the garage then dashed to his vehicle. He popped the trunk and removed a shotgun. But then, emitting a sudden gush of air, he dropped to one knee as Zina blindsided him with a belly punch, her adopted modus operandi. Ignoring the felled detective, she snatched the shotgun out of his hands and dashed around the far side of the house.

Several moments passed, all eyes on her crumpled path through the pachysandra, the silver edged blades of the little plants still trembling in her wake.

A tremendous blast pierced the night. A second one followed. Finally, came the pitiful sobs of a man begging for his life.

By the time Ross reached her, it was almost too late. Straddling Sergio, she held the shotgun to his bleeding head. A severed palm frond lay beside him. Scorch marks indented the house.

"Wait, Zina. Don't do it!"

"Do not ask for mercy. Saint Peter already knows your name. He sees you at the gate."

Ross attempted to disarm her. She struck his hand with the shotgun barrel, finger still on the trigger.

"Hey, man. Don't let her do it. I didn't hurt no one."

"Because you are a poor shot." Zina delivered a sharp kick to his midsection. "Unlike you, I am a fine marksman. Markswoman. Why are you here? Tell me or you're a dead person."

Holding his gut, Detective Leeks stumbled out of adjacent undergrowth and with evident skill yanked the shotgun free of Zina's hands. He then ordered the man to get up, telling him he was under arrest for attempted murder. Protesting he was not there to kill them, Sergio offered a hasty explanation. Back at the parking lot off Keystone, Sauer said he would take the three of them to Trine-Tree Emergency room. Unlike the others, Sergio refused to go because too many patients left the hospital with toe tags. Sauer wrapped his punctured hand instead. In payment, he ordered Sergio to shoot up Dr. Azzizzi's house, but only after Dr. Ross arrived later in the evening.

"Why were you to do this?"

"To scare the doctor. To remind him of his assignment."

But Sauer didn't tell him a detective would also be there plus a crazy female with a shotgun.

"Stop right there. Who is Sauer? The name is new to me."

Ross filled Leeks in as they returned to the front of the house. He kept to the highlights omitting any mention of fizzy soda or the thumb drive. In a major case of mistaken identity, an assassin by the name of Sauer was after him. It concerned a mix-up about stolen documents, a problem already resolved except no one had updated the assassin to back off. A dazed baseball fanatic, very accurate throwing Gideon knives, he possessed a unique skillset they wished to avoid. To evade, actually. It was the reason they visited Dr. Azzizzi.

"He knew we were here, however. This Sergio fellow is proof. He's also one of Sauer's victims."

"His own man?"

He nodded.

"Take a look at that bandaged hand. Sauer disarmed him

with one of his knives. It went clean through. Want to take a look?"

"That's okay. Don't unwrap it. He will need a hand surgeon."

"Call 911. Get him to Tampa General. You should also call for reinforcements. If he shows up, you're going to need more men."

"Maybe we'll get to him first. What's his ride?"

"Black SUV. Suburban, I think. He took it from Zalin, that phony FBI guy."

The detective made his call, issuing an immediate all-points. Until they apprehended the assassin, he would stay with Ross for protection. Gamel then reminded him of a Mr. Signet's instruction. When it was time to depart, he was to borrow one of Dr. Azzizi's cars and proceed with Theodora.

"Proceed where?" Ross said.

"He did not mention a destination. Only that Theodora would figure it out."

"He did not say for sure?"

"Those were his instructions, my dear. Just remember, Hatsheput was never afraid."

"Do I *look* afraid?" Again, she eyed the shotgun in the detective's hand. "Theodora took charge of *men*. Exactly like tonight."

"We noticed," Ross said. "What car should we take?"

"Your pick."

Gamel agreed to watch Sergio until the police arrived. Then, Detective Leeks, Melko, Ross, and Zina piled into the Jeep Cherokee. Tolerating no dissent from the disparate trio, Zina took the wheel. She shot gravel to the turnabout, swerved on to Gulf to Bay, and aimed north up Highway 19.

"Where are we going?" Ross asked.

"Quiet. I'm thinking."

Chapter 35

It was full throttle all the way. As she angled for the center lane, Zina sent her groaning cargo left and right during maneuvers. Unwilling to challenge the erratic speedster, other cars conceded to the Jeep Cherokee.

"Where, young lady, if I may risk a question, did you learn to drive?"

Having finally aligned himself in the rear seat, Detective Leeks found his voice. Meanwhile, Melko clutched his tummy, the roller coaster ride pure havoc for his innards. Preoccupied with his own agony, Ross dwelled upon the destination of this late night dash up Route 19. If he had to guess, Ms. Signet-surrogate already knew the answer. But, the constant distraction of possible collision did not permit speculation. As passenger in the front seat, he was much too close to oncoming action.

"On television, from Daytona." The Cherokee lurched left, preserving its scalp from a meandering truck. "Cash buggies driving in circles. Unlike them, I earn no money."

"Nascar," the detective said. "Or, the Indy 500. Where exactly are we going?"

"To my uncle's house in Tarpon Springs." She tossed a sideways glance to Ross. "Signet did not direct me. The decision is logical. Other than Grandpa, he is unfamiliar with my extended family. But, please, no one mention austerity to Uncle Stephano. The European Union and hard-knuckle Germans stole his bank account. Any talk of Greece would be unwise. By the way," she added, her eye on the rearview "a dark blue Jaguar has been on our tail since the underpass."

The three passengers had a look out the rear window. Sure enough. One hundred yards behind them, a dark, sleek vehicle was keeping pace.

"Blue, you say? To me, it's black."

Zina ignored the vapid comment and kept her eye on the road ahead. The question of the color was soon resolved, though, when smooth as silk, a blue Jag pulled alongside them. For a moment it matched the Cherokee's speed, then the front window slid down to reveal a grinning Sauer at the wheel. He raised his elongated middle finger in salute. After pausing a beat, he closed the window and, braking slowly, resumed his former position of pursuit behind them.

"I gather, I have just met Mr. Sauer, the man with the knives."

"I doubt he is a mister. But, you 'gather' correct, Detective. As for color, the Jag is blue. Good eyes, Zina."

"Thank you, *Mister* Melko. I appreciate that."

"Just Melko, okay Empress ... I mean, Zina?"

This brought them a quick laugh, but silence soon reclaimed them.

"Why do you think he did that?"

"To remind us he is there," Zina said dryly.

"He'll follow us to Tarpon Springs and tear your uncle apart."

"That's why we solve the problem here."

The detective removed his Samsung from an inside pocket, placed a call, and explained the situation. Satisfied with the response from subordinates at the Clearwater Police station, he disconnected.

"We're set," he said. "My men will erect a roadblock at the Tampa Road intersection. Five cruisers will easily contain this fellow Sauer."

Zina stayed in the middle lane, her determined foot making the engine scream.

"Good job, Ms. Palaeologus. Why your uncle, though? Why Tarpon Springs?"

Ross scoffed at the whole idea.

"Signet's influence," he said to Leeks. "From the grave."

"Impossible, my emperor. It is I, strong-willed Theodora, who now calls the shots. The unfortunate Signet cannot help us now. The beast in the jaguar behind us turned him into swamp bait."

"Why involve your uncle at all?"

She shrugged but maintained speed.

"We are safe in Tarpon Springs," she said. "Home to the largest Greek community in the country, a proud people with a terrific heritage. Once a sponge kingdom, living out of the Gulf, the area fell on hard times when sponge prices went kaput. But, the people survived. They turned the bayou into a successful tourist hangout. I belong there. And, don't worry about Uncle Stephano. Worry instead about Sauer. Uncle owns a shotgun."

"Orthodox Christianity. Now I remember," Leeks said. "You guys jump into the bayou every year to retrieve a cross. You also have a crying statue in some church."

"You are both ignorant and disrespectful. The event you speak of is called the Epiphany Festival. She is also not a 'crying statue.' You refer to the sacred icon of Saint Nicholas, patron saint of the Gulf coast sponge industry. No one but the very faithful has witnessed a tear in decades."

"You're joking. A crying statue—sorry—icon?"

"Not so long ago, a sacred priest saw the tears himself. Father Palaeologus, my grandfather, witnessed this moist event. He was also the exalted priest chosen to toss a sacred cross into the bayou. Epiphany, sir. We take our faith seriously here."

Silence descended, like a cloak over collapsed shoulders. Except for the high-pitched whirring under the hood, the detective's embarrassed cough the only sound in the car.

Lucky for him, Empress Theodora's foot was already

engaged. She might well have applied *Krav Maga's* chapter on "Annihilation of Fool." Fortunate also their driver's attention remained riveted on the Jeep's escape. She bypassed the man's sarcastic attitude with nary a blink.

In time, they swept past the empty Countryside Mall parking lot and, after the Japanese steak house, began the long incline to Highway 580. Appearing in the distance, a good mile further on, a line of flashing cruisers blocked Route 19's intersection with Tampa Road.

"Any time now, folks. The man won't know what hit him."

Ross leaned closer to Zina.

"This darn thumb drive is burning a hole in my pocket," he whispered, "What should I do with it?"

"A moral sacrifice is required."

Exactly what he did not want to hear.

"You mean like the footbridge dilemma?"

She gave him a look.

"What footbridge?"

"Two men are standing on a platform overlooking railroad tracks."

After checking the rearview, her mood lifted.

"Sauer does not slow down. Foolish decision. Railroad tracks? Tell me."

"Below the bridge, several people are standing next to

a siding on the tracks. They are unaware the switch is broken, that the approaching train will turn on to the side tracks and kill them all."

"Not if the man who sees the problem first pushes the other man off the bridge. He will fall upon and flip the switch. The train will then avoid the siding. The people are saved. The train problem. What about it?"

"Except this second person, the one who is pushed, will perish in the process. Same thing here. Should I abandon Glaucon to expose these clandestine projects?"

"I am confused. Are you making an analogy?"

How to explain this?

"I throw myself on my sword. I abandon Glaucon, the only copy of which is stored on this drive, and thereby expose Campesi and spare people the agony of his undisclosed and illegal inoculations. You know, sacrifice the one for the many."

"These projects are deeply encrypted," she said. "Colonel Bame and Mr. Campesi will work to keep them that way. How can returning this thumb drive expose them?"

"All codes can be broken."

"Yes, but by whom. Wait." Another rapid glance at the rearview. "Sauer approaches on our right."

They had long passed Highway 580 and were nearly at the bank of cruisers. Zina picked up speed, staying ahead of the Jaguar.

"It is treason to share those secrets with the media. If you keep them you also break the law."

"What if I toss Campesi off the footbridge? In fact, that's exactly what I should do."

"I like the sound of that. The fizzy cola is kicking in."

"So, that's how it works. I lose my fear of failure and do the right thing? Except, is there really a 'right thing'?"

"It must depend upon the situation. For example, when Sauer cut out that terrorist's heart, it was, for him, at that moment, the right thing."

"Can you imagine his buddies' reaction when they saw that chest hole? 'Something evil here, Sasha. Watch your back. You might be next.'"

It took a moment to recover from their suppressed laughter. He was no icon, but the tear he wiped away was real.

As was this intense discussion. Talking about morals with a Jaguar zooming up their exhaust pipe. Still, the problem nagged at him. It would not go away.

"Assume Mr. Campesi is the context. Will you really push him off?"

Presented with the actual situation gave him pause. Campesi was evil, but could Ross really do it? Watch out below! Man coming down! Uh, Uh. Didn't think so. Not quite there yet. Later, it might become the right thing to do.

"This is like the Nika rebellion," Zina said. "The vaccine, not Theodora, persuades you on a correct path of action."

Again, her loopy logic. This in no way resembled the ancient, Byzantine slaughterhouse inside the Hippodrome. He only wanted to halt the CEO's illicit project and preserve his own, very legal one. However, if he returned the flash drive, fell on his own sword, Campesi would persist with his deplorable behavior. Both outcomes seemed incompatible, particularly with Campesi the man on the bridge doing the pushing.

Back to square one unless his amygdalae were truly whacked out of action. Then, he might easily push the man to the tracks below. So to speak.

With a sudden whoosh of air, Sauer accelerated past the Jeep Cherokee, cutting off a U-Haul truck before screeching to a halt in front of the barricade. The Jaguar then made a sharp right-hand turn, zooming east, down Tampa Road, avoiding the police all together.

Detective Leeks smacked the seat.

"Goddamn! They set up on the other side of the intersection."

Recognizing their mistake, a pair of cruisers took chase, pursuing the blue rocket into the night. Zina crept through the resulting gap in the line, and a second later the Jeep resumed speed up Route 19.

Her gaze soon locked on the rearview mirror.

"Where did *he* come from?"

Her passengers turned for a look. Sauer had indeed reentered the highway, this time from a side road, cruisers nowhere in sight. Circling around, he'd found a way to elude his pursuers. Smart. One of Colonel Bame's perfect soldiers had analyzed the landscape, a deeply ingrained instinct to avoid capture, to snare prey. To snare them.

Melko groaned.

"Now what?"

Detective Leeks retrieved his cellphone.

"I'll call Tarpon Springs. Maybe they can catch him."

"Not enough time," Zina said. "I will lose him first. Hang on. Rough water ahead."

Not one to exaggerate, she crushed the pedal and the Jeep jumped forward, the speedometer, for a few moments, over eighty. Without warning, she hit the brakes and sent them sprawling. Fighting the wheel, she straightened out, and veered down a side road, passing rows of dark houses and broken street lamps before slamming the breaks, this time spinning left. She repeated this right-left exercise numerous times, plunging ever deeper into folds of impenetrable darkness, into a parallel universe of barren fields and featureless neighborhoods until, finally, tracking back the way they came, they approached the flashing orange lights of the Tarpon Road intersection dead ahead.

This time Melko wasn't the only one clutching a heaving gut.

"Are you sure this is the shortest way?" Ross said, fighting off waves of nausea.

"Shush. I'm navigating."

Nascar time again. A jolting dash across the highway. A split second lurch to the right. More unnerving switchbacks and jumped stop signs. In a blur, Ross identified the sponge dock, Aquarium, tied up shrimp boats, even Melko's bar and grill down an empty sidewalk. After a final squeal of brakes and a bumpy, pothole skid, they entered a dank garage somewhere east of the Anclote River. Only a rough calculation though, Ross's gyroscope long off kilter, his sense of direction wobbly. Yet, Zina appeared content. The only one still seated aright, a good thing.

With a snap of the seat belt, she disengaged from the Jeep, slammed the garage door shut then placed an ear against the side wall.

"No one out there," she announced. "Next stop, Uncle Stephano."

CHAPTER 36

The midnight moon was full, the air fish-tinged, smoky. They plowed on, Zina, like a miniature Signet, furtive, quiet, and on point.

She led them through back alleys and side yards, over abandoned lots, coiled ropes, past boats on vents, always keeping to the shadows, ear tuned to sounds near and far. A difficult trek for Ross, but for Melko, a struggle. He managed to keep up with Ross's help and Zina's hissed instructions. Having wisely accepted her advice, the detective had long departed for Melko's bayou grille on Dodecanese Street, there to wait for backup and a return trip to Clearwater Beach to retrieve his Honda.

After a painful twenty minutes, they reached one of the amoeba-shaped bayou inlets hugging the town. It was there, Zina informed them, pointing to the precise spot on the cracked sidewalk following the curve of the inlet, at this very location, beneath this sagging oak tree four and one half feet above the smelly bayou water, that she, with the assistance of Krav Maga, tossed four nasty boys into the bayou.

"Yesterday," she said, proudly. "Second time for them. Dumb boys, especially Stamos, who does not dive at Epiphany for the cross any longer."

Hands on hips, she paused to gauge reaction.

"Stamos was supposed to drive my van tonight."

"Instead, he paddled water. One hundred yards to a boat slip. He was a strong swimmer at Epiphany. Last year but not again."

She turned from the oak tree to face the path ahead.

"Bayshore Boulevard. Be careful." She pointed across the street. "My uncle lives behind those tall windows. Follow me."

At the sidewalk, she glanced up and down the deserted road then signaled it was safe. They went across the pavement and up a dozen stone steps to reach the front door. A double decker, the lights off on the top floor, but the front rooms lit like Christmas.

Zina punched the doorbell.

"Uncle is old fashioned," she said. "His niece shows up with two men after midnight. He might be cranky. Hmm. No answer. He leaves me no choice. I will bang the crab knocker."

As twin bongs reverberated inside the house, Ross glanced in through the jutting front windows. To his surprise, the interior resembled another museum piece, this one from both a modern and bygone era. Four overstuffed, plastic sheeted chairs faced a massive vase of purple, silk hydrangeas. Covering the floor, a thick, gold rug hugged the furniture and, on opposing walls, hung framed pictures of Greek gods. An odd feature stood out. Facing the street window, visible to passersby, a huge tripod displayed an incongruous poster of Superman stretching for the heavens. An hour earlier, Ross was steeped in Egyptian heritage. Now, a mere javelin toss across the Mediterranean, ignoring of course the anachronistic man of steel, he had landed in ancient Greece.

Hoof beats sounded beyond the door. It swung open and a sleepy, colossus of a man emerged to look them over. When his red-rimmed eyes settled upon Zina, he relaxed, burying her deep within the folds of his velvet robe.

"Zee Nee! How good it is to see you!" He backed off a step, studying her with sudden suspicion. "Is your rent due? Is that why you knock at such an hour?"

"No, Uncle. We have come for another...."

"Every month I sent money from Salonica. That apartment above the Aquarium has become too expensive. Move in here. Then, I can afford you."

"I cannot do that. I am on my own—"

"Adventure. Yes, I know. I read your letters. You cannot imagine the trouble over there. The government froze my accounts. They stole my yacht. They forced me to return here. I have little income to support you."

As an afterthought, he gazed over his niece's head and, seeing the two men, gave each a thorough vetting.

"Who are these vagabonds?"

"They are friends, Uncle. Can we please discuss this inside?"

A brief pause while Uncle Stephano adjusted. With a sigh, invoking forgiveness from the gods, he swept them into the house and shut the door. Shaking his head, still uneasy with his decision, he led his visitors through the littered foyer—luggage, piles of mail, and newspapers in the corners—to a rear study where Ross and an exhausted Melko collapsed on a leather couch.

To smooth the transition, Zina mollified her uncle with flattery and complimentary remarks about Aunt Sophia. Finally, as he relented, she explained about her guests. Each was a very important gentleman, one a respected physician, a famous innovator of eyeball cures, the other a retired detective who once apprehended criminals, who received commendations from the mayor of his town in Massachusetts.

She paused to catch her breath, casting an eye to the other guests. Wide eyed, each gave a thumbs up then witnessed a smooth manipulation of devoted uncle. Finally, he relented.

"Enough, Zee-nee. I believe as you do, each was beloved of his mother. Distinguished, worthy of praise. Of the two, I favor the freckled doctor. He cannot remove his gaze. Why does he stare so much at you?"

"At me? No, Uncle. He looks *through* me to tomorrow. He is planning a bridge party but not the card game variety.

Now, as I was explaining earlier...."

Uncle Stephano waved her away; he was more interested in Ross.

"I recognize you," he said. "Before leaving for Greece, I joined Father Palaeologus in an office visit. He insisted I meet his doctor."

"I remember. Father Paleologus wore a glittering gold bracelet. His visual field test revealed great improvement."

"Not so his behavior. Who is this Gina person? He came to life when the technician hugged him."

Strangely, Melko perked up, feeling a need, for whatever reason, to defend his friend's actions.

"Please, sir. Do not let a flirtatious priest distract you. This good doctor here restored his eyesight and gave him a second life."

"Ah. It is you, Mr. Melko, the owner of that grille. I recognize you. Perhaps we should discuss Saturday night."

Melko nodded, visibly disturbed when Uncle Stephano bit off the word *owner*.

"Yes indeed, sir. Please accept my most sincere apology."

"The priest, my father, is a man of God. We were there for dinner. You ignored my complaint about his behavior. You said not to worry. You insisted he was only some 'bozo' bouncing a waitress on his knee. It was obvious, at the time, you were unaware of his special calling, that you might think of him as bozo. Although he pinched a woman's bottom and called her 'honey,' you still owe both of us more than apology."

Although retired, the cop in Melko retained attitude. He accepted the rebuke, offered another terse apology about misidentifying Father Paleologus but reminded Zina's uncle the staff and patrons alike found his dad's behavior inoffensive and amusing. It was a lively Saturday night at a bayou restaurant, after all. What could one expect? At least no one was injured.

"Did you enjoy the food? Grilled fish is our specialty."

"The grouper was excellent, thank you. Very tasty. However, Father's behavior ruined dessert. And, his choice of clothes? Sandals and sailor shorts. I had barely laid down my fork when he squeezed the waitress. It saddens me to learn he is a regular at that abyss. Months earlier, before I departed, he conducted Sunday mass. Now, he conducts gymnastics at the dinner table."

Zina adjusted her position, gazing anywhere but upon her distraught uncle.

"A long story," she managed. "Later, when there is more time, I will explain. Right now we are tired and hungry. Would you mind if we pull the drapes? A gold fishbowl in here."

Ross took the hint and moved to a chair away from the window. Melko followed suit, selecting a plastic covered armchair across the room. It was wise to play it safe; although, since leaving Route 19, there'd been no sign of the Jaguar. It was unlikely the assassin would find them.

Ross could ill afford to be apprehended before he figured out a course of action.

Uncle Stephano vanished for a few moments. He returned with a platter of pita bread and sliced *kefalotyri* cheese that Zina helpfully identified as Greek and very salty plus a pitcher of lemonade with three glasses. It was all he could find, he said. Aunt Sophia, his former wife, had not prepared a proper meal since his return.

"She is unhappy Athens seized our assets," he said. "I fear she may yet steal my figurines." He indicated the row of tiny statues on pedestals around the room. "They are rare collector items. Made of gold and worth a minor fortune. Go on, Zee Nee. Explain your heritage."

Taking up where Gamel Azzizzi left off, Zina became de facto tour guide of Uncle Stephano's priceless Greek collection. Again, much resembling the pedestaled Egyptian artifacts in the time chamber on Clearwater Beach, her uncle chose to display his many gods and goddesses in a similar fashion. Unlike friend Gamel though, Zina possessed scant enthusiasm for any except her favorite deity, Priapus, god of fertility she added, blushing as she presented the bold statuette. She touched lightly on mighty Zeus, father of all the gods, curly Apollo and deadly Typhon, god of monsters and volcanoes. In quick succession, she mentioned Hermes, messenger to the underworld, Aphrodite, Athena, and Artemis until arriving at the final one set off from the others, a good size sculpture of a crouching Spiderman, his serpentine gaze filling the room.

Greeted by her uncle's mute applause, she plopped down next to Ross.

"He always makes me do this," she whispered. "Sorry."

He squeezed her arm. She nestled closer.

"Tell us about that picture," Melko said, drawing their attention to a glided frame of teenage Zina.

Spray-on bikini, sponge and diving goggles in one hand, a firm-lipped young female grinned for the camera.

"Uncle Stephano and me." She let out a breath. "One of my first dives. I enlarged the photo and had it framed. Happier day, eh, uncle?"

"You were skilled, an excellent swimmer. Too bad Father Palaeologus could not use girls at the Epiphany celebration."

She sniffed displeasure.

"Male divers, like this one, Stamos, who harassed me in high school. One time he followed me into a female locker room. For him that did not go well. He departed slowly, clutching his midsection." She let out a long breath. "Did you know he was Grandpa's favorite? Even as a man of God, he might not choose well. The same for Mr. Melko here. When I learned he was a diver, I decided to act."

"Zee Nee, Zee Nee ... You still flip bad boys into the water? What will your aunt say?"

A distilled silence followed these revelations. Just as well, Ross decided. It was late, rather, early in the morning. A grandfather clock bonged twelve times somewhere else in the house. They were tired and needed to rest. Except for Ross. Zina's comment about enlarging a photograph triggered an idea.

Percolating with renewed energy, he sprang from the armchair.

"May I use your computer?" he asked Uncle Stephano. "Do you have a spare flash drive?"

"No flash drive. I do own a laptop. It is unavailable because I loaned it to Sophia before I left for the islands. She uses it for inventory at her gift shop."

As there was no time to find Aunt Sophia and with Sauer hovering in the background, he had to enact the plan tonight. Staples, the business store. That's what he'd do. When it opened in a few hours, he'd copy the stolen documents. The perfect solution. Return the original to Colonel Bame then bribe Campesi with the copy, assuming Ross wasn't closed out or imprisoned first.

"You want to *copy* the flash drive?"

"I'll wait until Staples opens."

"Your idea to become another Snowden?"

"Absolutely not. I won't release anything online. I'll bribe the jerk instead."

"Excellent, my emperor. You have become that fearless man on the footbridge. Congratulations."

"The inoculation must be working. I don't normally bribe people."

"An MRI would reveal your amygdala to be Swiss cheese. How Dr. Braun described Signet's brain at this stage."

Like a switch thrown, his moment of clarity now vanished. Courageous bravura, so prominent but a second earlier, receded into a curious mist leaving a single image of the triumphant CEO standing in his conference room, cufflinks sparkling.

Glaucon belonged to him. He would call Ross's bluff, the misguided eye doctor no match for the vengeful man. His idea a complete nonstarter.

The sound of sing song chimes twinkled from the landline phone on the hall table. Uncle Stephano rushed to get it, listened a few moments, disconnected.

"My God," he said, bustling about, flashing his Red Sox pajamas. "That was Cousin Constantine. He lives next door. There is a peculiar racing car on the street. It crept back and forth three times before stopping in front of this house. What can it mean?"

Ross did not like the sound of this.

"Someone may be lost," he said without conviction. "Looking for a house number."

"Describe the car, Uncle."

"Constantine's imagination, I am sure," Uncle Stephano said. "Ever since deployed to the Middle East, his son appears as hallucination. Once he saw a cross in the sky. Such hope. Every night a vigil by the front window, he waits for his return."

"Was it dark blue? Think."

The suspense got the better of him. Ross rushed out of the room. He returned in a flash.

"It's Sauer. Parked at the curb, staring at the front door. I saw him clear as day. How did he ever find us?"

"Don't look at me. I told no one about Uncle Stephano."

"Who is this sour person?"

"A bad guy," Melko said. "I think I know how he found us. When you brought Father Palaeologus to Dr. Ross's office during the summer I bet they asked your name at check-in."

Uncle nodded.

"I am a family member. I signed the register."

"As the patient's son, Stephano. That way you updated the Palaeologus clan on their database. A simple matter for crafty Sauer to find your address."

"What do you mean, *clan*? We are not some tribe from the desert."

"A figure of speech," Melko said. "I meant nothing by it."

"I see. You are attracted to my *figure*."

"Zee Nee. This is not how we talk here. Behave or I will send you to your room."

The place was fast descending to a state of minor chaos. Despite their exhaustion and hunger, they could no longer dally with Zina's uncle.

On edge, Ross parted the curtain and examined the shadows of the rear yard.

"We can't stay here. We are not safe. Signet was wrong. We can't hide here any longer."

"You have come to hide, Zee Nee?"

Embarrassed, his niece nodded.

"Yes, uncle. We are hiding from that man in the blue car. Do not be angry. We will leave soon. And, for your interest, Dr. Danny-boy, it was my idea, not Signet's. By now, he is rot and worms. I hope he stays that way."

"A bit severe, don't you think?" Melko wagged a finger. "Didn't he introduce you to Krav Maga? That sure proved useful with Stamos and his buddies."

"Let's focus on this problem, okay?"

Minutes flew by. The clock kept ticking. No one knew what to do.

Uncle Stephano now took charge. He swept into the middle of the room, ushering them close, dropping into a conspiratorial whisper.

"I know the perfect place to hide." Suddenly conscious of his state of undress, he cinched his robe. "My former wife, Sophia, will take you in. No one knows anything about her."

"Except, they'll consult the same database that found you."

"She is no longer a Palaeologus," he said, voice tinged with regret. "She returned to her maiden name, Belisarius, after the divorce. I stayed away too long. Also, I stopped sending money. Probably why she no longer prepares me spanakopita. There is no way to link our family names. She cannot be on that database."

Zina's eyes lit up.

"That is right. Belisarius. Her family name is the same as Emperor Justinian's famous general. Do you remember him?"

Ross regretfully nodded.

"The Nika Rebellion?"

"Very good. Recall, he also defeated the awful Persians in the East."

"Ah, Zina. We are discussing where we might hide."

Taking a breath, she scanned three sets of bleary eyes.

"A great idea, Uncle. Sauer will never find us at Aunt Sophia's."

"Mr. Palaeologus, sir. About your spanakopita. My chef will gladly prepare it for you."

The two men, former adversaries, exchanged a hopeful glance.

"If it's no trouble for your kitchen."

"Consider it done. My pleasure."

Uncle Stephano now guided them to the rear of the house. They descended a narrow stairwell to the attached garage where they found a rusted Cadillac in a puddle of oil. Stepping with care, they got belted in. The uncle depressed a wall button, the door creaked upward and, after pushing his niece aside, jumped in behind the wheel.

At a snail's pace, they turned right and followed the alley to an intersection. Pausing for a quick inspection to either side, Uncle Stephano gunned it. Soon they were zipping down a long road into the murky depths of Tarpon Springs. Recessed houses, few street lights, and no headlights in the rearview mirror. The darkest night stretched out in all directions.

Ross asked where they were.

"Sophia lives up ahead near the Anclote River," their new driver said. "To your left, hidden beyond those trees, is the Gulf of Mexico. Over there, to your right, is the bayou. It takes you to the sponge docks."

Several minutes later, he glided to a stop in front of a split level home at the very end of the road.

"Tell Sophia hello. I will sell her this Cadillac. Don't mention an oil leak. Oh. Most important. Ask for a bowl of her lemon soup. She will take good care of you."

Half asleep in a sheer robe, Aunt Sophia invited them in at once.

CHAPTER 37

Two features stood out about Zina's aunt.

First, her choice of home, and its location. Situated on a spit of land, her haphazard split level stood submerged by an overgrowth of bushes and crooked trees, a dozen feet from the winding bayou without a neighbor in sight. A slice of unchartered landscape, an excellent hideout for the duration of the night.

And second, the woman herself.

Stout, with dyed blond hair, face worn with deep set, crinkly eyes, Aunt Sophia greeted them with a measured skepticism although, when she came to Melko, her gaze rounded in approval. Spotting Zina, she then burst forth with hugs and kisses, fussing as any smitten aunt might over a wayward and infrequently visiting niece. The niece fussed back with a fond flurry of her own. Like professional athletes, they performed a peculiar hand jive: left and right cross over knuckle bumps, finger tickles, under and over palm flips, and to cap it off, rubbed noses. Family. Always there for you.

In the faint light of the foyer, Ross made another observation.

Earlier in life, Aunt Sophia had been a knockout of impressive proportion, physical attributes noticed as well by retired Detective Anton Melcovitch, how he chose to introduce himself upon the conclusion of introductory antics. A light came on in his sagging eyes, hers as well, as their appreciation appeared mutual.

"Mr. Melko," Aunt Sophia enthused, rearranging an imaginary strand of hair. "Is that really you?"

Jarred to full alert, he doffed an equally imaginary cap, his manners a charming throwback not lost on Aunt Sophia.

"How could I possibly forget?" he said. "You and Uncle Stephano came in with Father Palaeologus last Saturday night." He turned to Ross, his brown and sober eyes alarmingly aflame. "This is the incident Zina's uncle referred to earlier. While assailing me with complaint, I chanced a glance around his immense shoulder and there, sitting demurely and rather becoming, was this most lovely woman, who I now learn is Aunt Sophia. From that moment on, I heard not a single word he said."

Assailing? Chanced a glance? Rather becoming?

He tried to get his pal's attention. Impossible, Melko already marshalling considerable reserve to 'assail' the 'rather becoming' hostess whom fate just delivered into his quaking hands. Girlishly ducking her head, her robe mysteriously parted to reward his effort.

"You wore that cute, black jacket," she said. "If it were not for father's pranks, I would have approached you. And, here you are now. In person."

Melko became younger by the second. Zina's aunt relapsed as well to salad days, and, as the years slipped by, Ross soon felt the voyeur of what amounted to a high school first date. The initial flirt, then shy invitation, an even shyer acceptance then, bypassing a shy shuffle to the likes of Uncle Stephano's relic Cadillac, a quick hustle to the top step of downward leading spiral stairs.

"Your dad is a terrific singer. A very energetic gentleman, livelier than our usual crowd."

"But, so embarrassing. Stephen later told me he grabbed a waitress and jumped to the stage. I was mortified. Thank the Lord no one recognized our priest."

"*Former* priest," Zina said, barging into the strange goings-on. "What is this about 'father' and 'dad'? He is *Father Palaeologus*. At one time a very distinguished, spiritual man. Don't be so certain he jostled ladies incognito. People know him. That is the problem."

Ross caught Sophia's worried frown.

"Come on, guys," he said. "We're here to visit your charming aunt, not to get distracted by last Saturday night. Plus we need to ask a favor."

Their charming hostess had already laid claim to Melko's elbow. With a gentle tug, she aimed him down the stairs to the lower level. During their giggling descent, Ross's twinge of guilt morphed into a sigh of relief. He was happy for his friend. Such a rendezvous was unheard of in the staid Belmont bedroom community from which he hailed. A rare encounter even for a restaurateur in Tarpon Springs. At his age, lady friends were as scarce as fresh sponges.

A filmy voice floated up the stairs.

"Zee Nee, dear. Feel free to use the upstairs parlor. A pleasure to meet you, Doctor."

Before she disappeared, he hurriedly explained his problem. But, no. Aunt Sophia would not be unlocking her shop that morning. Nor did she possess a thumb drive.

As a door creaked shut below, Zina took control above. Like auntie like niece. Ross found his left elbow in a Sauer-quality vise as he stumbled up a set of chipped wood stairs to the second level. Arms entwined, they stood in the middle of a dark and musty room. No lamps or wall switch. Only Zina lighting him up inside.

"She always opens the shop for weekends. She has now made other plans."

"You don't mean Melko?"

"Whether a good sign or not, too soon to say. It means, for us, the business store is our only solution. They open at eight. Until then, we rest."

✶✶✶

They were greeted by sparse appointments: an over-stuffed, Victorian couch, a stately grandfather clock, a few rugs and one table. While Zina adjusted shades on the front window, he sank weary limbs into absorbent cushions but not for long. His nerves forced him up. Together, they scrutinized the featureless landscape beyond the murky pane.

Empty of vehicles, the narrow road and its haunting foliage blended as a black splotch of desolate seclusion. Not one devoid of life though. An owl's eerie cry punctured the gloom while, scurrying unseen through the front shrubs, a rustling beast gave them a start. Raccoon, opossum or armadillo. More likely a coyote. The hungry beasts were conquering Florida, devouring stray cats and dogs as they migrated south and, if parents grew careless, unsuspecting toddlers might join the menu. Ross listened hard, photoreceptors adjusting, as he searched for Sauer amongst the shadows. Not there, at least for now. Maybe, just maybe, they were safe at Aunt Sophia's.

They sought the comfort of the spacious couch. Limbs akimbo, Zina leaned against him, lightly kissing his fingertips.

"You are tense," she said, massaging clenched fingers.

"Can't help it."

"We can leave any time. Auntie won't object. Mr. Melko may want to stay here. Her robe must be quite lose by now."

Heat shot from tremulous limbs to his face. The thought

of what was going on two flights below flared within his limbic brain. Thank goodness for the dark parlor. All systems full aglow.

"Correction. Not lose, but off. I hope your friend's heart holds out."

He hoped the same for himself. Zina crowded closer, launching round two.

"Don't worry," he said. "He survived a recent checkup. Auntie will have her hands full. We'll let them be while we copy this thumb drive in the morning. Then, it's off to Odessa."

His mood, for a moment whooping the sheets, went south, the idea, 'going to Odessa', noxious, chilling. The damper didn't last long, however. A playful hand caressed his inner thigh, teasing fingers adrift north.

"Have you reached a final decision?"

He shook his head, clamping down on her pesky hand. Undeterred, she ventured on, nuzzling into position, wiggling his earlobe. Once again, the typhoon of pungent fragrance, the wilting of fragile resistance. He squirmed with desire.

"Good to snuggle, my emperor. We are alone. No one to check our progress."

With a gentle twist, she joined them up, first, at the hip, interlocking legs and ankles then, after a full body rotation, their lips. He tingled with the soft and yielding kiss, the surging warmth, the relief of caress such a long time coming.

Zina repositioned his hands, already on the move. A deep embrace, the curve of her lower back now yielding. Another kiss. Nerves tingling, wired ... he was gone.

...somehow ... later ... they'd hit ... Staples...

...copy the flash drive...

...travel ... to Odessa ... Find Campesi...

...avoid Sauer....

He yanked the blinds on such intrusions. Already insistent fingers had made progress. His descending zipper sounded a xylophone progression. Then, his loosed belt buckle a cello tear in an unfamiliar musical mode. Yet, he held quiet his baton lest the couch couplet become unstrung. To fight off firm necessity, despite wonderful Zina upon him, he had to tame his sizzling, frantic brain. Off their leash and beyond frontal lobe restraint, hands seemingly not his own wandered over the frets of taut desire. God, he was ready. If only....

But no. The timing was all wrong.

With so much still unsettled, he simply could not conduct. Forgo this pleasure. Refocus.

He gulped the allergen infested air. He pulled himself together. He zipped up.

"Why stop, Justinian? We are almost there."

"I know. I know. My mind erupted. It can't stop buzzing."

With a huff of disappointment, she slid off his lap.

"Is that a problem? We are 'buzzing' now. Erupting will be good for us."

"I, I. Well, I have to copy files."

"Later in the morning. Right now, we do this first."

"But, only the Glaucon file. Not the others. I can't commit treason."

Disgusted now, she slid further away from him. Even in the shadows he recognized crossed arms over bare chest.

"Your project is that vital?"

"To treat and cure glaucoma? Are you kidding?"

"You already do those things every day."

"I know that. But, I need to make a *lasting* contribution. I want to be known as an innovator, a leader like Chandler, Grant, and Simmons and all those other greats. Even Kulifabo. My God. I can't forget Belcher. He has his own pedestal. A great man. Never to be forgotten. I need to be part of that tradition."

"On a *pedestal*, like one of the gods?" She shrugged, giving him a good look in the dark. "Maybe a god like Priapus might be okay. But, that's what it sounds like. Patients are not enough."

"Untrue. It always about patients. I just want to leave a permanent mark. I want to be remembered."

"Signet was right. You fear the void. That is what drives you. You resemble a man of god, except you don't write books to convince others and earn big money at the same time. Yes. That is what you are: a man of religion. Glaucon is your faith. Your belief system."

"Are you comparing me to Father Palaeologus?"

"Before he changed, yes. As a Christian, he pursued faith not money. Or girls."

She folded her knees beneath her. Lecturing now. Sharing a sizable piece of her mind.

"That swine Campesi poisoned Grandfather and destroyed his belief system. We know that happened. I see now Signet did right by you. Without that cola drink, you would never do the wise thing."

"My god, I was right. Mr. Zen-Security actually did inoculate me with that damn vaccine. And, what the hell is 'do the wise thing' baloney? Why does everyone keep saying that? Who the heck gets to decide what *that* is anyway?"

"Calm yourself, Dr. Immortal-man. Time for you to rest. Time for me to think."

She redressed, packing considerable charm and excitement from shadowy view. His heart, all that its feverish state entailed, throbbed the throttle down as well.

Zina leaned back and shut her eyes.

The room went silent.

Chapter 38

The minutes dragged on. He lost count. Like Zina, he drifted off. When she nudged his arm, his eyes popped open, surprised. Then, the granddaddy across the room bonged twice. He'd been out almost an hour. Her warmth, the perfume again invading.

Round three. He was ready.

"Grandfather claimed you are an exceptional doctor. Kind, compassionate. Does that not say something?"

"Grandpa was nearly blind. Fortunately, a sufficient number of retina ganglion cells survived. Following surgery, his central vision came to life as did his male stamina. He was happy with his doctor. That's all."

"Happy also with a brand new life. He sees clearly now. Or, so he claims. To be relieved of false and hurtful notions instilled by a deluded system. A seminary in the woods. Only priests and boys. Behave and God will whisk you up to heaven."

She paused. Shook her head. Laughed.

"In Florida, such people are more concrete. Snatch you from your car, they claim, maybe as you drive along. No wonder driverless cars are so hot. Go to heaven, no fatalities left behind. What Grandpa now calls another crazy notion inside crazy religion."

Again, a pause. A deep breath. She stared directly at him, a pair of blank, grey caves in the faint backlight. He got the message, though. Obsessed, needing to tell him.

"Grandfather no longer feels this personal connection. He is not one of the chosen few. Hah. Talk about a silly notion. Before birth even, God assembles your trillion molecules in a universe of trillion galaxies, our Milky Way but one. For him alone all these ideas became false. He has explained this trillion molecule idea a gadzillion times to me. For him, it makes the priesthood wrong. For me, it makes my head spin. You had a hand in this new outlook, Dr. Danny-boy. I concede, in his case, a wise decision had been made. You helped save him."

"I didn't do anything but operate on his eye. Campesi's vaccine 'saved' him, not me."

"You returned vision to an old man. That is saved enough. Now, he sees what his frisky paws are up to."

Ross left that alone. His turn to shut his eyes and lie back.

The parlor resumed its silence.

✶✶✶

More time crept by. With three gongs to guide her, Zina slid an arm behind his shoulder, pulled him closer. and their lips met. Minutes later, she caressed his ear with a smooth whisper.

"Had we time at Uncle Stephano's, we would be inside my bed upstairs, not bent crooked on this musty couch."

"Tell me about your apartment near the Aquarium. What's it like?"

She shook her head.

"A wide mattress, cozy. Tell me what is going on down here?" Ever so slowly, she maneuvered her hand to a spot beneath his fluttering tummy and gave it a vigorous squeeze. "We have a second chance. Let us put it to good use. Okay, my nervous emperor?"

He maneuvered her persistent palm to a safer location.

"You were describing your room on the bayou."

"Three posters cover one wall. Brad Pitt, President Lincoln, and Einstein. I read he was the guy who found the Higgs Bosom particle."

"*Boson*," he corrected. "Einstein was not the 'guy' who discovered it, either."

She laughed, resuming her caress.

"I know all about the Higgs Field. Scientists uncovered its existence in Switzerland. It's a scalar field, a basic structure of our universe. It is why we have mass. Why, I hope, our two masses soon merge. Like those two black holes and the gravitational wave the laser interferometer measured."

He sat up. Or, tried to assume a more respectful position.

"That's right," he said. "I am impressed."

"I read a science journal in your office while waiting for Grandpa."

She repositioned for a fresh hug. A near smothering embrace. He held on for more.

"I understand rockets now. The force to penetrate space. A laser to tear apart empty space. The idea space was at one time created. Along with Grandpa's trillion molecules. I once memorized the periodotic table...."

"Periodic."

"Ok, big brain Justinian. Thank you. The tabular arrangement of the chemical agents. I also do Sudoku when I have the chance."

He sensed the moment slipping away. Zina, on a roll.

"On another wall," she continued. "Are two empty picture frames. One someday will contain my high school diploma. The other, perhaps a medical degree. Or, if I am lucky, your beloved immortal's wedding picture. Maybe all three. Yes, Danny-boy. Since my inoculation, the world has opened up for me."

He noted the sly innuendo, the slippery, spooky assumption of wedding bells down the line. But, for whom will these bells ring? That, she cleverly left unanswered.

The suggestion they might toll for someone else sent his pulse lurching. Jealousy of an imaginary person? Impossible but still....

A strange jolt of energy shot through him. A jolt similar to the one experienced in Gamel's front foyer, where the intensity of colors, sounds, all sensations overwhelmed him. A jolt cousin to that which sent his hands in frenetic search of Zina on the lake earlier, grappling for purchase before being shot down.

Similar to those others but far more insistent.

Alien almost, a force akin to a hidden but controlling scalar field, surfacing, pulling him along, directing his full attention to the woman beside him. As if on autopilot, it propelled his hand to Zina's tummy and, like Lewis and Clark on a free-wheeling expedition, to previously unexplored, sacred territory rimmed with rich foliage.

He lunged, seized hold of Zina and hugged her tight. Because his heart was in it, he hugged again, a full body meld that left them both breathless.

"Ah, Justinian. Most beloved doctor, is this the time?"

"Come here, Empress Zina. I am ready."

"No more buzzing or mental eruptions?"

Never one requiring a hint, Zina wriggled into his lap. At that very moment, deep within his insula cortex, the place where higher cortical behavior confronted more primitive signals, a switch was thrown. Despite the hour, his fatigue and constant worry, all effort to resist proved futile. He had promised himself to act should an opportunity arise. And, so he did.

"Tell me, Justinian. Do you like my new scent?"

Nostrils buried deep up front, he inhaled a prolonged whiff.

"Very much. I'm aware this may sound peculiar...."

"From you? Don't be silly."

"I first detect a hint of cedar, very faint, like cut wood. Next, a floral aroma. Then..." He sniffed again. "...a penetrating, earthy essence..." He paused, nose elevating from the crevice. "So many sensations. What is going on here?"

"Shade of Night. A magical perfume. It binds us both, dear emperor."

He struggled with his crinkly chinos.

"We are nearly bound already."

"Let us wait, dear one. We should savor the moment."

They closed their eyes, the clock a quiet metronome in the darkness.

Once more his mind tripped back to tricky Signet and his fizzy cola.

★★★

Zina roused him with a whisper.

"There is something I must tell you. I have changed, from meek dropout to bayou basher."

He managed a nod.

"I got that."

"Fear no longer restrains me."

"I've seen you in action. Composed. Confident. You remind me of Signet."

"A compliment. Thank you."

"You realize, of course, from an evolutionary perspective, fear of shadows protected our ancestors from snakes and tigers."

"Hmm. Justinian, the idea man."

"Fear is part of our human heritage. That's all I'm saying. Why eliminate it?"

"We must rein it in when it overreacts."

"How do you know when that happens?"

"Take Franklin and his Big Lie theory. A story is offered to the media. The TV and internet repeat it. We suspect the interpretation is a lie. Who is strong enough to resist?"

"How do we know it's a lie?"

"If Tarpon Springs stays unemployed, the economy is weak. No matter what the radio proclaims, we remain in recession. Wipe away fear. Clarity resumes. I am now prepared to say, I no longer fear what you represent."

Fresh beads of perspiration lined his brow.

"I don't see...."

"It is okay to like you. Even if you keep your pants on."

He chuckled with that one.

"They are half off. Then, you stopped me."

"I know. We are almost there yet."

"Why then do we wait?"

"Pay back. I have snuggled up before. You take an hour to find me."

With little effort he found her now though. She unzipped him, and they wrestled free of clothes, her tee removed with a resounding snap, then shorts, the skimpy item underneath. Arms unfurled, Ross eagerly embraced her, welcoming in turn her assortment of natural skills including, he was convinced, several Krav Maga gyrations tossed in for good measure.

Meanwhile outside, save for the rare hoot of an owl, silence reigned complete. A distilled quiet, shrouding ecstatic groans within, symphonies of pleasure echoing from both levels of Aunt Sophia's split-level home, a comfy lair situated behind trees, on a spit of land at the end of a dark and lonely road, at the very edge of Tarpon Springs near the Anclote River.

A Florida first and, should his luck hold, not his last.

CHAPTER 39

A distinct *thunk* jarred them awake. They exchanged a look then jumped to their feet. A car door, Zina said, tugging on her tee shirt. Not *him* again, Ross replied, plunging into his chinos.

They went to the window. Dark as before, clumps of shadows difficult to dissect. Peering hard they finally made out the vague outline of a vehicle. Parked beneath a vast oak tree less than a hundred yards away, a vehicle Ross easily identified as the low slung, menacing Jaguar.

"Goddamn," he exclaimed. "How the hell did he find us?"

"You swear freely. The inoculation must be kicking in. You are also very jumpy."

"And, you aren't? That's Sauer out there. What the hell does he want?"

"You have the flash drive. He knows that. Also, you debate going to Odessa. He might want to kill you,"

He paced. Dust wafted up from the carpet. He sneezed.

"I'm allergic to this place."

"But , not to me. Busy at work you sneeze. With both arms around my waist. I was happy you never let go."

"What? Of you? If that guy weren't out there...."

He sneezed again.

"You are so blasé. What are we going to do?"

"I know how he found us. Auntie came along for Grandpa's first postop visit. Like Uncle, she signed herself in. The name Belisarius entered the database."

"You remember this *now*? Or, maybe you conveniently forgot, you know, to get us out here."

"Why would I do that? You insult me."

"Never mind," he muttered, "We have a problem here."

He returned to the window, edged the shade aside, and shuddered at the apparition crunching down the center of the road. Like an outlaw in a TV western, Sauer, in his inexorable march forward, booted stones from his path, the only missing item, a dog crossing his path.

"We're cornered. I suppose you have another relative to visit. Where the hell do we go now?"

"*Hell*, is it? Your basal nucleus must be gone. Soon, bad-word cells will dominate."

"Who told you that?"

"I made it up. Take my hand. Once again, Theodora to the rescue."

They descended to the lower level, not knocking on Auntie's door to warn them. Safer in bed, Zina mumbled, nodding a quick farewell and moved on. They rushed through a small kitchen, to a rear door to the backyard. Two small windows. A bolted lock. Freedom.

"Shouldn't we tell them?" Ross said, having second thoughts.

"Mr. Sauer comes for you, not your friend. With Auntie granting wishes, he remains in excellent hands."

She rehearsed their escape route. A fenced-in yard lay between the back of the house and Sophia's dock and her boat on the river. To reach the dock, they had to scale the first of two low fences, dash across a small sandpit yard, and climb over the fence on the other side. A path led through the shrubs to her aunt's clunker used only for weekend outings to Honeymoon Island where she sunned with friends. Already gassed, the sturdy craft lay waiting. The only problem, safely scaling two wire fences.

"Why is that a problem?"

"Don't look around. Just run."

Instructions tendered, Zina planted a quick kiss on each cheek and opened the back door. She brushed up beside him.

"Be brave, my emperor. Remember. Move fast."

"Wait. I've been meaning to ask. You call me Dr. Danny-boy at times. Emperor at others. Even Justinian. Sometimes it's just *Danny-ell*. Why the different titles?"

Hand on the bolted door, she paused.

"Dr. Danny-boy or Danny-ell for respect. Emperor and Justinian to readjust your focus. Like now. Think only about the sandpit. Jump the fences. Run."

She cracked open the door. They heard a scratching sound off to their right. Heard it again. Louder.

"He is at the corner gate, working the latch. Hurry."

The scratching sound stopped. A rusted hinge creaked open.

"Move!" he said. "He's in the side yard."

In a flash, she was out the door and over the first fence.

"Watch out for alligators," she called back. "The yard borders the river."

Alligators? What the hell?

Sprinting now, Zina hurdled the second fence and vanished through distant shrubs. Seconds later, the thump of timber boards when she reached the dock. Soon, a low grumble when the boat came to life.

His turn.

A loud boom made him jump. Again to his right. Very close, around the corner of the house.

Holy crap.

He glanced out the door. Sauer, making a racket, was half way over the chain link fence. He tore free and leaped to the ground. Only feet apart, mano a mano, giant to midget. Ross's heart skipped a beat.

"Your girlfriend made it. Not you, asshole. Time for the dark closer."

"No, no. Hold it. I have the thumb drive. Here. It's in my pocket."

He fumbled, diving for his pocket. Couldn't find the damn thing. Damn anyway. He put the chinos on backwards. In his hurry, thinking about the assassin, seeing Zina's silhouette in the window. God. What an idiot.

"Keep it," the big man said. "It's too late anyway. I'm going to enjoy this."

"You're off script. I mean, this isn't *supposed to happen*."

"There is no script. I changed sides. It's all ad lib tonight."

More than sand lot fences or gators, Sauer's mocking laughter did the trick.

He ran.

The psychopath read his mind. He arrived at the first barrier a split second sooner. He reached for Ross, arm prepared for a headlock. But he missed. Their forward momentum broke the grip propelling them, in a weird embrace, over the fence and into the sand pit.

Spluttering, spitting sand, Sauer fell on his face. Ross broke free and rolled off. On his feet, he scrambled for the second fence. But, the dark closer wasn't done yet. He lunged with his grappling hook arm and seized Ross by the ankle. Tightening his grip, he yanked Ross backward, spinning him like a toy on a string.

"Not so fast. It ends here."

Fist balled for the coup de grace, Sauer failed to notice the enormous shape materializing from the gloom behind him. He did take note as the shape snapped at his legs. Screaming now, he kicked at the slithering monster and forgot about Ross. The gator, however, did not see it coming. Unleashing a familiar maneuver, Sauer twirled around, wound up astride the alligator's back, and grabbed hold.

"Jesus ... holy effing mother ... where ... did *this* ... come from?"

One of the bayou demons had joined the fight. Evening snack. Go for it.

Ross hurtled the second fence and hit the shrubs when the commotion behind him ceased. Curious, he turned to witness Sauer's track and field exercise. With a firm grip around the beast's belly, he spun twice and tossed the gator into distant bushes. Catching his breath, he locked gaze on Ross, and the chase was on.

He stumbled down the teetering dock, again entertaining an absurd notion Aunt Sophia used a cigar boat for her outings, not the rickety fourteen footer he tumbled into.

"You're kidding," he yelled at Zina. "Is this seaworthy?"

"Quiet. Take a seat. We are out of here!"

He fell into the seat beside Zina in the captain's chair.

Surprising him, the craft lurched forward, creaking at the sudden strain, commanded out of its slumber, resisting with a couple of coughs, but finally bowing to Zina's will. Perched high in her seat, hand on the wheel, the captain cut a dramatic figure behind the plastic shield. Even in the dark, waves spraying on both sides, he was able to make out Zina's bemused grin, the curious poise she brought to this new mission.

"Look there." She pointed to the foliage along the bank behind them. "Your friend joins us."

On a parallel track, Sauer plunged through the underbrush along the water. A futile effort because they had already reached the midpoint of the narrow river. The dark closer soon became a smudge on the dark horizon.

"Nice Job," he said. "He can't grab the stern now."

She nodded, continued on.

In time, she cut back on the speed. For a while they bobbed along in the current, passing deserted docks and homes along the shore. Overhead, stars glittered in a moonless sky. The air was cool, a bleak yet marvelous night. The same damn night he was dunked in Lake Tarpon. No, he recalculated. It was early morning. Goddamn. Time passing all too fast. Only hours before he was expected in Odessa.

"Signet will be proud," she said. "We escaped two monsters. Sauer spinning. Gators flying. I am pleased you are alive."

"How does Sophia avoid those beasts?"

"She tosses pork rinds in the river. An easy throw from the top porch."

"You also said, 'will be proud' Present tense. Signet is alive. How is that even possible?"

She didn't reply, her attention riveted on the dock approaching to starboard. On the lone figure just then coming into view. Well over fifty yards away, Ross still recognized the mad assassin who had managed to circle the nearby bayou. Feet spread, arms extended, he pointed a handgun directly at them, details just visible courtesy of the dim light provided by Tarpon Tavern.

"Duck!" Zina yelled, cutting speed. "A Seal warrior, he is a good shot."

Proving her correct, a pair of shots slammed into the hull, the twin popping noise echoing across the water. Nose cresting the waves, the creaky craft took off. Zina slid from her perch and kneeled down, keeping a hand on the wheel for control. For a split second, she let go of the wheel and yanked him down beside her. The wind shield shattered where his head had been.

"He is relentless," she said. "He predicted our location."

"But, how? We might have gone down river instead."

"We cannot reach Odessa from the Gulf. He chose correctly." She resumed the captain's seat. "Sit with me. Your windscreen is gone."

No trouble with that request. Administering a sideways hug, he squeezed in beside. Bodies hooked yet again, a tight and proper fit. Racing with the wind, Grandpa's sparkling trillions stretched out above, he felt complete. Glaucon, his work, music, and now Zina. A perfect triumvirate, another first. In his heart he admitted the obvious. Tantalizing Zina was a keeper. If only, and he begged the fates, she felt the same about him.

"Can I ask a question?"

"No. You cannot. We will discuss your question later."

"Know what I think?"

"You squeeze so hard. I know exactly what you think."

"Sauer didn't plan to kill me at first. He said he changed sides. What does that mean?"

She drew away from him. Her grip on the wheel seemed to tighten.

"The man is unpredictable. Thanks to Signet, that much I know about the man. He was not to harm you, though."

"Those shots he fired were real. What 'side' wants to kill me? I thought all Campesi and Colonel Bame needed was this damn thumb drive."

"Please, Dr. Danny-boy. Not now. I must steer this boat."

Bent to the task, she closed him out, her usual ploy to avoid pesky questions. At the moment it didn't matter. They were zipping along at speed, the assassin fast receding.

Still they kept their heads down, hugging the shore as darkness swallowed the distant lights of the tavern on the dock.

Rounding a final bend in the river, Zina cut back on the throttle. The wind, raspy and biting at speed, settled to a cool October breeze. They puttered on, comfortable with a reduced pace that soon led them to the Sponge Dock, where a day earlier Signet had regaled them with the details of Campesi's despicable deeds, where the Zalin goons got a mouthful of Krav Maga. At three forty-five in the morning, the tourists and tables were long gone, an inviting destination to tie up and figure out their next step.

As frontal lobes wrestled for an answer, his hippocampal circuits reverberated with memories of recent events. First stop the most recent, in auntie's parlor with incredible Zina, then on to Sauer's rude intrusion after the sojourn with Uncle Stephano. And, before that, his visit with Gamel in Clearwater, his friend's time chamber and the encounter with majestic Imhotep, the statue's creepy gaze down eternity's endless lane.

But, that seated figure now triggered a sensed affinity as Ross floated beneath the canopy of stars, Zina his sole companion. A kinship where he seemed to enter a vast landscape he imagined Imhotep to occupy, a stripped down state devoid of sensory awareness, of an existence as some undefined speck along with countless others. A state inhabited by inconsequential entities of non-awareness, all nodes perhaps, a close approximation, through which thin, dark strings passed on a trip to and through other similar nodes, millions of invisible threads, shooting off as tangled star bursts at impossible angles. This, a system of endless nodes routing decisions charted long ago still continuously pursued.

A vast human ledger really, all paths charted, already known.

And, his own path? Somehow he'd been at this precise spot before, a journey begun long ago where wired sulci of uncountable neurons meshed with their counterparts outside this inner realm.

A oneness sensation. Fascinating. Fleeting.

"You have that faraway look." Zina jostled him alert. "Exactly like Signet behind his buried eyes."

Her pliant voice brought him back. He blinked, removed himself from the depths of the inner river.

...where Alph the sacred ran....

"Drifting with the current. That's all."

"I worried a bullet found you."

"Nothing like that. I'm struggling with this thumb drive. I feel the answer is already decided. I just can't locate it. At the tips of my fingers, gone."

She took her eye off the river.

"Another Signet moment?" Eye to eye. Lips close. "He spoke about threading a needle to solve a problem. It made little sense."

"I like his metaphor. Applicable, if you already have the thread in hand."

"Unlike you, Dr. Justinian. What is it in your hand?"

He glanced down. His hand encircled her narrow waist.

A wrap around, the same position of a few hours earlier.

"Sorry. A reflex hold. To keep you safe."

"The danger lies behind us. Still, like a Siamese, you hold on."

As she did, too. No inclination to disengage. She tweaked his ear, tapped his nose, then refocused on guiding their ship of fate.

The world of threads and fathomless nodes now receded. Like a trapdoor snapping shut, the glimpse of a greater unity, the sense he already possessed the outcome, that all he had to do was reach out and seize the obvious thread, disappeared as quickly as it arose. He had detoured into a mirage that was now mist.

The Campesi rendezvous in Odessa. That and only that, the predetermined node. And the damnable, elusive thread of correct decision? He peered out across the river in search of any clue to an answer. He scanned the predawn clarity just then drifting into view. But, in the waves of churning water he found enchantment but no solution to this enigma.

He remained as useless as a beheaded statue, expression sculpted blank, Imhotep's twin in the wind.

✦✦✦

Zina adjusted speed, sputtering toward shore. Silhouetted in the early light, Nick's Bar and Shrimp took shape behind a line of fishing vessels asleep at the dock. Like a casino that never sleeps, the bar thrummed with the zombie beat of nocturnal patrons.

"Oh, no! Grandpa!"

Coming into view, an older man mercilessly pawed a thinly dressed female at the rear of the dock. As the couple spooled from the shadows, Zina sighed with relief. Not the new age priest but a tattooed gent fondling an equally besotted specimen, her own flowery tats running to a long stemmed rose, gravity's gift, as was a wizard's face visible beneath a tightly caressed thigh.

As they neared the mooring, a third person slanted into view. Standing behind a tired palm, curled in a familiar shooting stance, Sauer again took aim at the floating target. Zina saw him in time, spun the wheel to port and sped on.

"How did he find us?"

"An obvious choice," she said. "We cannot go much further up river. Ahead lies shallow weeds and snakes."

"That's where we're going? Great."

A shot ricocheted off the hull and struck a beer can in the water. It rattled off as more shots followed. A bottle exploded at the shoreline. They ducked but not before another bullet whizzed past Ross's ear, the hiss of near death audible in the slipstream. The master tracker almost nailed him.

"The bridge!"

Zina nodded forward, then pointed. An arcing structure just then emerged out of the early fog. She gunned the aged contraption, the bow jutting out of the Sargasso sea, flotsam, all manner of debris striking the hull. Still, she plowed on plastering Ross against the seat. Caught in between, she swatted him away and pushed the groaning craft even harder. A metallic clicking sounded beneath his feet. The old gal was beginning to bark smoke. The captain ignored her pleas to stop. Relentless, hell bent for shallow water, she pressed on. Soon Ross identified discarded furniture, a dead cat in the shallows.

A sketchy outline at first, the ancient girder bridge came into sharper focus. It spanned a narrow part of the river waves now slamming over the gunwale. A gasoline can, bottles, even a coat rack and pair of sneakers floated by. Like someone dumped a garbage truck into the river. Sportspeople, Ross mused, quieting his tummy with the revolting mess.

Ignoring the swell of clattering refuse, Zina plowed on until her attention suddenly diverted to her right.

The Jaguar, she called out. On a parallel track up Dodecanese Boulevard, it bore down hard. Despite the rifling wind, Ross caught the roar of its angry engine. At full throttle, Sauer was aiming at the flashing yellow light at the approaching intersection. Skidding madly to a stop, he fishtailed left keeping the same rickety bridge in his sights.

"He plans to cut us off," Zina cried out. "Hold tight. This will be close."

The boat sprang to renewed life. Coaxing a final breath

out of the wheezing nag, Zina pulled the lever with both hands. To his surprise, the boat responded but not until after a death rattle beneath floor boards through which more dark smoke now appeared. They simply had to reach the other side of the bridge. If Ross remembered the topography, they would descend upon acres of swamp grass and miniature inlets, a watery wasteland for both Jaguar and man on foot. A dead end, but their only chance for survival. If they made it.

"Hurry!" he cried out. "He's right above us. Faster."

CHAPTER 40

Aunt Sophia's barge was already at max. Not close to chugging out of Sauer's range. Leaning over the railing at the apex of the bridge, he casually fired away, blowing across the muzzle, practicing what appeared to be a quick draw maneuver while always landing shots within feet of his squirming targets.

"See that?" Ross tossed a glance up and behind them. "He's enjoying this."

Zina slammed the wheel right, then a slow turn left. Still, bullets landed perilously close.

"Patience ... dear one ... remember ... the ... Nika Rebellion!" She yanked harder on the lever. "...like Belisarius ... with his sword ... goodbye, Mr. Sauer."

Something about her mirthless grin. He couldn't quite identify it. Anticipating the battle to come. Of all the time for that.

"Watch out. There. In the water...."

Zina swerved in time as a fleet of ducks quacked disapproval. "We cannot go faster!"

Her shriek seemed to shoot them further from the bridge.

"We made it!"

Jubilation, a brief emotion. Sauer kept shooting. Several rounds found the rear engine compartment. More smoke. More clanking groans. Ross imagined he heard the assassin's laughter. The slowly moving stern took a few hits then a shot struck Zina's wind screen. She initiated a slow and awkward weave, the lazy back and forth springing bolts from the creaking craft. It was all the old gal could manage. Still she kept responding to the captain's firm instruction. An elite marksmen, Sauer perfectly timed his shots, inching ever closer to Commander and First Mate each time.

Abandoning the wheel, Zina dropped to a knee and pried open a panel door, tiny concealed panel doors apparently a thing with her. She squeezed into a tiny cabin then pulled him in beside her. Knees interlocking, another tight and promising fit. Instead of Zina's other worldly scent, the stench of dead fish clung like barnacles inside his nostrils.

"Wait. You can't steer the boat in here."

"Quiet," she said, employing her favorite word.

She tugged again at his belt, this time with a different, feverish intensity.

"Give it to me. Now."

"It's my favorite."

"Brooks Brother's braided leather. I remember what you said when your pants came off. Please, my emperor. No time to quibble. We must escape."

He handed over his prized possession, stained and stiff from its earlier submersion.

Brushing him aside, she stuck an arm out of the partially open panel door. Stretching, she managed to reach up and loop the belt around the steering wheel. With it secure, using an equally nimble move, she seized hold of the lever. She gave the sign of the cross, raised her head above the wheel and conducted a quick inspection. Following a string of curses, she spun the wheel in an abrupt course correction. Downing its final slug of oats, the old grey mare lurched forward.

The unexpected jolt sent them deeper into the odiferous closet. Untangling, they waited. When the shooting subsided, she peeked out, sighed in relief, then flung open the panel door and reoccupied the pilot's seat. The bridge soon vanished far behind them in the lingering mist.

"We made it. Or, I should say, *you* made it."

He whooped and hugged Zina, marveling at her amazing improvisation.

She murmured a thank you, untied and returned his belt, ignoring the goose egg stretch hole in the middle. He looped it through his dirty chinos anyway smothering the urge to complain about the deformed leather. After all, she did save their bacon.

"Theodora, again to the rescue," he said.

At the helm, hair fly blown in the wind, she placed a finger to her lips.

"Call me Zina. I now reclaim my name. It fits better, don't you think?"

"What happened to Theodora?"

She slid her eyes in his direction.

"Too confusing. From now on, you are Dr. Danny-boy. Also, a fine ring to it."

"I sort of like Daniel. Or, Dan. That is *my* real name."

"Okay, then. Zina and Daniel. We will go far together."

So, it was goodbye to Empress Theodora and Emperor Justinian, appellations he'd begun to like. Change was in the air all right. All that remained was Campesi and his dark closer, what to do about them.

After numerous twists and turns past tufts of grassy land and shallow water, Zina beached their craft. A wise and timely decision. The engine compartment had long begun its death rattle. With a terminal grunt, Aunt Sophia's clunker gave up the ghost, its demise coinciding with a gradual beaching deep within the flat, inland ocean of deserted inlets.

Before disembarking, Ross rose on wobbly feet to get his bearings. In the immediate distance straight ahead, Route 19 snaked north and south across the hazy horizon, indiscernible save for intermittent headlights blinking through the high grass. To the south, on his right, stood the remnants of a closed mall. And, to the north, lay unpromising fields of grass and more water.

They disembarked, climbed a few feet to firmer sand and crouched down.

"Watch your head. Mr. Sauer might see us."

"Can't be avoided. He's probably already scoped out the area."

"That means we wade out of here."

"Again. Can't be avoided. I estimate one hundred yards to that parking lot behind the mall."

"Then what? We will be easy targets."

"We were easy targets on the river. He doesn't want to kill us. Not until he retrieves this damn flash drive."

"We fight. Is that it? Very good, Danny-boy. He needs a lesson in manners."

She was right. Sauer was one rude jerk. But, he doubted Zina, indisputably an accomplished fighter, would win in the end. The guy was armed. They were going to need help to get past the assassin.

He put the problem to Zina. Right off, she drew a blank.

"Let's call Signet," he said. "You hinted he was alive. Use your iPhone."

"He is in traction. Sauer broke his leg."

"Sure. Like, I believe that."

"What about Dr. Braun? She lives a few miles west of

Route 19. We can take Keystone. The intersection is right over there."

"She's no match for Sauer."

He raised his pal Melko's name. Zina shot that suggestion out of the marsh. He owned a handgun. But, even if he remembered to pack it, they'd have to unpack him from Aunt Sophia. It was also pointless to call Dr. Keresti. He had a pair of kayaks but was in Disney with his kids.

"Wait. I know," he said. "Detective Leeks will help us. I lost my cell phone. Let me borrow yours."

Zina reluctantly handed over her phone.

"Be careful. It cost Uncle two months' rent. Do you know the number?"

He rummaged through his pockets. Came up with a soggy but legible card. Placed the call. After three ring tones, the detective picked up.

"Hey, Mr. Glaucoma. This is your girlfriend's cell. Not a good sign. You take her hostage or something?'

He didn't think Leeks possessed a sense of humor. He glanced away until the laughter ended. Then, as succinctly as possible, he brought the detective up to date since his midnight departure for Melko's grille. The visit with Zina's uncle, the hasty retreat to Aunt Sophia's, the even hastier retreat up the Anclote River following Sauer's unexpected appearance, carefully avoiding any mention of his sojourn in Auntie's upstairs parlor.

Right now they needed a hefty infusion of help. If the

detective came to their rescue, he'd bag the twisty assassin and, who knows, maybe the Eckerd Hall murderer as well.

"That reminds me. I thought you alerted the Tarpon cops. What happened?"

Leeks sighed as the background sound of mayhem intensified.

"We ran into trouble with the local gendarmes," he said. "When the bulletin went out, all available uniforms were still buzzing about the walk-off three run bagger top of the ninth. I'm talking Red Sox, Doc. They thumped the hell out of the Rays tonight. Hey, hold on a sec. Kinda crazy on Gulf to Bay tonight."

He quickly filled Ross in. A pair of youthful druggies met the grill of a Mercedes doing eighty out of a topless bar while another druggy shot the driver who then crashed into a U-Haul van stalled in the middle of the road.

"The moral here, don't do drugs, attend topless bars, or stall out at five o'clock in the morning. Let's get back to you. You're stranded in the murky wastes off Route Nineteen, gators, snakes plus a bombshell girlfriend your only companions, not counting Sauer, of course, who is hell bent on murder and destruction. What's the problem?"

More laughter but short-lived. Reverting to form, Leeks then laid out a plan. Risky, he said, because Ross and his girlfriend had to reach the highway without being killed. After that, creeping past the mall should be a snap. Not to worry, though. The detective would leap into action, snag the guy before he injured them. Twenty minutes, tops. At this hour the trip up 19 a straight shot.

"Once you detour around him, watch for a break in traffic. Make a run for it. He's not getting away this time."

After the call, Zina retrieved her cell. Wedged it in a rear pocket.

"So, I am your 'bombshell girlfriend'? Never mind. We have twenty-five minutes. Let's go."

She took the lead. Watching for snakes, they waded from one grassy plot to the next. Minus a few watery mishaps, they gained a secure foothold behind the deserted mall. Angling east, keeping Route Nineteen in sight, they snuck along the row of storefronts. Finally, after slipping under a broken Bowl and Bread sign, they reached an abandoned boatyard fronting the highway. A quarter-mile south lay the gas station, their near destination. So far so good. Now for the hard part.

Zina depressed a knob on her wristwatch. A green light came on: five fifty. Ten minutes to show time.

They crouched in fading shadows at the base of the small incline. No vehicles up or down Route 19, the only activity a blinking yellow light at the distant Keystone intersection. At six sharp they abandoned concealment, scaled the steep roll of grass and strolled the sidewalk, a pair of tired, early risers out for fresh air.

Materializing twenty yards up the sidewalk, Sauer moved away from concealment and began sauntering, lazy as he pleased, in their direction.

"Nice going, guys." He stopped, feet spread, handgun held loosely at his side. "I watched you all the way in. Little lady out in front. Impressive." His expression tightened as he looked them over. Then the smirk appeared, the man loaded with violence. "I figured you'd wait near the boat graveyard. Fitting, don't you think? I stick your bodies in the Sunfish. You won't be discovered until next year. By the way. The Red Sox demolished the Rays. No need for their closer."

"We already heard. Who is their new guy?"

"Where's the Jag?" Zina said. "I don't see it."

"I thought I told you. Guy named Kimbrel. Big winner in the National League before coming over. They play again...."

"We are not here to discuss baseball," Zina interrupted, tone insistent.

Sauer shook his head.

"Afraid we are, honey. Dr. Ross is at bat, bottom of the ninth. Full count. Two out. Bases loaded. Down, two to zero. Time for the dark closer."

No one made a move. Zina whispered.

"You go right. I go left. On the count of three."

"Detective Leeks said to cross the highway," he whispered back. "Not dodge right and left."

"The trick is on page eighty. Advanced Krav Maga."

She was already creeping into position. She slanted left and, blindly obeying orders, he turned right. Meanwhile, Sauer stood his ground, smile grim.

"You're making a mistake, Ms. Palaeologus. This is between me and the doctor."

"Ever hear of the Nika Rebellion?"

"We talking Afghanistan here?"

"After I finish with you, read more history. That is, if your squished brain permits."

Continuing her slow pace to Sauer's right, she maintained a monotone for the history lesson.

"Ancient Byzantium. Fifth century."

"Why didn't you say so?"

A cynical laugh. Zina kept talking.

"It ended with a battle in the Hippodrome. Both Greens and Blues, political parties of the day, had joined forces. They trashed Constantinople. Churches, stores, parts of the waterfront. Then, General Belisarius, acting on Empress Theodora's order, slaughtered them all."

"No kidding."

She nodded, a barely noticeable twitch in the early morning light.

"The gangs threatened the entire empire. Something had to be done. Empress Theodora alone possessed the courage to act. Not Justinian. A cerebral genius, no taste for blood. Powerful Theodora ordered the generals to cut them down."

"In the Hippodrome, you say."

"The size of two football stadiums. Thousands murdered. Women, men, children. Yes, Mr. Sauer. Toddlers, holding knives. No one spared. All of them chopped meat. Historians called it a threshing machine, both the Gepid Prince Mundus and General Belisarius advancing from opposite directions. Theodora was merciless."

Obviously puzzled by his talkative adversary, Sauer paid her increasingly more attention, enough so that Ross was able to advance on the man's left. But, slowly, at a turtle's pace, heart in his throat. Zina continued on, drawing closer, feinting right and left as she reenacted the slaughter, until she was face to face with the bedazzled assassin. She concluded her story with a horrific cry.

"Attack *now*, Prince Mundus! Show no mercy!"

Only recently, Emperor Justinian. Now, a Gepid Prince. What the heck was *a Gepid?*

Equally perplexed, more absorbed in her story than he wanted, Ross nevertheless attacked, if one could label a tentative lunge in Sauer's general direction an attack. Distracted by a slim nanosecond, Sauer relaxed his guard, providing Zina the opening she desired.

The assassin's head snapped back with a roundhouse kick. The follow-up jab to his extended knee caused an audible crunch. Lurching sideways, stunned but still combative, Sauer never saw it coming. He succumbed to a chin shot delivered with a smooth shift of weight and a descent of Zina's free foot. She shifted weight again as her victim regained balance, but he did not long remain vertical. Zina landed a shot to the groin which ended the fight.

"For Kembrel!" she cried out. "Whoever he is."

Sirens filled the air. They brought Sauer back to life. He limped up and over the embankment and moments later came the low growl of an awakening Jaguar. A pair of squad cars now zoomed out of a side road near the Keystone Shell station and, like hungry hounds, gave chase. Riding shotgun, Detective Leeks didn't pause to congratulate either the beaming kick boxer or her bedraggled companion as he sped north into Pasco County.

"We were to lead him across the highway," Ross said. "Not engage on the embankment."

"His pain will delay him. A reminder, next time avoid the Hippodrome."

"Mind explaining Gepid?"

"A Germanic tribe. Offshoot of ancient Goths. Let's go."

Never one to stay put for long, she was again on the move. She took his hand and speed-walked him across Route 19.

"Masterful performance," he said. "Page eighty is a winner."

"No such page exists. I made it up. I hope he and Dr. Braun are awake."

"Who are you talking about?"

"Patience, my emperor. Ah, Danny-boy. It will soon become clear enough."

CHAPTER 41

There was no immediate response. He pushed the bell again. Still no sounds issued from within the condominium. Early morning birdcalls, a gentle breeze, and the unnatural silence got to Ross. He squeezed Zina's hand, placed a lingering kiss on her cheek.

"You were splendid back there. Just terrific."

"Three times already. You repeat yourself a lot."

"I don't...."

"Twice crossing the empty highway. Once on this front step. You were also a big help. General Belisarius will commend your stealthy creep when I inform him of our success."

"I see. The 'general' will be joining us for tea and toast?"

"He prefers small pastries. Let me explain our travels. Plenty of time for him to ask questions." She paused, closely examining him. "You always stare. After this morning on Auntie's couch, have you not seen enough?"

His passion threatened to reignite. The memory of a musty couch, a bonging clock, other images came to mind. But, standing before Dr. Braun's front door, his frontal lobe inhibition center threw a switch, reacquiring control. Hand in hand, he did not reach for more.

Still, she remained powerless to resist. Impaling him with tame hunger, her flashing green eyes appeared new to him. How, he wondered, had he overlooked not only this singular feature but also her perfect nose and smooth brow, the utter sweetness of this incredible, he had to admit, bad-guy-enraged woman. He reconsidered his conclusion. Perhaps incredible failed to capture her full nature. Challenging certainly. Even tantalizing. Difficult, most surely.

A crisp voice broke out behind him.

"Welcome dear Zina and you, Dr. Ross. I hear your neuro-modules have finally coalesced. Are you prepared to act?"

His heart pounded. His hand fell to his side. He spun around. And, there he was: Arriva's Chief of Security, attired as always, in a black shirt, trousers and cross trainers. A tad tired at the eyes yet fully alert.

"Zina said you were in traction."

"Hardly an injurious encounter. Sauer corralled you nicely. Once again, we are all together." He examined them as if they'd been the culprits who dumped him in the swamp. "One point eight," he added, leading them into the foyer. "The precise mileage between your Sauer tussle and Beth's condo. I estimated fifteen minutes. You took much longer. Therefore, you are both tired. And, after an active night, hungry. Come. Dr. Braun awaits you."

Active night?

More data sharing with "dear Zina"? Also disconcerting, the estimated mileage and the time. They both flew across Route 19 like herons escaping gators. By now, savvy to the misrepresentation, he knew it was just Signet reassuming control.

They found Dr. Braun beyond the framed bullfights and Toledo landscapes in the back study. Reclining on the couch, surrounded by the Heritage Bench and high back chairs, she'd laid out a tray of bite-size croissants and a coffee urn on the low table.

Minus the side table set for two, everything exactly as he left it on that evening of instruction earlier in the week. Instruction that, following a series of neatly choreographed scenes, discounting the Zina encounter, led back here. That is, if he could discount the early morning couch scene. For all he knew, Signet bugged the damn parlor.

But, he wondered. The Sauer attack seemed real enough. And, the blow below the belt very convincing. Was that injury improvised according to plan? Unanswered questions, like flies in the glue binding them all together, to use Signet's expression.

"Welcome, Daniel. We were expecting you. This must be the beautiful Zina, or Theodora or, as Uncle Stefano might say, Zeenee."

In a smooth and graceful manner, Beth shook beautiful Zeenee's extended hand.

"Zina will do."

Blushing now, she daintily seized a croissant and devoured it with a single crunch. She disposed of another in the same manner. Crunch. Crunch. Zina starved after an active night.

This broke the ice, if one might label awkward shuffling and disguised coughs as social ice. Beth made small talk, an exercise Ross never imagined possible with Zina. Signet then asked about Sauer, whether the raging psychopath had injured the wily gator Signet managed to place in Aunt Sophia's backyard.

"You mean the Melko gator!" Ross said. "Was there anything you didn't prearrange?"

"Ask Sauer when you see him. Now then. Hand over the flash drive. It will then cease indenting your pocket. Are you aware your pants are on backward?"

"Yes. I'm aware of that. At the moment, I don't mind the indentation. I'm still thinking about the matter."

A stillness invaded the room.

"Will you have coffee, Daniel?" Beth, aloof goddess, once more broke a spell. "Even though you've been running all night, don't blame Siggy. Zalin appeared from nowhere and so, well, we had to ask Sauer to ride shotgun. Unfortunately, he switched sides. Mr. Campesi changed his mind. He wants the flash drive. Alas, he also wants you dead. A nasty problem for us all. Well, mostly for you, of course. Drink up. A Colombian bean. Quite good really. It sharpens the synapse."

Ross politely declined.

"I'll pass," he said. "But, if 'Siggy' can spare a can of sizzling soda, I'll have that."

That got the security man's full attention.

"Are you sure that happened?"

"You poured the soda."

"Correctly accused."

"Empty Zonder Springs water bottles filled the sink. You mixed the two. You inoculated me."

"Have you considered it was only meant to appear that way? In fact, your entire odyssey was designed to help you change your mind. If you thought your amygdala was, let us say, rearranged it might be easier to think straight."

This person, this Zen-warrior-ear slicer never delivered good news. Yet, he confirmed Ross's suspicion. The week had been choreographed in advance. The worry resurfaced. Zina's warm embrace? No, he decided. No way. She'd been insistent and so very real. But, everything else, as he suspected from the start, organized and arranged. Still....

"I've experienced changes since drinking that cola."

"The placebo effect. You think you were inoculated. Therefore, you experience what you think should happen."

"Nonsense. I know what I've felt. But, that's not the central issue, is it? Imagine if I injected drugs inside your eyeball and never told you. For a physician, that is unethical. So was your cola job. Neither you nor Campesi sought informed consent."

"Grandpa and Zina were not harmed. He may yet return to the icon in the shrine."

Signet pulled up a pair of high backs. Told Ross and Zina to sit. He joined Dr. Braun on the couch.

"It is apparent fear still reigns. You remain uncertain what to do with the files."

"Which you stole in the first place. Why did you do that?"

"Let's examine your options."

"My *what*?"

"Option one: You hand the drive to Campesi as he requests. Without a reason to retain you, he will banish you to the woods. Your career will be sidetracked, who can say for how long. Perhaps long enough for another portrait to find its way outside the library at your beloved infirmary. Let us not forget Sauer, however. He wants to close you out."

"You forget I own the patent on the double tube. He can't develop Glaucon without that."

"*You* forget he owns the patent on both the nano-motor and biofilm-photon activating device. Any interested party can make tubes."

"Sorry. You're wrong about the biofilm. My idea. His product. One patent jointly owned. What I think will happen," Ross added. "Is that you will be fired if Campesi learns how these files were actually stolen."

"That brings us to the central problem behind this entire escapade: Mr. Campesi."

Ross feigned a sigh of relief. "At last. Let's hear it."

"The issue is not the theft itself. It is the *possibility* of theft, of precisely what has been stolen."

"Files of secret government programs."

"Plus your project. A small theft, I assure you."

"Thanks a lot. My life's work."

"To the Department of Defense and DARPA, your plastic tubes are minor. Not minor are the secret GENESIS programs including the detailed PTSD project. Of major concern is Campesi's contamination of the G-1 program which, at the outset, was a completely military undertaking. To create perfect soldiers. Hard, smart and effective. Primarily, just to remind you, to undertake the Eritrea mission. That is why we inoculated men like Sauer. To form a team of men for a specific mission. Then, afterwards, if it worked, to enlarge the program for the Department of Defense."

Eritrea. That tiny corner of the planet surrounded by crazed terrorists across the straits of Bab el Mandeb. Rawdadi, the insurgent. Saudi war planes, the surrogate war with Iran. And hostages. Benghazi all over again.

And, Signet wanted to go there?

"May I interrupt?" They turned toward the voice, sharp and commanding; the question, rhetorical. Beth wasn't asking their permission. "I have two things to add. First, Mr. Campesi cannot fire Siggy, or me, for that matter. We are under government contract. Arriva is owned by the United States government. That's why Campesi is the vulnerable one here. True, he is in charge of the post-traumatic stress vaccine. But, if his other projects are uncovered, that vital project might be in jeopardy. And, second," she added, facing Zina, her tone softer. "I was unaware Mr. Campesi added the inoculant to that bottle of water. I never meant to harm either you or Father Palaeologus. And, for the record, I did not distribute tainted 'fizzy cola' last night. This time I disobeyed Mr. Campesi's direct orders."

Zina patted her host's knee. "Apology accepted."

"From the beginning," Signet continued. "It was my intent to neutralize Campesi. A man of loose morals and questionable ethics...."

"Look who's talking."

With a flick of the wrist, Signet brushed away the sarcasm.

"Such an individual cannot be tolerated. To protect the PTSD project, to guarantee the Eritrea mission would go forward, I had to eliminate Campesi."

"You mean kill?"

"Exclude, remove, or jettison. All synonyms. Take your

pick. To accomplish this task, I had to convince Bame to do it. As the DOD's principal liaison with DARPA, he alone has the authority to eliminate your CEO. If government projects could be so easily hacked, if Arriva was leaky as a faucet, the man in charge must go. My first plan at Eckerd Hall was to photographically link you with Ravi Ravda's accountant, Newsome. When presented with evidence suggesting a secret collusion between a DARPA client, Arriva, and a foreign national, Ravi Ravda, Colonel Bame would deep six Campesi in a nanosecond. Newsome's unexpected murder proved an inconvenience, however. It left the main problem unsolved: how to convince Bame to reawaken the Eritrea mission. He had to be persuaded. And that, Dr. Ross, is where you came in."

"Newsome's death, an *inconvenience*?"

"Don't let that distract you."

"But it does. I was the intended target. Someone tried to kill me."

Signet's icy manner stayed solid.

"Regrettably so. I had nothing to do with that. Newsome's demise turned out beneficial though. It presented you as an alternative, perfect plan."

"Don't you mean perfect dupe?"

"Nobody is perfect, but I so have high hopes for you."

There was a commotion outside the rear porch window. A squirrel, whipping his tail against the pane, peeked in and took off, croissants apparently not to his liking.

"Go on," Ross said. "Tell me how I'm a perfect plan."

"Gladly. But, I will go fast. Not much time left to explain."

"You mean, my visit to Odessa?"

The puppeteer nodded.

"With Newsome dead, I turned to you. No longer would I need a photo suggesting collusion between Arriva and Simcoe, Ravi Ravda's India-based company. Instead, by having you steal files, most especially the Glaucon project, it would be a definite proof of collusion. If Arriva, a DARPA client company, could be so easily hacked, then the man in charge must fall on his own sword. Or, made to do so. Therefore, option one is out of the question. You cannot hand files back to the man who is to be eliminated. We move on to option two."

"I don't even know this Ravda guy. Why would I join up with him?"

"A good question. Soon to be answered. The point of my plan was to concoct a motive for you to join up with Ravda. To manufacture the possibility. Now, option two...."

Before proceeding, Siggy accepted two midget croissants from Dr. Braun. He devoured each with a deliberate bite, mimicking Zina's crunch while casting an appraising eye at Ross. The room tense as he slowly masticated a final morsel.

"Coffee anyone?"

Each declined Dr. Braun's thoughtful offer.

"Option two," Signet repeated, hands lightly clasped, the man poised, confident. "Let us say, instead of handing the drive over to Campesi, you keep it yourself. What then?"

"Simple. I copy the Glaucon file, hook up with friends in Boston or New York, even North Carolina, and I'm off to the races."

"Campesi will then continue with his independent inoculations."

Ross shrugged. Zina tightened the grip on his hand.

"Your problem, not mine. But, if I were you, I'd feed him to the Melko gator. After being hurled twice in one night, it must be hungry. Why include me in your mess? You take care of it."

Signet's head bobbed as he digested the questions. When he spoke again, his tone was conciliatory.

"You became the logical solution. I used you."

"Glad to be of service."

"For me to be directly involved, I would have to bypass title and rank and go above me. A pointless undertaking in the military. My accusation would go unheard. In an earlier day, yes, I would happily feed him to a hungry gator. Sever both ears for good measure. Yet, because of my own inoculation, a new way came to mind. If Colonel Bame were to understand a mere citizen, you in this case, had hacked a military server, then he would have to remove the man in charge, Mr. Campesi."

"You amaze me."

"To avoid the accusation of treason, you can neither copy nor keep any of the stolen files. Nor can you hand them to your CEO. That brings us to option three."

"Which is?"

"You hand the flash drive to me. At this exact moment, in fact. Then, when I call Colonel Bame...."

Startling them all, the kitchen door to the back porch banged opened and shut. Wearing his trademark Gandhi shirt and sandals, a toothy grin ear to ear, Ravi Ravda entered the study.

"Am I late, Mr. Signet? My, my. You have croissants. I really like them. Do you mind?"

The man grabbed three of the tiny delights and stuffed them, one at a time, into his not so tiny mouth. He chewed ravenously. Thus recharged, he wiped his lips, found an extra chair and sat.

"Where shall I begin?"

CHAPTER 42

The man's unannounced presence, not to mention his famished state, left them speechless. Signet's half-smile dimmed a noticeable fraction. A flaw in his otherwise perfect script? Was such a thing even possible? Corporal Signet, a.k.a. Mr. Security a.k.a. Master Puppeteer a.k.a. Mr. Zen to friends, acted astonished at the interruption. Or was this simply more planned behavior masquerading as a genuine human reaction?

Ross returned Ravda's friendly grin offered between giant mouthfuls. Scrawny, a man of bones, pinched features, and attitude, the man seized attention, immediately center stage. No wonder he easily acquired chanting acolytes waving signs and placards.

"Begin where ever you like," Signet finally replied. "Cover the details."

"Indeed I will, my good friend. Have you had an opportunity to share our good news? I am delighted we shall become partners with this good person."

Ross exchanged a look with Signet.

"Is this a surprise visit?" he said. "Or a delayed arrival."

"No surprise here. For you, perhaps. Mr. Signet invited me as guest."

A moment of silence, Ross more perplexed than usual.

"Do I take it, this is option three?"

Signet ignored him. How he always dealt with awkward questions. He and dear Zeenee alike in this regard.

"Ravi, please focus. Make your presentation. It is eight o'clock, and we have that appointment at ten."

"Yes, sir. Right away. I will get to it."

The president of Simcoe, Inc. sprang to his feet, various masticated particles spewing off his lips as he spoke.

"Allow me to properly introduce myself. I am Ravi Ravda, third son of Sami, a most important CEO and President of Simcoe Enterprises, a very large and successful company in Mumbai, India. Mumbai itself is also large and successful, a city prized by all of India. The home of Bollywood and many science institutes. Home to all our family and Simcoe, which has a growing subsidiary here in Florida. Maybe not quite yet a subsidiary. Now, it exists mostly on paper. That is the reason I am here."

He took a breather than launched in again, focusing lavish attention upon Zina.

"Signet has already explained so much about you. And, here you are yourself, in the flesh, so to speak, very nice flesh, too, I must add. Such pretty hair pinned tightly on your lovely head. The tight clothes truly impressive, but not as impressive," he added, finger to chin in contemplation, "as last evening in Odessa. There I saw you for the very first time. An empress in regal purple. I thought, how can this be a mermaid? Impossible, I concluded. You resemble nothing like those creatures at Weeki Wachee. Have you been there? So enchanting beyond the glass."

"Why, thank you," Zina said, courteously, succumbing to the flattery. "As regal as I may have appeared last evening, let me tell you about Empress Theodora."

"Yes, yes. That is how Mr. Signet addressed you."

"I am no longer her anymore. I am Zina, and this, as you already know, is Dr. Danny Ross, not Emperor Justinian as I once knew him."

This required a moment to sink in.

"Does this mean no more history lessons," Ross asked, "or reminders of the slaughter in an ancient hippodrome? No more General Belisarius wielding a sword against the Persians or the Blues and Greens?"

She gave him a thin smile. A distinct hint it might actually be true.

Signet coughed then tapped his Luminox wristwatch.

"The time, Ravi. Don't forget the time."

"Yes, of course. I have wandered. I am off track." Serious now, he resettled on his chair. "I sense we are all friends. Therefore, let me start with a question for you, my new and important partner, Dr. Ross. May I call you Daniel?

Good. Here it is. You are contemplating leaving Arriva with Glaucon. No, don't frown. Signet and I have long discussed this matter."

"You have? Since when?"

"Two months ago," Signet said. "When I first learned about Mr. Newsome I met with Ravi. I needed to find out if you were planning to abandon Arriva and join Simcoe."

"The answer I provided was a solid no. We had never met before. Nor did we discuss such a union. It is another matter now, though. As Signet advised, it is time to make the separation."

"He *advised* you about *me*?"

Ravda nodded. "He did and raised important issues. You must think ahead to when you shed Arriva. What will you do then?"

"*Shed* Arriva?"

"You have a colleague in New York. Another in North Carolina. Perhaps one in Boston. You might even consider a fresh start up; although, the cash required is huge. That is why my proposal is best for you."

Ross turned from the quirky gent in brilliant white to Signet, head to toe in black, impassively sipping coffee at the table. A pair of contrasts, with Ross, caked in dried lake mud, lodged somewhere in between.

"What exactly is your 'proposal'?"

"For a moment, consider this." Long, bony fingers stretched

for two croissants. They disappeared with a slug of dark roast kindly provided by the hostess. "My family and I have a busy business in Mumbai. With our main hospital clinic, we own an empire of outreach. I am talking eye hospitals, my friend. Yes, eye care for the millions. Quite an income, too, all provided by our strapped government. There is a huge problem though. Our dear country is mostly prehistoric. So, with generic medicines and squads of doctors, all trained in Boston, Miami, and London, we bring the very best care. Only, and this is where you come in, we have no method to treat bad glaucoma which is rampant throughout the barren countryside." He paused, searching for a reaction from his captivated audience. Emboldened, he took a long sip from his china cup and continued. "Your device will earn much money. As you do here in America, we will charge very high prices to the growing middle class. We will also sell Glaucon in Europe. Bypass all unnecessary FDA regulations and bring eye vision to many peoples."

Ross could not resist the pull of such an offer. It represented an answer to Campesi's raging predations, freedom to pursue the dream, to secure that elusive portrait on the wall and all it implied.

Another reality then took hold.

"Your idea sounds great," he said. "Except for one detail. I'll have to pry Glaucon out of Mr. Campesi's hands." He patted the flash drive in his pocket. "I can't copy it off this flash drive. If I do, Signet claims I'll commit treason. But, I need this file. It contains all the manufacturing details including the complicated method of producing BDNF."

Ravda laughed.

"BDNF is not a state secret, Daniel. This growth factor is widely used in research labs. We can buy it off the internet from companies like Arriva. Before Mr. Campesi seized control, it once produced and sold such biological molecules. We can also construct your tube device from cardiac catheter tubing. Be brave, my doctor friend. It is written."

"What about the nano motor and the biofilm? Mr. Campesi will never release the patents."

"Hmm, right. Those pesky patents do present a problem."

More silence filled the study. The dream escape Ravi Ravda presented had struck a wall. Ross was back where he started. A hot potato in his pocket. No place to toss it. Indecision alive as ever.

Signet laid his cup down with an annoying clatter.

"What has happened to your determination, Ravi? I told you not to worry. Have you forgotten so soon?"

"Oh, no. Not at all. Yet, Doctor Daniel has a vital point. The device depends upon those patents."

"Not if Mr. Campesi is out of the picture."

"So, we're back to 'eliminate'?" Ross tossed up his hands. "We just can't kill the man."

"There is another option."

"The 'option' man. This makes number four."

"Patience, doctor. There is time. Let it happen."

"Yes, yes," Ravi chimed in. "It will indeed happen. Signet has promised. I also have big plans for him. As security chief of our new Clearwater subsidiary, he will protect us."

"Subsidiary?"

"We bought an eye clinic in a pink building by the beach. You will be research director and Dr. Braun, senior scientist. And, Ms. Palaeologus—"

Interrupting him, the patio door in the kitchen again opened and shut, this time with a loud crash. Forbidding as a hurricane, Sauer entered the study.

"Stay put, everyone. This won't take long."

CHAPTER 43

"Where did you come from?"

"Quiet, Doc. I'm here for a reason."

"You are limping, big man. How did that happen?"

"Any more out of you, little lady, and you'll find out."

"Oohh, I'm so frightened." Zina waggled a hand. "Scare me to death, Mr. Sauer."

The assassin laughed.

"For a twerp, you got stones. You landed a lucky hit. Won't happen again."

"Are you ready for more?" Zina jumped up, assuming a fighting stance. "You ran away before I completed the job. I will take care of you this time."

"No, missy, you won't. Police sirens can't save you here. I'm not a high school bully you can easily push into the bayou."

"I pushed no one. I *whomped* their butts, then I tossed

them in. Don't insult me. Push is a joke."

Sauer waved her off. "I'll deal with you in Odessa. I'm here for that doodad in the corner. You're coming with me, Gandhi. Move over here. Pronto!"

Ravi Ravda froze, shriveled as if compressed in a vise, incapable of responding to the menacing psycho. Coming to the rescue, Signet slapped his thigh as if to announce the moment had arrived for someone, namely him, to confront the monster from the deep. He rose to full height, a good six inches shorter and two thirds again as wide as the bemused assassin. Undaunted by the size disparity, Mr. Security planted a finger in the middle of the man's chest.

"I didn't expect you so soon," he said, "Your job was to conclude back on the highway."

"Got a better offer. Campesi doubled your fee."

"A shame. I liked your idea of the dark closer."

"Still holds. I'll close out the doc and his girlfriend when they arrive in Odessa."

Signet nodded, offering a hand which Sauer shook.

"No hard feelings?"

"Uh-uh. I just got to take Mr. Bucktooth with me."

He again motioned for Ravda to join him. The frail man, anchored to the bookshelf, didn't budge.

"Me, sir? Oh, why no thank you. I am most comfortable

over here. Would you please toss me a croissant? I am having breakfast with these people, not you."

"Cut the crap, doodad. Mr. Campesi wants you out at his place. Now march, you skinny fairy. Get over here."

"I am no doodad, sir. No, not at all. I am quite a serious gentleman. And, I am certainly no fairy."

This drew a laugh from their dangerous intruder.

"We'll see about that."

Signet stood his ground, cutting off Sauer's advance as Ravda grabbed hold of Dr. Braun's huge bookshelf with both hands. For some crazy reason, he again poked Sauer with a dangerously exposed finger.

"Now that you are here," he said. "Maybe you can help us out."

"Oh, yeah. How?"

"We were discussing last night's Red Sox ball game at Tropicana stadium. They beat up on Tampa Bay. It appears Boston will take the series."

"I know all about it. Last night went to extra innings. Detective Leeks told me Tampa's new closer screwed up."

Both of Signet's ears twitched.

"When did you and the detective have this discussion?"

"Half an hour ago. Could be longer."

"Mind if I ask where this conversation took place?"

"There's a religious complex over that hill on Route 19. I led the cops there and, with Jesus looking on, made a deal."

"What sort of deal?"

"I promised him Newsome's murderer if he released me."

No auricular reaction this time. No subtle sign of churning or disturbance. Signet seemed oddly off balance.

Sensing the shifting wind, Beth went on the offensive.

"How dare you barge in here? You threaten this young man, glued with fear to the bookcase, and have the temerity to switch sides. Campesi, of all people!"

"He's not so bad once you realize he'll hurt you."

Dr. Braun vehemently shook her head, the back and forth dislodging a lacquered chopstick from her hair.

"That's not good enough. And, after all we've done for you."

"You mean, like pointing out my orkittal and lobar brains don't connect."

"That's *orbital* and frontal lobes. They're disengagement."

"Whatever. You guys always going back to that MRI stuff. And, please no more crap about some birth deformity your precious vaccine would reverse."

"I admit we aimed for a more constructive metamorphosis. We hoped you might develop moral scruples, the ability to tell right from wrong...."

"God damn, Siggy baby. Stop this deformation shit. You forget I'm a highly functioning psychopath. I know geometry. Logistics. Aerodynamic drift. I can hit a human target at 1600 yards with a Barrett 50-caliber rifle. Leupold scope. Semiautomatic. A deformed brain could not do that."

"Deranged, then. Extreme murder is not a good thing. Nor is ditching Corporal Signet. You two occupy a similar wavelength. To switch allegiance is disloyal and, and, well, not permitted. You know that."

Devoid of convincing logic, Beth's outburst fell flat. Sauer yanked Ravi Ravda from his perch, slapped a headlock on him, and dragged the helpless man to the kitchen.

"Stop resisting, you wretched ragdoll. We're leaving."

"I am no such thing. I have a wife and family. I am also wealthy. Where are we going?"

As soon as they were gone, Signet yanked a Krav Maga instruction manual from the book case. He retrieved a map of Campesi's Odessa estate taped to the inside cover and laid it over the empty croissant tray.

"Pay attention. This is what we'll do. Here's the main house and the shallow stream behind the patio." He paused, hand extended to Ross. "Time to surrender the flash drive. I can take over from here."

Ross shook his head.

"No can do. Let's hear your plan. Then, I'll take it from here."

It required a full ten count. Then the master relented.

"Back to the map, people. Don't say I didn't try. Hope it's not like Trine-Tree Emergency. There they ship patients out in a box."

CHAPTER 44

Autumnal Florida at its finest.

Countless birds swooped in and out of the woods bordering the cobblestones. Brazen squirrels scampered at his feet, as if expecting handouts, while insects, too numerous to imagine yet along with butterflies yellow, orange, black and white were soon-to-become meals for other creatures. A constant, shifting palette of color and sound, all drenched in midmorning sunshine, bathed by a gentle wind that coaxed mournful groans from flanking pines.

Perhaps not the invigorating vistas of New England but spectacular enough.

And, miraculous. An each and every day unassuming kind of beauty transporting him back in time, to a primordial spot of innumerable fibers, an infinity of nodes. The sort of timeless, undifferentiated space into which Imhotep delivered him hours earlier when he floated on the flotsam filled Anclote River, the bayou, and grassland swamp off US Highway 19.

And, now in reflection, these were sensations identical to those elicited upon entering Signet's private bower of soaring, whispering pines, and curious cypress swamp dwellers.

The bower behind Arriva's pink cube where he worked.

Mr. Zen, his captain now, voice in his ear, barking an order, get a move on. We are waiting.

Adrift on the Belgian stones, he picked up pace, relaxed and troubled at the same time.

Relaxed by the familiar location; troubled by the impending encounter with the dreaded—dreadful— CEO. What did Campesi want with both him and the talkative Ravi Ravda? Why labor so hard to bring Ross down? Questions put to Signet on the ride out, answers not forthcoming.

As he approached the portico, cloaked as usual in Samantha's wistful aura, he briefly glimpsed the wan and fuzzy image of goodbye. Then, the image retreated, slipping down a sulcus to a treasured compartment deep inside his mind. It was to her he owed the first debt, his chance to create Glaucon and a shot at fame; and, the second, the assault launched on his amygdala giving him the chance to develop a fresh perspective. Except for now, all he possessed was a faint outline of the path ahead.

Dark Thread. Where art thou?

The changes were real enough, though.

No longer did he covet Arturo's sparkling Lexus. Today, he viewed both it and his rusting Corolla in a new light.

The sleek sedan but one vehicle capable of reaching point B from point A. For Ross, an allure now gone. Sheltered by palms and Oleander trumpets, it loomed less imposing, less desirable this fine October morning. Despite unbalanced wheels and crooked steering, the various grinding noises beneath the hood, his trusty Corolla worked just fine, thank you.

And, embarrassing to admit, he owed this change of outlook to Signet's sneaky cola job. The tasty drink was hard at work reconfiguring his amygdalae, synapse by synapse, reshaping the contours of his mind.

Reshaping, for example, the recent sprint up the Anclote River. Though taking place a mere four hours earlier, it now felt to him, standing at the edge of the Odessa wood, as a slice of ancient history. A fresh time warp tightly bound him. Linking him, hooking him up with, an expanded realm of invisible threads which, like ubiquitous neutrinos, passed through his every molecule, every second. A timeless connection, a constant presence, this universal synapse.

A fresh perspective.

A rededication as well, to his eyeball heritage, Glaucon his personal contribution to posterity, that vast tapestry stitching back and yet further back, all the way to von Graefe, one of dozens of towering eyeballers from times past, and forward to modern greats, the Boston legacy a tree of light dropping pearls of wisdom across the country, an unbroken and glorious weave of famous threads. What more purposeful life could exist than to honor this tapestry by incorporating his own thread? And yet, and yet, the doubt existed, the suspicion, that despite all his efforts, he might just not be of that number. Glaucon, for all its promise, not good enough.

The best he might ever hope to achieve was to toss his invention into the mix, cross his fingers, move on to the next hurdle.

Assuming he recovered his invention.

There was also another equally compelling rededication. To honor the final wish of his angel investor, though it was more vanquishing scold than wish. *Yes, Daniel. Pursue your biofilm-tube device. Pursue earned fame but also retrieve the magic. Reach for both the gold and the ivory.*

The demand, that memory of promise too long simmering on the back burner of his temporal lobes, pushed forward now as he entered the resplendent foyer of dear Samantha's home. A memory dislodging ruffled neurons on its trip to Brodman area 10, the frontal tip of the brain, locus of all formulated plans. Following a solemn bow to the sheltered sitting room and the idle Steinway, he softly intoned his oath:

"I will do it. I give my word. Opus 57? I am coming."

"Hey, Ross. You *jackass*. You're goddamn late. What kept you?"

The CEO's foul scream boomed from the pool patio. Echoing along the cathedral ceilings, reverberating within chambers of Carrera marble and marvelous paintings, it jostled the ossicles of his inner ears, upsetting composure.

This from the treacherous ghoul who constructed a narrow passageway between the walls to spy on his unsuspecting and dying wife.

Treading his newfound path, he gave the man his due, refusing to be intimidated. Mental shoulders set, he wove his way beneath the spiraling staircase, across tracts of herringbone hardwood to the sprawling patio in back.

And, there he was, seated comfortably at a canopied table, slurping orange fluid from a crystal snifter. Already five sheets to the wind, he dangled a straw as Ross approached, disinclined to rise in greeting whether from too much drink or rudeness, take your pick. Dappled sunlight sparkled off his gold necklace and trademark onyx cufflinks while his mean, red rimmed eyes, scarcely shaded by transition lenses, chiseled into Ross.

"Don't get up," Ross said. "You're only the host."

The CEO laughed.

"Always the smart ass, eh, Ross?"

A drop of yellow liquid plopped onto his white shorts, an embellishment unnoticed by the tipsy terror.

"You've been a good teacher."

"The maid's off, or I'd offer you a drink. You're got a flash drive I want. For the record, I could give a damn about the copy of your precious project. Too bad saddle bags messed up yesterday's talk. There won't be any takers after that."

"Wasn't that the idea?" Ross had to laugh. Campesi's plan

to sabotage Glaucon had backfired miserably. "I heard Dr. Jose Calaban from New York did the rescue. Not bad. As Innovator of the year, his assistance and support a show stopper. So, don't worry about any takers. They're out there."

"Won't do them much good. Who do you suppose controls the patents?"

He gulped the last of his drink. Studied the bottom of the glass as if to find the hole. Shrugged, turned back to Ross.

"Hand it over," he said, eyes fighting the light. "Make it quick. I'm expecting Colonel Bame for lunch. Wouldn't want any embarrassing questions. He thinks we're airtight at Arriva. Better for all of us to keep it that way. Wait. Is that dried mud on your khakis?" Pretend belly laugh as he examined Ross anew. "I was told you took a midnight dip in Tarpon Lake. Brave lad, swimming with the gators."

More laughter. More disdain. Ross had a reply wrapped and ready for delivery, but a commotion erupted behind him.

"Hey, Dr. Danny-boy. It is me. I am over here."

Voice a watery gurgle, Ravi Ravda was calling to him from across the pool. Ross hadn't noticed the Simcoe man before. He did now. A chilling sight.

He'd been tied to a plastic chair by a green cord, its free end wrapped around an adjacent palm tree and held by a sadistically grinning Sauer. The assassin was lowering the doodad inch by inch into the pool, the coiled cord in one hand, a black knife in the other. Already half-submerged, head bobbing at the water line, Ravda screamed again for Ross to save him before he drowned.

"See what they do to me? I cannot swim. Or breathe beneath water. Give them what they want. Set me free!"

His plea spilled out in a torrent. And, for good reason. Sauer looked prepared to complete the task any moment.

Worried now, Ross checked his watch and scanned the woods beyond the pool.

Where the heck were they?

Signet and Zina were to have already emerged from the stream at the back of the property, the plan being to first overcome the assassin and, afterwards, deal with Mr. Campesi. But, they were late. Ravi Ravda was almost swimming with the fishes.

"Oh, dear God. My chin is under water. Help me, Dr. Ross. I am unafraid to die. I simply wish not to drown."

"Sounds afraid to me. Your turn next, doc. Waterboarding's a specialty of the house."

"Yee-ow, Danny-boy. Please explain to these peoples. We have no scheme to join up. You and me, we are innocent. Hurry, please. This water … tastes awful…."

Unfazed by the torture session, Mr. Campesi sucked cubes from his drink.

"Don't believe a word of it," he said. "Lower him all the way, Sauer-baby. Your pal Signet claims they are collaborating. We can't tolerate that. If you want to save your partner, hand over that flash drive."

Collaborating?

"Forget whatever Signet told you. I don't know why, but he's lying. Mr. Ravda and I have never—"

"Cut the crap. Give me those files."

"They are encrypted. No one can read them. What's the big deal?"

"Encryption can be broken."

"I also didn't steal them. They were mailed to a friend. I had nothing to do with it."

The CEO nearly choked on an ice cube.

"Signet warned me you'd say that. Who the hell's lying now?"

Not a simple matter of lying, however. With Campesi, it never was. He operated on a more insidious level. A sociopath to the core. The picture, once drawn for him in sharp relief by Signet, seen clearly now. All remarks shared with Ross over the years, pure deception, baloney or as Sauer might put it, bullshit.

Congratulations, Daniel. Great work. Dr. Braun setting up experiments, teaching bio-statistics, helping to comply with the FDA.

Atta boy, keep at it. Real progress. Dr. Braun perfecting the biological preparations.

At this rate, you'll be innovator of the year. A collaboration, really, Dr. Braun at his side parenting everything.

Comments designed to harness Ross to the lab, to the smelly rats, to the increasing toll on his sanity, but worth it because it led, in the end, to the payoff: a long scheduled talk summarizing work to date, the future ahead for his creation. But, at the crucial moment, snatched from his hands....

He refused to go there again. Ms. Saddlebags Myla almost did him in. But, quality in the form of Dr. Calaban captured victory from defeat. Long ago, he should've shifted back to Boston, even to North Carolina. But, he stayed put. The sociopath had read him like a book.

The opening theme of Opus 57 roared out of the bushes at his feet. He jumped as Beethoven's rumbling brilliance surrounded him, the trills, the powerful syncopation, the overwhelming genius of the piano sonata pouring out of the concealed sound system amongst the shrubs. Campesi clamped his ears, fighting off the intrusive noise.

Allegro Assai, the surprise electric.

"What the hell is *that*?"

In another lucid flash, Ross at last saw the way out of the entire mess. He was not the man on the bridge or anyone below. Because, thanks to Signet's doctored cola, his triggered musical neurons came to life to save him. A fresh new reality took hold. He reentered a realm where fear no longer claimed him. He disowned the obscuring emotion. It no longer fit.

All week he'd toyed with the slim notion Campesi would finally relent. This, a false dream buried so deep within the convolutions of desire and self-deceit, it seemed real.

He knew the coming gesture was futile. This pompous ass controlled the ballgame. Yet, he would not succumb to the incomparable jerk, an immoral man who had to be stopped.

If not now, when; if not by Ross, by whom.

Do the right thing? Damn you, Signet. You figured this out all along.

Energized, he dug deep inside his caked pocket, twisting his hand to enter the reversed opening. He grasped the thumb drive and tossed it high, flinging the damnable thing over the deep end of the tiled pool, tendrils of attached fear forever severed.

Other research labs would invite him in. Another time, another place. He was free.

Not quite.

Sauer launched a counter attack. He darted across the flagstones and soared above the water, his arc, timed with characteristic precision, to intersect that of the thumb drive. With balanced ease, he seized hold of the drive and, with a flick of the wrist, tossed it to Campesi, who managed to catch it, as the assassin struck the water.

Aware of the stakes, Ross launched a counter-counter attack. Too late, however, his dive bringing him, when he reached the water, into the muscled arms of his worst enemy.

Nighttime on Lake Tarpon, Act Two.

Except this was no alligator infested lake but a chlorinated swimming pool. Sauer held him high, allowed a brief intake of air then dragged him straight to the bottom, there to hold him an eternity of hell before shooting to the surface, Sauer grinning madly as Ross gasped for air.

Eventually, he struggled to the stairs and pulled himself from the pool. Taking advantage, the second poolside sadist stomped his fingers.

He cried out, still dazed by the unscheduled swim.

"Damn. What was that for?"

"A reminder. I own Glaucon. I'll keep you in patent court for years. Just where did you think you were going with this?"

Across the pool, Sauer re-secured the chair dangerously lower in the water.

"Please, kind sir. Pull me out. A very nice dive, by the way. The performance of a champion. You have what you want. Let me go!"

His plea fell on ears attuned to the rustle of leaves coming from behind the patio. From Signet, in fact. Always prone to a dramatic entrance, Arriva's Security Chief edged the last shrub aside, displaying his own chilling, calm precision.

The volume from the shrubs diminished as the first movement ended. An expectant silence settled over the patio as Signet sized up the situation.

"You are here," he said, casually.

"As are you, amigo. You misjudged me."

"And, you, me. Twenty seconds for the rope tie. With the gator under a drape, it required thirty-two minutes to Aunt Sophia's."

Sauer cracked a thin smile. "Got the picture. A calf tie at the rodeo. Neat. Hope your passenger didn't ruin the seats."

"No problem. Good work taking out Zalin and his crew. Maybe it will make up for saving Ross."

"I guess. Got to like him, though. Nerd dooby from the ivory tower. I felt bad leaving him in the lake."

"Commendable performance."

"Now what?"

Eyes locked, the two adversaries stepped away from the palms. Like gunfighters at high noon, they inched closer until face to face. Instead of exchanging blows, they perpetrated antics similar to those undertaken by Zina and Aunt Sophia although more intricate. First, the odd series of flip flop fist bumps, twisting palms moving at alarming speed and intermixed so that, at one juncture, it appeared the smaller security man had suddenly sprouted outsized baseball mitts for hands, forearms also briefly involved in brief rolling hip hop gestures, the entire vaudeville act mesmerizing but soon concluded. Exercises no doubt perfected long ago on chilly Afghanistan hill tops. Mirror neurons at work. Both men inoculated. Both brains lurching down a track in roughly the same direction. Master Zen and assassin, as Beth pointed out, on a similar wavelength.

Then they spoke, words caught by Ross's now over sensitive ears.

"Haul him out. Towel him off. Wait."

Sauer nodded, hesitating.

"Took your time, Corporal. You're late. Our doodad is almost dead.""

Signet nodded.

"Stumbled near some rocks. Twice. But, you have the situation well in hand. Mr. Ravda is correct. A perfect dive."

"You were right about the doctor. He tossed it in the pool."

"We should help him. He got us this far. Let's complete the bargain."

"One he was unaware of. You chose well."

"Circumstance served him up. The colonel will be impatient. And, please save Mr. Ravda."

Signet studied his Luminox wrist watch.

"Let's wrap this up. Then, lunch. All this climbing through the underbrush has stirred an appetite."

While Signet aimed for Campesi, Sauer delivered the shivering Ravda to the pavers, a squirming fish, but one with a better future than a sliced fillet. After untying the grateful Simcoe man, the dark closer joined his companion to corner their common prey. Oblivious to any danger, Campesi cradled his empty snifter.

"What is wrong with you?" He pointed his straw at Sauer. "We're almost home free. Think of the profits. We sell Genesis III back to the D.O.D. Jesus, man. Get a grip."

Tranquil as andante con moto, Signet issued his own instructions, changing rhythm and key.

"As of today, your project does not exist. Your role at Arriva is terminated. Next stop, a padded cell behind bars."

"What the hell? I'm giving the orders here. You idiots are about to be mustered out of the organization."

Determined to retain control, a pugnacious CEO lurched to his feet.

He poked a finger at Sauer.

"You forget how you got here. I'll inject you again. A double whammy will eat your brain out. Simple as that."

Astonished by the outrageous posturing, Ross stood back from the evolving confrontation. Either of the two Special Forces operatives could squash Campesi with a pinky.

After a suitable pause, the pair of closers exchanged a look. Signet then waved at the French doors on the far patio, signaling to come ahead.

Ross then witnessed what he never thought possible. Cowering, Mr. Campesi blinked twice when he recognized who emerged from the house. Shoulders hunched, he dropped like a stone to his chair. Arrogant, insane with power one moment. Crest fallen the next.

Bracing his shoulders, Colonel Bame strode up to them. In full regalia, a chest of medals sparkling in the sun, he at first appeared unfriendly, the executioner prepared to claim his prize. The breeze, anticipating trouble also came to a brief standstill.

Ross misinterpreted, however. Bame's attitude reflected only disappointment, peering down at his quarry with more sympathy than regret.

"Arturo."

"Bennett."

"I did not come willingly. I explained that when you fetched me at MacDill."

Ross flinched. He was reminded of that moment outside Arriva's third floor conference room. Looking back he realized the colonel's bark reflected disappointment, not the dressing down of incompetence by a most senior officer.

"The corporal claims you jumped the rails. What the devil is he talking about?"

"Sir, I have already submitted the evidence required for dismissal."

Colonel Bame held up a hand, silencing Signet.

"I've examined your evidence. Frankly, I don't see a

problem. Who gives a damn if some Greek mermaid now beats the crap out of town bullies? She ought to be given a medal. And, what's the big deal about a priest becoming a pervert playboy? Where's the harm in any of this?"

Talk about going off the rails. The colonel's outburst, like an eruption of tympani, stopped the conversation. Always on point, Signet spoke up.

"Imagine the publicity," he said, voice a soothing melody of restraint. "Investigative reporters will have a field day."

"Not if no one tells them. Tell me, corporal. Do you intend to receive a pension?"

"Of course he does, Bennett. Now see here, all of you."

Campesi made a valiant effort to stand. Exhausted, he fell back, knocking his crystal snifter into the shrubs.

"What I'm trying to point out, the colonel is correct. No one has been hurt. We have an energetic, former mermaid. And, a frisky priest. Hell, he's getting a taste of what he gave up along the way—"

"But, the stolen files—"

"Hey, corporal. Screw off, okay? There are no stolen files. Misplaced, maybe. But now returned. No harm. No foul. Episode over."

"It is not over," Signet countered. "They were easily downloaded. They could just as easily have been copied. This, in itself, is pure negligence. May I remind you, Colonel Bame. These are highly sensitive government documents."

"But, encrypted. You made sure of that yourself. Dr. Ross possesses neither the intelligence nor contacts to crack the code in a million years."

Keeping his distance from the insult and the angry warriors, Ross shifted weight from one water logged foot to the other. He'd been a pawn from the start. Let the big boys settle their mess. He was out of it.

"Simmer down, for Christ's sake. A tough ass mermaid and a fruitcake priest? What the hell is wrong with you people?" The colonel ran a hostile eye over his disruptive troops. "Now, Corporal Signet, can you guarantee this goddamn thumb drive was never duplicated?"

"I swear on a stack of Army Survival Handbooks."

Satisfied, Colonel Bame pried Ross out of the shrubs.

"Signet has brought me into his confidence. He needlessly involved you in this military matter. Your role, if we may call it that, is over. Even though you possessed top secret documents for a while...."

He paused, taking a closer look at the shivering individual before him.

"You, ah, transported this thumb drive on your, ah, person?"

Ross shuffled nervously.

"Don't be fooled by these chinos, sir. Of the highest quality, uh, Brooks Brothers apparel...."

"He is merely trying to say he guarded the drive with his life."

"Uhmm. Thank you, corporal. I am sure he did."

"I think the doctor is concerned these documents are labeled stamped Top Secret."

"Yes, yes. I understand. Doctor, let me assure you, no harm will ever come to you because of this matter. The corporal chose well. You are a credit to your profession. To your country, as well."

He was speechless. Still, words of reassurance did not reassure. Treason was treason. An enterprising prosecutor at Justice would have a field day.

"There is more to this issue," Signet said. "I implore you to reconsider."

"Stop. We are done here. There is nothing more to discuss. The case, if there ever was one, is closed."

"The security at Arriva is porous. That is a major, unsolved problem. As is this man's unauthorized experimentation on the public. The lives of the 'mermaid' and the 'fruitcake' priest were compromised without their consent. If this were to hit the newspapers, the trail would lead straight to you."

"If you're insinuating—"

"I am *guaranteeing* your job and promotion to Assistant Chief of Staff will be jeopardized. You must eliminate Campesi. With him gone, there will be no threat to the public. No reason to ever disclose this horrible secret. We will then be able to proceed with our other mission."

The color drained from the colonel's face. He paced, hands fiddling with a bronze belt buckle.

"*Eliminate.* Are you listening to yourself?"

"We cannot afford another Benghazi."

"Ah, I see. This is all about those hostages in Eritrea."

"Their lives hang in the balance. Every week the local population flees by the thousands. Their young men are forced to enlist. It is a terrible environment. Yet, our government does nothing to—"

"What can anyone do? Intelligence claims the ambassador's wife is dead."

"True or not, this putrid dictator has incarcerated Americans at Assab, an easy reach from Bab el Mandeb. I've explained all this in my report."

The colonel held up his hand.

"Your proposed rescue mission is too risky. This is also not the proper venue to discuss it. Arturo Campesi will remain in place at Arriva."

Signet again waved his arm, this time in the opposite direction, at Samantha's magnificent veranda door on the other side of the house.

"You will now learn why *that* decision is too risky."

"You are insubordinate. When I return to Washington...."

The colonel's voice trailed to a whisper. He had caught sight of Zina and Detective Leeks emerging through the French doors to the veranda. They joined the group, all smiles and self-congratulation.

"Did you enjoy the choice of music?" she said to Ross. "It was the top disc on the CD player."

Lovely Zina, off script, gave him a not so furtive hug.

"Did you bring the pictures?" Signet said.

"Detective Leeks has them. Do you mind, Colonel?"

Whether he did or not, Zina stood at his elbow, allowing him sufficient opportunity to look her over. To sniff her over, too, his nose wrinkling in delight.

"You must be our mermaid."

"Call me Zina. I no longer hate you. I forgive your secret inoculation."

"You are mistaken, my dear. I had no part—"

"My name is Zina. Is that so hard to remember?"

Unaccustomed to rebuke, the colonel stiffened.

"I am fully capable of remembering your name. As for the 'secret inoculation'. That was Mr. Campesi's idea, not mine."

"An offshoot of your project, though."

The colonel sniffed, nodding in approval.

"That scent," he said. "It is new to me. What do you call it? I would like to procure a bottle for my wife. I think she will like it."

"It is called Shade of Night." She tossed both Ross and Signet an enigmatic glance. "Others have liked, or should

I say, benefitted from it as well."

Ross's heat shot up like a thermometer. From Eckerd Hall to Aunt Sophia's Victorian couch, the same scent assaulted his nostrils. Colonel Bame's turn to be distracted.

"It so happens, I have a small vial inside. I shall get it for you later."

Ross looked at the security man who winked. Damn. The guy winked again.

"I shall look forward to that. Where is your grandfather this fine morning? Out on another escapade, I hope."

Zina was not as receptive with this remark.

"He is still a priest," she said, *molto espressivo*, dropping to attack crouch.

"No, no, Zina. Please take no offense. I meant nothing by it. I only wanted to meet him and apologize."

Still incensed, she began circling in an all too familiar, pre-strike mode.

Sensing trouble, Signet separated injured pride from a tunic of medals.

"Allow me to introduce Detective Leeks," he said, *andante con moto*, with a smooth transition. "He has several photographs he would like to share."

CHAPTER 45

The detective sprang to life as Signet made the introductions. When it came time to shake the colonel's hand, he shook Leeks off like a piece of lint. To emphasize intent, he wiped his hands clean as if contaminated by the air itself. When Leeks offered a knuckle bump instead, the colonel, in rare form, shrank back as if dealing with a dead skunk.

"No offense, sir," he said. "I abhor germs. What have you got to show me?"

Leeks produced, from an inside pocket of his disheveled jacket, a small manila envelope. He shook the envelope open, removed several photographs, and, while the group closed ranks, described what they were viewing.

"Everyone will recognize Mr. Campesi." He nodded toward their besotted host. "He's wearing a blue blazer, I'd guess from Walmart. Not that it isn't stylish enough. I hear they also sell name brands...."

Signet tapped his shoulder.

"Let's move to the second photo. What do we have here?"

"Right. Okay then. The lighting is a bit off. The photographer shifted to his, rather her, left to capture the shot. That, center frame, is Mr. Campesi's foot. As you can see, it is raised with the heel sharply indenting the victim's throat. The victim had just opened the door and turned to his left when, wham, that's all she wrote."

He passed the incriminating photo around. Refusing even a mere inspection, Campesi handed it back to the detective who displayed the next photo in his portfolio.

"This punishing maneuver speaks for itself. While the vic clasped his neck, falling to his knees, Mr. Campesi delivered the coup de grace. See here. He's moved behind him to snap the neck with another kick. An unnecessary blow according to the coroner. The first impact crushed the windpipe. Why break the neck? Mr. Newsome, ah, the victim was already suffocating to death."

Detective Leeks shuffled the pictures back to their folder. He removed a pair of handcuffs from his belt, waiting.

Angry now, Colonel Bame seized the folder and reexamined the photographs. Hands quivering, face contorted, he returned them to Leeks.

"These photographs are fakes," he said. "They are grainy as hell. Probably photoshopped. I am not convinced. Not for a single moment."

Zina thumped the folder against the chest of medals.

"I took these pictures myself," she said. "I witnessed

the entire thing. I saw Mr. Newsome's look of surprise and horror, the awful head blow, the perp's escape as he ran back up the stairs and out of sight. Not 'perp', "she corrected herself. "Mr. Campesi, this *awful* man, is the murderer. The pictures are not grainy. They are plain as day."

"You don't say. I want to know who put you up to this. How did you even know to attend this particular event?"

"I went to meet Dr. Ross. Signet said he'd be there."

"Signet, you say? The man with a mission. Hmm."

"Two missions, sir. Let us confine the present discussion to the first. The need to stop Mr. Campesi. The man is a threat to the United States defense establishment. To DARPA, not to mention, to society."

"That is quite a claim. You exaggerate, corporal."

Signet shook his head.

"Not for a moment, sir. Let me explain. I admit it was my original plan to eliminate this dangerous sociopath by securing a compromising photograph of Dr. Ross and Mr. Newsome at the concert. Such a picture would suggest the CEO ran a loose ship, that the doctor was sharing state secrets with a sworn enemy. I never anticipated Mr. Campesi's presence at the concert. Or that he was sufficiently brazen to secretly pass a message to the doctor in order to kill him. Newsome's death was shocking. We are, the doctor is, lucky the accountant intercepted that message. Yet, we have the necessary photos. The man must pay for his crime. He must be removed from Arriva."

A stunned silence. Zina squeezed the lucky doctor's hand. Signet offered an obliging nod. The colonel scoffed.

Yet, it was an impressive performance. Following an unscripted mishap at a Beethoven concert, Signet managed to engineer a precise series of events for the ensuing week, an undertaking made possible by annihilating Ross's amygdala, and all designed to 'eliminate' the nasty CEO.

Mission over, as far as Ross was concerned.

"Because I myself was unable to take these remarkable pictures," Signet continued. "I made other arrangements. This involved Ms. Palaeologus. I spoke to her that very afternoon, in fact. She knew about the concert. She also knew her favorite doctor would be there. I asked, as a favor, if she would photograph him between sonatas. She was unaware of the purpose, however. She unwittingly witnessed the grizzly execution. We are lucky she possessed the presence of mind to take the pictures. What happened was a surprise for us all."

Campesi finally freed himself from the chair. He grabbed and shredded the incriminating photos, tossing the fragments into the pool.

"So much for your so-called evidence. We all know they weren't real. Anyone could see they were doctored."

"Don't be an ass," Detective Leeks said. "Ms. Palaeologus retains the originals on her iPhone. For some reason, she waited until the last moment to forward them on. They arrived just in time."

From the back seat of Dr. Keresti's KIA on their ride to

Clearwater Beach. That's when she sent them on. Ross well recalled the moment. One second a hand on his thigh, the next two hands on her cell. But why then? Signet's instruction. Had to be. Supposedly dead in the swamp, still capable of transmitting messages.

The detective produced another folder, removed a single sheet of paper which he thrust at Campesi.

"A warrant for your arrest," he said. "You're coming with me."

Surprised, Campesi pushed the document away.

"You're out of your mind!"

"Am I?'

Signet, with a skeptical frown. A quick one. Ross almost missed it.

"This, Dr. Ross, is a civilized way to *eliminate* a problem. Take him, Detective. Lock him up. Throw away the key."

Complexion torrid, the 'perp' was having none of it.

"You can't *arrest* me. Think of the consequences. In a public trial my testimony will hang the Genesis programs out to dry. Including the PTSD vaccine project, better known as GENESIS 1. I sure as hell won't go easily into the dark night."

Another standstill. A septet with broken strings, none of the players confident to proceed. Except, as expected, sostenuto Signet, propelled them onward.

"He is correct," the corporal conceded. "At trial, he will provide the media an endless revelation of damaging secrets. That Arriva conducted unsavory projects he was directed to conceal. Colonel Bame, his liaison with DARPA and hence the government, coordinated these projects. And worse, all such orders come directly from central command." He paused for a concluding beat. "Which means a public trial is out of the question. We shall arrange another path for you, Mr. Campesi."

Grabbing hold of Colonel Bame, Signet invited the detective to join them for a private conference beside the pool. Should Campesi attempt escape, Sauer was to have a Blackhawk Gideon at the ready. The threesome then moved off. Holding the baton of command, Corporal Signet conducted the trio, rejecting with a vigorous head shake, each objection offered by Colonel Bame.

Meanwhile, Ross waited calmly amidst the pachysandra with the others.

"Curious about what's going on?" Zina, sotto voce to Sauer towering above her.

"For Campesi here, nothing good."

"They don't scare me." The CEO chortled. "I've got a fleet of lawyers to tear these guys apart. That reminds me. Why did you return to Signet? I offered more cash."

"Didn't trust you to deliver. You'd take off once you had those files."

"Damn straight. I'm not afraid of you either. We created other assassins. Got an entire platoon of you guys, in fact."

542

"Yeah. We got to find our way out to Eritrea."

"Shh," Ross said. "They're returning. Let's see what they came up with."

Expressions firm, the three men surrounded Campesi's lounge chair. He turned away, fuming in disgust.

"Sorry, old friend," Colonel Bame said. "The game is over. You're coming with us. Take him, Sauer. He's all yours."

"The hell it is." Now furious, the CEO spun free of the assassin's grasp. "I'm not going anywhere with you. I'll take my chances with the cop and his phony evidence. This is a travesty. It's a goddamn joke."

His pathetic outrage fell flat. The detective wasn't about to arrest Mr. Campesi. He was going with Sauer, exact destination unknown. No one voiced an objection. The violence flowing through Sauer's veins guaranteed an unpleasant departure.

Still, the CEO resisted. He swiveled about, searching for a nonexistent opening in the foliage. He was trapped, no place to go.

He faced Ross, eyes fierce.

"I should've had Sauer take you out when he had the chance. From the beginning, you've been a major pain in my ass. If Newsome had not taken my note, Ms. Palaeologus would've caught your neck snapping, instead. Best laid plans. Shit!"

"Did you hear that?" Zina said. "An admission of guilt. The pictures are proof. Case closed. Next stop: death row."

Campesi snorted.

"A vodka confession. That's all. The charge will never stick. My lawyers will see to that."

The indignant bluster had begun to falter, his situation clearly hopeless. He examined every shrub and path through the bushes, even probing the clouds above. He searched everywhere for the escape hatch that did not exist.

"What I really regret, Ross," he said, finally, "Is your blissful, your relentless confusion. It's a joke you never made the connection. And, forget the mix-up at that stupid concert. It's true. I really wanted to beat your ass. That's in the past. Let's think about Samantha, my late wife. Her story is also in the past. But, it lingers on. I should never have listened to her and brought you on board. She had this misguided belief you had promise, that you'd be famous one day, who knows, maybe even have your portrait painted; although, where you or anyone else would hang the damn thing beats me." He smiled, very pleased with the snide remark. "To be perfectly clear, she brought you in, not me. I would've trashed your ridiculous letter. Yet, before I could pronounce 'nano-glaucoma-technology,' there you were, *inside my company* with your goddamn idea. Hell, inside my house and, for all I knew, my wife. A double tube, growth factors, a neuro-regenerative attempt to cure the incurable. To think, I bought into this nonsense. It boggles the mind."

"Your mind maybe. The data speaks for it...."

"Stop, okay? I heard that crap before."

"To set the record straight with you. She asked numerous times, but I never violated her vows. Not once. But, she wanted me all right. God, how she begged. 'If not for me, do this for Beethoven, your patron saint.' Broke my heart, Arturo. I cared for her too much. I had to turn her down."

Okay, he told himself. That was thick. For all her charms, Samantha kissed him only once, never more than that. A kiss of sympathy, in fact. He messed up a Chopin etude. He'd played terribly, in fact. An exercise of embarrassment, of being out of practice.

There, there, Daniel. Parallel thirds can be a monster. Even Arturo, bless his black heart, knows that.

Next thing the smoocheroo. Lights out for a quick moment then back to the keyboard for him, back to the settee for her.

But, the suspicion of more was Campesi's Achilles heel. Time to inflict his own pain for a change.

Then, he reconsidered. Even for such an egomaniac. Cruel.

"Look, Mr. Campesi. None of that really hap—"

"Buzz off, asshole. I don't want to hear it."

"Me, neither," Zina said.

"None of us do, Ms. Paleolugus." Sauer slapped the CEO across the ear. "The guy is lying. Anyone can see that. Where were you, man? Your woman was suffering. Hell. You resemble my old dad. A military wife gets a rotten deal."

Signet laid a comforting hand on his companion.

"Let him vent. Where he's headed, he won't have the chance."

"Such a wiseass, Signet. I was an idiot from the start. First Samantha convinced me. Then, after she croaked, the colonel made me keep you on. But, you, Danny-boy, win the double tube cake. Glaucon will never fly. My name is on most patents. Without my permission, the project's dead. Or, if I disappear with maniac Sauer, Glaucon also go down the drain. And, if I'm around when the nano dust settles, the project will stay put at Arriva. Yeah, keep frowning, buddy. Didn't think you'd like that one."

The patents again. He'd discussed them and the subject of royalties before with the CEO. Because Glaucon was developed at Arriva and Arriva is a DARPA contract company, Ross would never realize a full return, or anything close to it, should Glaucon become a big seller.

Today, this worry did not concern him. He was a new man. He'd tossed his project into the drink. Hell, he wasn't entirely sure his portrait belonged on that library wall.

He was home free on all accounts. Forget the double tube device, nerve growth factors, the miracle bio-film-nano-motor. He'd leave Arriva, patent a three tube device and use injectable nanoparticles of stem cell factors to cure, save and sprout neurons. Definitely, home free. Come to think of it, a small portrait might yet be in the cards, say on an inside wall near a water cooler.

"The patents are critical," Signet agreed. "However, we are dealing here with a more critical issue. The CEO of a DARPA-licensed lab temporarily lost national secrets. Details about immune development, the GENESIS projects plus names of soldiers, their injuries. All highly classified documents. The colonel is obligated to notify the FBI as well as his superiors. Once informed of the nature of the problem, they, like DARPA, will work to keep the matter buried and away from public disclosure. And, here is where we might find a satisfactory solution to our combined problem."

He pulled up a deck chair and positioned it near Campesi. He sat, hands folded as if discussing a sporting event with a neighbor.

"You know, Arturo. A deal would be to your advantage."

"What sort of deal?"

"A simple exchange. Wherein charges of treason would be dropped in exchange for a release of your patents. In the name of national interest, this could be arranged. You will remain sequestered, however. No chance of media contact whatsoever." Signet now addressed the detective. "Mr. Leeks, am I correct to assume, the man will never stand trial?"

The detective nodded.

"My guess, the murder may never be solved."

"What do you say? Fair enough?"

Campesi gave them all a measured look.

"I've been accused of murder. I'm a citizen. I demand a trial."

Colonel Bame pulled up a chair. Adjusted it near his old friend.

"What you'll get is a federal trial," he said. "No jury, witnesses, or reporters allowed. You'll be found guilty, sentenced, and never leave prison."

"How is your 'deal' any different?"

"All charges dropped. You'll be jailed in one of those white collar crime country clubs. Big difference. Be smart, Arty. Give it some thought."

In the end, Arty came to his senses and agreed. All charges dropped in exchange for release of patents and, the hard part, indefinite prison time; although, with Sauer now gripping a deflated CEO, it was an open question whether Campesi would ever see the inside of a prison. The inside of a gator, more than likely.

Ross caught up with Sauer and his charge at the edge of the woods. As a courtesy, Sauer granted them a few words.

"Thanks," he said. "I appreciate it."

"You want to *thank* me on the day I disappear?"

"Actually, I'm curious. Wasn't the PTSD project enough for you? What were you trying to accomplish?"

It took time to register. The vodka, whatever it was, delaying his thoughts.

"Excellent question. GENESIS I was not enough. I'll tell you why. After I inoculated Samantha, she did not improve. She remained scared out of her wits."

"You *inoculated* her with the PTSD vaccine?"

"I wanted to know why, if it worked with war vets, the vaccine didn't touch her."

Ross was horrified.

"What you don't realize, cancer patients experience a form of traumatic stress all their own. She had no peace. None at all."

He wracked his brains. How had he missed this?

"Finally, I convinced her to get an MRI. To my surprise, her amygdalae lit up like bonfires. No veteran brain looked like hers. They were in terrible overdrive. I asked a neurologist for a consultation. His conclusion was a stunner. Distant effect from her cancer. Fucked up antibodies attacked her brain. So I took a different approach."

"Now I get it. GENESIS II. Knock out the amygdalae altogether. But, wait. Did she go through with it?"

A well of sadness drowned his eyes. A side of Mr. Arturo Campesi he'd never witnessed before. The husband truly loved his wife after all. Now, a surge of remorse swelled inside Ross.

"I wanted to but no. She rejected my suggestion. I never got to spray the vaccine into her nostrils. You want to know why?"

"Afraid of failure?"

"You were the reason. It was the day your damn letter arrived. It lifted her spirits. Then, before I knew it, you were shambling over the threshold. The soon to be clinician-scientist and lousy Beethoven pianist captured her heart. After that, intranasal inoculation was out of the question. So, no, I never got the chance to help her. It didn't matter in the end."

"I had no idea."

"Your presence seemed to revive her. You rekindled her love of music. Who knows? Maybe that strengthened her immune system. At least for a while. Then, with a vengeance, it reclaimed her. And, as you so kindly remind me, I was not there at the end. She spent her final hours with you."

He wiped away a real tear. The crying icon of Campesi. One had to wait a near lifetime to witness the impossible. Father Palaeologus waited for his. And, here was yet another. A streak down a stubble cheek. Shoulders hunched. Onyx cufflinks shining but a lot less brightly now.

"There is one thing I will never forgive. Why I've always despised you. You took her heart. Your absurd charm, all those lumbering arpeggios, won the day. Before your visits, she primped at a mirror, fluffing near invisible hair. Why the hell did you ever show up?"

His gaze wandered, over Ross's shoulders to the pool and patio beyond, coming to rest finally upon his glorious home where he and Samantha dreamed up Arriva, Inc., the production facility for the PTSD vaccine itself. Arturo Campesi, a lost soul, remained trapped in time.

"You wanted to prove efficacy of GENESIS II with Samantha."

Campesi's eyes flicked alive.

"Exactly. I wanted to help her. When she said no, I still wanted proof. Eventually I moved on to Father Palaeologus and the girl. I, I'm, sorry. What can I say?"

Sauer ended their talk. More gently this time, he took hold of the CEO and led him away.

"I'll give you one thing." The prisoner bit off his words. "She found solace in those damnable sonatas. You just lavished them on another man's wife."

"I didn't 'lavish'. I honored her requests."

"At the end, parallel fifths and Chopin Etudes failed to console her. Plus, you stopped playing. The Glaucon project consumed your time. Unimportant now. She had a terminal disease."

They were not so different after all, Ross thought. Both husband and interloper possessed an aching absence uniting them both. Each, in his own way, wanted to help Samantha. Each, in his own way, failed. Very much alike indeed.

"Dingbat," Ross said. "An improvement over jackass, asshole, and hot shot."

Campesi appeared not to hear.

"It wasn't enough for you, either," he said. "You abandoned a productive practice because of that crazy device. Yeah, buddy. We both wanted more."

He soon vanished behind the shrubs without another word. Ross waved goodbye anyway. He hoped Sauer would make the final exit a quick one.

Signet ambled up behind him.

"Worried about the CEO?"

"Kind of. Feeding him to the gators seems extreme."

"Sauer is escorting him to federal lockup. He'll be okay."

Ross groaned.

"I forgot about the flash drive. He still has it."

"Had it. Sauer picked his pocket while we examined photos. Right now the colonel is in possession of what you stole."

"*You* stole those damn documents. Why do you insist...."

Miracle of miracles. He shook Ross's hand. Clapped him on the back. Damn if he didn't smile. A genuine, but exceedingly brief show of pleasure. Gone in a flash. The shoulder crunch lingered for a bit, then it too was gone.

"To lunch," he announced. "Zina is serving. The idiot won't know what hit him."

"Mr. Campesi?"

Mr. Security shook his head.

"Colonel Bame. No frivolity at lunch, Doctor."

Signet strode off toward the dining room. Then Zina, after giving Ross an inviting kiss, fell in beside the corporal and slipped into the dining room on his heels.

CHAPTER 46

Twenty minutes later, obeying Signet's terse command, Ross abandoned his seat at the dining room table to find anxious friends in the kitchen.

Clustered around a sixteen inch monitor on the marble counter, courtesy of Signet's advanced planning, Melko, Aunt Sophia and Zina, were closely following the action in the dining room relayed to them by the wireless nanny cam their fearless leader installed in the crown molding.

"We saw the entire performance," Aunt Sophia said. "Mr. Signet is quite the magician."

"A perverse one," Ross added. "And, in good form today."

The black and white picture on the screen displayed the setting in eerie clarity. Framed in a wide angle view, corporal and colonel sat stiff as boards at opposite ends of the polished mahogany table. Trading compliments and barbed remarks, a battle of wits for weapons.

Currently sparring, sharp words exchanged between mouthfuls of Auntie's Avgolemono soup, they exchanged comebacks by jabbing the air with dripping spoons. The corporal, having won the round, helped himself to more soup while his superior's utensil paused on its path to partly parted lips.

"What are they saying? Turn up the volume."

"Not yet, Aunt Sophia. Wait until Zina goes back in."

From what Ross extracted from the scratchy sound system, Signet was dishing out a canned talk about the requirements of Special Operation missions, what Auntie correctly called a "performance," and one resembling many others of its kind Ross endured all week.

The action in the kitchen also worth noticing.

Hands entwined, Melko and Aunt Sophia wore goofy grins their attention alternating between monitor and grill. An occasional frown with the goings on of one, smiles of contentment with the progress of the other, sea bass and parsley, the latter according to a secret recipe of their chef extraordinaire.

Ravi Ravda the condiment of surprise. Precariously perched to one side, he still wore the expression of a prisoner released to the comforting balm of the everyday from the swirling vortex of a moist death. The man a frightened doodad with whom Ross was now curiously connected. Altogether, a fascinating scene in what Ross hoped was the end of the play, awesome in scope, and to judge by Signet's verbal pirouette, twisting to a conclusion.

"See how they slurp," Aunt Sophia said. "Lemon soup complements the sea bass. Uh-oh, take a look." She pointed to the monitor. "He signals for a second bottle. Here, Zeenee. Take the creep his chilled Dumol. I hope he chokes on it."

Melko patted her shoulder. "He's is not the one consuming the chardonnay, dear."

"That's right," Ross said. "He wants Bame sloshed for the curtain call."

"An appropriate description. Luncheon the prelude to the finale. Our master can wait a few minutes. What he really wants," Zina added. "Is this."

In her zany, seductive way, she produced a small vial of perfume from the front folds of her hip-hugging server outfit, purchased by Signet for the Odessa shindig.

"What, may I ask, is *that*?"

"A gift," she said. A mischievous glint filmed her eyes, framed by the upward arch of purple, caterpillar eyebrows. "Signet was explicit. Meet me at the piano concert. Bring your camera. Be certain the good doctor takes a prolonged sniff. Well, I did as told, but the detective interrupted. I was only able to share a departing whiff."

Her head-swimming perfume. His first exposure. Unforgettable.

"Leeks barely sampled a fume. You had a better dose."

"I'm not sure I'm following...."

"Signet's stolen documents brought you to center stage where you finally attracted Colonel Bame's attention.

Time now to seal the deal."

They were interrupted by a polite cough.

"It is time I must be leaving." Ravi Ravda stepped forth from his niche beside the fridge. "I am liking these moments so very much, but my wife awaits me. She has prepared lamb curry, my favorite. Please convey my sincere appreciation to the corporal. I am very fortunate to have found all you people, especially my new friend, Dr. Ross. I am confident we shall work well together."

"Please explain. How will we work—"

"As President of Arriva, I shall conduct activities as protocol demands. We will make many discoveries, you and I. It shall be marvelous to occupy our new Clearwater building. Are you aware it once housed a men's clothing store?"

With that, he glided out of the kitchen leaving Ross bewildered.

"What the heck was he talking about?"

Zina patted his hand.

"Signet had wanted to explain himself," she said. "Before luncheon, there was no opportunity. In the nutshell, DARPA and the Pentagon will need a new face to run Arriva. After reviewing options, Colonel Bame accepted his corporal's recommendation. Because the military seeks a new airbase in India, Ravi Ravda's Simcoe became part of the solution. DARPA owns Arriva and therefore Glaucon, making a merger with Ravda logical. Not only will Simcoe provide a market for Glaucon. It will form DARPA's cover and liaison in India."

She paused to preen in a small wall mirror.

"Who is this new face?"

"You, Dr. Danny Ross. These important people at DARPA have concluded, well, to be correct in the matter, Signet convinced them, that your light activated delivery device is revolutionary. A perfect example of translational science at its finest. The PTSD vaccine for veterans. Glaucon for veterans and civilians alike. A win-win all around."

"Then why the fancy luncheon?"

"The colonel thinks lunch is for celebration. It is not. I have a surprise for him." She kissed him on the cheek. "Auntie, where is the Dumol?"

"And, my role in this...."

"Silly boy. You stole vital documents. If Signet could convince the colonel this was the CEO's fault, the colonel would remove him from Arriva. Goal number one has been achieved." She shrugged, the exaggerated movement momentarily exposing more skin. She tucked things back to normal. "The mosquito in the jelly...."

"Fly in the ointment."

"Fly. Exactly. You were always a step ahead. Always the mastermind at court. Where was I? Oh yes. The fly is Bame's fear he'd lose an important promotion. This is where I come in."

"Signet said I was to change Bame's mind. Now, he's using you. Makes perfect sense to me."

"Your theft brought the colonel here from Iraq. Before his return trip, we must win goal number two. He is only here for a final meal because of you. Do you remember Theodora's magnificent general?"

"Belisarius."

"Ours is Signet. You and I, the skilled Hun and Herulian horsemen. We have lured the Persian to his trap. Now is the time to sink the knife, rather the vigorous whiff. It will perform the same function. Tell me if I pour too many glasses. Or, the gods forbid, I lean too close."

CHAPTER 47

She did both.

Meandering up and down the long table, seemingly oblivious to the bloviating interchange, she refreshed glasses. As always, Signet led the discussion. In the kitchen, the audience listened close.

"I hope the spanakopita is to your liking," Signet said, his words distant but clear through the intercom. "'I instructed our chef, a Mr. Melko, to prepare it fresh."

Spoon poised in midair, he peered down the table, past the pitcher of Zonder Springs sparkling water, rejected by both men, to the colonel just then patting his lips with the pink, embroidered napkin.

"Quite good, Corporal. I am honored to receive this last minute invite. I am short of time, however. My Washington flight leaves MacDill in three hours."

"It is my honor you are here, sir. I am told we shall enjoy Aviva beets with the bass. A combo to die for."

The ear slicer was in rare form. Sometime between leaving Ross and Colonel Bame to examine Yannis Stavrou's mystical *Bleu Blank Rouge* above the credenza, he'd donned his former uniform, secured from his Arriva hut for the occasion. With Zina in the room, the resplendent diners confined themselves to social chit chat avoiding any offensive comments, acting like perfect gentlemen. On several notable occasions, as she plied their goblets with chilled wine, Zina provided a full display of her décolletage for the colonel's pleasure. Upon each exposure, he leaned closer, nostrils wiggling as he again inquired about Ms. Palaeologus's special scent.

"So distinctive. So absorbing," he said. "Did you find that vial you promised?"

Zina threw back her shoulders with whimsical pride.

"My boyfriend claims it whispers of faint breezes. Of promises yet to come."

She did a little bounce and the tip of the vial appeared in her dress. She dropped it into his muscular palm.

"A remarkable, lingering fragrance. Thank you for sharing."

A chuckle erupted in the kitchen.

"I pray Uncle Stephano does not hear of this."

"Shh," Melko said. "There's more."

"I am positive my, ah, wife will savor your beguiling perfume."

"Why not open it now. Take a remembrance whiff for your trip back home."

The colonel's color changed to a darker grey on the monitor. Aunt Sophia poked Melko in the ribs.

"Please ask Zeenee for another vial. I have yet not tried her new scent."

"Wait. Not now. They're arguing. That was fast. They were palsy-walsy a moment ago."

He was right. Ross had missed the colonel's remark,, but it set Signet off, his voice firm, sharp.

"...I disagree, Bame. It was not fear of reprisal that made him drown the flash drive. Just the opposite, in fact."

"Bame, is it? You are crossing a line, *Corporal*. Your insubordination is uncalled for."

"Stick to the topic. You know what you have to do."

"What you *think* I have to do. I want that promotion to Assistant Secretary."

Zina flashed across the screen. She had repaired to the senior ranking officer and refilled his glass. Though deeply involved with Signet, the colonel took a moment to refill his nostrils with the server's exotic aroma then waved her back to the kitchen. A moment passed. The men resumed speaking.

"I agree. Your promotion is critical. You'll then be second in command, in a perfect position to rebuild and restructure our armed forces. We *must* return to a nation respected the world over."

"Christ, Corporal. Promotion or not, I'll entertain the same reservations."

"You know that is pure baloney. Do what Dr. Ross did with that flash drive. Use your own free will. Do the right thing. May I remind you, lives hang in the balance?"

"The *right* thing again. That tune is now monotonous."

"Only because you refuse to pay attention. As I've explained before, homo sapiens, our unique species of bipedal hominids, is endowed with an innate capacity to behave correctly. It has nothing to do with morality. So don't cop out with that old dodge, the military is a war machine story. We behave out of self-preservation to protect the tribe. And, our tribe, our country, our *forgotten hostages* need us to think and act clearly." Signet let a moment elapse, adjusted the wine glass at his elbow, then continued. "The trick is to access our important talent without contamination."

"You're talking Genesis II again. The invincible soldier-warrior project. Why is your Genesis IV project so important? Aren't II and III sufficient?"

"To willingly return to battle? Only a psychopath without an amygdala would repeatedly volunteer to fight terrorists. Let us move on. Genesis IV can wait."

"Why then did we send Campesi to federal prison?"

"To protect your ass, sir. Stay focused."

"Damn it, Corporal. I warned you. I will not excuse—"

"We need appropriate men in place."

"You mean, brain-altered soldiers capable of killing that baby you always bring up."

Aunt Sophia gasped and put a hand to her mouth. Melko hastily explained the colonel's comment. Not an ordinary baby, he whispered. A make-believe baby. They were referring to an example of moral decision making. The one where three people are hiding from terrorists in a closet. A woman with sleeping baby and a stranger. Both man and woman know if the baby awakens and cries the terrorists will find and shoot them all. If they smother the baby, though, both adults will survive. But then, Sophia countered, her voice tearful, if the man kills the baby the mother will cry out. End of story.

"It's an imaginary situation about moral decisions. Let's listen, okay?"

On the monitor, Signet continued to lecture.

"Culture-dependent morality is based on fear. In order to make a proper and *correct* decision, fear must be recognized and checked. A dead mother would be of no use to her other children. She must sacrifice one. We are not talking about people in closets, however. We are speaking about—"

"Dainty Dr. Ross perhaps? That weakling is a perfect example. I was certain you'd bring him into the discussion."

"He had a lot to learn. I nudged him along."

The colonel laughed.

"Nudged. I like that. The poor bastard."

"Nothing like that at all." A quick glance to the top molding above the pantry door. Signet fully aware of distant spectators. "I used him, true enough, but not in the way you conclude. He lived at the edge of a precipice. He wanted to get to the other side. I pushed him over. He flew instead."

"Whatever the hell *that* means."

Signet shot another glance to the top molding.

"Forget the doctor. He's fine. We're speaking about hostages."

"Have you ever considered the intelligence might be wrong?"

Signet shook his head. "Impossible. You installed two attaches in the compound. Both Yemeni. Both trusted and skilled counterterror experts."

"Both dead, thanks to Saudi bombers."

"They died weeks after confirming the hostages were abducted. This Rawdadi fellow took them from Yemen to Eritrea. A violent wilderness of a country. Five men, including the ambassador and his two children. How can you not try to save them?"

"You forget they were all housed in the same building with our two agents. They have to be dead. No. Not another word. The Secretary Of Defense will not authorize this."

"Damn it, Colonel. It is up to you to *convince* the Secretary.

We have no other option. The lives of those hostages are on you."

"And, what if the mission morphs into another Blackhawk Down?"

"You express a situational bias. That was an isolated incident."

Colonel Bame shot to his feet. He downed another jolt of wine. Glanced at his watch.

"I don't see the moral imperative here. Just where the hell is the sacrificial baby in your equation?"

"The baby is a metaphor for fearful bureaucrats."

"My colleagues at the Pentagon?"

"Colleagues who downsized the military. To protect the country, we rely on Special Forces, on men exactly like Sauer."

Screeching over the speaker, the colonel's chair scraped across the wooden floor. He bolted around the table aiming for the door to the front hallway.

"I cannot do this. I am up for promotion. This conversation is over. Thanks for lunch, Corporal. Goodbye."

A very distraught Zina shot to her feet.

"He cannot go. There was more to say."

She grabbed hold of Ross, and they ran down the pantry hallway. They met Signet at the front door. The colonel's SUV was already moving down the cobblestones. At the street, it veered right toward the main highway, disappearing in a spray of pebbles.

"All things considered," Signet said. "That went well."

Ross was surprised. The corporal exhibited little concern with the colonel's abrupt departure. If anything, he appeared relaxed as he stepped away from the porte cochere, basking in the wan, early-afternoon sunshine.

"Inform Mr. Melko and Ms. Belisarius the bass was superb." His calm gaze fell upon Zina. "Thanks to you, our frightened guest is off to a fine start. He pocketed the vial, unaware of its secret magic. A superb suggestion about taking a final whiff. Congratulations to you both. Definitely a successful mission."

"Will you kindly tell me what just happened? What was that business about flying over a precipice?"

"Metaphor, Doctor. I find them useful."

Zina hooked him with her arm.

"Signet showed him the door. It is for him to walk through."

"What precisely does *that* mean?"

"Colonel Bame is afraid," Signet said. "For the Eritrea mission to proceed, he must overcome this fear and convince the Secretary. I am happy to say, his transformation has already begun. He doesn't know it yet."

Signet and the purple seductress exchanged a knowing look. The corporal shrugged, stating it was only proper she tell the doctor. By now, the doctor has had several experiences with the new perfume. He deserved to know.

"I disagree. It is more appropriate the emperor's most ingenious general share the battle plan himself. Justinian would have demanded it of General Belisarius."

"Stop it, guys. I don't care who tells me. Enlighten your emperor, for god's sake."

"Very well," Signet replied. "I shall do the honor. Dr. Braun has for some time now succeeded in transferring the Genesis II inoculant to perfume. Whether the aerosol is carbon dioxide in a bottle of Zonder Springs water or the molecular constituent of a complex perfume, the concept remains the same. Beth merely added the vaccine to a small vial of perfume, gave it a gentle spin in a centrifuge then transferred the fluid back to its original container. The result, a very pungent aroma both you and now Colonel Bame became particularly fond of."

"And soon, his wife."

"In the chest pocket, beneath his nose, he will have full benefit on the flight home."

"That darn perfume. That's what this is all about?"

"Your first exposure was at the concert," Zina said. "Several others during the week, the most important one while we, ah, waited on auntie's couch."

She stretched up on tiptoe. He leaned down and met her halfway.

"Yet, if you inoculated me at Eckerd Hall, why the fizzy cola?"

Signet gave his shoulder a tiny squeeze. Another show of, what, friendship? The second of the day. Amazing.

"A diversion," he said. "I wanted you to think of it as inoculation. Doing so served a purpose. Do you recall my remarks about mirror neurons? On the Tarpon Sponge Dock, they informed me you would succumb to misplaced fear. I refer to your need for that portrait on the wall in Boston. I knew you would weaken and return the stolen files to Campesi. But, if you believed you were inoculated and fear was on its way out, you would be free to make the correct decision and blame it on an altered brain. Which, at the pool, you finally did but only because you knew, deep down, it was best to sacrifice the baby."

"You tricked me into using my free will?"

"The ploy worked, did it not?"

"What if the partial, Eckerd Hall dose actually took hold? Maybe you didn't need a fizzy diversion."

Puppeteer and purple lady shrugged.

"Perhaps it played a role. Regardless. By your own hand, we eliminated an immoral man. As a result, the irony, you reclaimed Glaucon."

"It is now up to Colonel Bame. A lot rides upon his transformation. As Signet said, lives are at stake."

They flanked Ross, the three of them staring down the driveway, at the faint cloud of dust framing the colonel's departure.

"Do you think it will work?" Ross said. "Will he overcome

conflict and convince his superiors?"

"So far, it works for you," she said. "I'm confident it will for him. I placed a drop upon his neck while he inspected territory."

"You see. His change is underway."

"The perfume is our best shot."

"To silence his amygdala against his will."

"We push the man to the tracks below. We smoother the baby. For the greater good, Daniel. Just remember that."

Signet stepped between them and corralled both with his lanky arms. A true first, a kind of unity experience all its own.

"Soon we will know for certain. For now, patience. Time will deliver the answer. Until then, we wait."

As there was little else to say, they remained for a short while on the cobblestones.

Then, they went inside.

EPILOGUE

It was a time of many changes. The two most noteworthy took origin at the same location and time of day eight months earlier. The location, a split level bungalow on a deserted spit of land bordering the Anclote River. The time, an early October morning that previous autumn.

The first change, earth rumbling and unexpected, came with Aunt Sophia's and retired Detective Melko's wedding on this fine, June Saturday afternoon. Engaged two months after their initial encounter in the bungalow's lower level, it no doubt inspired the subsequent engagement of Zina Palaeologus and Dr. "Danny-boy" Ross, occupants of the upper level, that fateful morning of entangled limbs and twin commitments.

Both events scheduled to take place in the same, sun baked gazebo in the lake park behind Melko's restored Tudor. All interested parties save two were now assembled. Zina and Daniel, hands intertwined, looked on from the back of the gazebo, while up front Auntie and restaurateur were being hooked by the emancipated Father Palaeologus of the Church of St. Constantine, Tarpon Springs, Florida.

Though not as thrilling as a sail in the Charles River Basin, or as magical as a trip to Vermont's White Mountains, for solitary gents from Massachusetts, the moment sang out, cheerful and hopeful. A day lovely in all respects.

Still the occasion alarmed Ross.

Did Signet and magical Zina truly whack his neurons with either fuzzy cola or perfume or both? Was twin happiness a product of altered neural pathways, his current course aligned with invisible dark threads, this gazebo a node through which they all traveled?

It sure appeared that way, the perfume playing the major role though, a goodly dose now wafting up at him from his new love perched at his elbow.

"Who would have imagined." He tightened his grip on Zina's hand. "A retired cop and a fussy, bayou woman."

"Be still, Mr. Fiancé. They exchange vows."

Heat soaked his brow. His chest surged while his sulci went savage in confusion.

Fiancé?

He could scarcely believe it. Yet, it was true. He and Zina would tie the knot.

Distracting Ross, forcing him to glance off, a sunlit reflection had slipped into his peripheral vision.

They were coming, volatile visitors making an entrance after all.

In sonorous tones, casting an affectionate eye to the playground swings where his girlfriend of fifty-eight voluptuous years giggled happily, Father Palaeologus, in full church regalia, completed the exchange of vows. His purple vestments, out of sync with Church custom, were worn in honor of his dear granddaughter, the instigator, so he claimed, of his welcome madness, the former Empress Theodora, from a court far, far away, that despite her best efforts, remained mostly forgotten.

The priest's latest MRI revealed partially annihilated amygdalae, the main portion gone but sub-nuclei still there, attached to anterior cingulate and dorsolateral frontal cortices, a discovery accounting for the man's peculiar mental state and sense of humor.

Not attributable to rearranged neural circuits, Melko's transformation was of a different sort. Gone, the flowery tee shirts, rumpled slacks, and bemused manner. Today, he insisted upon black tie and shorts, plus easy to remove, hearts and flowers tattoos, all the while basking in the radiating glow of his new mate who blossomed in peach pastel with honey braids and pink sandals.

There was a tug at his elbow. Franklin. Another in a new day of wonders.

"Shall we begin serving?" he said, balancing a tray of bubbling flutes. "Or, should we wait until after the receiving line."

Talk about metamorphosis. Tightly groomed in an Armani jacket and pressed shorts, the young man exuded the image of respectability. And, to everyone's relief, he spoke little of The Big Lie any longer, accepting his fate to matriculate into the halls of higher education in the Fall. A Cambridge education enabled by a mysterious influx of cash from his hedge fund father. Somehow, following a donation to the university, his prosecution for fraudulent money manipulation did not seem so onerous.

Ross made a mental note to speak with the lad. Glaucon and the Clearwater Research Laboratory were always in need of more funding.

"Serve now," he said, espying the approach of the newlyweds. "First, champagne for the Melkos. Then, guests. Don't forget yourself."

Franklin departed for refills as Aunt Sophia, quickly tipsy, twirled about.

"What do you think, Zeenee? White is so *effete*. I couldn't resist!"

She came to a stop facing the wrong direction, discovered her mistake and flipped around to face her companions.

"Melky went for semiformal. I chose modern chic. Does it suit, doctor?"

"Perfectly. You both look fantastic. Congratulations!"

He bear hugged the peach fantasma.

But, *Melky*? Ross would be a goner if he ever used this name. Box his ears. Book Ross for verbal abuse. Even poison his souvlaki. Melko was now capable of revenge. For he, too, had changed.

They'd all traveled a long distance out of the way to come back home correctly. Home being, of course, their new reformulations.

Sophia now addressed her niece.

"Soon it will be your time, dear. Are you not absolutely thrilled?"

"Hold your horses, auntie. Autumn will be soon enough. By then, Daniel will have remastered Opus 57."

The throaty roar of a braking vehicle seized their attention. Polished to a satanic shine, the black and red striped Escalade slammed to a stop just short of the gazebo. Both couples descended the side stairs to greet Signet as he exited the rear seat.

"You made it!" Zina cried out.

With a resolute frown, Mr. Former-Security Signet accommodated her sudden embrace.

"All the way from the Middle East. Welcome!"

"Yes, my dear. Glad to be here. One hug is adequate."

It was *Colonel* Signet now, a promotion following his latest success in the field. But, he made it clear in his text message accepting the invite, he would always remain Signet amongst friends. Still, the rank of colonel was a significant elevation for the Zen warrior. In the aftermath of the Eritrea mission, they'd not been in touch, however. Signet and his second in command, *Corporal* Sauer, insisted on maintaining a chilly silence as they sprinted from one international hotspot to another executing clandestine missions. Not so long ago, the Tampa papers carried a story about a particular incident in the Eritrean capital. Certain terrorists lost their lives to a land mine as they exited a brothel. Rumor had it unnamed secret operatives wept at the funeral.

Signet presented Aunt Sophia with a pink carnation.

"May I?" He briskly pinned it to her waistline. "Not that anything supplements natural beauty."

Extending compliments now? Neuroplasticity sure left its mark. As it did for Ross. Against all odds, he was engaged.

Signet next produced an elegant watch. He handed it to Melko.

"From an insurgent in Yemen. He will never miss it."

Never miss it. No imagination required about what happened there. Perhaps it was premature to think Signet evolving in a more civilized fashion.

The groom appraised the gift from various angles.

"A knock-off?" he suggested.

Signet did not flinch.

"Read the inscription on the back."

Melko did as he was told.

"'To S.B. from B.B. With Love.' This insurgent fellow stole it from someone else."

"The American attaché in Sanaa. When ISIS arrived on

the scene, this insurgent fled. A Shiite, wary of angry Sunnis, he escaped across the strait to Eritrea with the attaché, his wife and several others in tow. Naturally, we followed."

"I can't keep this. It would be, I don't know, wrong."

"After we liberated the insurgent of his theft In Masawa, we returned it to the owner. In gratitude, he handed it to Sauer, and he gave it to me. And now, to you."

"Why did he give it to you?"

"In thanks. I allowed him to sever Mr. Campesi's ear."

Aunt Sophia shrieked. Signet quickly consoled her.

"I apologize," he said. "It is by training and my nature to misrepresent. Actually, it was I who claimed the ear."

Two hands across her mouth, the new bride stared in disbelief.

"You didn't...."

Melko handed back the watch. "I can't accept it."

Signet returned the timepiece to him.

"The attaché would not object. He would want you to have it. The initials can be removed."

Another pause, the groom again inspecting his gift.

"If you really think it's okay."

The front door of the Escapade opened and shut with a resounding thunk. Wearing a ferocious, dark-closer grin,

Sauer sauntered forth and presented Zina with a small box. He withdrew, standing tall and worrisome.

"For you, our former empress," he said. "A special remembrance from times past."

Ross shook his head. First, the Zen warrior, newly gracious, and now the assassin, a poet?

Zina fingered the velvet box, appropriately secured with a purple bow. A box identical to the one Gamel Azzizi gave Ross that gruesome night on Clearwater Beach many months earlier. Untying the bow, she daintily removed an oversized bronzed ear bearing an engraved pedestal beneath the lobular lobe: FROM ERITREA. A TROPHY.

"You're kidding. An *ear*?"

"A special antique." Signet offered a vanishing grin. "From special-ops. For a special person."

"Such a strange gift." Zina weighed the bronzed object in one hand. "Did this happen to come from that horrible Mr. Campesi?"

Signet steadied his former protégé by the shoulders.

"He will not miss it. Except for a large scar, he bears his burden well."

"Do I also have Sauer to thank for this?"

"Correct again. It is he who performed the, eh, dissection. Not a pretty sight. The prison guard said he accidentally severed an artery."

The tall assassin did not deny the accusation.

"I lie again," Signet said. "Another soldier performed the harvest in Eritrea. A well-tanned ear, one which lent itself well to the magnificent bronzing. It is heavy. A paperweight, I thought. You will need one when you return to school."

Smiles appeared on both warriors' faces. They chuckled. Then laughed until tears lined their deeply etched faces.

"I mislead again. A terrible habit. The ear is but a sculpture. A reminder of my former occupation."

Inside the gazebo, a familiar island combo was warming up. Enlivened couples shuffled feet, ready to dance. Succumbing to the beat, Melko and Aunt Sophia now returned to their reception. Soon, the huge gazebo rocked with the joy befitting a fun wedding.

After a moment, Signet invited Ross and Zina to join him on the dock a few yards down the path.

"Time to catch up on events."

They followed him along splintered planks until reaching the water. Hands on the railing, they watched a pair of speed boats streak by, wreaking havoc upon the lake, propelling a wake that rattled the timber beneath their feet.

"I gather you enjoy your new job."

Signet nodded. "You gather correctly."

Their last contact had been on Thanksgiving Day, before

Signet, under precise orders from *General* Bame, the new Assistant Secretary of Defense, journeyed to far off Eritrea to undertake his long planned mission. Other than three short notes, they'd not heard from him since.

"What have you two been up to?"

"Traveling," Ross said. "Next week we're off to Mumbai for the Indian Glaucon launch."

Thanks to the FDA's sluggish review of trials, they felt compelled to seek approval elsewhere. The European Union prudently registered the device in a marketable Class 2a, leaping at the chance of curing a potentially blinding disease. To date, nearly two thousand Europeans had received the miraculous implant. The next target: a looming glaucoma catastrophe in the sub-continent.

"Very pleased to hear this," Signet said. "What else?"

All eyes shot down to the water beneath the planks. A five foot alligator was heading for the seagrass. Fishing from shore, anglers sought bass at the same location.

"The Clearwater subsidiary is prospering. We were fortunate Ravi Ravda bought the place after foreclosure. Even for physicians, it is painful to be forced out of business."

"New health care laws forced the concierge route upon them. Fortunately, regulation is more sensible abroad."

To avoid the local healthcare mess, they registered Simcoe, the parent company, in Ireland. Still, to comply with Miocene midgets in Washington, Ravda was busy complying with the FDA's outdated demands. Trials and more trials, patients' eager acceptance notwithstanding.

Ross entertained high hopes anyway. Following several glaucoma symposia, a multi-institutional study was underway. All glaucoma titans had attended, even his magisterial mentor, Dr. Chandler Seemanz, in retirement on Cape Cod.

"I was informed you two are to be married."

"How did you…?"

Signet waved the question aside.

"General Bame. A font of knowledge including the news you study for your GED, that afterward you will join Dr. Azzizzi and become a certified technician."

Zina stiffened.

"How did *he* discover anything about *me*?"

"The general has connections. Let us say, in repayment for that wonderful perfume you, ah, shared he, from quite a distance, has kept in touch. Did you not also put his name down on your mortgage application?"

Zina tapped fingers on her sleeve, nodding with reluctance.

"I did. And, thanks to you both, we now live in a large home in Myrtle Point, a snooty community up lake from here."

"With a parlor facing the lake."

"Thank you, Daniel. With your Steinway on a Kashan carpet no less. Now, there is no excuse. The Beethoven should be warmed up for the wedding."

Ross tilted sideways to kiss her.

"For my immortal beloved. Opus 57 will be indeed be ready."

Speed boats then zoomed by on a return performance. More waves washed beneath their feet, the gator long gone, off and hunting.

"Danny-boy now learns French," she said. "For his visit to Brussels."

"In truth, I butcher the language."

"You now devour curry, speak Hindi and, as CEO, lead an international company. The previous Dr. Ross was incapable of that."

"I had no choice."

"You had no fear. Hence, you make *correct* decisions."

Zina held him with her tinted eyes. He succumbed to the enigmatic force field reeling him in. Heart to heart. Better than mirror neurons. A more secure connection.

"Speaking of change," Signet said. "Does Arturo Campesi's fate interest you?"

Nodding in unison, they listened to the astonishing tale. The former CEO, a genuinely bad fellow and in defiance of all odds, had found God, his conversion serving both spiritual and practical needs. Confined in total isolation, he discovered life in Federal prison to be a desolate existence, but one that helped concentrate his mind.

"Being a resourceful man, he discovered a solution to his fate." Signet produced a sardonic grin. "The insanity excuse. It is quite amusing."

Ross and Zina surfed in on a tide of laughter. They rode it for a spell then let their storyteller continue.

One fine day Campesi asked the guard for a Bible, a request the guard could not refuse. Then, a week later, after much pretend reading and audible reflection, he requested an audience with a priest. Following tears and prayers, he claimed the Lord provided a special assignment. Community service. He asked for absolution so he might qualify to fulfill his mission.

"Clever lad. A way to escape solitary confinement."

"There is more."

This ploy did not work though. The priest, knowledgeable about the supplicants' many transgressions, properly demurred. Then, the former CEO called for his lawyer.

"Denied absolution from a priest," Ross said. "The atheist next tours a legal venue."

"Another dead end. The assigned military lawyer was also unsympathetic. But, the evil magician had another rabbit up his sleeve."

"Don't you mean, in his hat?" Ross said. "Magicians pull rabbits from a hat."

Zina laughed as well.

"What they have up their sleeves are cards."

While they chortled, Colonel Signet snapped to attention.

"Very well. Laugh. I refer to what we forgot. Mr. Campesi possessed another patent. And, that concerned the manufacture of a BDNF related component for the PTSD vaccine."

This ended the merriment.

"That's a DARPA program. It doesn't relate to the Glaucon device."

"But, what does is the cost of securing the human growth factor component, not the usual one on the market. Fees paid, in essence by Uncle Sam, to Mr. Campesi's account. Fees he has now offered to you, Dr. Ross. In exchange for regular fresh air via community service."

"No kidding."

"The fees are not huge, but, in offering this exchange, he added one final detail. You must donate these monies to Veterans Affairs."

"I don't follow...."

"A cynical ploy, so like the man himself. It amounts to a deal, basically. Feed the underfunded vet health agency in consideration of speedy approval by another agency the FDA, of your two other Glaucon biologicals originally denied. A fast track for your gizmo, as first planned."

He paused, to gauge reaction.

"Will the feds go along with this?"

"Thanks to General Bame's intervention, the deal is done. He has become very persuasive. Remember how his return trip to Washington turned out."

Upon landing after his rushed Odessa luncheon, the colonel complained of a bad headache. Treated for a while at Bethesda Naval Hospital, MRIs revealed inflamed amygdalae nuclei at the base of the brain. A strange virus infection, his doctors concluded. One with a short life, it turned out. After ten days, he was discharged a changed person. Kind, assertive, even polite, quite unlike his former self.

Two days later he went into seclusion with the Secretary of Defense. Upon reemerging, the Secretary announced that the Pentagon, in the future, would rely on elite special operatives for overseas missions, omitting the crucial fact they were actually mercenary-elite assassins. Not long after that, under cover of darkness, Sauer and Signet conducted their lethal Eritrean extraction. As a result of their rescue mission, Colonel became General, Corporal became Colonel, and Sergeant Sauer became corporal. Secret medals deployed. A commendation from the President. A complete success.

"Zina's perfume hit the mark," he said. "Next I must tell you what General Bame is up to. He calls it GENESIS V."

"I thought he was terminating those secret projects."

"All but his new one. He plans to perfume insurgents captured in the field."

"Shade of Night?"

"Is there any other?"

"Who benefits by creating a fearless enemy? Besides, isn't that a type of torture?"

"He reasons, if not already psychopathic, a disqualifying diagnosis, but only delusional, well, such an insurgent would make a suitable candidate. Bame's hypothesis? Upon inoculation, such a person would become peaceful. Still an insurgent but one unwilling to kill the baby. He would give it a bottle, instead. Hardly torture, Daniel. The opposite, in fact."

"You're joking."

"I have more news."

Difficult if not impossible to decipher the puppeteer's half-sneer, half-smirk expression.

"Let's have it."

"I wrote a letter to your famous institution."

"To the Boston *Infirmary*?"

"I attempted all manner of persuasion. I suggested the monies pouring into your new device might support needed research programs."

"You wrote a letter to the *Chief* of the Infirmary?"

"Curious about her response?"

"Well, sure. Did you mention the painting idea?"

"I did. Sorry to report, she was noncommittal. That is

why I sent her a small gift. A tiny vial of a most precious scent. The second letter came from you this time."

"You *sent* her Shade of Night?"

"Assuming she applies the small portion provided, she may yet change her mind. After General Bame, we adjusted the dose-response curve. He may have sniffed too much. We cut back the dose."

"I was only following your instruction," Zina said. "He really liked the scent."

Signet squeezed her hand.

"You did exactly right. Scientists might call the colonel a Phase I study. We now have the dose just right. I estimate two weeks for an effect. It is now mid-June. By July, we will have an answer."

His cerebral circuits went haywire. Signet *secretly inoculated* the reigning Chief of Ophthalmology at the famous infirmary? What was next on his platter of indiscretion? A tiny bottle of cologne to the White House?

As always, their leader wore a bemused grin, his focus trained to the distant shoreline. Speedboats veered in their direction before zooming off. Waves lapped amongst the weeds. A gator downed a slender carp for early dinner. A moment of quiet confidence on the wavering dock.

"Do you think the perfume will work?" Ross said. "Will she overcome hesitation?"

Silence. No one knew for certain.

"Patience," Signet finally said, voice hushed, wisdom trickling forth. "Time alone will tell."

"I've heard that before."

"And, how, good doctor, did that turn out?"

Sometime later, they left the dock, wandered up the path and rejoined the party.

It was in full swing.